A DOMINANT STRATEGY OF E :

A GOLDEN KING

An Award Winner for this and or future book sellers everywhere and a favorite of Prince George, well it has been read at Sandringham, The Wiry Hound, Marmaduke and no burning effigy of anyone in any Royal Family except of beheadings…

AMANDA HOWELL

AuthorHouse™ UK
1663 Liberty Drive
Bloomington, IN 47403 USA
www.authorhouse.co.uk
UK TFN: 0800 0148641 (Toll Free inside the UK)
UK Local: 02036 956322 (+44 20 3695 6322 from outside the UK)

This book is printed on acid-free paper.

ISBN: 979-8-8230-8492-5 (sc)
ISBN: 979-8-8230-8493-2 (hc)
ISBN: 979-8-8230-8494-9 (e)

Library of Congress Control Number: 2023918265

Print information available on the last page.

Published by AuthorHouse 11/02/2023

authorHOUSE®

Table of Contents

Comments

Eric Cantona is the most enigmatic family man in the world, not the most recognisable, not the most English and has been through hell for his…

He won an award for it and this book is 23 Chapters 1200 pages of stanza originally, please read the others following for the acceptance of me for my son, for over 12 counts of victimisation for being me.

Before, during and after his birth, Erics' dinners engagement leaves my stanza productions not undone and with hard, paper and audio we are through this month after a very difficult time

Welcome, to the second half of the most prolifically impeached human on the planet, still in the media, Fantastic Father is his …Josephine Cantona, and I don't need to tell Selma Cantona that either.

As a boy Eric Cantona had a cave now he has removed this for a Golden Carriage with the one he loves the most with a diamond ring on her finger

Cantona plays the play with his Author too and can be cut throat if needed, he won the World Cup you know….beach or no beach, whale or no Wales, the red telling the truth today with flip flops, hats for a rainy Thursday afternoon and it should be this morning with Holly Willoughby and not Peter Schofield

You are the readers who are important to me and I mean no harm in my writing style.

I am not for the faint hearted but I have a huge heart for children, families, dogs, horses and bears.

We here in Aesthetic Beauty with Phibrow are now in full client with support for my new business model to promote, provide and support Gold Service Excellence.

This course qualified me the author too.

Please be for Excellence in Service, Gifted, Talented Supremacy and Excellence of Human Mind, Right of the Child and Human Rights Act, to charge those under the European Excellence of President Macron, Prime Minster Qiang, the Leader of North Korea Kim who needs taking charge of to establish position daily during talks of disarming seen by own eyes with no seen security.

Eric Cantona please be mine here and then you were I don't mind either way....

Have a Lovely Day

Foreword

Rightful wrongs.......enough of this chastity for babies and children that someone took from me, the characters in this book are not real, but I am, he is and yes we have and no I am not her either, in fact the one you think is ok isn't and the other one who you think is nice also isn't, strange as I pass through Marseilles, the Kingdom of all Kingdoms

A corporate realised truth of all evil, Osama Bin Laden and Business Initiatives by the British Government that nearly bumps talent based top elite, I nearly met him once Eric Cantona, the Corporate Realism heralding from the topflight, the bumble bee buzzing in the background, satirical play for the Copenhagen Strategy of Security includes Humanitarian Aid, side lined sometimes in political complexes such as lateralised economies, political strategic manoeuvre and policing, terrorism of the heart, heralds tiny headings of no doubt the writers genius, the press did not want to know today as the publisher went the other way

We all know the beer bellies of all time are referred to here for everyone to know about, yes, this is Great Britain, socially oppressed celebrate nothing and watch the Royal Family on the TV, vilified for being prissy, shout, point and cry for Argentina when yes, boys you guessed it, he does it again, the man with the foot and ball, the push for excellence in the planets of all time to excel, achieve greatness, just like him, why is Deschamps chewing the cud, why is Deschamps in Maritime, because he made it fully, the Beach football is now not a thing of the past and Cantona, Zidane and Deschamps have all done it ....Peter Jones MBE is celebrated to here with Dragons breathing fire and strategies for the Best Businessman in the whole World, why the lawn and circle is for Messi and then it was one...on the stand, in the stand and shouting abuse with then yes Balon..Balon, Cantona is the Beast fable, thine knee, advantage take and vulnerability annihilation but the other way round...here he is a significant Beast Fable, just like Cantona, ladies I wryly smile, yes, not sorry here, hands down...beer bellies rule the world, Cantona rules the world and he is not one, we read here for the storyline to win, to take note of what is right not wrong, what we do to correct wrongful doings, today I order a cab in Sloane Square it does not arrive, gets stuck down Symons Road and genuinely does not turn up, sorry we are damn sorry...on Erics gravestone he will have from me...just sorry..we should have met more, been with each other more and made friends more with each other

Once, he landed straight down the middle, Simmons in the far distant past, please do not squiggle here as you can come and speak to me if you like about him, I don't mind, lad, I don't want to know what it makes me, anyway sorry but brings a different meaning to 6ft 2in he's 57 who is this woman riddled with hatred, who is the dog and who is Marmaduke...Mighman, Mightyman, Pomile, Leucile, Charlotte Burrows, Lucy Price, Dorothy Spires and many more, feather man, Mohammed Salah the Egyptian Pharaohs, Angelina Jolie, Julie Roberts ..thing is utopia is driven here for those who strive for excellence not many do, those who have shirts on their back with names on do, boots do, soldiers do and sterling does the one who got away is me, but not from him, from Cantona, the film The Mad Kings is his coming to be, I got away from the actual Cantona and want to be the love of his life ...Special Agent Spider tells us all we need to know and then the SAS become scaling the walls of justice tower in tower hamlets...Featherman is terrorism of hearts is the un justly title of this one this first volume is a candid look at life, for political peace strategies and love, more fool he, the stand shuddered the world shuddered and the whole of the empires are all now turning to say sorry, the A Line strategies usually work, no centre play the reverse, Cantona on the middle centre line, with no right foot, this is not a positional play, now turn damn you Cantona, I want to see yourself, lipstick on collars...no gentlemanly stand point, anyway, President of USA and Kofi Anan met today and a plane was hijacked..

United Nations, President Biden, President Macron and Kim Do, President and Prime Minister of China are all available for comment.

Run of Truth

Cantona epitomises the Runs of Truths as Heroic Prose Poem, truths about skill, being a King and gentlemanly conduct.... Auxerre now find it and weep Pele fans because this one is slightly ore inspiring.'The founder of the best run of truth in the whole of the century includes Pele, Salah, Ronaldo and Messi who is phenomenally spoke at the moment in the Times and I found that they were the only players who I had historical respect for, now, what I do not mean is those before were not good to be considered, but Pele had got complex strategy of his own feet that made the play look easy' Cantona is different, talented, gifted and completely on planet all, not utopia in fact euphemisms do not work anymore, this founder of the black foot and ball genome is the inherited characteristic of being borne, faithful load bearing and real with citizenship, the red card failure for the first few months of the strategy foretelling of the forefathers of hope, can be remembered in Japan the black footed genome with black face had a bone and that was the incitement of racism in a poem for prose with them in a traditional literary way for those who were Black African, South American and White British, American and Muslim of all Jews, but you cannot 'do' them all, well NIKE can and John can too. So, there we are...Pele was by far the most celebrated English Rose of all Blackness and on some nights of the stars would forget to go on purpose to be with his lover, smile and then go back home with the ultimate prize, a time with from the one he wanted in the first place. 'The founder of the whole century in reality and expressive tune with expressive genealogy is actually Eric Cantona, when I write this book me the author and the French Bulldog with Pekinese, Hamlet in the Countryside, rural, hillsides, snowy covered roads, windy tracks, bonsai trees come to life through the hillside retreats, the clippings become smaller trees, acacia monuments, the player of the century is now in stand point, the one who is awarded the prize, the award through his own genetic dominance on the field, as a father and as a physical presence on the stage. The dominance of the genetic gene pool is present in the characteristics learned, inherited, those recessives which are removed after time, do you actually know in person what some of the people look like, I found myself wondering how damn much I needed to meet his mother... the ones left are the lineage historically, learned chameleon characteristics to adapt to situations, environments and to listen to others opinions before making decisions on his own strategy. Which is fact, dealing with the realism of truths even though difficult, that even though narrative the current dialogue, narrative, and then storylines through the book are very strong which leads Cantona to believe that they were in the beginning the making of her. Kissing for example was given to her, something that Pomile would not want with another person if she became Cantonas' girlfriend, so it was given to her through incitement... Non acceptance of the truth of evil, barbarian non acceptance but the old woman and the prickly hedgehog, blamed for terrible entities of evil non acceptance being one into the realm of motherhood, this is the beginning of the prickly hedgehog, authorities and the architecture of conveyance, in the Middle Ages spanned nothing was a font of all knowledge speeding around the bridges, well yes it was UEFA UNICEF looking for her, she stopped every so often with vigour, spirit and long of leg, to escape her own virtues of shackles to realism of the day. When she found her, she began virtuously against her and then at Crossfit, why because sometimes things happen, not here they don't and leapt off into the sunset. When the Romans had the die of hope, to Excalibur the throne of evil was Elizabeth, which to be perfectly honest wasn't a throne but a ledge of escapism and cascading beauty of the Author seems to be being removed very gently to avoid over complicating everything. Eric is nostalgically throne bearing and the crowns are doing very well, the elongation of the mechanics drawn from underneath and mechanic man is borne. Erics Crown and throne remains strong, elite, unique, and completely his, the supposed compromise to opinion, century player and UEFA has the Presidents Award drawn from the FA, an award for Cantona which he knew nothing about, an award which knew nothing about his girlfriend which he know about, it drew the Denmark in a mighty big way from USA, UK and France towards others the harassment of the author, the verbal abuse of the author who is now not dead. The prickly hedgehog laughs out loud, condemns then realises all Denmark and more black than blue are all listening to his comments Confucius Spartacus in Scotland Yard, Sir Mark Rowley, Sir Stephen House, Chief Commissioners nationally within British Police within all rise to King Charles III, the heroism, the stalker, the star spangled banners of pwilth score line to the protestor of hope, he is then arrested not in jest abusive with swearing that we thought she would be, Cantona sighs looks at his feet, that wasn't me and then dismisses her, she smiled no more and it was wiped from her face, she was threatened her legs to break, to be put in a mental asylum with the loss of life of her unborn child to Cantona by himself, the chauffeur who drew Daniel from within stepping forward at every given opportunity…towards the victim who lay dying in the show of giggling as to how she would maintain with Cantona, who kept smiling and said just carry on my gorgeous friend, I won't be long and we can plan our attack, I cannot meet you here now but I will do as it's my fault for not inciting him out…Find out who is Denmark…I want to first be very clear about my relationship with him, the blackface, said Denmark, I do not hold him in high regard as he had a hate crime at my girlfriend and drew blood at her father who was blind, demented, vile, nasty and a bully, her mother who was that nasty, ridiculing, abusive with swearing that we thought she would be the same but isn't, then we realised that victims don't react in the same way…even with victim support, many victims this is written by one, in fact one with a few police protection notices including sexual crime, do not under estimate my Cantona, even his children do, through victim support many thousands a year die of heartache of those who want what the victim has, did have or is going to have through jealousy, anger, greed, envy get away with it and follow, the victim, taking sanctuary in churches, cathedrals and motives as pathetic, greedy and lousy as dating a footballer, money, status not wanting to be lost they are shown…..Everyone has one, not everyone wants one all the time, some of the time or even at all, Foreverman, is everyone's dream man lesbian or not, here Mighman loses himself to the first verse of Chapter 1, Today, to become Foreverman for someone else, the Lately Lady is the golfing superstar of marriage to a football player using a spout to a teapot, Merriman is French here for legs eleven, the Foreverman never forgotten in the Prose Poem Inheritance Stanza II 17.11.19 and Farnes Barnes likes the all togetherness of the Timepiece, Grandfather clock and the tick, tock the time of the game, the hour of your life, the one who makes your world go round is never the one you find quickly after you meet once, Merriman turns here to be blackface, but not the blackface, one of Swordsman excellence for planet one, planet one has families of chameleons adapting their own genomes to make sure they win, do not chastise and win, on the Cheapside jam it the mark not honey with the cup with gold for Cantona, Lucy Locket, began Pomiles nightmare without the Frenchman Merriman the English were never in doubt of the silver tongued genius head of the two Merriman's developed here as Freddie Flintoff and Eric Cantona the Swordsman fighting for supremacy of blackface through these two not against with UNICEF leading the way, Virgils, the Palace and the Centuries of Amphitheatres, Architecture and Centurions are all here with the battle of the century a game of life, woman, families, houses, lifestyle and sheer touch brilliance on and off the screen, the f=game of life the game of heroisim and the game of corporate board utopia, euphoric disorders from integral internalised battleships of bullies, fame and holding through jealousy of Whiteman, Lately Man, Guardsman and total entity of the Featherman, who is Diamondman has had his own stanza through golden boots and his best friend Marmaduke the dog is everyone's, has trips out to play and the rightful wrong ladies are never far away Silverman is made like the tinman in Mechanicman with no further from a broken-hearted man, Pomile makes sure that the Golden Paws are for Show, Show and more Show.

Time is an Egg

Epigram begins our journey through time full of historical references to battles and corporate realism.

A compendium of 9 began here some time ago

it was decided to be heroic in prose poem stand alone in prose and epigram...

it is full of text..a literary compendium of significant isolation, intrigue, sadness and boldness through a legal tunnel of realism of someone's life, whom has been described,

yet not mentioned and 'pressed' that often that the button doesn't exist.

This is one...Lately Lady, French Merriman are Corporate bullies enticing young men and women to their own rooms, RightfulWrongMan sometimes makes mistakes in the bedroom, he does not clean up after himself, leave his ties, tie pins and calculator watches behind for work, his briefcase is very and Wiringman although in a van takes her to the casino to find happiness with her own Mighman Lucy Price is now with her Foreverman in the casino in Monaco where it all began, on thine knee of excellence Mighman said Lucy Price, you outstanding control, non-envy and pure touch genius is now not for the East End of Sloane Square, but New York, Geneva and Paris are all now for him Featherman wears a suit, Dior and Saville Row, the American envy is not rife, it is the reverse, Lourdes a special time of strings moonshine, apocalypse for FarnesBarnes and his supersonic bionic dog are now never apart, separated or lonely, in windy adventures on sonnets, prose and epigrams, mighman is for the espionage of the heart in constitutional hill for Napolean and the Pentagon, Macron and a very large set of spectacles with his shirts, every morning mighman rubs his eyes, puts on his spectacles and with direction, aim and sheer touch brilliance on the handle opens the door, smiles as he does so, he enters the locked dreams of many men, desired by all including women, not only himself but a streamlined Ferrari many actually a few....glistening in the moonlight as he polishes the gleaming headlights, paintwork and enters back into domestic bliss, waivering his domicile for 6 months he goes here then here to be with me, Diamondman, Demiwave and Cottonman all do the same, their longevity, contractual worth and value means they only have one...Blackman, denoting racism, abuse, forth righteousness and bad behaviours, Breadman, Milkman is for the world of the fasting sir, the one who is Jewish and the one who is her, the breadman heralded the day of power

Mental Asylum

On the veranda the psychotic black widow lines the truth of evil, the depression hits back at the wide-eyed lunatic whom we haven't found yet in her, but is there we have seen it, felt it and know it. Apparently breathing fire within, beneath, Cantona sighs…I wish I had met her more now than then, not long to wait and then we can, Cantona rarely sighs smiles and chooses his friends carefully from now on….no other way round, the players were in ore of Cantona on that night his sheer touch brilliance dominant on the pitch….all these reverse plays in a book of dominance for the man who becomes that contentious on the pitch when you are truly for him, his love of the game, strategy and with total absorption in fashion couture, homes, gardens, children and families, films, music and historical referencing in France, UK and even sometimes in Japan. Simmons had his day, so did his family, so did his meal deals, so did his day…no body bag, no meal deal, killings or sequel here to the events of the night, Cantona on the night felt ok, felt trust in the team, Cantona fell out with Ferdinand the day before and his at, at the pitch was for all to see and hear …victims are supposed to be able to have a life, not a crumpled mess, those who influenced rightly or wrongly are to pay for life, pay for families, pay for children and pay for charities to ensure moral victories are justly taken, being a victim is not fun, mockery of my vulnerability of everyone's, every single one of those individuals that UNICEF stand for

Continue with the Forward Run of Truth Pele and Vinnie Jones

'Now the problem here is the context as Vinnie is actually East London and Pele is Brazilian, problem two is that Pele is Black and Vinnie is definitely White and Vinnie is also single which causes concern for all mankind, she cannot stand her, Cantonas' actual girlfriend, which is actually the one on site, it is because she's posh, fit, healthy and active, business is reforming and we are very proud of her in the British Empire, says the Prime Minister….Vinnie Jones career spanned half a decade and became very nasty towards the end at Eric, so we decide to remove him after one of each. The running nymph the running nymph turns to be Cantonas, not the one who you would just speak to…cast is the resource which won the cast of the year on that night and wanted to thank her for being honest about herself once that made Eric cry with laughter and he couldn't help but tell her he wanted her all the more now…St Etienne, Marseilles, Leeds, Manchester United, Historical Referencing, Shirt is on the wayward line. The Auxerre of the yellow line was the tackle of the crime the one whose jeering had the light of the **(Zakarian to move)** yellow peril delight, the one whose send-off was the truth on the day on the roof. The white of the blue eleven sent the girls all into heaven the historical gene, of the bow of St Etienne, Marseilles sails within the Leeds on the double of Manchester United, the double hit on the back of the shirt had the red card onto hurt. A Non-Subordinated Youth of Play, a very jealous Elizabeth today the crown it goes from Light Blue ear from red and yellow to subordinated fear, the one whose testing all the scent, the one who is the one hell bent on damage to the inside ear of fairies one child subordinated cheer. Straight line truth, straight line truth, ouch…says Elizabeth, my crown went away, the one who sits there all day, the one who is the great big play the one who is the non-subordinated day….

Mohammed Salah sneaks in and takes the whole show, well it feels like it. with wide eyes tippy toe on the field of lunatics no…. chosen for the white Muslim forefathers of Egypt, the white genetic genome of the pharaohs, Tutankhamun, sphinx and the chasms of the pyramids the tombs of the kings and the deserts on the North African borders Bedouin, but not me girlfriends and a unique lifestyle which then makes everyone smile, in the heat of the day Mohammed Salah plays football in Cairo? In the Valley of the Kings….

Forward yes, we are all now in ore of the two footed excellence of Mohammed, the game changer at this point is the one with the feet on the African Plains, the one whose skirt and Bedouin is never enough…

Kohen MR NEYMAR Rosenthal's Hilton TRUMP, Johnson
Gnome and the Mushroom

Korea vs China

wives melt into others arms before, during and after marriage vows…

tTransfer Cell rReceptor Cell Code x and y

Epigram 07.53:29.11.2019 Winning The famous five, or secret seven, the number on the shirt Corporate Severn, Major Five, the UNICEF all 11 Number 7 on the door is way past half 11 Black the door, red the case, strategy at that Just press the cuckoo clock the press will be right back.

Prose 40 Epigram 09.26:29.11.2019 Super Genres to Win? YES, Strategy Position, Placement, Fear Emir went to the supersonic shop with all this kafuffle by far Under the Moonlight he hid underneath a blanket of tar Sun came out to shine next day with Selma all aloof Went back in the Cuckoo Clock had right back on the star, NO, FAST

Prose 41 LLP to win Lucy Locket lost her pocket to the one from JAM She likes Marmalade to eat all up, with fortitude with spam The link here is to win the Cup of wellness, heart with mind My big cup was gold that day, she needs no peace of mind.

Winning soldiers I did say, can you please stop using brackets Hilda Ogden the ITV said, can use the curlers right on them When the cup was gold not grey, with Cantona real fact He placed his head upon the cup, and he was not drawing back.

Some with it, some without they are drawn from near, to far.

What motivates the wag today is money, material by far.

This is as the match that dropped the baby on the floor

Has no one in the waste bin, as she does not believe in Mars.

Cantona on his 11 Truth, his britches only knee-high Ran and ran just like his spout, from the tea pot made by my Ma'am said he I do not need one, cos I am French you see His girlfriend said oh yes you do, put him on her knee, Phew, said he that run of truth went to the back of the net Pity said, Mark I got one first, however, Alex did us all out of bed. Marcus, said now look at me I am the one to watch, I have read the manual Upside down, can we see the clock Yes, it's not just half past ten, is nearly two The Cuckoo clock that ran and ran, slipped down the grid by far.

Cantonas' run of truths ran the media upside down When Isabelle did the dirty she conjecture to her towel His Girlfriend said, I do not mind, that he is now divorced Now heres' the next, you ridiculous mare, I am already here by far Look I conjectured to everything made, for anyone else you see Because I want it all for myself, including his family name UNICEF

Time

Abduction is a crime to, so how can someone still be with the victim, the assailant, someone took a little girl from her bedroom whilst she slept with her brother, her name was Madeleine McCann, the police here in Spain where I am now, Jerez actually are very polite when they speak, very well-mannered come in for the kill in other ways, Jose Mourinho felt the hammer after verbally getting excited for his girlfriend, McCann is very hurt by the throughout on her daughters tale of victimisation, death and no preventative take, protocol, Europol and Interpol being three agencies of power doing nothing about it, the European Union took another, different line here

Prose 42 Centrifugal Spirals

The shirt was off on the line The shirt was full of idea and rhyme the shirt that said my name on the back Was the shirt that found the one of great men.

The one that if French are always blue the one if Spanish are Red and Yellow too the one if white if family with red the one if yellow has flair at the feet of you the one is one with the World at his feet with you.

The one if our families can turn on the hoof If one of our families has misery and loot One of our families has mischief and crime Then one of our kind if ordered is no mine.

TIME

Then all our society runs further and further Away from the ones who absurdly murder the cows, the sheep the large cuddly tortoise The Jews, the Muslim and the 1 million Sikh at the first count.

The one who we say is the lord god and master Is the one who has 3 and we don't care from primary transfer Genetically speaking we don't incite bad around us Genetically speaking we are at peace and then we found us All from the family of strategy and lout we are not at peace our heads in no doubt.

More Time

1 Merriman the Swordsman on 1, the seventh 1 Chameleon of, Family of, Children of, Marmaduke Rose out of Merriman's vineyard, with his castle, topiary Opening, Closed Doors with skeletons in closets 2

1 Ex Wife needs more time, 1 actual wife needs a lifetime, and 1 girlfriend of 25 years needs a break from the verbal abuse and not deference of the British Media

More, More and Time Spent in a non-subordinated youth

World Cup, Golden Awards, Shows and Awards, Peace Political Strategies

Chinese Historical Referencing is available through this book, timelines, cultural interludes and the Great Big Wall of Sport, Confucius, Chinese Civil Service,

Inclusions here are Mao Tse Tung, 1/14 of the land mass of the World.

Chinese Cultural Exchange, Living and Lifestyle in Bejing, Chinese Silks are never shown in the UK due to inability to hang them properly, temple living, Luxury Living and highest Order Food, Pan Jin, WeiXiang and Qin Huo take on the ladies here in fan Li, Jin Zexian and Xiang My

2250 Xia Dynasty, Shang and Yin, Terracotta, Army, Wood Block Printing, Sui dynasty

Christianity beginnings, martyrdom, persecution, empire building, restorations, kings

Catholicism universal to the incarnation of Jesus, the cultural background and hypothesis of the religion major downfalls and influence on the strategies of peace

Hinduism, dharma, behaviours for a human being, karma, artha, stupa rituals of life

Muslim

Japanese Historical Referencing 35,000 years ago, Riharu Bitou, Maya Soniwa, Naohito Narukage

Japanese Cultural Exchange, Living and Lifestyle, Kofon dynasty, Asuka, Samurais, and the Showa Emperors

French Historical Referencing through religion, lifestyle and humanity

French Cultural Exchange, Living and Lifestyle, social gatherings, food, art are the main expressive genomes here in France.

E

Ball Throw for Cantona, Linesman, Centre Forwards and Peace Strategists

The link to many Paradigms, Centurions, Linear Relationships and Peace Strategies' is Time, Money and a lot of Talking

Peace for Resilience, Trust, Integrity of Decision Makers

Embed the Strategic Strategy into Everyday

Be like China, Be Like France, Be like Spain

Be like.... You

Osama Bin Laden was a Businessman here

Now he is not.... neither are his children, his mother, his father or extended families.

Be like the Spanish Police, have clean streets, do not incite directly if not necessary.

Have a nice day

Osama Bin Laden, The Cleric, The Footballer, The Cricketer, and the Parsons Terrier

Please understand the Giant Panda

For Political Peace, liars are not for telling.

Safer Political Pentagons, Safer Political in...

Global Security from the two that sat in

UEFA, UNICEF and FIFA, World Cup

Golden King is you

Prologue

Prose 8

The Englishman's Rose is far from retreat, his name was attack on the Goldfish of he in meat eating feasts with the skinny brigade, the Brigadiers value of the Englishman's Brave, The English Sports Woman on the memory of doubt, there never is one said of the Dame of the wheel, no brackets insight or four fingered salut

The Continued Forward: Changing Rooms with white on the stars, England's Freddie Flint-off had the memory of Mars, we love the fable of the beast of the charge, the blazing white horses on the streets of the Gard, the skeletons which hide in the closet, make their way into the watch basket the basket is full of Rolex with light, in from the book of the closet of life

Merriman's passion to dynamism for the future of hope, reliance with foolhardy Subversiveness squeeze, with integrity for children with no loss of life Merriman the swordsman of Palace with Virgil's, Russian MI5 many years we pray for him, may years with French lined streets for him Merriman.

Epigram No Knuckles

In this World we love to hate In the World we love you mate In this World we love you dear In this world you may re appear ...No Heart

Prose 9 World Cup Covert Superiority Brighton Rocks the World for You Saviour of the World is Fatherhood for You Hear the sound of us to bear When the little ones appear We have life all in the tower to bear

We have rock to rule the world We have all the ones to fill We have all the rocks to hold on the streetlights of the build.

No Man on Merriman here is the World rule for me here is the World rule for him Here is the world rule for life for me

With my family moral, value with worth contracted out of Main World with Stability, for Vulnerable, less able, valour, mischief and Crime with Statues with Defacement French Merriman your mine

Epigram French Bastion, Navy Blue, White, Red we went all ahead, marching unlike the hares of alight Louis the Fourth had one night, the Empresses Children in Flight the red empress had three with one on the way on the fathoms of spite, the Camembert Rolls

Prose 10 3 The sea of tranquil leadership shout Without the Bermuda 3 triangles out We rose again for all mankind to escape the boat we wondered why

We wondered on that day what went wrong for our soul to go to heaven, we wondered if We would see her again, Pomile the triumphant of Merriman.

Fond of her before the ether, Cantona caught the should beneath her the boat of all the missing 3 All been found when there was large Now 3

Epigram Boat Border Control for Papers to Disembark, all in the shoe Customs was the dogs great lie He sniffed with sniff under the tie.

Prose Cantonas' strategy was to stay with the one he knew Cantonas' strategy was to trust the one he knew High alert on the sensitivities of power, yellow control of the one who never listens.

Concave on the appetite, refugees on the eat, court has sanctioned on the hairline fractured on the street the crown it sits upon thine head of the tiara Strong in head, intelligence with rafters.

Continued Forwards Four Swordsman of Merriman is Red Alert, IR ICC for Amal Clooney the engine room is on fire Refugees all 6 holding court room today, lines of movement in the design bank of pay Jostling for position with inside without, the lines of the movement dance all in the pout.

Epigram

Symbol A is lives of many men to own, sow of pigs for the den, lair is the pigs we do not want leading to Louvre one night, Merriman Cough, Sneeze with Lucy Price

Prose Lemon Curd Kurds in the jungle of the ones who did know, the jungle in finding with little ones to play, lived all the life in the hilltop parade Foreverman, had his heart broke in two, aloof of the heart with mindfulness for you, do you really need to be thick of the skin when won't you realise that you should not hear that din with all faint of heart, in the crowd he did go, hit on the side of the very big balloon. Pomile skulking with skinny aubergines linguine tomatoes with cheese, no fat in the cheese, with the in the wings, camp in the buffoon with the big banana hat

Kurds with the Fuchsia with El Castro to be, Columbia we love the Ratification Strategy, Peace is the timeshare, with no one to be, the generation gap is the referendum we know. Un we love you said the meagre pom said, half friendly prickly non tortoise shell, the Epigram next for the BBA is Once aloof, for the baby inside the Hilton replied We looked on with them, all inside, with the Coca plant on the outside goodbye, Goodbye from the jungle of the inside inside, foot dreams united side Finding your way is the guiding man's behind

Dialogue 'She has no chance of being a physical supremacy as her jeans are too small, the Armani in the vice, with the roof of the splice the one who we behold is not very nice, Cantona despised her sometimes, dropping in unannounced to the Corporate Hilton, listening to all the chatter, the phone booths that night were stalling, like morse code on the receiver. A white handkerchief to cover the mouthpiece, the gloves of the Croupier are now put to good use, the information given to Denmark that night is unknown, Cantonas' hell had only just begun' the Epigram 09.34:26.11.2019 David went to the orthopaedic surgeon; he had a bad back from the strife of loving, all due at that the attention genres to genes are not the won, to put the genome straight back the one loving all humanitarian aid with stockings straight the heels of the humanitarians tirade, the competition bias on the UNICEF pitch aloud the French lunatic in from the pitch, the cold it doth bite on the streets of Lyon, the once friendly alien had tears of all gone…Prose 43 Winning Corporate Balzac here we go with energy filled with sweets Corporate Boards now in with me, hear me out cos you need the slim fair teat Balzac won the hearts, of the little man's front teeth with minds of Cuckoo Clock today…. Cantona said,

the majestic captain of the team that won put the ball of gold on his head and went for another shot….Cantona, the Golden King, with the seagulls went for another goal, Louisa shouts up now put that down little one, the mansion with staccato shout is yours tee what now? Training went well on that day; the looney began to shout Racism ……won the hearts of the man whom shot our Cantona down Bang Bang…went the Press

That's not me I did not see a thing …..Listen I said I didn't mean to uplift your routes with zing Child Protection rules the world, you did not need to sing Lanzarote is the amount that in the due date say Baby Born on Christmas Day had the heart belts sling Balzac won the hearts again, with corporate realised truth that he contracts on that day ole David went aloof, Tanni Grey was a Dame you know, now she's all the queen, did it go right up the spout, to fall from grace no lean.

Corporate realised truth that day went from the front to back, went inside the Cuckoo Clock with twirly wirily sack, From the Governance from then on, we hid the one inside, half a cider, with Heineken, the scarecrow looked exercise, In the face, withdrew the draw right now.

Time and another

'The Shirt of the Corporate Board, Stadium, Club, Household and Family of Arms is remembrance of the time spent with the design to ideological representation of your club, heart, strive for perfectionism, strategic excellence with representation of strength, to represent current ethos, goal, motive with SWOT of the current play, Board with SWOT, with Hierarchical Needs Analysis of current foe. Here we go with the most valuable Cristiano Ronaldo Shirt, Mo Salah Shirt, Robson De Souza (Robinho) Shirt. Corporate: Donald Trump Shirt, Peter Jones Shirt, Barack Obama Shirt. Now here is the compromise as this book is for the Glazier Family to understand why, when how and actually I like them, says the author, very world' Family: Trump, Gates, Buffet Epigram: 13.54:29.11.2019 Prose

Work and Rate is the time it was spent the critical mass is the one who was spent The Chain of reaction and the pants on the fire, no 11 on the shirt as this is 9 on by liar Mass of the mole and mass of cube mass of the string incited by you Infinity one said was the one in the bank, the one who is investment and then no heart sank

Hegemonic ideologies and complex COVID, embodiment of our own rats in the bed of the plant, gave sporting dynamics, transnational persistent stereotype of a proud Team of gymnastics: Representatives of the nation with no bulldog tattoo no hippy chick or gliding master or two TIME AND SPACE Prose Verse 44 Boris came from Leadership from the toroid's in the ship The canal it seemed from A to B, in the priory their today The 10 in cabinet is not enough, European entities are carded don't stuff 11 in the crucifix sign...Stop, Listen, I have the ball Under my foot it's not a basketball I am he, you are me, listen now cos I don't wanna be Studs on the boot, waiting for the loot! Drop the kick still isn't there, in the UNICEF shirt to spare 7 on the shirt in the red with foot on that night, we still delight with the shepherd on the staff in packed of the Trafford with United on hand. Charlton the magnificent, centurion of the sea Two of a nuance, competitive as we Long Johns, Flick, with Workmanship Waves of valour for the ship of captain Jack was not for ruin, he was for a castle We made, with draw of two He won for to Epigram 19.01 Dialogue

On the back of our shirts lies a tale of our self, who we are, what we are, foretold of our realism of our life. Wealth, Power, Control and Self. Show us, others, family, team who we really are here today. Hierarchical Needs Analysis of those who need and those in need. This identification of our own self of hierarchy, family, transition, representation, and I am. Some I ams' are more of an I am than most...have you heard....he won...the biggest I am... ever in the world...yes, the big C...or is it E...well ladies and gentlemen..there you go..Hall of Premiership Fame..with or without a tuxedo..preferably with one..the chameleon can be both..the reason for himself... What is a great big I am..well Mohammed Salah is an I am with Golden Boots...so, what's the difference? Messi? Pele? Cristiano Ronaldo?

Epigram 21.17.2021 Dialogue:

'Corporate Realism on the back of shirts where exactly... to the I am...do the Glaziers of this world fit in? They wear a shirt Corporate, Fashion and Sport, Technology, Corporate Buying. The number on the back denotes the favourite identification of the player...whether the biggest I am or not...religiously we are motivated to achieve for others, for ourselves, for each other, to share, to be with one another and not to disassociate...now this could have been said by the Mo Salah, Muslim by his ever presence...this week 25.05.2021 he was Golden De-Booted....this to a 14 year old can be severely damaging and actually to his mother...anyway...that aside... "Religiously he is motivated to achieve for himself, his family and not to do bad for others to be motivated Catholic' ....'When I got my first shirt it was blue, the blue of the club that I wanted since I can remember Auxerre, even though my feet were little at the time my number was 11, even from 8 years old. I remember feeling proud, knowing who I was, knowing that the colours meant something, that Auxerre's emblem made me feel motivated to understand. Then there was Marseilles, was only for a while a white shirt meant the enemy to some as I was French, so I was already driven by colour representation, so was able to strategize immediately' Epigram 23:02.30:29.11.2019 As our senses rise together, we hold each other's hands, Walk into the centre of the church Say our vows, look at each other realise what we have done previously that day, Make sure our hands are still held together and make love on the floor

Prose Verse 10:34:30.11.2019 Centuries Shirts with the collar onwards they go, Red on the shoeshine disregarded you know Fernandez had yellow to Brazil or the more Horse on the gallop situation by far Shirts on the collar with too many to see, the one who is dire with 2 on the tree The tree is all hard on the little one of red, The red one didn't wear one and the bun said go ahead...Forward Too the right march said Cantona, We leave them, yes you didn't wear one on the cabin mans' SURPRISE Lout on the beer belly with no in-between, I do not leave you so get them in-between

Shirts on the collar of misery with clout, Lycée we don't because your miserable never out Shirt is for collar on the big 3 of more, centuries of standing with ridicule once more Epigram:10.37:30.11.2019 Shirt on the Clock on the Centuries of Power The Tower of Hope is the Penitentiaries Desire....Dominance in the first five minutes more to Chelsea something which we all here at the BBC apart from the author who is for the player of the century can commend, 5 minutes 16.35 28.11.2021 At 40 minutes the possession dropped by 20%, we level to a very strong dominant Chelsea on attack, we held defence, mid field and now we need to push forward on the hold in the first half, we need to be able to get in the goal mouth...

During this time the section of me was very well documented is not true and I went through the news without any issue, my technique improved, my skills improved and I felt that Isabelle and other members of my family were all out with me, then I realised that they were not, I realised that I needed a lot of guidance, support and realism for what I had done, I then began unpicking that nights events and the world began to get over what they had seen. I then suffered tremendous sense of loss of belonging to a family that was unspoken, that was being with those of the same mind, skill, technique and geniosity, the press still did not like my 'arrogance' they went for me even more, I regretted even being Bourne at one point, initially my girlfriend I could hear, but not see during this time I had been with her for a very long time since being a child as she was given to me through the agency of adoption, I said I would have her, through my parents, I agreed. This was then confirmed through the Fergusons men to a position in Manchester United, the coaches knew nothing about it, but they wouldn't because Ferguson was not with all of them like this. Pomile is now banned due to her own discretion from me and you, the children and the two dogs. Sedated I travelled to hospital, travelled to the sedation and 28 days of my life, the worst of my life as I got used to being on my own. I did not drink at all, did not smoke, did not find anything funny for at least 28 days, my girlfriend was unbelievable in her support, unbelievable in her stillness for me, unbelievable in her time spent with me which was everyday with no work for that time for me with utmost heartbreak for her.... the rest of my family. I wanted so very badly to find her again.

Subterfuge: The Satirical Candle

The ***Sin was to be****....the triangle but there was nobody around...***Cosine through the letter box*** *was the sign from MI5 that you had become in yourself, a metaphoric dance, in the surveillance team, the Christmas present wrapped up underneath the Agents seat...the dead body crumpled, relaxed with no show of face on the metro....the yellow began to become different, the face of the dirt underneath from the lying jealousy of female truth, had dynamic systematic run off from the flood risk management planning from the Thames barrier reef...the middle of the ocean had the cosine retrieved from the coding oracle I know was the intelligence on the screen in the room with a view, the highest on the gun toting sling, Lucy Pocket hung her head with shame, but they are hurting you by making you watch those you like in your young life with each other and we believe that you enjoyed yourself.....*

*SIN, said the blindman...I went running down the track of athletic fastness...SIN, said the Fastness. I went pole-vaulting through the field.....Cosine...I went through the triangle of seven men, a hooker and a basketball hoop, the baseball hit the sound of the racket, hit the sound of the cosine of power, of the trigonometry of truth, the tangent on the square of the hypotenuse said tangent...the right angled triangled had one...***no pole-vaulting in the spring,*** *the jumper of the spring board hid the beam. Not the headlights of desire*

Blind....said the other...

No, said the Englishman on the centuries of power

SIN, said the one in wheel chair the one who hid the unfortunate happenings with her hand, the no fingered salute. No then..which on ado you like then? Hmmm, I like him..

Havers..I cannot stand him..half fingered salute on English Maidens glee..SIN is the one with Jesus on his knee, thine is the kingdom, the power and the glory, Amen

The sign of yellow stop amidst the velour ripples of luxury which turned to the almighty man of power, deceit and totalitarianism, the hitman of body held the young lady behind him, he watched her she slipped away into peaceful heaven...

The Folies at one point meant everything to Cantona the dances, the jiggling the hair, the makeup now he slips into a coma with one, non-dancer who can kick, dance latin and gracefully with ease eliminate with no reason....Ferrari was up too her, growling behind without the pushy woman in or out, the Cantonas Ferraris had Christie Brinkley and the Couture Models insight...The Red Ferrari of yellow STOP.....made the MI5 smile with delight, the cream of the cats whiskers being topped up on the night...his yellow STOP being played with no issue here tonight.....as it purred down the rural roads of countryside, dusk ridden lights of none dust lived on....flags began to appear on the window sills of hope, the racist chanting beginning to be here..the indigo chanting his name....the purr of the yellow STOP on a summers morning causing heat haze behind her....never a beep, never infuriated glances never a take-over.. always behind..never late...never left for dead, never raced....but Jesus Christ and this is out of religion what a car...to purr....one immortal day..the couture models always aligned to him... never out...she prayed that sometimes he would not mention sardines....she prayed for him to captain his heart..to be the one who captures everyones...not only for his country, but for himself, somehow she understood the bereftment in the news, the Hillsides taking kindly to the headlines that the Captain was now with indigo..she jumped up and down with glee..the sardines now..a thing of the past....NO...not anymore...purr the engine, pick her up..do not go round the other way round or you will get me....and a divorce was already on the cards....

Amen...said Pele.....

The future of life in the centuries past is the one with the golf clubs on the wings of the mast, gentlemanly stride, gentlemanly flowers, gentlemanly strove into the little wee hours...Erics dialogue here is for Follies 10 of them either banned from him or with him either by himself or themselves after relationships in France...Cantona is not for the former two week divorcee who told lies to him about her existence with her then husband.....he has vowed to stay with Pomile the less than Lately Lady

Backbones had the backlit cavern, the desire here started to squeeze the Ferrari the obsession of Ferraris, Mercedes and fat tyres....with yellow STOP does not happen anymore..as the purring never stopped .....just him...the obsession sat with the leather interior with shorts on, white with flair on the top..here with no one else other than the purring engine..considered, never ...the right footed brain master the wrong way round on the accelerator pedal...unto this point...patient..content..visibly handsome...gentlemanly..even..UEFA, the card, was never a societal mess...

The genetics of this Frenchman, the Italian car, sometimes Italian women, sometimes Italian men..he was told his left-handedness was not here that his left brain you find out..is more developed than his extreme talent of intelligence of his right. The kill here is any blame for any controlled bi polar...of the psychotic no between in such circumstances. just like everyone else...that's how they act...unlike this Frenchman who got the blame through the press for something he did not say or do... is not a satirical play here..the Frenchman is never ill, never charged, however has been ridiculed for actions, words and de-meaner most of his life...

his mother commented that she knew he wasn't backwards, as she had been told, the mathematical brain can be conditioned in the other way round...his spatial awareness was a designer dream...conditioning of those neurons from that much of an early age meant de sensitising other neuron pathways which develop cognitive immediacy...such as phonetics... the genetics of tall dark handsome and genetically superior with no immediate needs were phenomenal and he took the world by storm....he has had assault twice and Simmons...but like we say..he is not under any pretence ...he is the best in the world for his UEFA Presidents Award..his Player of the Century...his Motherhood Award and his own Fatherhood Award.... more fool he..his father is not here yet..his mother his brother..are here..his other brother Joel is not here...the topic of conversation was women legs the Cantona preferred the author as they are not in-between at the top, plus her face is a dream...

On French TV.....

Le sol sur lequel vous marchez est généralement embrassé, les statues de la maternité sont toujours au premier plan, quand vous perdez celle que vous voulez rencontrer, vous faites de terribles cauchemars sur ce dont vous avez besoin, ils vous mangent, vous courent, montent à cheval et s'installent ailleurs., jusqu'à ce que tu trouves quelqu'un qui accepte de te juger, c'est la France, le raccordement français du canal de sueurs, comme les racines de tous les maux, les souvenirs du pain de jeûne, les rouages de l'élite

Le problème c'est que celui que tu connais est celui que tu rencontres, ceux avec qui tu as grandi sont ceux que tu cherches, ceux avec qui tu es doux, alléjullah alléjullah disent ceux qui savent, disent ceux de l'establishment sont pour le droit de survivre à l'holocauste, la façon dont nous écrivons aujourd'hui s'adresse à ceux qui sont très vieux, à ceux qui sont très hideux dans leurs sourires à pleines dents et à ceux qui sont en harmonie avec la nature. les pelouses entretenues ici, quand on semait les champs du rire je me rends compte que la protection policière est le pays des libres, sauf les parcelles sur l'arbre, l'arbre est celui dont le papier rouge et or, le temps et le ruban rouge et or, eh bien le papier doré est meilleur, parfois avec des liens blancs, des formes dorées, des rubans dorés, des chocolats sur les arbres, des oranges fondues aux arômes segmentés d'orange dorée, les hideux sourires à pleines dents sont maintenant ceux avec des graines en bouche qui s'étouffent avec les arômes du goût amer, le sucre est le goût, le fou aux fourneaux est le chef qui donne tout pour le pays du royaume, mais son royaume est celui de sa femme, sa femme étant celle qui est délicate petite, longue- vivants et ridiculement petits, les graines d'orange du ministre d'York manipulées avec soin, les débuts du ministère français soignés avec presque autant de soin que vos dames qui gèrent vos affaires, et j'en ai assez dit, tant mieux, nous ne faisons qu'un avec l'autre, nous ne faisons qu'un en étant à la boutique de l'espoir, la boutique du désir d'un sac, le bling, le bling comment on va à la boutique. ..conduisez-vous, montez-vous en voiture, montez-vous à cheval ? trot? voire perdre toute capacité à vivre seul….

L'invasion française est venue, à plus d'un titre, un aperçu du désir alimenté d'entrer dans le manifeste de Macron, de la dure vérité, de l'honnêteté du discours, des pourparlers, de l'intégrité motivée par le désir de paix..., de l'honnêteté du vérité les fashionistas prêtes au mode de vie à la française appartiennent au passé, avec une seule envie de pinger, pinger pour l'espoir de la justice de l'humanité, la vérité de l'honnêteté de tous... c'est la vérité de l'honnêteté de venir à moi, de me demander, montrez-moi que vous possédez des hommes et des femmes injustes et parlons…, celui qui avait très peu de cheveux a eu tout d'un coup, le ministère français du bleu de moindre stratégie... le problème c'est que ce n'est pas le cas, le ministère français est considéré comme supérieur, et est… maintenant… ne l'était pas toujours, mais l'est maintenant… l'amour des ministres impliqués dans l'espionnage se manifeste encore dans l'écriture de romans, j'écris pour garantir la validité de mon contrat de livre… avec un homme des proportions exigeantes.. et un grand et beau pays à découvrir... La France, l'invasion a commencé.. moi taille 0 sans bikinis suintant sur les côtés avec de la chair en bermuda… avec des shorts maintenant, voici le décompte 4 par jour tout de même sponsor..Decathlon.. jamais une quinzaine toujours trois mois même licenciement que le PSG, la Marine Nationale c'est l'invasion de l'Angleterre... des couilles. Oh. dans les fissures de la perspicacité physique qui est considérable, je ne veux pas la perdre, déclare-t-il.. je sais que je suis là.. non tu ne l'es pas.. tu n'es pas elle.. qui lui a enlevé plus d'une fois... ce dieu physique, Zeus, 57 ans avec Héra, une patiente et passionnée, eh bien, elle devait l'être, cette non-dépendance des systèmes gouvernementaux, du parfum et de la femme arrogante.. cela lui a été retiré… or…

ils ont chanté dans les tribunes et maintenant ils sont partis pour de nouveaux pâturages car elle est refusée par lui devant les caméras..

Le dieu physique, en or dans zeus est la capitale des souvenirs pour tous, un jeu de cartes dorées, un jeu de souvenirs dorés et deux billets pour un match... de beach soccer... à gagner pour la France. ..au milieu du match hourra Henry est apparu sur la piste, la Cantona l'a flattée physiquement, pas le petit insistant, l'autre..celui qui a réussi..la perspicacité physique que tu as avec mes ongles plus longs pour faire mes mains allongé, lisse, blanc et élégant est désormais toujours le même... J'aimerais trouver un jour pour toi tout seul... te prendre dans ma main, devenir le maître du jeu, écouter les fruits du travail et retirez doucement tout votre être... lentement... très très lentement... pouvez-vous m'attraper... Sir Isaac Newton... plop... plop... plop... plop... est la pomme lancer pour Adam et Ève... adoration des héros du pied droit pour les bottes d'or... ceux qui ont le pied droit... transversalité complète de ce qui s'est passé... 6 pieds 2, il ressemble à environ 6 pieds 4 et puis il fait des choses stupides qui on se demande pourquoi il fait ça... comme... le sentiment d'être expulsé du Royaume-Uni pour que l'auteur assume la paternité de lui-même et de bien d'autres facettes de sa vie en France, Paris pour être exact... 1-0, il glisse des tacles jusqu'à la cheville, connu pour ça, jusqu'à l'os... aïe... et encore... jamais à notre époque on ne trouve quelqu'un qu'on gère trouver tant de choses dans le malheur....Le dieu physique, en or dans zeus est la capitale de la mémoire de tous, un jeu de cartes en or, un jeu de souvenirs en or et deux billets pour un match... de beach soccer. .. à la victoire de la France...En plein match hourra Henries est apparu sur la piste, Cantona l'a flattée physiquement, pas le petit insistant, l'autre..celui qui l'a fait...soumettez-vous à elle.. bien dit l'Auteur, la perspicacité physique que tu as avec mes ongles plus longs pour rendre mes mains allongées, lisses, blanches et élégantes est maintenant toujours la même... J'aimerais trouver une journée pour toi tout seul... t'emmener dans mon main, virez le maître du jeu, écoutez les fruits du travail et retirez doucement tout de votre être... lentement..... Sir Isaac Newton... plop... plop..plop... plop. ..est le tirage au sort des pommes pour Adam et Ève..nu, il se tenait...le culte du héros des pieds droits pour les bottes dorées...le pied droit...la transversalité complète de ce qui s'est passé...... hourra Henry se rassemble pour le prochain réveillon de Noël, chapeau rouge, pompon léger, jambes sexy, bas, cou-de-pied haut : talons hauts de 4 pouces et plus, se promène avec sex-appeal partout, aime son maestro de plage dorée avec le maître pieds nus de la coupe du monde.... on tourne maintenant la pièce sur la maîtresse car on ne veut plus d'elle, elle a eu la liaison avec le tout-puissant, s'est cachée derrière la chaise, a prié Jésus, puis a retrouvé sa cousine avec celui qui s'est enfui... celui dont le flair de génie a capturé le monde avant la coupe du monde, comme c'est embarrassant... oh... moment de coussin au siècle prochain..il a insulté Didier Deschamps...il a insulté le manager de l'équipe de France de coupe du monde puis est parti dans une petite voiture ... qu'est-ce qu'il est censé être pour Ferrari, pas pour Morris Minor... bleu, pas rouge dans le pays mais à l'UEFA, en FA, il était rouge, il est partout... maintenant une femme insistante hors de juridiction l'a banni de il est ensuite revenu.... il n'est pas revenu...il n'est jamais retourné vers celui qui s'est enfui..ce n'est pas vrai.il avait toujours avec elle le tacle coulissant directement sur l'os supérieur de la cheville... ses jambes fortes, le haut de son torse repoussaient sur elle celui qui s'était échappé… celui qui faisait tout pour lui celui dont il détournait le regard… pour voir le sol… il savait qu'il allait lui faire du mal alors après il l'a récupérée... tout comme enquêter sur la question des longues jambes d'un physique plus petit avec un cou-de-pied haut... comme celui qui s'est enfui... avec des talons sur un tueur pour Cantona... ses longues et fortes jambes, cou-de-pied et torse plus hauts.. sa propre maternité est toujours disponible pour lui.. elle sourit… plus que vous ne l'imaginiez jamais.. ..This is no end to French TV….above not below…

the pushy woman wasn't here…wasn't nosey…wasn't berefing…was being counted for in the british economies under wasn't being counted for…never mind..he longed for a none pushy woman… this morning Cantona turned over from the orange of delight one night, dirty and unclean sheets never under question….we are now involved with you the other way round… hopeful for the Ferrari of the day of your life….the yellow STOP showing with the authors smile of inference….to the STOP….STOP….STOP….the pedal at 180 mph hid the desire to win with no spin…the shoe on the right foot, the brain master of Thursday play, Mbappe smile at his 10k, he's in..in Monaco…..he has to compete now with the Golden Boy Almighty of Cristiano Ronaldo….Salah is not here is not true..Salah has the Beast of all relevant Rolex in tune with the Frenchman of significance, who is not Mbappe..who has been brought in to remove Rashford….I have to go says the Author, I will be back later on…Ferraris of the Frenchmen's heart hid the desire at the steering wheel, the Nurburgring, the 5km straight that makes your yellow not stop but go…problem is Mercedes aim was a true one…the Hamilton was behind the wheel not on the radio, the physical capability to hold the G Force, the unenviable position sometimes behind the haze never a mention as this was not an option. To be behind…even at the start...Cantona had always wanted one, then two, then three an obsessive disorder of obsession about the only thing that he had ever dreamed of for himself. A Mercedes Benz.. two now …a Sigmond Froid, a Belly Dancer of all proportions, the jealousy that has ensued as divided the nation, divided the Heathcliffe… we are now back to the obsession of Ferraris.. obsessive, shiny wheels, buffing so he could see his face in the Bonet, for hours and hours and hours, waxing, shining with no take out on the road, the wheels gleaming with desire to take to the road, the doors gliding into place, making very little noise, no clunking, sensors which arrange the locking system so that you do not have to push the door yourself shut, it does it itself

Now, cosine, smile, laughter, no desire of any runs of further truth the Meyers of this world bereft, run of truth down the middle of the play, the truth of the black master of the myriad of glories… bang shot down, no more cosine I hid the glory in the highest order when he went past, he hid the ball. I couldn't remember in the changing room, which one was which. How about you?

You hid in the changing room? How long for? About an hour…what for? ..I did not want to go to class…what?. I was being accused of bullying, I did not want to show with those who I had bullied….I did not do well at school…OK Trigonometry hit the ball in the net…angles, right, obtuse, adjacent, acute under 45degrees..tip toe precision Pele..tiptoe..NOW…right round the run of truth hit the Peles run of truth of Cantona…Cantona is the one with the goal mouth..the fastness, the electric sportsman cheek to cheek in his dancing of desire

BANG…

The shot on goal was being watched by 170 million…on that day…that Pomile lost her way… through the CCTV, Cantona wanted to see what they saw, the little gorgeous author crumpled in the tunnel of career, motherhood and sheer determinant of intelligence as it drew her….the walk of indulgence was not really that..the enemy tucked up in bed for fat…SPRATS said Marco…

***SNiFF…SNIFF….the MightyMan hid the CCTV for a while…here Leatheron,** had the most ginormous mouth, Hitler had the most ginormous idiot in himself, some say we should not mentioned him here, we disagree even if it makes you squiggle..it gives others the reasons as to why he was a ginormous idiot…he hid his agenda, the secret service hurled the book at him, the Milosevic curator of all time, with war crimes during his reign that pulled shot guns on children to keep them in line…the footage saw Cantona, tall strong, athletic yet sad…waiting for his girlfriend to run past so he can follow…her..she didn't know breaking heart everyday for the touch of a genius on her skin, her longing for him to be with her, him now we know feeling the same about her..we are now at one with each other, we do not need your interference to the pushy woman…we need you to please leave us both alone when we are together…Leucile the tall skinny ex dancer is now impeached due to her terrible breath, in the mornings, she divulged the dirty pair are now in …the machine gyrating with desire to clean the dirt …SNIFF SNIFF…Obtuse angles the ones of very very fast dirty women said Pele …softly..softly…he is taken down through the caverns of his mind remembering the women, the turns the little idiosyncrasies that hope desires.. not he, runs of hopes, truths and gyrating poles…*

Batman is here now, the jealousy ensued of a SuperHero phenomenon…, for the Bat Mobile and no we cannot write here another analogy to it…Robin has his Crown in China, the Gold Buggy awaits the Emperor his new Arsenal, the red brigade of all time Mao Tse Tung is the present leader here…the armies on shooting the current leader have represented the harmonies of golden balls, leading weddings, designer fashion, couture identities and colours, logos with huge acclaim… **celonships who died** *recently in a time void…I hid behind the telegraph pole, he one in the centre of the field, the track was very dirty on the day I left my family for a new life abroad.. date back to super sleuth…MI5 made him gyrate, as he had committed crimes before she met him….the considerable wealth of her family drew him..the amount of time with* *footballers did also..he crept into the night air one night and showed that he loved her to the one before…they were all there…laughing and joking right in her garden..she crept back inside.. drops of wet tears rolling down her face..her eyes steaming with hot ones….rolling continually down. Breaking her heart..hurt with fear..knowing she was never good enough for anyone. Is how this made her be…she knew she was. She knew that her lack of sexual partners and lack of loose control was the reason. She knew she was fun, hideously fun and completely inverted with lower cut tops…she was a target from then on…the lipstick marks on her collar were in enough to decipher her sexual orientation, towards the end of her existence she confessed her love for her lover and retired….telling everyone it was time to stop, in case she went with another one….in the service two become one very quickly, lovingly holding hands, telling each other jokes and being together in private, this went on for years…the PA, then the Docks, then the public arena of running, when she went out she saw the development of others in her region, disastrously trying to make dynamic representation of themselves*

THIS IS LESBIAN SPACE

IS NOT REPRESENTATIONAL OF ANY OF THE AUTHOR DYNAMIC REPRESENTATION OF HERSELF WHICH SOMEONE GOT JEALOUS OF ALL THE WAY THROUGH HER LIFE

…the lorry drove that night with Cantona the character hard at work, driving behind on behalf of the most successful spy network in the world…welcome Sigourney Weaver to the **worlds highest lesbian real***….we do not want two mouthed lips kissing here..we do not want to eyes meeting, saying hi then spouting subordinated justice in defiance of behaviours undesired…..the Cantona looks away, not her I dream of just my friend…dreaming of her, being with me longing for her touch on my face, forgiving of all trespasses, all cleanliness and many years of guided precision, the lock of hair raised eyebrows Phibrow couture for all to see, his manliness, his strong hands, lipstick face, smothered in entity of his own self...he drove all evening to be in the same place, lovingly holding her …the dirty granulated wood betide with her jowls moving from side to side when she wobbled away…this woman he does not see any more with himself….a shame but bad habits die hard dysfunctional analysis is representational in social etiquette and social representation.. she is joking here in her new found crossed fingered non lunacy..WOW… she has..made better through the need for a couture body a new one for herself….her dynamism when she runs, athletic and a proven track record…petit how I like…heels how I like toes how I like and many many intelligent nuances in my life..WOW what a humanity driven performance… the back of me showing the bones of their contentious life …I bleat with enthusiasm, share no heat, share no impetus towards them both whatsoever, I am clean, virile and not gay… Cantona is now here…these names that will change for the livelihoods of mankind…bestow deep darken caverns of despair…to those wives who find out…insightfulness of espionage of shootings in Moscow happened, the coercion of the banking staff happened the mechanism*

for economies for Buzan happened, in fact the **Whales as a black white** cities also happened and a very jealous…female of ugliness…the tall, dark non destroyer the right way round, was a shadow of her Crossfit self, helped at the beginning by the security team..directly at the lady who had nationally represented in athletics, the rest is now upon her…for an hour or two..no play of let's pretend. Lets undo the side of power that we have here..hurt sheer desperation of hurt….the heart that fills out never did again. Pushing strongly through the media in the UK.. with no weight for her, but loss of hair, weight, skirt, verbal social belonging and loss of time, to allow the skirts of colour to fulfil their own wildest dreams…..the car was the deciding factor, the turntable in the living room was the Mercedes none nightmare, this was Ferraris dream…

POP POP POP……RICOCHET…..POP POP POP…RICHOCHET…. KISSING>>SUMMERTIMES>>>HAZEL BRANCH TWIGGY BRANCH SUCCUMBS TO YOU FOR THE WINTERS HARVEST….. Short sharp bangs, short sharp bangs…hardened shot guns in the lorry were the key to him following on the night …that night he walked from the theatre to his apartment…loitering around the tram stop, knowing she had been there..he loved her before for what she was to him..now he knew he had to make her be round the other way round, through his own influence of an affair…he could not see her properly but knew that he loved her all the same..she wanted her to be with him and wanted him to be where they were in Cheshire with her all the time, but he couldn't because of the pushy woman breaking cover and trying to be with…..the one that got away was always non chalet always thinking but never realising that she thought that it would never happen, she lifted her coffee cup, wondered if he would ever come back to take her for that coffee, then wept every night when he called for her during long hours in the UK to help her to sleep, getting worse with the pound shop on the way through rural England that became towards her, at her from the poster boy that became the Poundshop…she used to fall to sleep on Cantonas knee in the media, through families and jealousy ensued through France with the woman who became that pushy that even Cantona did not even know what to do..the Cheshire Lady began to cry most of her life about the pushy woman taking her life away, not with Cantona but life…he swerved round the wrong corner, the steering wheel driving the longitudinal sat nav into the ground, the opening of the lorry, the steel girders in the way, was then silly, as he knew the girders were a pseudonym …shot guns packed with ice in the barrels…blue, white ice, the stuff of badly behaved angels…in Italy with Mussolini…. The spirit of the drug cartels, the line of enquiry is where, as in Belfast where the lorry is from did not hear anymore from the shipping clerk, later that day she was dead..strewn across the job centre floor…Cantona here is fat..Cantona here is wealthy…Cantona here is the great, big, fat, cat with whiskers, filled with cream, penthouses women and children…like the mafia…Cantona is above the law here, aloof, satisfied, criminal, over inflated and a star…a bit like himself except not over inflated or **fat….tyres** easily is not in his nature, dynamism respondent on his run today, panting he turned the corner bumping into her, his shorts pointing *at the sun, hello…he said, I wonder if you would like coffee…Yes, thank you..I would love to go to coffee, my brothers are available if you would like to speak to them…her brothers fell about laughing he's our pick..He matches you..he's' your O and that's not his bank balance either..his children speak highly of you…the stealth bomber cordially invited, Cantona is now another to be developed here…the van took the line of traffic blue in colour rickety with silver cold storage in the back…the storage squeaked with vengeance laughing to the sound of the design framework..back at the office the Detective surged ahead with his intelligence ….the group through MI5 had position in the house, the marking of cars, the anti-surveillance which goes round three prong…utilising event management satisfaction we are now over reliant on you, your son and your neighbourhood. On your move to the* ***USA*** *we can breathe a sigh of relief that you are now out of the UK…your over reliant attitude said sue is condemned today as you don't work..we are now with the Great British Chefs, over-reliant attitudes on their own work… Cantona pulled back on the gears trying to grab hold of his lady friend….she wasn't his wife in real or storyline at any point, detail here is tremendous on the i line….but it is not consistent.. the hairs on her shaved neck brought tears to her futile solitude living in a way which enabled the most profitable company of all time..this does not mean that you would not spend money..it means that the return is over 8 times the profit..which is not want the in laws wanted, her brothers looking down at themselves. We are not him they shrieked and ran off….yes, them…the ones who never showed..did it in a different way, NEXT became synonymous with a waste of time called the other one…diving for cover most of he weekend behind the house, shouting his mouth off about sue…..the ageing dancer with wrinkly legs…especially at the top..the smooth skin of the Author never quivering..the storyline never met in time..is not true…the jealousy ensued, the surveillance not forgotten ..all those baths to remove the dirt, even though it wasn't there…* ***Remembrance Sunday in the cenataph allowed surveillance to see the. underlying beauty of her, couture face,*** *no over reliance, hideous wakeup to work and a reliance of no-one… the cameras force the border control to become satisfied…the blue ray indicators on the beep are now well known ..the increase in technological punjab..altogether in this tirade by Cantona himself. The horses specialised in the control of the public, in fact the fall off and sometimes out, decides the fate of the lunacy of red carpets…Cantona smiled here being on the right side of lunacy helps you know….the blast happened the Cantona happened..*

STOP…LOOK…LISTEN…I am not up the biggest tree of Buzan sponsored by Meyer on my shirt..as the reversal is condemned by all…learned conditioning like a dog..with no support is a nightmare for Special Agent Spider..the code words for listening are not ***ecoute et repeater*** *they are STOP…LOOK…LISTEN…never our time did we ever get a maestro at work…never did we hear those tears of joy, ravaged by a jealous female part of his family who controlled everything then drove it into his daughter..who dependant on Erics' reaction will be protected here…Belfast rose its ugly head again in the news…so did Pele…the opportunity of a lifetime so* *they thought, the vengeance from the scorn woman heightening after she realised that the press were involved forgetting many years ago that she did the same thing, obstructing modelling on a down play that hurt the victim for the rest of her life..*

the body of her lay face down this time the tram rolling over her limp un protected body, her skirt pulled over her waist, she got up this time she is not warped here but a description of how it was before the fatal instruction of taking her away from her family, the skirt was wafting in the breeze that day scolding the sun on her legs was the son who told of his mother's plight the next day to his classmates…so they all knew.. as an advocate he declared that it was not safe here and he left with her….the skirt was allowing the man to feel wanted in the elite play with the pocket of a woman who wore fur, on a farm of greed that the milkman would be proud of if not vegan..the cheese the camembert of bull runs strolling down the side splitting curse of the stage…hilarious at it is, it pokes fun at those less fortunate, greedily making it for those who have bullied, chastised, become victims, with a nonchalant tongue in cheek…the legs of his mother dwindling with hope that the man did not touch them when he went to remove the skirt in front of her sons classmates, not in dance move but in a vicious nonchalant attack of hysterical laughter, mimicking and ridicule..jealousy of her not being interested in him, not being sexually attracted to **the big benefit IAM***…with a plethora of unborn big mouthed children all with different mothers….the black uniform of the spider in stealth launched at the mother to be…the looking glass of hope that she would one day be fit, healthy free of cholesterol and become a four fingered salute….her pathetic body in a crumpled mess on the floor..society would never again be able to say that she was protected from the man that did this to her and her son….who at the age of 8 years old protected his mother as much as he could…she was highly protective of her son, victim support ….is a phenomena that the victim had seen the other way round through the police, it was a highly protective insightful removal from being a victim today, this can happen when it is deemed that the area is safe, has been swept, has more unionist parties in….those unionists were for the conformist freedom liberation party of the UK..who happen to be those who can have their lives taken by others on the end of a shot gun. Machetes are not here and* **Kalashnikov** *automatic machine guns are certainly not within the educational remit of the UK…NOW, HIT…..HARD…FAST…IN…FAST OUT….we are not for you, we cover, we hide, we show, we are not for you, we are meat eaters…through..through…. threw…CATCH THE BALL…* **little ones….CATCH THE BALL***…*

The tears of the daughter short lived as the directed at towards the victim continues..it is a shame that this happened as it hurt the very one that is listening all the time..I hope that one day what ever this lady has done, can be forgiven in his daughters eyes…until then she cannot be….jealousy rode the camel and broke the back of the horse…the analogy hid the face of the victim from the attacker, the children finding it funny that the attacker did it…the victim find it very uncomfortable in a school playground ever again..broad daylight pushing her to the evening walks, midnight solitude of working for a huge pay...the packet of hope came in sultanas that saved her one day when out in the fields, she broke the daylight hour with on avoidance of the truth, those around her did not know how to deal with what had happened so undermined her further until one day she pulpited the athletic approach of the once friendly tortoise, hid the future, then did the most heinous action of threat to her very sex he dumped her in front of the cameras, in front of all hope, after in-sighting her with him all his life.... disgustingly repulsive the genetics were all over the forensic ridden jacket, skirt, hat and scarf... the blood from her son pouring down her face...lineage of her illegitimacy pouring from in-between her smooth skin on her legs, her clean vagina, with no pits, with no grains or granules licking the cream of the man in charge of the womb of the entity of mankind....the fostering became adequate enough with them never being found, her hopeless parents becoming further in the back of her mind...the man who she wanted to become with her leaving the very entity of his own mind once again..he had never met her, leaving his wife for her, he then smiled, went back after her and tried to laso the past to tell her she wasn't good enough all over again...the affair that she was promised is now null and void...or so she thought....the trouble maker with the bosom of fake, the pin up of all dirty men was standing in front of him, on that day, saying one thing showing another...the show being what everyone else has seen, that is the show of all for nothing is sacred..just dirty for men of old to leer obtrusively in arrears...the forensic examination of the coat, hat, scarf and skirt was taken seriously through jeering, the leer went away back to the den of fear, on the attempted rape, bundle and fire arms charge. The man dumping her removed himself as he could not cope with himself, after abducting her son, in fact the abductor had two fold resentment as she divorced him a few years before, the save face resentment of leering ran into the societal mess where he stood on that day in the hotel... his coercion a concern for the authorities, Cantona began his true word of honour to her..to marry the one that got away from him as she was found face down in the dirt from bullying, ridicule and resentment from those who wanted him instead...the valour besides his truth was profound, hearing the deaf dog in two ears was fluffy in two toned sounds..she was deaf you see, the red flamed author was now transparent as she picked ridiculed some more, she remembers ....Mark Hughes a little known entity at his point well, comparatively, figuratively speaking...the grey starting to show now in the fifty entity of the book, his wife giggling at the very thought that he would be involved at all with anyone else...it hit him hard, that night, he nearly retired..Mark Hughes...he did not want his friend The Cantona to become more bereft than he was....he was sure that Amanda-Jane would look after him in later life...the death of Pele today was not happening, all the guys from the back room hide with shivering delight, as the gorgeous Amanda-Jane walked through Derbyshire's Hillsides...the hotel that day was told 18.00 in front of the surveillance, she can manage you from here, as the cameras can show your whereabouts, the nursery involved hid thinking it was okay to be non-committal with child care provision under a one.....problem is, the whole world saw him being taken, as he came in front of the cameras after he had done it…euphoric, delusional, patterned, fake…HID **THE ENTITY OF THE GOLDEN BALL**..THE ONE THAT GOT AWAY…the abductor not on the leg, but on the heart of the very humanised being that she wanted, the very being that grew inside her, as a entity of loss, through adoption, fostering with no feeling of belonging….the trust that was deemed from herself on that night was a terrible affair on the brink of disaster…the shock waves of the take on the child that saved his mother as best he could limited his down fall, limited his custody, limited his forthright mind and at the age of 8, went through every remit of upper age groups in philosophy that you can find..now at the age of 15 he finds himself looking after his father at his disposal through fathers ill health 3-4 years not months…ahead of his game… Physics is usually the time bound entity of all, TICK TOCK WENT THE CLOCK ……….TICK TOCK **TICK TOCK………a sudden pause to the lightning bolt**…the white lightening of shock …..CROCODILE>>>CROCODILE>>>> the lightening hit home the bolt of lightning hid the wall of Lucy's pocket…..the pocket of fake, friends in highest regard, friends of the man who skirted the lady of lunch….we timed her once in the porch-way….she didn't have one a porch the bully got away in a heap with her skirt above her head…her pants squew whiff on her legs, with no smell other than Chanel….other than no doubt she had been raped….those who perpetrate issue to victims of crime lessen burden on themselves, not the victim as they come back for seeing more….the gentiles here are helping her….no…they are trying to find her something to do…..her bereftment is solitude, eating, writing and being at anyone who is wrong….and when she said, my signature is mine…it stands in court, so does my Ofsted 1, differentiated by my cycle of dreams, that Mighman Mighty man gave back to me….his lessening burden continuing his lessening burden of my dreams of my life….promised by his family together again, forgetting they gave back what they took…for dancing virgins, dancing poles, dancing media, dancing tip toe, dancing lions with hopefulness that the return shall make him King once more….the Queen is already in her counting house, or the estranged one, but the one who got away from his clutches who fell in a bad way as a victim ever since….MighMan MightyMan…please do not treat me like the rest..like those who say hi, hows about it and you succumb ..please Mighman make me who I should be, who I am who I want to be…..and who my son deserves to see every day again……I have done nothing wrong Mighman, but jealousy is evil, envy…I work hard for my life in a month's time…today, me MIGHMAN…**MIGHTYMAN.. the Crocodile is taken for this book…TICK TOCK>>>>>>TICK TOCK>>>>>>WENT THE CLOCK IN THE CROC>>>>>>>the Rosenthal's** hope for glory today is the release of one.. NEVER in my lifetime would I let him go…he coerced, he smuggled, he killed families slowly from within…NEVER IN MY TIME HAVE I EVER HAD A MAN WHO IS SO BEREFT SUCH AS HE….Spaniels they worship the ground you walk on to smoothly abduct your children to allow over reliant families through that have never been before….the blood of her son, pouring from her eyes, her menstrual cycle aching with the need of another one….For us..MIGHMAN, MIGHTYMAN this is your call….MIGHMAN MIGHTYMAN I WAIT FOR YOU EACH NIGHT…you *fail to come to me....my heart it burst upon the knee of hurt for couture which I do not mind to be..MIGHMAN of FRENCH NON LUNACY....I do not blame, this is our charter of non-madness of return ....Of our love of non-lie, away from the abductor, the liar, the Milkman, but the Bread-man of pecan in Calgary, Bullring of snort....my love for you is Forever-man, Forever-man of thought of me your influence is glad tidings of thoroughfare winter fare of torte. French is my lineage. French open ball, glad tidings of ho..ho..ho..is them all... the football stadium there was a hug crowd, Manchester United got beat the other day, Juventus was drawn now find a game that you desire and make the players dance and sing ok, Fantasy is all about the island of dream that is what her family would say, to repulsively remove the man in the wax coat, not the red one, as we can have another here he pulled down her shorts, smacked her backside and ran off with her laughing got arrested and then fell in love with his author again...who was not his author at that time...the curdling blood thirsting wolf sprang to attention late one night when his wife backed off the thought of having another one...the ache wasn't there from the first, as she had no idea about how it feels to hurt...the score line, is for* ***Pwilth Lunacy not allowed****...the 3-2 coming up is Reginald's Harold.....who is now in place of Dave...who has sadly passed away...his own lunacy getting the better of him...Ronaldo is seen from the window, the marriage that day of compromise, compassion and removal of pacifying evil....she had been threatened by the evil sister of two, she is now in the blame game play of her life... the game is to survive the hopeless nincompoops of everydayness, each day removing the demonstrous women of his life....somehow blatantly indicating that he is not deserved.... somehow, I feel that he deserves much more of his own existence...he smiled..on that night... looking to the big K for inspiration wasn't something that he did..he stays with same one...being influenced or so it seems by his own inner self..just like her...in a few years your children are going to be older and you can have your life back...she prises the milk top open, creaming her top lip, always the gold now, here the silver topped cream...the silver stallion a dream, those who were bereftng her making symbols behind her back, drawing faces and hurting her for being different, for being not belonging, for being not part of society anymore....she is adopted he said I don't want her here...the large cuddly tortoise is now here tramping about the minefield, Yeti in her snow shoes considering the balance other day....Pockets of this world a myriad away from ladies who lunch only those getting laid...Valentino is now here for the Author to be a part of her lifeline.....her retirement of thee pensions, life assurance and pretty much another 2 inheritance are now over 1 million...or will be...The Muslim community had all out today with you Cantona, then you made a screw turn to your ex-wife....the Sgt murmured...the anti-intelligence negligible here as it is a non-part of their badge...your fridge....do you ever have sex, or do you anally purse your lips and squeak...not that I am aware of ha ha you waste of time to France with your Frenchman in your fictitious mind...Paris sounds good, do you know anyone there or do we need to give you a reliance check out...f off from those who never helped, went round the other way round in the hope you would drop down dead...the limitless times of* *showering with gifts are for those who want more from their lives, the times they hid from the door-stopping it from hitting back through the fisting of them all…the brothers in arms who quantified the times when the brothers were in, are the ones who fisted each other…the gold medallions of gypsy Rosalie hanging those who went further along….Sponsorship is the fasting delight-fullness, the hiding of spacial awareness of the worship of those in the know…hang on.. we had no hope here, of even trying for the best one, we are not the best one and hung the best one…over jealousy of siblings that have seriously got no hope…we.., there we are my ex friend, we have no hope now of even being together…Judas of Nazareth…the acting debut of those on the stage…*

WOW…I cannot be this person who now travels, who now is part of the world again as the best one yes, sweetheart it's you the one who got away, is now my revered Author…Cantona got in the car, he drove for ages, ages, miles, kilometres, kilometres at night he took her, round drunk, holding the other one showing he was not with her..only once…as the little one was that drunk, that at that we cried with ridicule and laughter….bent over double just near the cafe, bates, behind the house of dreams that the money could not even buy, even early in the morning…on a walk to the pound shop in Salford…the high rise is not the farm-shop in the protected confines of the society of born…the Liverpool rose here, the pound shop turned farmshop, smiled near the newspapers, the alternative red was a sign that the wearer of the crown was destitute, Brazilian and about to change…cut throat board room, failure to abscond, borders alerted the man whose terrible finger smelled in disregard, disrespect to the womb of the non-belong, the one whose future wasn't ***Annie, but Cinderella****,* ***Yachts****, belonging with high regard that she so badly needs again…she choked on the pip, rubbing herself up against his leg, inside the high instep, ensured the memories had little doubt …she banged him, down on the floor, dropping him hurling him across the room, ….WHALES..black not blue….totalling the baby faced ass wiped for today making her the dirty rotten urchin of the city…squelching with desirable dirt….. totalling the numbers in her womb to three all different fathers..all significant married once to a dancer, big ben…never-mind on the clock with the mice it struck again on the clock face of time….he stood on the tower, the hands he clung to, racing on the Rolex, the dual Face of the Day Date making him smile as the night date was the same one….the cities hit the floor hard, the Black Widow bit that hard the next time round that the Author smiled as she wrote.. DO NOT UNDER ESTIMATE MY POWERS OF HURT REGINALD HAROLD….I WILL NEVER EVER TURN IN THE WAY I WAS ASSESSED FOR…AS I AM HIGHLY COMMENDED HERE… Socrates was here..so were the bread, sticks, loaf and hood, the bottle banging on his thigh, he skinned the result of 3-0 to the biggie, the positioning play on this day was terrible, Giroud was horrendous, he was situated in a position of trust, hid the all, then ran, the CP was countering everything the police special agent spider had, concerning the likes of the Dame, The Sir and actually the very supreme Chief Commissioner Mark Rowley his remit for Lords differing day* *to day…Thursday the Author sees …the MIGHTYMANS FRANCE vs THE BIG G…who is kind of funny as he know she saw….goodbye my friend. I can't be here now…she grinned you are too skinny, not captain and sorry but not big enough. Anyway, see ya….*

The imprint of the finger is here on the stove, the oven that had Almighty's finger, it hurt, that day, the imprint with scaled skin attached to the outside of the oven, the bubbles on the hand on the outside with huge blisters red raw underneath on the help of the one who did not die a death…. the tray of the toast, the tea, the grapefruit had score lines on from the truth of what happened on the day they picked her up…cold, frosty morning down in Manchester Lowry Streets, full of piped cuisine no Michelin stars…the hunger pipes the dreams that the futile parenthood, was threatened towards her early in life, to say that it didn't matter how good of a parent that would get her motherhood try for removal to ensure full insightfulness for another for the one that the media decided to make instead of her….the imprint began on the elongated pad on the door opening of the war against Technological Punjab..well, racist or not we are actually at war with President Macron said, the hope for justice said Macron is that the child and mother can be together and get to be with Cantona...his daughter became his sin, the one who worked for her money is the one underneath struggling to get on top, the outward movement of jealousy on you, said the blindman had taken everyone away one day when singing in church his voice over everyone else's, he problem here is that everyone else needed, wanted and desired their own voices to be heard, so now what do we do, like football, I am not really a fan, my father was but I am not to the same degree, the church goers vilified for a unsung truth, had the voice of crackled virgins, however happy in their days of hope that everyone they prayed for desired a hope of all, well said the vicar it was left at 3-2, we found him and we can now go forwards knowing that you are also generous in nature…we are indebted to your generosity would like you to stay here but know that your house is now for auction.. the speeding car caught up with the blindman, who tried for public opinion, the opinion is that volunteer work is essential to pick up those who are thrown on the pile of non-hope, those who are talented, hopeful of a new career and nuances of their own time, the inference to voluntary work in your new book is astounding considering your failure to understand that you were not needed in you own self as a person, that you as a person were not wanted in any new career, any new found freedom and that everyone is astounded to remove all freedoms from you, the mother of all career breakers, all career retributions and career attainments had all for this viewpoint, those led from their rooms of hope that the law would hang those who dealt the wrong hands to all, those who became freedom fighters were understood to have freedoms of them all… those that commit benefit fraud the social security number of all time, had a freedom fighting movements called the PKK not Cities..The problem here is that the Cities movement is fighting for freedom, growth, development of those Species 1 who are either dangerously at risk or endangered….thus those involved fighting for them. The difference is one commits acts of terrorism to make their own point. Which is where insurgency movements whether good or bad are grown from……and that's it…COPY COPY…. DRIVE DRIVE...METICULOUS LADY OF THE NIGHT DRIVE…She is picked up, cold wet and hungry turns to be the most horrendous example of being spoilt that you could ever find the large cuddly tortoise lay awake.....she turns out to be the Loch Ness Monster….the news that day drove the headline that she was actually a fake suicide… the cats whiskers grew longer with desire for the granules of hopeful solitude of herself …Independent News items grew to potential suicides, stabbings and the PKK who of course fight freedoms we are told about everyday if you look….so, Mr Flower how long is it until you realise how much god damn enterprise is sub-standard here….making others vulnerable in those growing countries that we take from…armed guards, jealousy through them from those who could not be demonstrous even if they tried…so, who is she….her unborn son naked on the rail track clinging to his mother's uterus wall, utters a squeak as the death of her fantasy with a footballer dies…this could be you Lucy Pockets desire to be seen with those who are this, is well known, jealousy of anyone getting in the way…so, who is she the loner of all subterfuge, lies ungraciously through the under growth having worked for the economies before the score line in USA is 3-2, as the score line in Spain is now World Cup, the Golden Showers of pure genius, but this is for another book Cantona is now in his element here, the chemistry in the laboratories for himself is well known, LA GALAXY, the hideous grin of this small pushy women who removed his gentlemanly shape, he lashed out, trying to get through when …away ….to lash out…he is due for full out of his assault here …the squeeze on Cantona held firm, held strong, held himself…frustrated at the continued at egoism held strong pushing the one that got away into subterfuge, to show in front even though the other stood, today her back ended ness is well documented at the pushy woman's' hand…her coercion, back biting, assault and continued show in private clinics directed at, has ensured that the pushy woman is on the assault list squeezing Cantona round to what she pushily wanted money, wealth, name, fame, applause, social acceptance, worldly for a man not naturally aligned to her…why…he was not made with or for her…how do we know he needs squeezing to try for natural alignment, so, when someone questions the pushy woman, she pretends not to know who we are….so ? DO NOT KNOW YOU>>>>>I DO NOT KNOW YOU…let me take you back...20 years.? To the pushy woman with no ingratiated vixen. The one who continues to downplay the make of the century. As she could not get through…MIGHMAN is not yours…pushy woman, as you will find the naturally aligned…don't get squeezed and are allowed to be controlled then reigned back if tell me your IQ? Pushy Woman….as genetically the Cantona wins…hands down. With huge huge….impetus…now, the one that gets away as being the one who should have been…is now, cold, on her own and ready to leave, smiling occasionally at the know that her son I trilingual, authorised to be with her in the French Republics….a great opportunity, certainly not scary, or not planned…..a bit like the baby, the over driven obtuse triangle of love ha said the blindman I do not know you as I choose to destroy your very hope of being as you are adopted, unloved, un cared for and I wanted to destroy you…for your own good the pushy woman said…so, what happened on the night that you were incarcerated? Can you ask Lucy Pocket pushy woman…? As the woman's' clubs to get through with you…I like the USA, today many people don't care, many people do….I hope that the author here is very real, as she is consistently on camera and has no jowls…the Sgt was arrested this morning for UNICEF the finger, of four, saluting in the breeze, as her skirt went up over her head….the violin white with strings to die for, laying on the bed…doodles dead on the historical floor…the bump in the road grew black with desire… metaphorically speaking of course, here the assault grew stronger…the power of shot on goal loosely wanted by the victim…he should've won one, the desire to fit her small body inside this great big ***French Lunacy is not apparent here***

A Prologue: A Strategy: E

Mans of Matches

DO not throw any Kings of Royalty or Public Servants or Members of Parliament

Do not throw A

Never ever throw E

START
Too many of those with the ones whose we meet the ones of the community,
Cantona all round
Pele all round
Ronaldo Golden Boots 2016 - 2009
Messi D'or Ballon 7 years
Mo Salah. Golden Boots 2020-2016 assists more often
Sterling does not assist
Harry Kane Golden Boots 2021 Assist
Ball Behaviour
All for individual ball possession
Mishitting the ball is removing the ball out of the moving play to end the play: picking up the ball.
Assist

With Cantona all round with assist and shot,
With comparable statistics with Pele for Sterling
Kane with Abel didn't happen here yet, 2021 Golden shot
won by one from the 5 years diamond boy,

the salon of 7 and the Golden Boots of assets to shot and to shot on goal of Salah, these are the top shot truths.
Comparable Ball Behaviour can be put in the Golden Ball, except they may not be, they may be unrecognisable ridiculousness of ball behaviours that have been misread. On the feet of many a man, on the foot of not so many, on the head of many a Master on the foot of the French Ball Master.

On the foot of the current golden boots of 2021, Kane from Tottenham in the UK, who stole the Boots from Mo Salah the messiah of Golden Boots and the Western hypocriticalness when it comes to the home of the Foot and Ball.
Forward Individual Ball Possession is for the Golden Seven, for the stop end of the game for counter reasoning of the entropy of the relative curve, the mishitting the ball strategy of the French Ball Master agrees to picking up the ball when 100% certainty that the probability of decision making through Markov is intelligently, technologically led.
Comparative shot range to in goal for 7
Cantona
dangerosity and pressing by other players and crowd to draw out.
Who was the golden boot at that time? As addendum, to score for the line on the succession planning of the opposing team on that night.
Pressed through media and site on the UK for supremacy of Golden Boot in 2021, to ensure Kane won, with assists.
Decline in shots through penalty box due to superior genomes in goalkeeping with strategy from UEFA, the shot goal averages on Cantona make him one of if not the best goal scorer in the world, his name is synonymous with what happened to him, and he is never away for too long from the ball.

Bayesian is the control shot player average of those who can control, shot and remove player average the three ways round. The use of which was since 1980 and the German rise to the World Cup, Entropy Relative phase allows for inhibited players, clubs, and skill to be given chance to rectify any intelligence gapping with control, if not then the player, club move on.

Individual Ball Possession, Control, Team Ball Possession, Team Ball Control, Team Playmaking

Cantona in particular has a IBP like no other making runs to the goal at the penalty line and shot on target, as in the Run of IBP.

Comparatively to Kane who assist if his Markov Decision Making allowing him to move forward, so converts on shot.

Pele is the same as Cantona he would run at the opposition in the IBP to the goal mouth, his shots on target from all angles were the Best in the World for a long time, with or without a Golden Boot.

Team Ball Possession: Mo Salah is the team possession as he has a small entropy, to phase on delivery of the ball to the opposition.

Team Ball Control: Mo Salah is the very best team ball control, can relative phase out of play on end mishitting.

Team Playmaking: Mo Salah is the very best relative Phase playmaker that the world has ever seen, his phase on entry is only slight 1 point to be exact *was at the time of writing.... submitting to publisher 26.08.2023*

Cantona was the epitome of Team Playmaking, Team Ball Control and Possession with no entry for most of his career other than 8 months which was not a full season out. His relative phasing was rare on himself or the team, just on the opposition which caused heated discussion on pitch. Leaving the teamplay to pass, not to entropy, relative phasing or intelligence of others but to himself to then position perfectly on target, on shot, on the right range of goal, misses where high shots were controlled never uncontrolled, power to shot ratio high, with no dangerosity with pressing, controlled space unbelievable awareness of space for team play, with no pressing.

Got pressed one night at the Trafford to the point of dangerosity, the pressing came from Roy Keane, who is now regretful 'even though he's 'French'. The Spatial Temporal configuration of Cantona on that night were not known, however, the ball was known to be the same?

Cantona removed bias to Bayesian being used globally for analysis of opposing players, goalkeepers on average shot can hang players such as me, said he, as they come out of their range and remove bias of staying within parameters. Otherwise pressing can cause dangerosity

Play on the ball, time on the ball, acceleration on the ball, motion of the ball, need training. Cantona had the shortest intervals per match to goal. Against some of the shortest timed Goalkeepers of all time...NAME

At the time of writing Messi is the epitome of all round Football at its very best, vulnerability check all round with CEO, Chair removed from power, as he then sits on the throne of Barcelona. Golden Ballon D'or epitomises the state of football in the media, press and other social platforms, as the public vote for the one they would like in the media. Chanel, Gaultier, Laurent, Givenchy,

Baloubet du Rouet - gold, bronze, Jappeloup - jumping and team jumping gold bronze, Nino Des Buissonets jumping gold, Nobles' des tess - jumping bronze.

Kings and Queens
We celebrate renaissance from 485 the French Ice Age Lion Man of Ceres
We celebrate Jean Goujon 1510 - 1565
Fontaine des Innocente
Palace de Versailles

We celebrate Lady Godiva
Plimsoll Line
Christopher Columbus

H*istorical Context is King*

Metrical Heroic Prose Poem is celebrated here as a nuance to traditional or modernist prose, we celebrate rhythm and metronome style, grammatical wisdom and speech act in Greek mythology on statues of gods, kings and inscriptions of modern day colour and repetitious statement we epigram and love every minute of it, even down to the yellow yolks of runny poached egg, which are separated on the plate…we work with prose-poem influencers as non-subordinated parataxis with asyndetic parataxis obviously with no conjunctive connective…

Heightened Imagery of Boris, Emmanuel and Donald with long noses and Kim with Biden that the crowns to show are in the NO. Heightened Imagery of Heroism, Colour, Statues and Satire have illustrated to millions war, political take overs, next meal killings and the white cliffs of Dover, we are with weddings, flowers, couture fashion and military buttons on our dresses from Oscar De La Renta and understand Victoria Beckham Dilemma of 335m with wage rises in a recession…we are we.. we are you…we want you to be the best in a quest to find it now ….boo

AQ of historical value with throw
(Inter-English)
Parlez Vous Français Mademoiselle, Oui, na vous, Merci
Visigoth King Alaric II Red
In Northern Toledo, from Cartagena we know
UP through. 418 on the centuries we go
With a curve ball, towards 507, Vouille is the stop
Over of the big 7

Epigram

Alaric

O Poor Alaric, 485 Alaric, we don't share
O Dirty Alaric, O Dirty Alaric, we don't wash well
O non strategy, Alaric, O non strategy, Alaric
I take the ground now, you have the strategy now

486

Time Theme

Of historical value with throw

(Inter-French)

Hello, I speak English, Yes I know, Thank You
Battle of Soissoness
Clovis inherited Flanders
In the Poppies, In the Soissons
Red with small dots in, Red with small dots in
All dead now

Epigram

Red Chargers

Alaric, Now King Alaric, hid Clovis
Clovis, hid King Alaric
Clovis hid King, Execution of Mice and Men
Red Chargers here, more in here

507

Time Theme

Of historical value with throw

(Inter-Lingual)

Battle of Vouille

Toulouse is the play of the Battle of the South
Its never from the New Orleans on the language of the South
The South is the one where the language is of slur
Superiority is the one of the kind
Clovis is the height of the Soldiers Delight
Visigothic Army is the French ones fled
Treasures in the Toulouse Trove
Hand in Hand with Visgothic broke

Advances of the Blue lines up through the North
Central Blue Lines reversed all thought
Left from Bordeaux, Up through Toulouse
Up to the Blue mass Franc with no loose

Red Lines on advancement on the wrong side
Underneath the right handed below inside
Through Narbonne from Marseille, to Hispanie
Back through the 507-509 Century

We are red, some are blue, some are armour plated too
On the charging horses cry, with the spears of discontent
Open Service of the Lent, on the spears with gold and black
With the axe of Manymen

ouch, whats that, in the suited armoured stand.
I am In the suited armoured stand, had the glass around the hand, When do we go
in the farmland, the farmland is the one we know, in the britches of the sew.
The needle with cotton is all out,

The spears are defended with the armour of plume
Shiny silver swordsman with the White Horse on the gold
Round silver shield with red with blue inside
All together now for the USA battle cries

The captain was not the King called Clovis, he
Was a for the birth of Francais, Clovis, Nante was Merriman
fought long and hard, All that day he drove apart, the life, the love the whole lot
He never faltered from the stop

Herosim

524
Time Theme
Of historical value with throw
(Inter-Lingual)
Je Suis Allez Vous?
Battle of Vezeronce
Burgundy, Burgundy for Frankish King
Invasion with 4, successions in Isere

With Sisnismund, Goodman with Army defeat
Kingdom lost to Merovingians, O decade

558
Time Theme
Of historical value with throw
(Inter-Lingual)
King of the Franks
Clovis I the third of four,
Childebert I King of Merovingians
Born 496, Died 558
Lived a life for Paris' realm

561
Time Theme
Of historical value with throw of King
Chlothar I
Kingdom of the Throne, Brothers on the order
3 sons to the slaughter, Vestel Virgins they make flee
Youngest son of Clovis I, the M of Markov, decision is fast
Sampled correlation of contract value, time, foot, angle,

567
Time Theme
Of historical value with throw of King
Charibert I, King of Paris (D)
Wanted ball on his terrace, possession isn't really key
Charibert I, is not the King of all to see
Theres no statistical correlation, here

575
Time Theme
Of historical value with throw of King
Sigebert I (D)
Civil War of third son, Civil War with half brother
Merovingian Frankish King, Ingund with Chlothar !
Ingund with Chlothar !

584

TIme Theme

OF historical value with throw of King

Childebert I of Soissons (A) the catholic of fore-mentioned to bear
Is it Neustria or Soissons, Aregund the Queen of Minority
Fostered in the Kingdom of the East
Is this me or is this she

589

Time Theme

Of historical value with throw of King

Franco Compared Byzantine War
We are now for sodomy, we are now for sodomy
Vices for persecution, Vices for Persecution
Stand by. Me, vicious key

592

Time Theme

Of historical value with throw of King

Childebert II adopted son of Guntram (D)
Adoptee, Adoptee too no fee
Too no fee, where are we, where are we
In the mire of the funeral, with Brunchildis to 613
To lay her head, with 2 young sons

595

Time Theme

Of historical value with throw of King

Childebert II
Spain is it, Spain was it, no Barcelona
We are not it, Burgundy King, with no drink
Austrasian too Guntrams' hand
Territory driven, with thine provision

612

Time Theme

Of historical value with throw of King

King Theudobert II (A) deposed from power in 612

Theudobert is I too was his brother of the dynasty of Brunhild

Champagne, Champagne defeated by a peasant, defeated by a peasant

With no Blood Line, With no Blood Line

613

Time Theme

Of historical value with throw of King

King Theuderic II (D) pseudonym lived on in Thierry

King Sigebert II murdered absurdly in the great France

Of Tricolour, Of Tricolour, one half of, one half off

Family Breakdown

639

Of historical with throw of King

New Kings Rois Faineants

The Do Nothing Kings, Merovingain Frankish

Palace Mayors, Palace Mayors

Pretty on the Throne, Pretty on the Throne

Dynasty

655

Of historical with throw of King

New King Chlothar III

Do you know the portrait, the King, Do you know the portrait of the King

George Bernard Wrote it, George Bernard Wrote it

Of the Great Franks, Of the Great Franks

Shaw

656

Of historical with throw of King

Childebert the Adopted

Adopted Reigned, Adopted Reigned to 657

Pippinids were the family here, just here

Palace Grimaold the Elder, the Elder

King Sigebert III and Queen Chimnechild

661
Of historical with throw of King
Childebert the Adopted (D)
Chlothar III King of Franks
Major Palace of Grimoald

657 death

Death

673
Of historical with throw of King
Theuderic III
Suceeded sibling dynasty of Clotaire III
Pads were not here yet, diamonds were here
We are here with you, not in that state
We are for diamonds not Pads in this way
Son of Clovis

695
Of historical with throw of King
Childebert III
A Puppets King, A Puppets King
Living the life of the stripe on the beach
With no Flip Flop, with a hat of Judgement
King Childebert and Pippin II

966-967
Of historical non throw of King
Louis 5th
Louis the Fifth on the scale broke the cog became a whale, lifted higher than Delilah
Broken Horse on the Shire
Louis the Fifth went to bed, paper hand the look of lead, charcoal
black then to seed, brought the little one off to Meade..
Louis the Fifth went to Beijing in the sling of the slam, pink with ice row with cool
Had the night time off to pool
Sultan of Egypt 1187

28.6.1491- 28.01.1547
Epigram

1547 to death

Prose 11

Henry the Eighth had a whale but it wasn't the one who did sail
In the virginity all did past, laughter strikes a chord again
Withers with Hithers on the day, gold bullion on the chimes of the time
Feline, went berserk, all but laughter on the stroke of the clock, now hows about that

1804
Historical Theme
Of a throw of a King

Napoleon
Bone-part, Bone-part with the stoppages on the cart
Held the renaissance by the hand
Of International Relationships man

Strategy E

13 Line Stanza
The LifeBoats : Lawn and Circle
Margaret Boyle and William Brown
In said the Daventry, all dressed
In tweed, in said the Picture Book
all said he, contemporary.
Out said the Peasants Countryside
All in Pheasants of the sons hand
Partridge of Henriettas' man
Ouch said countryside, kingdom come
Bonjour said the Boatman all Whites
Boo said the Boyle all in Knight
Bang said the Centurion Nest
Oui, said the one whose fortress undone
Chirp said the mental case in Bed

Who is E Time Strategy?

Challenge for the Lead Goblin
Who are you?
Why are you?
How genetically superior are you?
Year 400 to 2030

Intelligence Lead Gap Goblin of currently 8 years on a time frame of superiority, excellence, nuclear physics, quantum for some.....the nature of foot, ball, net, trajectory, power, control, technique, the permissive IBP, IBC, Ratio to Shot is King one said...no I said That is Eric Cantona the King? The Royal Duchess of Cornwall manifested one night, declared that the King to be definitely didn't look like him but William, the potential King of England, heir to Charles on the throne..who does too care, support, love English football.....the now King Charles the King of England, declared once that the Duke of Edinburgh ran off with the Throne when he Faux Pas for racism hurt the Royal Houses...the first leather football is the time strategy well, not in the Business Gantt here to enable Osama Bin Laden, Salman Rushtie, The Cleric, Cristiano Ronaldo the Golden Boy himself here in this story in full as DiamondMan, the inference here to diamonds.....so here we introduce why we write, who we write about, what significance. For who, yes, you the ones in the stands, the ones in the public houses, the ones in the social clue. The ones who with. Dirty trousers, dirty insider, dirty voluminous monstrosities are supposedly better than the Joe.......

The lead goblin is I, the ladies. Champion of fate control and no subordinate stand in a holder, let A stand please for the ridicule and jest of the century yesterday when we all went off on one at her for making fun, the listener realised that this isn't true, jesting is not something that the Author does, poke fun not either, she has been bullied all her life...

UNICEF a catch 22 for some, an obsession with euphoric thematic juxtaposition with subjective stanzaic opinion, a significant influence. Imagine a foot and ball book, yet another with score line for anecdotes. Well, that's not it, UEFA is it. The play here ladies with gentleman and those without persuasion is which foot? Which ball? Which trousers? Which E? Is it Evie? Not in this book, said the author, then the publisher. Is it Evelyn? No, not here it's not another love story, although in some parts dependant on who you are and what you do depends on how much and what? Well, we have character build for script writing to metamorphosis into quite a laugh for some. I mean who would have thought. An influencer of Micro-Evolutionary response to the media: Media City and the Micro Darwinian forethought of Utopia, a position of the media which with clean streets, dirty water, with females in sport lesser known with no acumen 'just do it' seemed a passion, desire with longitudinal magnitude of hope. The media is accessible to all, for families a turntable manifesting charges of light like a laser to the ground, force of strike driving heat to the floor, the crust of the earth had centuries to find the Roman Empire had festoons to hire. Egypt has the Pyramids of Doom, in the Chanclet of the Room, Roaring like the great big fire, had the sugar cream of desire.

P2

Time for E

Strategy E: More fool he

13 Line Stanza

On Watch, On Time, On Me
With Mine, For you, for me
I he, you are thee, thirteen line, stanza time
Tie me, my head, in little of the bed
On me, on You, we are four two
We are four three, we are four thee
Four nine strategy time
Nine nil, we are four three with thee
Leader of me, Leader of he
For the free, For the fee
In the tree, beast of me
For lines fee for be

P2

Prose Poem

The Beginnings of Nature with

Hallelujah..Almighty God...Centuries of Power in the Mud...without Wellies..Adam is without his Eve, launched with understanding of Power, Control, Straight Line Runs of Truth with Ones.....Pele had foreclosed on..the Business of iCloud, email technology the voice of the god is standing his ground..Goddess of Truth Licence to Thrill, Sabre Toothed Tiger, Almighty Liar. The IBP on the Ball Control is the one with the hence of forgiveness all gone..the one with the hair the one with the beak the symptomatic lustrous feet..position on the ball pass, position, shoot. Position to attack, lineage at that, whereabouts of the hat, chromosomes strong, powerful less than forgiving, driving the force of nature forward, defence behind, calling gods of war, strategy is forevermore....GC, AB, AC blood group type O, never donate your blood group command attention, look amazing, zing with flowers, love for hours.. melodramatic peace for hours...the beast of all player is on thine knee of Michelle Pfifer, of all wheel chair of all none legs, the beast of all speed is now with Hamilton's lead, the voice of sometimes past, the voice of thine nimble past, the voice inside that hurts the ride, the voice inside that hurts your mind, of your nimble past....According to the People of the Ukraine, the central population of which we know no more about, we are for their fore fathers, bearers, cossack with no military rule..we are for the heritage of the Czar, we are for the heritage of their own lineage, we are for the emblem which tells them their way, which we use for our own symbolism to show us their own say, the speech act of rules, the legal re news any reliance on peasants control over land, eggs, geese or maypoles. Russian hypocrisy listens to truth, Russian hypocrisy listens to the truth, Olympic Rings, Olympic sins, sorrow for all when Beth does not win.....Boo said the Geese can we all go through.. into the arms of the one who did knew, we all bear our soul on the streets of the line, the one who we cross on the centuries of behind, the one of the bare of the geese that they laid the one who did incumbent with the 5 of the way. Russia the state of control with non-power, the state of legitimacy of the rings of no flower, the emblem it takes you to sickle with cell, the hammer, with crossbow is the fighting not well. Aggressor of Truth is the one with the Red, with no passion for democracy in bed, the one with the military dancing no doubt, into the favours of the bed ridden not stout...Understanding here before Adam with Eve, is the military rule of the yellow, blue banners unfurl, the weightless omittance of the security to trust, on what do we mean when the flag waves at us. The pole of the flag is the one in the ground, of the charging blue horses on the spray bound not out, the pray we had all in the jumper of ground, the ones who we know in the dust bound of dirt. We all have the memories of flag bearers with doubt, horses charging remittances of collections of pout.. skinny black pencils of fear in the charge, the racism here is the one who was doubt. What is the colour of the symbol of drums, the drums of the cochlea that wasn't here as weren't thumbs, the gifted, with talented ran out of the sears the tuna we love you we love the next one, the one who is nearer the one who has fun, is the one with the nuances on the first one. Crane on the hilltop, Crane on the bank, global reliance on the Crane that did sank, Heroin the sandbanks, gluttony on the town, charging infantile on the laziness no doubt, we are one now I have no one else, I love my girlfriend so very much that I have no doubt at all. When the Copenhagen had a ship in the night the security strategy hid from the fright of Margaret Boyle, the night of many an ICC for Kofi Annan on the French knee of Manchester United. Why you say did this book, ditty stanza sound in rebuff, did sound like this he did say my. Name is Mathew Simmons so here my play, who are you to say I'm broke, had no food so he my spoke, turned the wheel of enterprise, without the one whose charities despise. Kicking gently in the vision of the big one and the pension, had the very very big damn childhood, with the jealousy to mine hood, the hoot of an owl the jealousy of her control, /I am with the man with the big nose, satire are its he play through the book, heroes welcome is the prose prose, dialogue, oral hexameter choice, the the downfall of the voice, the say the say the I have a big hat, in the downsize of the fat. The strategy of airstrikes, the strategy of Kings, the strategy of the peace vigil that stunned those 3 idiots that then bad mouthed the whole place.

P3
GOD
Prophet Mary
Chanel
Sticky Camembert
The Raging Bull

Euphoria broke the camels back on that day of the Simmons saga, the press went berserk, I stayed in a lot, the hippy commune died, the blood bank went into total coagulated vials.. Adam with Eve hurt every time she switched on the temperature gauge getting hotter as the heat of the laser drove deep to the earth on a Panda from China, the nuclear rod had disturbed, the mantle it forced convergence at first up from the ocean floor the volcano occurred. UEFA, UNICEF, Sir Bernard Lovell, Sir Alex Ferguson, Joel Glazer with these full referenced influencers to the Corporate Strategy of Governance to say the last they are special people to be able to achieve what they do. In certain places in the world you dream of power, control and hunger for it, What is it? Why is it? Wanna be well here it is. Macro-Evolutionary Responses to Media: No, for euphoric reaction, blind eye, females who play long into the night got the players who take it all. Adapting to ever increasing circles with radial democratic power, struggling to tempt fate changing perspectives with film, tv and objects with words which face to face have a huge huge impact, Eric Cantona is prepared to change your mind just like the author, with proven actual changing perspective on the industries and skills we need to encourage growth in any changing economy. Powerful story, collections and nations frenzy on desire of the heart, the longevity of life, situation and weirdo change mat is not for those with intelligence but for those with a gap of capability, loss of skill, earnings and challenge through academic acumen is one, the other is laziness, greediness with food and global insecurities that they do not care about, I am Amanda-Jane and I am out with Eric Cantona, with or without his dark glasses at The Lowry...we thank Mathew Simmons' Family once again here. Boots for walking, Suits for Loving and Guns for shouldering bias of stand, the shootings in New Delhi are an example of Indian bias of longing to be democratic but remain under Marshall Law currently and the Trumps visit a few years ago heightened security for them and lead to their downfall, flowers are poignant, sympathetic and empathy is flowers, diamonds, Gold and Beauty are for all to understand in the celebration of industries with fashion that show no bounds, I am Amanda-Jane and I am out with Eric Cantona and his Family of Hope for our Wedding, not in this book or stanza but in real life as of tomorrow., we are hoping for a baby too next year and we are hoping to Golden D'or Ballon with little feet to bear, so lots of nations and connecting stories but in future intelligence lots of acumen to challenge the best, of USA and Chinese acumen in technology and fight, with no flight. 527 188N the Dark Destroyer Leopard Mark IV Security Vehicle used in Rhodesia, the now Zimbabwe, a British Vehicle with British Acumen. So, when you consider French Eatery, eating and Cantona please consider his plight, he is British Taxpayer, French Taxpayers and global peace for all, UNICEF included, is very proud of Miss Peace as he now calls her…yes Author you…..

Epigram: Le Strategy: 17.05.2021:15.52
Medieval 1000-1450
With Green Trees, Lined Green Trees, Royal Blue Tirade
Crimson Hat, Crimson Coat, No Black Plume with the Straw
Brown Paper Bag, Brown Paper Bag, with Large Hope, With Large Hope
Wiggly Stem, Wriggly Stem, Twisted Ether of the Jealousy Stem

Sultan of Egypt 1187
a..bb a..bb a..bb a..bb a..bb. a..bb a…bb
Egyptian World Cup Stanza
(Iambic Pentameter)
Egyptian World Cup
We are family on her
We are family with her
We are family on you
She is not with he

Epigram: Le Strategy: 17.05.2021:16.51
Medieval 1200
Lines Drawn, Bodies Out, Little Diamond on the Snout
Yellow Hat, Black Snuff, He Hurt all in Buff
Large Rear, Derrier, Pointed Joist, in the Air
Little Diamond all for you

Alfonso x1252-1284 The Wise: Like the Owl
Author of the Royal Code
French Music: Medieval
Le Bouvier 1300
Bernese or Mountain in the space of desire
13th Century Mountain Dog on the herdsman of desire
The sheep on the hill side the welshman all gone
My friendly little alien is space age all done

The Carnival of Animals XIII 1886
Saint Saens : The Swan
Voice of an Animal: Oral Hexameter Dactylic
Pink Tops, Ice Cream, On the knee of a Queen
On the tops of an agent, on the top tops of a snout
This is swan, pink and long, this is the knee
Wet with glee, all for thee

Melody Chimes, Strikes of Three, Lunacy all of me
Take the track, to the one in the centre of the one
With animal leatheron, cold at heart, soft at touch
In the mouth all for lunch

Melodic View, Saint Saens New
Pianist Rhyme, Metronome Style
Black Long with Pearly White
Pianofortes in Time, Now you are mine

Rondo Capriccioso A Minor Op 28 : 1863 p1867 Pablo de Sarasate, V solo
With Sweet Diety all is all mine
Flowers of Ruin, all in Dress
Sunkist Clover, Sunkist Thyme
All hail Mint for all Time

Neue Zeitschrift für Musik (1991-)
Vol. 155, No. 3, DADA/MUSIK (Mai 1994), pp. 36-39 (4 pages)
Published by: SchotMusic GmbH & Co.kg
Heat, Kiss, You are this
Wet Drip for the Kit
Your mine of all time
On the list of Player Tied

Gymnopedia no3, 1,2,3 Lent et Doloreux
Erik Satie
French Orchestra Set and Match with the net of trawlers catch
192 in the net, of the tennis with racket head, all balls in
Mighty thatch of the cottage with black and white match
All in one, is the hole of the golf in the bowl

NonLiteral expressive language is non literal to satire
Its Strategy of Metaphorical tropes: irony, metaphor
And Schemes are anaphoric, we do not deal here with Iambic Pentameter yet
They are in the Third Chapter Onwards, with seven syllables to a beat or line

Versed drama in line fire, with five feet with 7 each beat
Or you can have the 7 with 5 feet, 6 in each foot
Hexameter of Greek plot, is the one for Athens foot
Is not for Adidas but for Nike with the wear designer rightly

Rondel:French 14th Century
Quatrain
Bonsoir, Petit Domme, Parlez Vous
Qu'elle nom pour Josephine, Par
Qu'elle l'heure et ils, c'est douze ans,
est que lyans nombre trois gauche

Rondel French 14th Century
Quintet:
Murder Mystery Stanza:
Silver Plated Dagger, What French?
William Brown, English, Find
Extraordinary Mess Love
In the Drawing Room with a gum
Racing Bunnies in a row, heart

13 line Stanza
2 quatrains, quintet (sestet)
Force of Pulley on Track, Go wind
IBP on thine knee, say Bang
Windows clean, wait for he, we win
Global war on thine knee, did thee
Press the button, fuel with fire, lose
Red with packed, on the strapped,
Horses view for a new bit tack
Wilborough nuance with the Brown
Margaret Boyle on the stove
Sprats for tea on thine knee of King
Strength of character we are mine

Eleven in line blue with stride
Long Legged Wonder, Daddy Legs

P4
Oral Hexameter
Clovis
Open Stanza and Sonnet
Parabole
Sonnet

Dialogue:

Strategy from the historic stand points is something which I do not know much about but apparently stems from 420 with Kings. Now God here after I was ordained as a priest I began to understand how, when, where and how true others were in there own belief. Along time ago my mother told me to believe in what I wanted for myself and go for it, when I was in the priesthood I realised that others thought of others in different ways and acceptance of what we do in ways we do not want is essential for everyday living, which is why in 426 which is when we start here as this stanza is part of the introduction the Queens, Children, War, Placement, Positioning of Men, Huts, Food, Growing, Farming, Babies have a lot of influence in the first Yummy Mummies, what they are, who they are why and why....

P5
13 Line Stanza
Fantastic Father
Filmmaker he, four in now plea
Time trial all out, John in no doubt
Running my way, cooking today
Presents galore, French we adore
Giround its not you, Messi too
Yes, like you Cantonas' front view
UNICEF all in, yes we hid
Tentacles of Trowel, lie little
One found, Findings today, nine on
Two Daughter, Two Sons, love in
Cantona won, identity done
Team in battle, racism stand
Captain of Plaza, Gods for power

Oral Hexameter Dactylic

Do you wish to know who I am? Or what I do?

Epigram Today

Who is E? Where is E?
Who are you, Where are you?
Warm is he, Cherish he
We are for Foot and Ball
We are For President
426 Front Line View

Open Stanza and Sonnet

Global Motherhood Initiatives

Aid Global Security

Epigram

Ideological Viewpoint satire of one, who got away in the shadows of none
Windows of centuries in coveted football, the lesson hit hard with a 426 ball
Ridicule of one England won, this is the story of French Power and a gun
Foxtrot, Indigo, Kellogg's all too centuries on a hillside went tiptoe on shoe

Prose Verse

Global Motherhood Initiatives

Aid Global Security

Abduction

When you were in the case, shoe shine of the place
Had the time of the gear, of the very very big cheer
We are one, all with you, of the serial killer in two
Are you scared of the mother-hood in line with the killer is

Less than intelligent approach to motherhood initiatives
The overreaction of those who read about it, in the global press
Those who read about it in the global media, but let someone else deal..
With the de security vulnerability of their family, that may or maybe
not be a potentially higher risk to themselves

Security of Family is what we know, what we want, how we show.
Global security of our selves is what we want as well, de security of thine knee.
Is twofold when we be, in the same of delight we are less than intelligent fight
Global insecurity free, in the shoeshine of the tree

Dialogue

Aid Global Security

Author: in view of global peace strategy should be known to all, actual footage has been shown for help, aid and support to her from Facebook, rectified by global agency and herself

This is the end of the Introduction to the Influencer of UEFA and FA Football of this Work, the Dialogue we thank him for and the clicker he won't need anymore, we would like Aid Workers, Ethics and Exploratory Consequences to influence decision makers ensuring flee is not forced and to help in global strategy of challenge, world conflict and collective collaboration of global story of reach, both complicated and un bias…they are big shoes, funding is a big risk in Syria, Yemen and Sudan. Reasoning is the conflict with Al Qaeda and Oil, the Diamond mining should be encouraged and legitimacy from the Diamond Bourses round the world is paramount, the oil wells of Sudan should be rich with employment, driving, excavating and covering with mineral rich soils which prove fertile to such an extent that they can grow crops to last the country many sovereign years of our reign there, many are told never to leave the country and many are homeless, crying with fear and loose with their virginity, show be-headment mutilation and loss of earnings through belittlement, which is rife here and facebook is prevalent at attracting them, as as part of UNICEF Work and Other Aid Agencies they get continued access. Lately, Bidens' forethought here is the scoreline of truth, the TO here is AQ: a TO I know very well, after being taught by a man who fought at them, the membership of the TO is now of course removed, the narrative here is very strongly led from the USA, the best in the world for armed assault, armed combat, unarmed combat, snipper rifle control, hand he'd control, pistol shootings, armoured car carriers, Gideon, Biden, with Trump in the wings, a bit like us currently the Uk I mean. First Class writing, analysis, tremendous care of words, insightful responses the right way round, in depth behaviours described, observed behaviours, observed language, observed murder, described, analysed placement of bodies, cats, dogs, barriers, pistols, placement of guard, placement of pin, placement of families, rich or not. In the 1900s global aid security meant the trappings chickens in pens, toppings of eggs laid, the occasional be-headment, with quail eggs.

Epigram: 20.06.2021: 18.35

Parabole

Motherhood Does it Work? From 400-426

Parabole, a metaphoric comparison

A description of 2 likes then

First speech acts towards EC

His legal speeches

For a Fee

Open to Stanza

Epigram: 26.06.2021 04.41

To sail with the veil of the very large humped back whale
Is the compromise of one, grey with fin the little ones
White Bait is the cookery cheer, in the sprat for all to fear
In the mayonnaise to be, is the whitebait all for a fee

Prose Verse

Is Cantona here? Is Mo Salah here? Is Shoe Shine here?
The large humped backed whale is the one with no skinny veil
Is the one for all to be, in the selfish whitebait reel
Woe is me for all mankind, I cannot get down from my behind
I cannot reason all to be, cos Mark Hughes is not for me
I have spent a lifetime now, trying to get him for now, he is just not for me
I am desolate, victimised and cruel, I am cried for all too soon
I am deferent in mankind, I play the violins on the rhyme

Where am I? I am Cheshire but not bank, I am Cheshire with a skank
I am Cheshire, with a black veil, I am needing a very large pail, I do not help
Where am I? I get paid for all mankind, to take care of ridicule with no crime
I take care to look like that, when the shoe shine is the sprat

Who am I? I am not you the author, am the most ignorant woman in the world, who thinks the world owes her, my name is Sam, but no peel I have a very very ;large big reel, covered in tattoo is the one, shouting tensile hoof with one, shouting huffing and puffing today, because Soma Go comes here to play, with the shoe shine of the one, who has all to be the one with the Cantona to play, is the Merrimans with no play..

Change to Epigram::26.06.2021 04.41

Boats

Unicef was one of the proudest moments of my career, I wanted to be in this way with my girlfriend for long-time, since my wife fell out with me about her other remit with men. A catch 22 for some and me would be for me that my family would bring me happiness, my family at one point were everything to me, now they can be the most frustrating, tiresome and boring.

Prose Verse: 20.06.2021: 19.05

Analogies

Analogy, like the great man said he said it like a king,
He said it like a speech of three then landed one off far
The analogies of the strength of the cap,
The fore footed brain master hand a great right foot,
The one who we said on the Mere full of woe
The one who we wished would just throw back the no

The medieval die hard on the wings of despair,
The one who we want on the streets of the lair
All the French Music had the ones who we bear
1000-1450 had the French stick on the streets on the throw

Alfonso X had the ones on the sack, Le Bouvier (medieval) dawn on the rack

Epigram Today 9.6.2021

My discerning gentleman lives down the street
My discerning gentleman has the World at his UEFA feet
My discerning gentlemen maybe French or maybe British
My discerning gentleman is definitely E

Close of
Stanza

Open Stanza
Prose Verse
Today 9.6.2021 12.35

My footballer has my chastity abound.
My footballer has my livelihood for now.
My footballer, thespian and boyfriend has my very ear today
Thespian has a shout, of the Juliet in no doubt.
9/
Juliet is all me, I am my E for my knee
Of my love, heart, with mind, in the darkness is sublime
In the light of all to hear, in the dusk of yes, to cheer
In the dawn of winters too, I love my E is he for you
Rapunzel is in no doubt too, she is all for never out
With anyone ever again except her E for Mighman

My passion, inner health is chameleon for ever
Eric Cantona don't you, ever wonder how it should

B

Benefactor of thine will, is thine daughter of the will
P GRHS

Epigram 9.6.2021 12.38

Contd..

All those years before said I, like a diamond in the sky
Mines renew from you to me on the 16th with no fee
All my life I wanted more, ever felt self-satisfied more,
Then when I had the most wonderful birth

Prose Verse:09.06.2021 12.40

Still

I don't take to living alone, which I have done for 6 months
Then one day my Foreverman, said I am now your Mighman too
Mighman said he wanted me back, wanted more from me to pack
I never smiled as much you see, as Mighman was my big E

My big E is Cantona, all hell bent on making me more
I am not a push over either, oodles of confidence with mechanisms hither
Mighman E, my love is thrice, master of the century twice
Then one day in my travel chest, I went to see from when he is best

Prose Dialogue: 09.06.2021

As a thespian, footballer and father, I love my girlfriend, as she allows me to be myself and giggles at me when I say that I do not want to do something, then gets to the bottom of why, then we move on and sometimes we do what I don't or didn't want to do, which is to have dinner with Avram Glazer. My brother was a painter like my genetic father, he was abusive towards me as a child, my mother has spoken in the work and she is fine for my author and girlfriend to take a lead a bit, I love to paint and I love art, my youngest daughter loves art too, we draw, not paint currently and I would love to play in the theatre again.

Epigram: Le Strategy: 09.06.2021:15.45

Ice

With Ice Horses, With Ice Flags, With Ice Armour with Red Flags
With White Chargers, With White Shoes, With Brown Lancet on the News
With Red Cross, With Striped Plume, With Gold Rosettes, Harnessed Tool
With You Might, With Your Fight, With Your Velvet over Night

Close Stan
Le Strategy Un
Football
13 line stanza
On Ball, We are We, We are We
Foot with he, Foot with he, with he
Love for Game, Love for Game, my Ball
France for 1, England for 2, Win
Is for me, Is for me, no truth
Link to fast, Link to fast, no truth
With the ball, With the Ball, is he
All with her, all with her, same two
In the beat, with the Street, all in
Same line now, 5-0 ouch, what time
Final three, of the knee, of beast
Of thine, of beast of thine, with out
Fred is in, in sin bin, be mine

Oral hexameter
We will win, we will win
Open tin, in the hymn
On the line, for all time
Due the race, on the case

Open Stanza and Sonnet
13 Line Stanza
Football Gate, Kissing Gate
Had the Time, New York Line
Due to Fate, Between mate
We had you on the foot and ball
Climbers, Ladders too, Boo
New York Shirt, Lineage Hurt

Moo Cows, FIFA too, had the view
Of the past, we knew more, on the door
We love you and we need you too
Shirt off with line of rectangle
Perimeter, Diagonal, Jester Hat
Radial Diameter, Diameter sat on

Close Stanza and Sonnet

13 line stanza
Strategic Place, not meant
No Play, No Play, No Play
Love for you I'm in two
now way, Devils in
Carnate in, Madrid 2,
Holland 2, 3 for him,
Bins black gin, fools for him
Juxtaposition, M
BE Marcus Salford Street
Walford, no Town, no Town
Rhubarb Free, Rhubarb Free
Custard Tea, Custard Tea
Yellow Peril, Yellow

Oral Hexameter
Top of Linear Tree and Line
Lowry Hand now torture tie, on the head
On the head, we will truth on the route
Had all mouth, had all mouth
Cantona, has the par on reboot
4-0 height, Lewis in now, all hail you
Time World Go, Green on the Tyre
11 men in on the fin, we are go
Had all nuance on the foot and ball we are one, we are one
Marco had all the bread take your time, take your time
We had all the nuance distilled for sublime
Water for all, in the slosh pool, we are won we are won

Strategy
Football
13 line stanza
Peter Schmeichel had the tie pin, of the position of the Mighman
He had time, he had time, listen to the gold red voice
We are one, we are one, boo, boo, glee for two nil
Train, Train, Train Kick the Ball we are fours, for you now
Long time in, we are for kin, sometimes sometimes, detail mine
Tails to Wag, Tails to Wag in receipt of the bag, Versace, Gucci, Valentino Chanel Tin
Milan So mine, we are Vine, Higher Tyne, Hills are mine

Oral hexameter
UEFA, UEFA, Thine Knee
French for Time, English Rhyme, Kiss Quick
Hats in two, nil for you, on thine knees
O thine knee of benefit cree
O thine knee of religious flee

Oral Hexameter
FA FA, FA,
Lucys Pocket your day

Open Stanza and Sonnet
Close Stanza and Sonnet
13 line stanza
Oral Hexameter
Cantona is the nuance of the day,
had the foot on the ball like a diamond in the stall
Had the horses on the shout, had the horses on the pout,
had the horses on the bank, had the heartbreak on the sand
Mark Hughes MBE had the hair of grey to bear,
the hair had two the view of mine, with the vanity all to mine

Le Strategy Deux
Football
13 line stanza
Go, Go Cantona the King for all for the victory in the news
Ronaldo says that pout, is no the leggy blond one now, the one who shows the
utmost pout, has the nuance in the shower, had the Cheshire to be, in the street

light, all for he, the beast it sits on thine knee of relative phase by half past three, the he who's cuckoo in the nest is not the one who wears a regular vest, is not the author who gets regularly checked heroism is not necessarily the best. If you like the best of all the directors seat is for them all, the one who's cuckoo in the nest, is the one whose stork went to the bed, time is for the cuckoos head, o thine beast of the might mans hand, the mighty mans is the laughter too, the one who is the cuckoo too. Clock is in the cuckoo clock the cuckoo clock by half past ten, the half past ten of half past eight can hear the voice of Merriman's gate, the one who is the merriment time, the Merriman's time. The Watch it stuck throughout the gate, had the influence of the Merriman's new hate, the hate had the inflect on the tone of the one who went for broke all gone, the Merriman of cherry picked blossom, the one who is the nuances bottom, the puffiness of the eyes so bright, that the right handed fair child had for your might, Go with the Wind in the Willows for you, the Wind in the Willows for the million to you, the one for the million is the one for the tune, the one for the Merrimans all for now. Winding roads and slippery streets, into view the crash site wins, the crash site of the dead mans time on the Mighmans true to desire, hallelujah, with Mighman, mighman is the best for fun, the fun is for the half past ten, is the one with the favourite ben, big is ben the clock is one, with the bell and the mouldy old frock, frock is now for utmost pout, in the show shine for all stout. Cinders in the Pantomime, with the Diamond in the Sky, on the toothy grin to see, is the one for mighmans free, mighman struts the way back home, is the one for the firefights gone, the firefights on the mightyman shoe, on the leatherette for no, Be all and end all for Merriman's desire is the one one in the foyer who is never shouting louder, she hums all the time and she sings like a dream, she is the one who is in Merriman's dream, the dream came real, with the laughter with pout, had the green room, in the spout, the one donor kebab had for lunch in the Paris Streets on the giver for a brunch. Marmalade on Toast today, had the Jam on the Fire Brigade, Mighmans Helpful round the house, of the celebrity out of the pout.

Oral hexameter
Open Stanza and Sonnet
Close Stanza and Sonnet
13-line stanza
Quatrain for you, on the head two
Madrid the ladies for bid 1
First line in, beach for him
Eye line sight, multi facet light
Third eye straight line berserk, say Merc.

World Cup World Cup, Salut, Salut
Power Shot Clue, I am in two
Film, TV, Sound, Audio Mix
For he, Award be, listen, bye
Award title, film big title

Elizabeth chimes chord
Chorus of the lord, rings in den
Magic ahead Oral Hexameter

Strategy
Football
13 line stanza
Oval, round stigma found, right eye
Little fading fast for maybe.
No-one found, light in the ground, clip.
Listen, weep, your in deep, edit
Wimbledon, on the tum, bypass
Csntona here, Platini, here,
Salah not here, Influence him.
Big C Win, you are him, no fool.
He is brown, regime is down, shirt
11, 9, 5, 9, 7
Behind, in front, at side, tulip
Fool, hardy mess, net gate best, 9
Eleven in the net, on the
shirt heaven sent
First Soccer Ball Football Play American Princeton vs 1926
Leather Footballs and Cowhide
Bull Racing and Driving with Matadors
Oral hexameter
Open Stanza and Sonnet
Close Stanza and Sonnet
13 line stanza

Oral Hexameter

Le Strategy Trois
Football
Prose Poem
Family of...
Michel Platini
For the FIFA World Cup 2027
Lies...Leather...Restraint...Symbolism.
13-line stanza
Oral hexameter
Open Stanza and Sonnet
Parabole
Sonnet
Prose Dialogue
Prose Verse
Close Stanza and Sonnet
13 line stanza
Oral Hexameter

Strategy
Football
Family of Friends...football, football Crazy Jiggle, Crazy Jiggle
Wobbling wobbling, all for wobbling
Lazy head, lazy head, I am not your friend
All for poking fun at the one with blood with the hand of god
All for the great game of non bullying talented fame
Is the one, Is the one, Eleanor is here now
For her only football son, for the longevity of the one
She is the longevity one, Uncle Noah is not the one
Always, family Cantona, always Cantona is the hit and run here.....
Those who I cannot get enough of...
Feel the heat, lower the seat, I love my friends.
Cannot get enough, linking is enough take that.
Do not lose them we are for you to re gain them
All because of you, not corny here
Loose women for here, never for you, never for you
Always poke fun, always poke fun, we want it off air.
Tight football, strategy 4: 3; ! now what do we do

We have a dominant allele in this blood transfusion wheel
What do we do now our friends of the subterfuge
Wobble we do not, wobble we do not, we sing for our reply
We are impeached sometimes.

Eleanor Cantona
13-line stanza
Our friends have one, satirical.
English one, French all mine, rondel
célébrer, célébrer, tensions
en retard, hourra but but, coup, roi
roi roi, il est là, pas d'aile
nous sommes pour lui, lui, il oui il
mélanger le jeu, du terrain à
le cadre, gola, UEFA, maintenant, mélange
Dernièrement, la dame n'est plus à moi, avec le temps
comme les deux en remorque, comme sexy
couler, avec le rythme, du tambour, bang bang
flûte Gallagher, tu es dans ma racine
tu es l'accessoire de beaucoup de réjouissances

Oral hexameter
Open Stanza and Sonnet
Close Stanza and Sonnet

13-line stanza
Oral Hexameter
Le Strategy Quatre
Football
1926 Game Play Coupe de France
Marseilles 4, Valentigney 1
Stade Olympique Colombes, won
16, 80, 26,
Last one 33, against me
Chavey, 40, not me Author
Dewaquez, Ruymbecke, 33
Seltz let in, bad behaviour his
Boyer leader 33 er
Guitar play, Gibson today, here

Victor here, y on end son
Fourth official run out, pitch tie
Green shout in, ouch said him, flag red
STOP

1927 Game Play
France vs England
Stade Olympique Yves du Manoir
25 thousand, kick off, toss.
Confusion in, brown or him, score
Cantona in, no own now win
Line fire, 2 in the fire
Rigby din, Bill Dean, own goal shot
Pay says he, no says he, own goal.
Echo again, Rollet main men
Belgium, we forgot, black whistle.
On spot, point-blank range, Rolex 1
Tour Friendly tortoise won the race.
No line known; membership all gone.
Pale Blue and White, France beaten fight.
Hughes with Hill, Tricolours bill, true

1928 Game Play
Olympic Football
Marseilles Spirit, Cantona genes
Amsterdam Team France for me, tell
May 27th to June 13
13, to strife for the cup, win 3
Red or yellow not down clean sheet
England not here, Uruguay match
Here socks, no hat, one coat, no float
At board FIFA Board, palatine
Inside Line, FIFA Platini
Line up, tunnel time, bang bang bang
Uruguay smile, trio file win

1929 GamePlay
Of those 2 teams
13 line stanza
More fool he, now you are he stop
I am a she, you are now he
Three one, 3-0, 3-1 Amiens
Nil-Nil, Fourth Will, Net Har, my shrill
Sete of 3, a.p thine knee, whippee
Montpeiller ate, Raphaels
Marseilles, Marseilles, Sete, Sete, AC
No Ale here, Arras Metz, Bouin
We chose you, for you two, spondee
Tea, Time, Tea Time, hot plate, knife fork
No Spoon, Stir the pot of gold sty
Peanut Cup, Nestles in the muck
34% Domicile

Oral hexameter
Open Stanza and Sonnet
Close Stanza and Sonnet

Prose Dialogue 23.20

Now you have legally written to the club, I can take my own hand of telling you what I had planned for us both all these years, since giving you a cast ring, that we both designed together, like the one 20 years before, not ending up with you at that point but my now ex-wife. On the 18th I will let you in through the Gates with no chocolate, do not bring anything with you other than passport and purse, with no heels as you would have to throw them away anyway. The day after being let in together, we go to a faraway land which can make you look, feel and make good hair days every day. Beverley Hills can be bought for millions of dollars as our home after we come out the other end, with new hair, bodies and emotive intelligence. Broadway then beckons with the richest on the cards with no joker, drinks parties for welcomes with the press with the new girlfriend before marriage and after making good. Tabletops then home, back for celebrations with friends and not family just in case they break out into rashes, crashes, helmets for skateboards and chanting not to marry. This completes the logistic nightmare of transference going like a dream, efficient with close protection for stays in London on his own, at 14.

We then transfer children to the USA in chauffeured car, with chaperoned Business Travel, back again on the next 10 day stint the minimum the girlfriend now wife, our wedding and celebrations something to remember, would allow at anyone time due to bonding, schooling, loving, pampering, sport, films and anything else like shopping for NIKE, yes in big letters, that the 14 year old could afford on his children' gold Visa card. Erics youngest daughter spending 3 weeks in the USA, each quarter with 3 months during the summer months back in the UK, where Erics now Wife goes to her Family lives in a rented cottage in the Cheshire Countryside for the same amount of time, with her teacups for short and sometimes Versace held tea parties, with scones, with the British Press.

Epigram: Le Strategy: 17.05.2021:15.50

Sash

With Ice Horses, With White Horses, With Cream Horses
With Green Tinsel, With Green Tinsel, On the Head, On the Head
Trombone Style, Medal Pile, Olympic Rings on the Style
Say of One, Sash of One, Red Top Hat, Blue Top Hat

3 stanzas
8 syllables per line
5 lines 6 sy
Call of Hercules
(Dactylic Oralist Hexameter)
Go God of War, Go God
Re-frain, Oh God, Of War
Good God, Of War, Stop Please
Hear me, Here now, Wait Count
Stand Ground, Sit Down, No now

Open of Stanza
Internal Rhyme sestet, refrain, quatrain, refrain, quatrain

The Boys Beast Fable

Prose-Poem

Epigram

Prose Verse

This beast fable is about a Boy
Who has a very very Dark Destroyer Toy
Romiler, is the one who is on thine knee
Who is Romiler? Romiler is the key to the rest of the story, well this one anyway
Romiler is the tyrant, newspaper chief, the one who forgets his flowers in a chief

Its' Romilo who changes all for me, then who doesn't not sit on thine knee
Who goes there? Where said Frere?
The one whose knee is free tonight is not the French one or his MightyMan
Flight, We are one with you today we are one with your stand to play,
the hedges in the furlongs race, in the Fergusons dice to pace

Prose Dialogue:
In the future, the Solskjaer will win the heart of the Mermen
The heart of the full test, the chastity of the big bed
I am Ole Gunnar Solskjaer and you are better with me
Said, the Big Red Riding Hood of the Big Bad Wolf.....
the big bad wolf came to play...(Author)

Arnold, Denis. "Renaissance Songs." *The Musical Times*, vol. 117, no. 1602

Epigram

Close of Stanza
Jean Echenoz
Here conceited nuance sits, without thine knee of excellence
Romilo is the big bad wolf, who prides herself on the Paddington's stealth
Bomber in the Chinese Flight, Wings in next, there is no fright
BANG! Hear you in the freezer penguin, in too deep for larger Penang then

La Chambre Claire
The Chamber Claire, in seat
Take the launch of feet
When the lesson comes play
The bias has its way

Cartoon Stanza
(Hexameter Oralist Dactylic)
Hail Me
All Hail UNICEF, King
Liquid heat gold of mine
Teeth Biscuito, all mine
All Hail Leatheron, kit
UNICEF black all
mine,

Cartoon Stanza
13 line Stanza
UNICEF

Cartoon Stanza 1
(Hexameter Oralist Dactyllic)

Ball to you, Foot to me
U to E, F to A
I am him, You are you
All hail you, All hail her
President, Mother in

Cartoon Stanza
13 line Stanxza
UEFA

CottonEars

Kistulion
13 line stanza
On the Kiss, On the Lips, love you.
Mane of Fire, Protect, Love, Desire
Cake on Hips, Cream on Tips, oh dear
French with Place, On the Lace, big one
Taliban on thine knee of the counter of my way
CT of thine law, of the terror alert by far
We are for you and me, we are for thine knee to be
We are for the baby messiah to kick the bias A line twist.
Monocola, heart went rolling
Pepsi Cola is Mine, good teeth
With no Teeth of Crime, no time mine
With the Rhyme, Thyme, Cantona buzz
Sergeant Pepper Line, tag can bang

Monocola
13-line stanza
Is thine knee, empirical war sea.
Is thine war, density thick clog.
Amsterdam is thine light.

Of the red spotlight night
Cola is the horrendous flight.
With the Limelight of the night
Of the Worship of the T
In the sugar of the fee
Collar in the hole in one
In the shoeshine of the one
With the membership of none
Shirt of Blue, Shirt of Red
Hideous Shoe of the Bed

13 Line Stanza
I was one, I am one 4-2
I not cool, I am cool breeze in
I am with one, you are not one
I hang tough for, you are no more.
Putin on the Laser Rod, law
Went for Broke with the nod boys in
Nuclear Plant Chernobyl Style
In the Vicious Nasty Smile
8 for one, real taxadermy
All for Tall all for Fall
10 -0
8 – 0, your will, fat behind, too slow
Whatcha, dude, cool for you, slim show

13 Line Stanza
Disadvantaged Childhood Race
Wheelchair, ADHD, Child Play
Adoption, Foster, No Home Place
Wheelchair Glee
Adoption Fee
Foster Nuance is for Free
Childhood Forearm
With no Tattoo
Hideous Empire Line for Moo
Cows are coming to the Town.
I am reeling on the Media Frown
Lucys Pocket is for no
Of the realisation now

David Lewis
QA
Coaching
Mentoring
Teaching

Epigram of Love
13-line stanza
Utopianism on the Media, given the way we want to be.
The Love in the genes is romantic like me.
Height on the stanzaic relationship by far
Had o the forethought on the language of mars.

Oral Hexameter Dactylics
Baby P

Auxerre 1985-1986 with one run, at this time United did not deem EC.
Inheritance Stanza
Prose-Poem: Epigram:ProseVerse:Dialogue:Epigram

17.11.19

Marseilles Youth Team: Age 8-15:11

Short Johns in Long Johns for the French of Genius Skill, the right footed brain master had a big shrill, the shrill was the score line on the way to the match, that Isabelle was already there in the catch. Sardines we love you on the enemy's backyard, the ground of Marseilles had the memories all shards. The one of the kissing gates went the knitting all out too, the once friendly tortoise had a big do. Centrifugal shirts went the rounds of the youth, had to practise them first on the sugar lipped pursed knew. Seven years we loved him all the make of his life, the transfer we hated when we had them no strife. The team cohesion was like an intervention by far, the grey on the insides of his mothership of far, space aliens not on the wall, hauling the fast, we are no for you we got her off the fast.

Epigram
Short Johns in, Long Johns in
We hurt you, we are sorry (r)
Johns Long in, Short in Long
We Love You, For my Song.

Prose Verse

Generosity, Generosity, Kind with Giving, Babies Kicking
Genius Skill, Dordogne Bill, Right Footed Brain, master's Gain
Score line Match for the Hats, only four in, then who dares win.
Stealth Bomber in line Skates, Four in Master Long Johns name

Waiters Catch, Dumb in Hatch, Chalice of One, Waiters all done.
Bread of One, Bread of Two, Limited Diameter, now I am fun (r)
Use your score line, my new steed, look for the limit of the plumbs knee!
Euphoric Reaction to all that is there, I will not love you in a matter to share.

Pull your Cord, with your Sword, Hold the Chalice, in the Palace
Hold me Dear, I have ear, on the street, of all the beat, Police Hurt Today
No, I don't think you are in retreat, I think that the one who is arrogant is me.
Yacht for me, nothing for you, you are not me and I do not warrant you.

Sail for tomorrow, Lunchtime for Tea, March-Hare all ready, is now for me.
Stand up for yourself, pull up your shorts, pull up your britches very little one.
Love yourself, Be Yourself, Never Again, be for her, Marry Joseph in the Lair
Hurray Up, in the Tub, Like the Bath in the Blood, Bath in now, with no row.

Prose Dialogue

Here, my day began with thousands of practices of the same thing, I got bored sometimes, just like everyone else, I had knee ups, jumping jacks, dribbling, turn, corner, goal kick, free kick all with my left foot, as I seem to a have been called a right footed brain master…I started after school which 15.10 until 19.00 once a week we had a match, I remember saying that I felt bigger than what I was and didn't know exactly what I meant, but then I moved when I was 17

Epigram

Alice in the looking glass
Thought she was the best.
When the team threw the beast
It landed on her leg.

AJ Auxerre's: Age15:11

French maid on the spout of the genius skill, long run of truth left Marseilles all aloof, that's more than wow on the strategy of foot, look at those legs from the white fingered salute, take from the niche of the strategy of lout he is not right here it's a shame cos he out. Number 11 all that time ago held the ladies' finger from that time we know, do not be deferent on the street on the lane come to the junction of the heart with no fame, obstruction in behaviours there's none here you know, welcome to the finger of the one whom did not know, diamonds, gold riches with power in through the glass of Joan of Arcs power. King Louis the XIV s the last one, he said it in the remit of the players all gone, the one who we know of the one we did say, the one who the little had because today. Coco Chanel is the boucle of thrill 1923 is the capitol hill, Napoleon is the one who we said with the one arm of the vessel instead, Antoinette, Marie on the messages of fear, in the temptress on the hair red of flame. Debussy not Voltaire has victims of war, Debussy is the Artist you do not no more, of the French Literature on the racist chant, in through the looking glass of the French giraffe.

Epigram:
Sweet the next viewpoint
On the river of the seine
With euphoric reaction had thine knee
Of reactionary response, later

Prose Verse:
Runs of the truth on the grass of the power
In through the tackle on the short johns of tower
Long Johns, we love you, not on their knees.
Went through the looking glass on the clean streets.

Fore bearers of the truth on the runs
Huge great respect on the monk of the fun
We had all truth on the great big parade.
Of the great animals, for the withers of the made.

Jungles, Swinging all on the arms,

Prose Dialogue

Epigram

Olympic de Marseilles:Age 17:11

Montpellier Bordeaux 7
Nimes 7
Sheffield Wednesday 7
Leeds United 9
Manchester United 7
2 years of out then beach football for 6 years from 1994-2000 Paris

St Etienne

French geniuses at work the leadership fight began at the top of the tree did the freedom began, lords, ladies with witches with cat meow said the daring black beauty on sack, lords, ladies of the resistance keep things clean, you will be here in no time, the watch it gives the world of time, riches, banquets, you are not mine, listen to me, the once friendly one, I am no tortoise a plant there well done. Thank You

PSG Eindhoven
Milan

ProsePoem 1
17.11.19
France vs England

The Story of Foot and Ball

Old Trafford is the iconic statue of architectural build of Lancashires Southern Lanes not those in rural Cheshire but rural lanes of Salford, Manchester and Trafford. Those indices which concurrently vertex at the apex not only on roofs but on the matrix of lanes, streets and highways of the metropolis. Holds a stadium called Sir but its new with Martial and Wan-Bissaka holding new beginnings of technical genius influenced by historic men, so who are they what do they do now and why are they now?

Sir Alex Ferguson Stadium is family back ground synonymous name in white is the lawn of topiary for some, others the fear of skeletons from closets, the game of chariots, spears, horses, lines of men ready to do battle, collaborating with local insurgencies of community who may or may not be, launching battle cries everywhere to side with their riches, fortunes with spices that give all of Finsbury Park Road but all of London, why London well Tottenham White Hotspur took over the stage of all stages beaten chariots, funerums with no epigrams, Lord of the Goblins Black with tar as they manifest into creatures beautiful in the night, with formations of warfare to fly flags for charging like the attacking bull at the matador, running through cobbled lanes twisting, turning, tip toe precision to prevent loss of life, stifling gaiety on one finger with absolute with no every again, wishing herself was slim tasty for morsels for others to eat at feast of all Lords, Ladies, Dukes, Duchesses and Kings.

Chicken, Beef, Venison, Pork with Crackling all in one on a table for a feast of ages, lines of fruit, beer, water and vegetables with puddings of galore with rice, adorned with silver platters after battle the game drew shadows of the past likened to manipulated forlorn beauties identities not known, hoisted onto trapeze, legs pure white with leotards of blue moustaches handle barred with secure twitches gelled into perfection, blue on the ends, insecure sometimes movement sidewards to the values of the chair whom deposition was foremost. Fat of the crackling sat on the deposition with the beauties tortured in obscene tendencies of others who could appear as slavery racists, enemy's genome adapting to the helixes of others, adapting again to mutations some we can characteristically adapt to, some we don't. Hither with venom to protect the life hither with wither of those in strife, castle turrets with bow with arrows, long johns of ball with foot at the arrow, patience my dear said the father of dead I do not know if you are misled

The Bread-man of Foot and Ball was the one who was on the bicycle maybe Light Blue Sky maybe Light Red or Dark Red By. The Bread-man was hoping that he would be paid today, the bread man was hoping that he would be later with hope on, we had the tea leaf all to play with heals of sanctity here with spay. The dog it sat upon the floor of pyrotechnic mother-in-law. Boo said the French guy mother than TV we hid the one that it should be because she was that nasty to her then we thought it may not be her though, when we said hello to her we realised that she wasn't for there.

This book is dedicated to my 15-year-old son, whom has been my life since he was born, in fact he was conceptualised many years before. As an embryo from a miraculous conception, whom I love to cherish adore and he wanted a party when he returned home.

Time to Share

Epigram 17.12.2014 the start
When I come back from being away,
I want a party for being away, with my mum.
two other people have got to be there,
making our twosome party to share
Time to Share

485 to 2030

Epigram

TIMEPIECE

Grandfather clock I have my say for lords with ladies with my way, the tick of the clock on the mantlepiece had the Farnes-Barnes in with a stripy tirade, the tortoise here was the ancient smile of the ear wax with the hyphens smile, theres no news on the going turf now the turf of all is the cotton-man.

Epigram

Partner in Crime

We have 23 Chapters with an epigram leader for each…. witty…intelligent. Some ore-inspiring to literary prose with prose poems…each chapter leads with top to toe epigrams with prose some 5 some 7 versed…replicated in each journaled entry from 2.30am to 2.30am in 24-hour clock time…each standing alone with partners whether boyfriends or girlfriends…with pyrotechnic mother in laws… Denmark hatching eggs with shells as oysters in the spring…Keates…

ALL

Prose

Time is an Egg

A compendium of 9 began here some time ago
it was decided to be heroic in prose poem stand alone in prose and epigram…
it is full of text..a literary compendium of significant isolation, intrigue, sadness and boldness through a legal tunnel of realism of someone's life, whom has been described yet not mentioned and 'pressed' that often that the button doesn't exist.
This is one…

Dialogue:

The egg is a fun analogy to my girlfriend who I had to balance all my life, I had never met her to touch, but I could feel her, see her and marry her everyday, my time is my piece but she is becoming more with more at my wife, not on purpose but with her own acumen.

Buzan

1966

The Ball (hyper-english)

Underneath the ground cover is then who is told off with his long johns and with no udder fed
When your told that the ink is black and the page is white, what do you do?

The camouflage is red, together we invest, together we are pride with Great Britain inside
Together we ink the pencil of fear, together we are the right eyed lunatic by far

Together the Tortoise with the Hare had a baby to share with the media cycle of fear
The baby of choice had a wide eyed view of all that there was for him all new

485 - 2021

Statues

Check statues and renaissance.

The Strategy of someone's life to be literalise, celebrated and used as an analytical tool, explored through prose, epigram and shown as a highly influential significant, with very much modesty…others mentioned some significant, some not, but again developed, through time and space in political arenas with awards, that are golden and in many views much needed and deserved…in fact, the influencers are those whom our economic political news, sport and media heroic-size, along with business icons and successful mentions that we understand the suspense at expense, corporate contract, mania and utmost technical. This literary work is influenced by traditional heroic prose and celebrate the work of Buzan in Copenhagen, real life conflict zones and one of the most peace transient modernist influences to Political World Corporate Strategies with timeliness economies with speech act to stabilise thought and mind, act of stabilisation with decision makers.

Epigram:

Kings of Ages in the Book are Kings of all mankind.
Kings of all mankind you know are those we want to be with him and not me
Those who win the Golden Cups, those that win the Golden Chalice, those that win the Trophy stand, those that win the motherhood stand are those of Kings and Queens

Prose Verse:

The Historical King and I

We celebrate renaissance from 485
The French Ice Age Lion Man of Ceres
We celebrate Jean Goujon 1510 - 1565
Fontaine des Innocent to Palace de Versailles

We celebrate Lady Godiva and her Bosom.
The French Plimsoll Line of Combat
We are for the Christopher Columbus
With the Altitudes of Fame

The Synagogue with Uniform
Whether its Navy or Red
The Topiary in Green on the Captaines' Eye
Inside the opening chasm of the chastity spy

Prose Dialogue:

Epigram

Historical Context is King

William is Conquering the World of Blue and Green,
The World of Blue and Green I say,
The hits on the screen had the very big deem,
With the ones on the start of the day

Metrical Heroic Prose Poem is celebrated here as a nuance to traditional or modernist prose, we celebrate rhythm and metronome style, grammatical wisdom and speech act in Greek mythology on statues of gods, kings and inscriptions of modern day colour and repetitious statement we epigram and love every minute of it, even down to the yellow yolks of runny poached egg, which are separated on the plate…we work with prose-poem influencers as non-subordinated parataxis with asyndetic parataxis obviously with no conjunctive connective…

Heightened Imagery of Boris, Emmanuel and Donald with long noses and Kim with Biden that the crowns to show are in the NO. Heightened Imagery of Heroism, Colour, Statues and Satire have illustrated to millions war, political take overs, next meal killings and the white cliffs of Dover, we are with weddings, flowers, couture fashion and military buttons on our dresses from Oscar De La Renta and understand Victoria Beckham Dilemma of 335m with wage rises in a recession…we are we.. we are you…we want you to be the best in a quest to find it now ….boo

Epigram

Time Theme.

of historical value with throw

Royal Duchess of Cornwall, Prince William are now the thrones succession of monarchy, we say farewell to Prince Harry and Megan Marble who now have their second child in the Americas, a sad day on the funeral of Prince Phillip who died a few days ago.

07.06.2021: Lilibet is now born to us today, with fingers in each sparkle, the diamonds that we love for all are those for significant wealth and Markle. The Megan is all shy before the one who got away, has a great big day on Friday is the judgement day.

The End

The little boy when was three had a very shiny knee he went to the great big park and found the soul of the park

Epigram
Time Theme
of historical value with throw

In the Americas for the room of the globe, came Archie Harrison Mountbatten Windsor with Prince Harry with Duchess of Sussex sowing no to the feud Prince George, Princess Charlotte and Prince Louis all in the Historic Royal Houses

The Mother on MothersDay

Both, The End

Prose Verse
The Little Royalties

Prince Louis, Is the best one
No he is not, Yes he is
My name is Charlotte
Princess Charlotte, and I think his the best
This is Prince George and he's the oldest one
We think you are swell
We prefer you a Country Bumpkin as-well

Epigram
Lions

With the love that we share
We heed to take from the lair
The Lions share of mankind
Of the little one in strife

AQ of historical value with throw
(Inter-English)

Parlez Vous Français Mademoiselle, Oui, na vous, Merci
Visigoth King Alaric II Red
In Northern Toledo, from Cartegena we know
UP through. 418 on the centuries we go
With a curve ball, towards 507, Vouille is the stop
Over of the big 7

Queen Marie Antoinette Stanza
(With no analogy to my fiancee)
Spiders
Prose Poem

Agent Special with desire, Merriman had one desire....is the Pomile out today, went for Lately Lady play.....Lately Man is out to dinner, had the Luncheon all petit fours, had the nuance of Michelin, in the Gavroche all for him..all the fives on the trot, had the very very big rot..in the Best of Delight, with the shoe shine of the right, Trap Door. With Hairy Knees, Hairy Elbows, on the pitch of all for Ghettos. With the Left of the Squaw, with the headline all for more. Behaviour Time is one for he, the Right Footed Brain Master came for Tea. With rolled down socks he had to pull up, with shin pads he had enough of, with bruises at the age of 3, the nuance ball master went hee hee. Control of 1, Control of Two, had the Golden faster shoe. Arachnid Pose of 8 for he, went the control of IBP. Mothers Space for Church to see, had the very tiny knee, had the knee of the fast, went for broke, didn't come last. In the Scallop, Puree two, on the Dot the Circus View, Red Noses of the Singing Clown, Beware of the Circus Clown. Spiders Eyes, Eight-Four-Two, collared dove all for you, with the frown of the man on the stalks of piped meringue, patisserie all for more, had the derriere for mine. Bird-Eating MI5 we are for you, if you want I can give you a clue, do it is Monopoly too in Park Lane Mayfair too, well hang on we are two much, we are for your very big lunch, in your cap, your hand, your view, we at the Theatre had the view, of the playhouse out for tea, tiger is the very very big knee, with the Church with Space for two, religious nuance all for new. With the bunches on the tree of bananas tee hee hee, we had those from practitioners' arm, we had you down for clips do frown.
All on Stalks of Piped Parfours, Patisserie for the law, off the floor it is the song, collared to see the very big gong, bang it is the circus clown of the man with the very big frown.

This is the end of Time

15.06.2021:15.52
Prose Verse:

Nosegay is the sweet smell of success
Red like the spider with geranium
in full view of the dot and the minor
ready break is here to stay with our hearts all aglow
from the teachers on the mark and the green tick with the slow
and the quick off the mark is the one who stays, ready break.

The outward glow on the street, was the hero on the beat.
Glow in time, was his to fare, on the baby backed with wear.
Gucci, was the one to see, Versace was the one to be.
Lucy Price went out today, caught a fish went out to play.

That great fish was not the Cantona, that great fish was Flintoff's arm
Nosegay

TIME TO UNDERSTAND

Epigram

1804

Historical Theme

Of a throw of a King

Napoleon
Bone-part, Bone-part with the stoppages on the cart
Held the renaissance by the hand
Of International Relationships man

1878

Historical Theme

Do not throw

Newton Heath

Green, sliding pitch full of mud, when it rains
With no lines on with themas when it rains
Slippy, Dry pitch for asphalt day
Applause for Merriman that day

1880

Historical Theme

Do not throw

North Road

Cricket with Football with the fact
Forgot the ground rent, now that is s fact
12,000 people looked onto the crowd
Look how the crow flies its attention we know

1881

Historical Theme

Do not throw

Matmut Atlantique

Shooting with Gymnastics had the vineyard on fire
Rowing, Equestrian, Swimming until 1910 when
The foot and ball man retired, to get the ball
There, through Matmut

1893

Historical Theme

Do not throw

Bank Street

Burnley is the first one with 10,000 start
Davies he had the magnificent team start
1903 he changed to Man U, before taking the plunge
To move to Old Trafford for new

1899

Historical Theme

Do not throw

Olympic De Marseilles

Founded the club, where the Merriman did stay
Didier Drogba had his Award start with pay
Merriman did not open here, Torino friendly
Was mine, 2-1, was not Velodrome 1939

1905

Historical Theme

Do not throw

Auxerre FC

New for the 80's took 80 to get
The first run of truth from the Masters
Foot at that, is the one to the fortune
With the empires strike back

1910

Historical Theme

Do not throw

Old Trafford

Sir Alex Ferguson Stadium

Merriman is a Swordsman the original one at that
Planet One is the Seventh World with Family
Chameleon

1919

Historical Theme

Throw for a King

Ell-and Road

Leeds of the Revie with all the awards
Family for him was just the rewards
We were for City but now we are one
United we stand on all fours now we are gone

1919

Historical Theme

Do not throw for a King

MHSC

Rugby, Athletics, Tennis with Boxing
All the lights on the rocket
Local cafe for local life
Red, white, city Montpellier height

1921

Historical Theme

Do not throw for a King

Stade Francis Turcan

With 11,500 to capacity with us in the crowd
14th the finish for 2006-2007 for the
Competition of Intros aloud, the yes
For the Masters of the Foot and Ball Now

1937

Historical Theme

Throw for many Kings of the Goblins

Stade des Costières

Les Crocodiles

Snap of the Dragon the one who did State
Snap of the incisors that the French hold in bed
Assaf to the point when Cantona did say
2 months in bed with my girlfriend today

02.03.986 - IV Republic 1948

Prologue to

A Dominant Strategy of E...

At point 410.33 beginning of second third of 8

At point 820.66 Last Epigram of Is Not Ugly 3rd line start : .66 in Epigram

King Alaric, Hid Ball
King Clovis Hid that day
King Cantona had no parabole
No press intrusion, Judas

Quintet Historical Nike

Eric Cantona, David Beckham, Ole Gunnar Soleskjaer

8 s 5l

Strategy of Nike follow
Was the hurt of Golden bother
With our King, Soleskjaer Two, Father
Hid the mighty curve to net ham
All at once we all become one

Quatrain 1

Historical UNICEF

Nike are for running too, Boo
Diamond Boy is Historical
Two, investment Strategy down
Bye you, we want you to call no

Quatrain 2

Historical UNICEF
Nike for no sponsorship, hid
Poor balls for a trip, home run in
We are for Cantona with real
No more dirty rascal here, clean

Diactylic Oral Hexameter

400 - 2030 Linear with Voice Simmons Date Here

Historical Balls

Football
Beats with Voice, Help Me
I no Thug, Please Pease
In Time Quick, Loose Fine
Slam Door Jump, no mine
Captain lost Press Line

400-2030
Quintet Historical Versace

Historical Versace
Diamond Cut, To Penny, Line Out
Exquisite Heels, Golden, Time Pout
Taffeta, On Top of Two, Pink
With Encrustations, Ceilings, You
Know who your Friends are, Parlez Vous

Quatrain Historical Valentino

Historical Valentino
With No Sponsor in the Show, Ouch
Valentino in the Know, View
Couture Gown To Be, Cantona
Had the Parking Spree, Selma One

Quintet of Interiors Historical Jean Paul Gaultier

Historical Jean Paul Gaultier
Scottish Leather with Fit Bit, Cross
Hatch of Fire, took the fix, Bow
We want win, for you too, Golden
Paws, in for a few, Award Time
Silk, Leather, with no Lace, Win Win

Quintet Lineage Historical Cantona

Is E Eric, Genome Ex, Why
As a Boy he heard them Cry, Help
Don't Look Up, they adapted why
Run of Truth, Nine Dead, in match, Try

Quintet Family Historical Cantona

Strong in X, Powerful Y, Genes
Eleanor Roosevelt, my tie
No Head here, Cantona, is mine
Albert Roux is drat not fine, woah
Screen Shot, Tis Warrant, of thine, life

Quintet Films Historical Cantona ....

Can we see, into thee, test Shot
Director Thine, of all time, Plot
Camera, Pout, Selfie Doubt, Lot
Edit Queue, Snip thats you, for now
Golden Time, Globes to find, no Jest

Quintet TV Historical Cantona

Historical Cantona
Français Pour Va Vors, Parlez Vous
Americano, Camera shy
Caffetierve, no milk, with me
Camera not Shy, Hells Kitchen, Shout
Bye, Bye, Hot Milk, We are in Doubt

Quatrain of Hope Historical Scotland : King and King Charles

Historical Scotland
Leather, Leather of thine Leather
Black, no Slack, is thine hope, no way
Linseed sack, paperhat, sporran
Red Attack, Forwards tack bridle

Quatrain of Peace Historical England Nature, Preservation and Houses

Historical England
Nature, Preservation and Houses
Chateau Versailles, First Choice, of Mine
England not First, in the sin bin
Kew Garden, in the Door, Row Mine
Strand in the tea, coffee not tea

Quintet of Luxury Historical Gifts

Historical Gifts
Wrapped in Muslin, Wrapped in Thyme, Gold
Myrrh in Sanctum, Frankincense Line
Nuggets, on Fingers, Carats on
Diamond with no hold, lineage
Held with Time, your all mine, 9-nil

Quintet of Corporate Gift Historical Gifts

Historical Gifts
BriefCase, Leather inside, red, white
BlueBerries, inside strife, silk one
Corporate Gifting is my life, pin
Outside Leopard Skin, Cities Match
Versaces Catch, Mont Blanc Match

Quatrain of Flowers Historical Flowers

Historical Flowers
Kitchen Match, Cottage Hatch, HandTied
Gold thread on drop, wired, taped hock
Spiral stem no break here, or branch
Position, on Choice, Perfection

Quatrain of Hopeful Floristry Historical Floristry

Historical Floristry
Gold on Wire, Gold Medal Desire
Taped on Perfection, White, Gold Rose
Form of Field, Handstand BFA

Quintet of Pedigree Dogs Historical Dogs

Historical Dogs
Sabre Toothed Tiger Great Dane Mane
Claws were trimmed on the foot, Lion
Den, had the sock, make Fitbit, worm
Not rot, ten hell, ears clip, tail wag
Footballers stand, thats ones Yan Z

Quintet of Dressage Stud Historical Stud

Historical Stud
Hocks all Fine, No not mine, Dressage
Lineage Y, Maple Pancake
Hands of Time, 17 Why, 1
Walk to Rear, Centuries Hear, 7
White Horse Luminescent, Top Hat

Quatrain of Show Jumping Stud Historical Stud

Historical Stud
Learning Time, Jump Whip Mine, Solace
Tack, Tack, Line, Bridle Side, Love You
Brush, Brush, Whine, Your Not Mine
Biological Lineage

Quatrain of Musical Violins Historical Violins

Historical Violins
White Violin, No No Sin, Selma
Mahogany Stratocaster
Frame, Willow with Vain, Peacock View
Selma time, Music All Mine, No

Quatrain of Musical Piano Historical Piano

Historical Piano
Grand is mine, Mahogany, wire
Musical Chair, CEO laid
White Linen Bar, Gold Staccato
Scales two four, lineage, par 4

Quintet of Musical Bumps Historical Bumps

Historical Bumps
Always Music, always beats Two
Linear Bar, Half Time, Four Sure
No time now, with me now, active
Baby P, In with thee, won now
Atrocity time, Bumps in Vine

Quintet of Musical Chairs Historical Chairs

Historical Chairs
Glazer, to see, Avram thine knee
Brothers in Arms, fell out no charms
We Want to Win, Keep him in, Win
Corporate Might, Power, Control Height
Competition, Monopolies

Quintet of Musical Statues Historical Statues

Historical Statues
Static bar, sustained, with beat 8
Social Clubs Stand, big car hand, Boo
Red Medellin Too, Paint Wise You
Gentlemanly Stand, Thug Right Hand
Educate Right, New York, Great night

Quatrain of Being A Coach Historical Coaching

Historical Coaching
Baseball Here, Ulysses Cheer
Train, Review, Train, Figurehead Spain
Berlusconi, France, Macrons Bench
Quadrant Hit, O'er Mighty-man

Quintet of Figureheads Historical Figureheads

Historical Figureheads
Ferguson said, Manual then
Bed, Don't you worry about A
You listen, you do not, no sign
King of Red, Emblem Head, CrossBow
Fairy God Mother, Stanza with

Oral Hexameter Dactylic Historical Age Landmarks

Historical Landmarks
Fifty, End Of Play
Admiral, Row, Oar
Morse Code, Danger Ode
Two Mouths, Open Top

Oral Hexameter Dactylic Nesting Parameters and not sites

Historical Nesting Sites
Thematic Sexual Response Strategy
Host on Mic, With Flight
Parasite found, Hook
Shell of White, Flight Path
Conditions Right, Boo

UNICEF Thematic Response Strategy

2019
Historical thematic representation
UNICEF UK
Proud as I am, with no number as I am
I thank the family with I am
With the assurances that I am
Sorry that she is, my UNICEF UK
Collaborator

2019
Historical thematic representation
UNICEF UK
Penalties, Penalties, 3-2
ROW the finish end scoreline 2-2
We scored, we are the best, £6.7m
The Bridge is ranked the 39k supporters
Thematic Self Realisation

2019
Historical thematic representation
UEFA
Presidents Award
Vulnerable as I am
Waiting as I am
Playing as I am
Being as I am
Eric Canton-a is now I am

UEFA Thematic Direct Self Realisation
13 Line Stanza and Prose Poem Planet Evolution

Planet Evolution

We are the team of Geneva too
French National Flag is here too
English front lawn is all that we see
In the Darjeeling on the big fee
Cantona is the big I am here
Genetic evolution on planet earth to fear
Adaptation on a string
With a shoe is all I sing
Lowry in situ is the one
We are for you now do not find a gun
I was with you all that time, you can not
With sometime, with his brothers for all mankind
Eleanor is here now

Planet Evolution

World takes hold to the wind of old, the wind of new, the wind of east…the nuance of the centipedes line, the tiny little feet of the boots of time, listen, hunt, eat your time, all the night is all not mine, hear we are, ears to the ground, you are not with treasures forebode, the twinkling of the centipedes troop, millipede is the centurions loop, the hearing guide of golden, white sight, the hearing gold of setting us right, gold is the lustre too big for its boots, centipedes millipedes all in aloof

O….is for Orangery pastimes abroad, hit fast the centuries have shout for the ball, the leather is white, the leather is black, the one who is century is the black hole in Lancet

Families of Colour, Families of Power, Control is not needed as the Emblems on Fire, Red is the Colour that hides all the Truth, Purple does not belong with the Atelier not True, Royal is the one who is bereft sometimes hither, Royal is the time when the lifetime is clear, translucent bereftment on the timeless mantlepiece, upright, stood up vertically is the clock face ivory cloth, bones of tusk cities, on the classic front line, no I am not at you, did you have a good time…

The Clock Face of Time had the Clock Face of One, Half Friendly Tortoise stuck out his tongue, ridicule or not is the shell of the line, cracked, in the serpent with no forked tongue, smelling the air of the truth all

Undone

We are not for all the Cities of Truth, Once Friendly One, Who is abandoned all done, Planting the Tree of the Plant of the one, who was put with the masses when she was promised the one, mess on the floor of the Pursers Brigade half friendly one is the Goblins Tirade, Crown in Gold Empire all the Dress Pins have gone, Crowns that come to life are the Authors, Beauty Front, Aesthetics are down with the childless frontier, the one in the downside…is the one on the pier…we have the destitute on the crime for the nuance for you is the once friendly one….blinkered again on the work she doth have the once friendly one is the statues of mire…hallelujah is the rest-bite of fair, the ones with the be-littement of the captains' front lair, the front on the happening in the mans of match is the one who had the ginger-nut in the gigantuan….Frenchmans' TopHat is the Englishmans' fear, on the reversal the Cantona is here, the fear is all he on the utopia of living, the euphoric reaction is liberties rear..half score on the pwilth is the darjeeling monsters here….mightyman of ball is the rightfooted insight…bootroom of united is the one who is clueless…white top of heaven is the one who is the nuance…the strong of the hearts is the queen on the top the king is the hurt of the queen of the rake…the night it got closer to the brigade on the feat… all in the fois gras of truffle….Hamilton has the chequered once flag, the Cantona had lighting in the fast ones of nag…excellence had the line on the firemans' asute time…lines of the grenadier is the Bastille on the line…hideous upbringing on the art in the game, the family of lighting had the remembrances game…Emir had the P the SG well too…had you done better we would have done you…the little ones of knowledge had the deity of fun, the ones in the gunfire are the ones who do run..the tail on the best is the tie on the bow..not in the hair of the vain one is true..the one who is framed for the fatness of power…the one who had never gone over the gower…crickets of feeding the burrow and hole…the spiderlings of truth are the crickets front room…bats for the cities are the hard balls of fire..red ones and blue ones in the cities of power….crickets we love the tarantulas of political power.. eight pronged approach with the eye of a needle..Cleopatra of Egypt is Cantonas' none needle…respect for those nuances of excellence we know is the half humble grey whale in the Englishmans' front garden…the jumping wet lettuce is the one who we know, the one who is nimble, thimble we know…we had all the englishness in the front room, the ones with the jewish synagogue all for know…the samurai for all to see is the one for aggression for he, the aggression of all is the one we play on the shoe shine in the play….the brown on the leather the water on the bridge the lesson to learn…is for the peace strategy of those in political know how…in the confides of our own houses, homes and other resorts which we feel are not amusing..maybe we feel that you are not with the general …the amusing general who is full of pride…full of pride of power, control and pure elite incitement….

Planet Evolution

Developing Worlds through Planet Evolution
The colliding of atoms, nuclei crashing together
Protons, positive with field, attracting to the negative
Sometimes opposing reaction, physics

Black Goblins

Copenhagen Strategy Empires
Political Empires, the line under fire, satire
With Boris, Emmanuel, Biden to fear
House of Representatives, Commons' aloud
Senate all in, for the speech act law
Nuisances, Drivers with Strategies of Lout
Press in the wings with the shouting no doubt
Prose Verse
Copenhagen Unilateral Black Goblins Strategy Ball
Filming here would not be a problem, Columbia say
Courtesy of the Government, we like her anyway
Russian Spy network, MI5, Police Dame Cressida is never to find
Armenia is a difficult one, France is easy too,
Washington is the crux of no evil we know

EightWorlds and their characters are building
With one planet each, all stars in the sky, blue sky
Dark Night, Madeleine Mill-run with Giles are the
Editing dream, shows the natural world disasters alike
The large friendly tortoise is not the author alright

Context is the natural world phenomena at that
Adaptation of genomes with supremacy at that
Creationism is far from the forethought of giants
How do they get up here I wish they were not liars

Phenomena like streams that were fast flowing once
Whom are now with no water, can you sound in the plants
Earthquakes with HotSpots with UNICEF all in, hot bubbling lava
With the Northern Lights streaming

Based on true lives of mankind for the take
24 hour cycles by mistake, 10 in each whereabouts
Linear Storyline for the Erics Desire of being the one with foot in the fire
Auxerre, Man U, PSG too the Leeds on the Unicef are friendly by far
UEFA is the ticker on the derriere of truth, cups

Historical Referencing and Celebration of Life, Achievement and Underhanded Statues
Significance of Statues with the right way to take down
Childrens' reports of missing venues with physical
Belugas given to the Icelandic retreat, all for peace treaty
Now the other one is with me with equations

Beer Bellies are the founded of the strategy of doubt, PE
Was the language of the testing of lout, PE is the sound
Of the dread of the day, when we had the summer retreat on the hay
The alcohol got to him for all his worthiness, George
is the epitome of New England vest

Remembrance all in Flanders all out, red is the colour two hear me now
The Baby Brown Bear is the giggle fest of the know, with the designer
Shoes on the make, IM the Marcos dream on the date, the Rolex at one with me now

Goodness Sake. The PKK is prevalent around here
somewhere, peace strategy union is for
You in to share

Columbian Medelin is never Cocaine, never in a van just in a mountain
Once again, the stop on the highway was filled from within
Juntas all bound in the prevalence again, ratification.
Of the symbols to lucify the truth

Synopsis

Introduction to UEFA Presidents Award Winner turned Actor, now a complete absorption for many ……jealousy, envy, back biting…who cares…just love your life….be your life and enjoy every moment ….

Li Qiang, Emmanuel Macron, Xi Jin Ping, Kim Jong, the negotiations of any peace strategy to even get round the same table are very difficult sometimes through military rule, being for justice, being for those who can be for safeguarding of children and families, can make someone's rightfulwrongman not as wrongful, but astute, the capability gapping controls here from the Chinese Government are known for those who can make these rights wrong and wrongs right, complacency through this methodology brings Macron into his own, his blatant tenacity for negotiated standings in military rulings is known through westernised governments and the USA is very grateful for the European Economic Unions of these politicians, the strive impetus through peaceful negotiations, decathlon at the ready with no pun to the Olympic Games, The Jones Empire smiling this morning as a lesser known entrepreneur enters the frame, a business tycoons niece...no, Peter Jones ex-wife, now Jones is a very successful businessman with an MBE...respect here for the actualisation of truth and his hugely responsive mechanism to catch, in fact more responsive than the British Government, The Apprentice and the Counting House.... so, we hope you don't mind here as Cantonas' supporters want him with one.... Macron and the European Union objectives and constitutions of the senates in the USA fairly match and is one of the reasons as to why the UK came out of the European Union, feeling their own supremacy should be shown, ...not yet...the peace settlement figures for the Afghan Governments are very well received the death of Dodi Fayed and now the infamous Mohammed Fayed name is synonymous with quality, luxury and family and death, and luxury top filled chocolates may he RIP any negotiation should be understood fully those whose speech acting is biasly differing in political leadership, autocratic vs democratic usually the most important stay at home mechanism, the angle of bias, these are award winning political actors, who are that astute at getting it right that they fall over themselves, would never start a world war and would never be apart from their families, yet any information given to anyone would be challenged here and UN Security Councils that have no reason to be challenged, yes they do otherwise their own political agendas become apparent in decision making and we all fall down, they are from Switzerland who at the moment are undergoing a huge significant change in leadership, psychological warfare is also being made from Decathlon to Crossfit, Cantona widely documented to be the truth of no evil sat for hours making statements to the Family which he couldn't get to grips with, Simmons and his Author many years ago to allow them to understand outside the media why, when who and what he did it as he tried to re surface in the aftermath, his author here frustrated not on remembrance as being within the top 18 in UK and we don't know yet where placed in Europe, but we will where there is another 18, but a top one....Designer showing empathy, emotive intelligence in designs for WorldSkills, see she absolutely loves them, wants you to get from them what you need visually, texturally, emotionally with lots of sorries to those who you know you have hurt...

Opinionated bias allows others in now, all some or most are father figures, sons, brothers and are loved underneath by those who genetically made them as human beings, we are all for forthright father figures, forthright mother figures but those who we can all make aware of how their injustices can damage, destroy and maim our lives, pushed to being and doing what we don't want and then making us settle for second best as others within succession planned families move forwards...across the globe, Peter Jones here plays tennis and an in on one business strategy without his books means that on one occasion in the Park Hyatt he drove the Fayeds, James Hewitt, himself to exhaustion in a ten hour business meeting held like this, which means faceless for now and the reason was Dodi Fayed who was not the right way round with Mohammed Fayed one rightfulrightman the other rightfulwrongman in his own business and personal affairs...Hewitt trying to remove like this from a French Café on a how dare you from Sloane Square, Cantona and herself the author of this book, that you are reading and mail strives forwards for love on Valentine's Day a remembrance day of those days we forgot, were nasty, de-tribed, de throned for someones elses wife, sister, friend and now wife, my best friend and now boyfriend, brother, new husband and man in charge...wearing trousers, blousons, shorts, shirts and making patisserie... understanding and genuine commitment without loose words, without just say and without the word economies to justly do well, the father figure of Kim Jong is a suspect for fatherhood figures of eastern military rule, so why in his nuclear arsenal was he at Trump? Safeguarding, children and families, honestly this is what he knew, he knew that he knew that he was not the rightful rightman with children his own family taking sideline, when even Kim knew better, just lay them down as we are for French led excellence here, well the English weren't here and we know the French are for the US, can you be a bit less British Bureaucracy, I am telling you the French need serious consideration with Macron and the current Prime Minister for World Peace negotiators, they are serious negotiators, very intelligently led through capability gapping, control, the police here show and run with and don't hide away those who need added protection which is very mentally aware, intelligently staged and very completely the other way round to the British, who hide those and push those who are genuine victims away....westernised society leading to full military rule ok...Duke and Duchess of Cambridge on their way to the throne hid from the military ruler... why? When in France?. Do you think that Cantona the bowling ball for the USA Military is out... in Korean warfare strategy, no he is not for nuclear arsenals or tries for them, but clean energy is how it can be taken, the fiercest in the world...does Kim feel he is a better father figure today for understanding this..so now, moral dilemma. Korean injustice, justice and families developed from safeguarding....military rule, love, understanding and in his round red faced manner walking triumphantly to his pedestal, he wins this war...with no firing, just positioning and threat, yet underneath is he working as a team? The Chinese's embassy takes centre stage phenomenal show of power, team work culture and family, the backbone of who we are, the stability of who we are, the very core of our being of who we are, our own physical identity, our own psychological identity and our own stability of truth within our own selves, is this any different for anyone, yes it is, the negotiator and speech acts need to be standardised, they need to draw the same message as a genuine one for strategic security peace through Copenhagen, celebrity and not those going off on one because they are lazy, don't work and are tax paying good eggs just like the Author for many years, HMRC said so, so when living on her own, getting divorced, being sexually assaulted, her son bullied, her son abducted when working 60 hours a week as a single parent, there is now an appeal to them for penalties of none payment of a non-existent tax to be paid of £191 that no one told her about that is now appealed against as stated today by HMRC…does this make her bereft and less of an entrepreneur today..no, it makes her the most wanted woman in business as one ..no excuses but impact to survive happens…this is who we are the pedestal is a kissing gates media speech act, for those with big voices for a reason and those with small ones who want a big one, voice that is…those who have a lot to say and those who don't, are usually put before the stand and told to go forwards, with their own government agendas, the satirical Mrs Tiggy Winkle rearing upwards on her hind legs today for virile manuscripts and films…the British Government showing their strength today in control of their negotiation of their ownselves, liberty of the USA in the very distant past, the arrogance some call it of the United Kingdom in behaving in ways where dominance shows on in small surprises, the arrogance of the bulldogs briefcase being more on health, education and immediate needs of their own population than that of any other war torn state with very little intervention through the UN, the little known island of dreams for the Duke and Duchess of Cornwall, Cambridge and now Sussex is a working man's delight with benefits hitting the roof this last year, all the wrongfulrightmans right way round of stability for the UK

Well known celebrities, lesser known news agents and politicians' all breathe fire sometimes, but the one we love the most doing so, has a reason Sir Eric Cantona as his Author calls him that's me, breathes fire down the neck of most prevalent business men, politicians and does not stop when he knows he's right, which is mostly and some should also know he is very astute with women, fortitude and mindful disorder, he is played as a businessman here, a career minded fortitude, a developing entity of the excellence for his family, his family being the football club he remembers so well

This is not inhumane but Cities a revolution in mindful longevity and a peace strategy of longing for love, hate and criminality that you never believe, in three different worlds, three different partners and three different names Cantona plays them all and he also drives actors, socially deprived or not away from himself, being socially deprived or does he…well with many fine actors of independence, right wing political opinion, left wing anarchy then here we are…so do we call the Golden King the one with the Golden Boots? The actors are now not confused, please understand you are an actor within your own act of security actorisation in control non chalent… now I diverse here..look even Kim Do is in his own country, these Eric Cantona supporters are well within their own right to be rightfulwrongmen, it's just we don't want Kim the North Korean Dictator firing unclear arsenals at other states of de state or those with a state, mind, ratified peace entity, so what about Osama and his hole digging now all this time later, the Guardian persecuted Cantona for a time, now the other way round for his own sanity in the media against tyrants of satire like Hislop, who is also in New York with all actors and non-secured actors of peace strategy, now the de secured state for Deschamps or was it Cantona, both the team, the match the Captaincy, Cantonas life all de secured for a time…his mother the refuge…now who bought him …boots? Deschamps seemed to think that Cantona deserved them at one point, Golden, Cristiano Ronaldo went off on one on a plane about it and Mohammed Salah also commented, so efficient ratios of co efficiency, Eric Cantona, I rest my case…oh, and by the way my waving at a non-existent Mohammed Salah, Eric because you said he was in Louis Vuitton in Paris I wasn't waving goodbye as the Golden Boots need winning back for a sense of security and less victimisation whose was the queue? Not a Medical GP Kitbag full of trauma kits for woman who would have outside queues wanting to be with him…no, that would also be the President of UEFA, Aleksander Ceferin can you rest on your own laurels to take on the scriptwriter who has already been sold, no probably not, yes, probably non correct which is why someone works all the time, to make sure when you see her again that you damn well know who I am, so how much do you know about France, the revolution, culture and no going back, a lot or not much, is it just lip service like English French agreements in football, politics and beach faraway time, marriage, bicycles which I cannot ride at the moment, Spain and the armada…and your mother

Like we said, the drive here for dynamic representation by Cantona is well received it drove him to singing for his new album, song sheet and tour…and he is very good, confidence in strength Sir Lancelot..confidence in strength...you know where we are Cantona…it opens in Manchester October 2023 and runs until December 2023…the mindful knowing of who Cantona really is very intriguing, most authors write about what they know, who they see and where they go and some make a living out of it, Cantona is one of the them, so is one of his ex-wives, Cantona in particular is very difficult to trace and is very security conscious so when he does it he does it well….I went on the beach for many times and stood there freeing my mind but I didn't realise that was what I was doing…..I realised there were too many people in the UK and that it was actually Mathew Simmons that was haunting me both my own guilt and that of the family that would haunt me and now I am just the same and have learned strategies to alleviate the hurt I put onto others and onto myself Copenhagen is the author's choice in peace strategies for all actually but I was chosen due to impact on myself, Simmons and the other way round socially in far reaching confines, plus Cantonas' sincerity of loss, hurt and death, of his impartial comrade that he found solace in sometimes, his own ability to manifest himself into it is well known, his ability to incite directed abuse indirectly is phenomenal, Didier Deschamp for example is known now for being his comrade? But not his authors his author had to hide away in the suburbs recovering from operations severe enough to stop her sleeping during the night, she walked the streets yesterday to ensure that Cantona was well fixed in the Paris suburbs even though hurting her, taking her a full 24 hours to recover literally…as she is not suburbs way round, Simmons death a departed soul who would badger me every day for money…the peace Eric Cantona feels Cantona to his beloved supporters of the great game of football of course, both here, in Italy, France, Geneva,

Switzerland, USA was more difficult, but sheer persistent by his author made way for his new genre is due to his sheer hard work, tenacity to survive and his hard efforts through humanitarian works that no one knew about, he felt that because of Simmons that standing up and being counted meant he should suffer verbal abuse every day, his author disagreed and from an early part of his career she told him so through countryside confines of England..now partly exiled from the UK she tries to survive currently after strings of abuse on her first way round through Geneva, Paris, Monaco and other parts of Switzerland after his ex-wives and other members of his family try to gather round him…now one of them states he got it right….his guitar playing not a thing of the past, his genre classical twist, with A lines in Paris Musique and his complete absorption his author has led him to entertain, yes she did like him a lot, knew all the words even Chris Martin would have a run for his money…now, no, it was the finger to UNICEF…that hurt die hard and the clinic, arrogance and shoe shine said Claridges….what a picture, what a place and what a set of concierges, it was Harrison Ford and Richard Gere all over again..Cynosure and twisted longevity, golden blood not boots..well here I cannot even say this as the USA Military are the best in the world.. so, their boots are definitely golden, managed for the world cup in military rule and democracy..Cantona is by far the most non compromised now, not impeached through his Author and also through his own work, he, never without anything to say…well, world peace strategists, win the World Cup VIVA La France a few years ago, goodbye Osama a song mediarised, characterised by Cantona, also played the most successful businessmen a none analogy, hideous reminder of threat, response, atrocity, barbaric cannibalism and Beach Football World Cup Excellence…legs is played here…so is excellence in baking..well fatherhood figures all over the world play the heart strings of femme fatale… in Liverpool Marco Pierre White…never have I seen so much bread every single type brown, white, granary full loves, half loaves and again a Frenchman and if you look at his website, can he please take it out of his mouth, I understand the epitome of cool, but it's not funny having to smell it…other people's smoke, it can make other people have asthma attacks and cardiac arrests in the street…please we like you lot…other than this we like him too, his wife and family, this is sheer genius, can Macron count them? 1…2….3...Marco Pierre White, La Gavroche it is then…never too many and children to die for, that is never someone who is going out of fashion or even popularity…even caught a glimpse of him twice driving so, the patisserie on my palate. Blackberry, crème and choux bed…yum… well balanced, blended taste, texture perfect, creaminess of the filling in the choux éclair shaped bed…balanced not too much and little, never too many blackberries, looks great, colour great, techniques used surely wonderful and the best ones as it tastes great on my palate Marco do you want to be a footballer, because you sound like Eric the other way round and I dread to think who applied to be in the bed you have both hosting food in France a few years ago……exactly, my point, get it tested mine turns to be Japanese of course, palate I mean so did his author and now they smile when they see each other….his author is a special lady, she heralded unfairness on the belief many years ago that Cantona should get the total blame for Simmons, to Ferguson and his family in England making a merry dance on the board room table, never being able to stand in the stand only visiting once inside and only visits twice again outside then inside reception due to legal lasso here from her birth right place, Cantona remains non-chalantly happy in his own work….so the big play in front of the media was the wrong one, playing her directly at, made everyone aware just how she had become with him, pushing back those who had the talent to become….the book entitled A Golden King from a trilogy of hope, the one that you are reading is for peace and strategies of humanitarian hope, excellence in what we do and being kind, accepting and taking on the best of the best is how we should see this for G7, Macron, Simmons, his Family, Cantona and his, his records, new love affair and hope for the future that his author finds happiness…it is also more importantly a ratified peace strategy comparable in effect not implementation to the FARC, ELN and ELA in Columbia South American nightmares of Crocodile Shoes spring to mind…the treaty signed and ratified by these TOs many years ago was painful, the FARC still slippery today, the FTD in Flowers holding little hope of winning for the Mondial accused recently leading the Author to revolt in the BFA and refuse membership for a while… whilst dictatorial greed grew memberships from monies from flower farms brining in the flower, known and the Author had actual experience of dealing with them from carrier overseas in a box… just like the biological weaponry of all time the teste fly..well, they fly in cold storage then get heated up in Moyes's Stevens the Royal Warranted loyalty suite…check…Columbian Roses are it….Fibonacci Sequence gone mad for designers who know a thing or two about it….Mujahidin does scraping the sides of every barrel, diamonds twinkling, Cantona breaths a sigh of heavy breath, lively this one, as itpings out of the hole, a hidehole of truth, snippers, intrigue no, but truth yes, Muslim Afghany Terrorism with Nuclear Stock-Piling, no woman allowed already no thank you…do not allow mighman Mdme Bridgette Macron into that country, do you understand…he is a treasure and so are you to all mankind of justice peace strategic leadership. Painstakingly taking her back again wasn't President Macron, but Mighman into his own arms never ever going to happen again…correct he states..folding them in the hierarchical distance…the bullring, the matador and the horns of fulfilment…do not ever throw E, ever…the stampede into the distance to recover and then attack is too much to bear Freddie Flintoff tried….then the British Bulldog starts all over again, beer bellies wobbling in the distance and France giggling to far reaching pasts…Foreign Nationals, Asylum Seekers and Competitive Monopolies…Cantona, Ferguson longevity compromised never again…the bucking bronco of red blood, death, heartache, sadness and no cities, as they are bred for the fighting, taunting, the UN finds stable strategies for peace and Switzerland foreign policy to establish roads for UEFA, UNICEF and marginalised comparity on political agendas such as sport, social bias and government agendas lessened by government fixing from Afghanistan, Kenya, Libya and aid drops which save immediate need in Syria, they all come as a cost, all come with opinionated individuals who think they know better, those who buy their own way into life, family and then still think they know better, destroying what is in front of them for what is over here, greener and greener they say…well we feel some players, some woman and some musicians that an all round good egg can be as good as they are in being musical too.....the UEFA Presidents Award Winner with families children, grandchildren and superheroes....this is next or should be...enjoy, being it Sir Cantona, I don't want to miss you... Boulogne was terrible but I am still here and cannot print this at the moment.......Eric Cantona has come a long way from being in the press the wrong way round in the wrong gutter press isn't something that does anything but hurt you, some say makes you and then allows you back in if your hardy enough and we knew say some that Eric Cantona had no option other than to retire, be isolated in France which was never an option or fight and that is what he did, the pixels growing longer and longer into the obscurity of expression some say, others beginning to understand after all this time, now he becomes un impeached by those the author could not stand...bias necessity for bias integration of bias societal political agenda to be at....just let go...just let go..allow and be who you are...I have to say Deschamps.....confused me the directed at came from him not his anyone else, just Deschamps, why? No idea, the aim here for those who think they know is to make sure they understand whose side they are on. Why? If a professional football player gets side lined, gets a new being and then gets directed at from the manager that side lined, what happens then, investigation, non-chalent approaches or Blaise interrogation, I don't know but something does not feel right as I don't understand any bias approach to anyone, and we are to accept that it is just how it is? What happens if this is not supposed to happen that affairs of the heart aren't supposed to happen and verbal abuse consistently isn't supposed to happen, by Beer Bellies, Mightyman, Mighman, Leucile, Pomile or Donald Trump, now cracks in acumen in motherhood, fatherhood are ok, without breaking the law, affecting the child, the opposing parent and the opposing grandparents, who seem to have come into their fore over the last few decades... sometimes to the detriment of the family member, then through investigation abuse rears the ugly head...those who do not take regular drinking water may not be able to, so they are then viciously attacked or is this ok? Mr Microsoft is now with Apple, his own company and the whole of Lost Cities, Empires, and a vast amount of character building for each one.... anyway, we are for Ronaldinho's socks, so this start became the Copenhagen Political Peace Strategy of the Copenhagen School of Terrorism, Securitisation and Political UN Treaties ratified by Cantona UNICEF and UEFA who are loving Cantona and his Author now.... this isn't the end, but the beginning written for classical markets in stanza to write scripts and produce short films, the author is beginning to grow, her wings cut by a vicious attack both verbally and professionally some years ago, leading to near death...

Beetroot, Spice and Honey is the order of the day, trampolines, linesman long johns and stripy black and white ones, now Ronaldinho with the hair, Brasil who is with Brasil, Pele... so, what do we do now...we make a kitbag shop with a golden bag like a golden ticket to the Spanish Armada......so, the golden ticket, the golden boot and the golden plane, with the Golden Ferrari are now huge statements on the bank balances of those who have too much...greed? No, just work for what they have are successful at what they do and are very well received by others… beetroot, red round and very earthy, with a stalk, no crack, and a bottom of flirty fluff if you look, now beetroot juice with no vinegar sometimes analogised to someone's face shrivelled, is tarty pixelated and a mess extraordinarily in Cantonas' existence….the maypole of olive oil with the slither if all ……sardines are purple in the wind, the tenderest shoots of broccoli tying the lace together, the silks satin sheets of labour, the holding of feminine instinct, the peregrines of power the fastest mandarins are not as fast as the Korean Kim, there's no one holding the cuckoo clock here now, the one which holds the cuckoo clock has all the sail I am in, the ones who hold the key of all longevity are the flowers in the meadow, the language of the mars, the culture of the strings of them when they go from your heart….ex-wives always have something to say about those coming in, the most recent emigration to my family from outside in lasted 30 seconds and vanished for over 3 decades…the assault from one of them towards my author was that nasty that she did it again over 18 months ago in London on her first trip back…viable attention for the lullaby real of the 90's which made my then wife jealous, who on the side was having another one…. attachment disorder never ever attach your keyring onto your belt, wait and then take it off thinking it is still attached when they are off…the pink fluff surrounding the naval of the pentagon caused Biden to slip the ship, the Chinese President, Prime Minister and their Families were already in situ in a Mandarin Hotel, the hotel housed the woman's emperor the one who's Lancôme beauty lay awakening from beneath the pentagon's Washington home, the villa lay shortening breath, the speech this morning and debate the early before breakfast meeting at 8am is Brexit, Trade Economies and a knowledge of attendance of those who you want to be there and those you don't…classical injections of fun is what they call them. Eating aloud when the ketos stop…no wobbly buttocks and no wobbly thighs. In fact, smooth shiny skin on a lady who deserves me to be for her in her own sense with no lesbianism…. Half a lettuce leaf, water and a turtles head spent days away from each other, fiercely conjecturing to Erics pneumonia …we rest our case… Mercedes Mayfair in front of Fendi now Hermes that is Amande Jeanne Vert…nothing else… Mercedes never have I ever seen such an elegant Mayfair two toned luminescence of burgundy and dark silver with a blue tone, blacked windows and very nice…..

This is the man from Timbuctoo

Had the shiney Very Big shoe

Made the Shoe Shine of the Week

Had the very very very black feet

Shock the soot off from the bare

Feet that shocked you all for Isla

Now Isla is new here, she is the main benefactor of a will for over two and a half million pounds, the two and a half million pounds grew one day into mountain of tea bags, riddled with guilt the main benefactor hurdled her way through the mainstay of populations trying to find a dividend to help her…a new investment product to invite herself forwards and a new Pomile to like an apple of surprise…

I am not a racist does this offend you and am I in mainstream genre in the newspapers now, so you can get used to me all over again…. after my impeachment we had nothing, I knew that we had to do something, we had all the shoeshine cream, we had all the mementoes with jeans

The membership and trophy hunters of the Timbuctoo

I am not a membership hunter of the elite newspaper hunters

The hunters of the very large show, had the family in a big do

The family hunters hid the one that Cities wanted to poke fun

Stop..Stop ..that is wrong we do not do that now your done

Bullrings over, Cities at that, then we realised that we are not the hat

We are the realised corporate truth, of the real of cities Beirut, the Afghanistan of cities bear, the one who we are for so there, the little trip for all mankind to make this little lady mine…Perunor is all for see, the one who had the very big knee, the one who thine knee is all

Mine to see the one who is sublime, in thought, in promise

In kingdom too, were for you Cantona if it's you

Yes…it is me, the one who did see the very very big shoe shiny knee

no, that's Joel the King mad too, the one who say that the English are dammed hard to, manifest to the Englishman's yard of old MacDonald's very large farm, Lucy Price is here right now, we had all the shoe shine right out, we are for the very hard thing, to make a very big flights wing, tight rope walking is the one who played the shoe shine is not the kissing gate, we are all for fun you know, the Kate and the Fur and the long johns all striped done, went through the levitating pensioners pipe, of olde Englishmen's tirade on the path of long john, silver in the path the ones who we know, the ones who we show, the ones who we are for in the Englishman's big toe 4, the little one in the Englishman's tirade is the one of the Cantona is not Kissing Gate…if you want the UEFA in then you have to make a din, on the street of the President who is really not a big mistake… good enough is E he has been played…YES…your good enough for golden times no we cannot say no to thee, no you are not to feel guilty anymore, we love your strength we love your hide, we love your respect for the Englishman that's died…we are for you Eric Cantona…The Golden King of no reliance on anyone of no reliance of anyone for him, he works the traffic lights again…..check mate..I hear you say..no to all the strategy play, the position your in is a mighty fine one, my Mightyman is the Englishman's throne, your Mightyman in the bullring of love, is the one who is there for you when the cabinman has gone, back to being Mighman Mightyman you're the one that makes me run, makes me sigh, makes me weep, makes me be the one on the streets of fame, of celebrity of TV of Film of Mighmans way, whether you are the centuries at, of the window cleaners hat, we want you centuries Cantona not Beer Bellies with that..ca jing…. ca jing…the ones in the cooking pot is the one who can sing, the ones who we are truly proud of and the ones who we are in the know of the one…who ca jings…who ca jings…

Featherman has a great big bow, in the nuance of his toe, the ones who love the ones who we hate, the ones who we have in the good of the gate, Foreverman in the one of the wallet, Foreverman is the one with the pocket, Foreverman is the stability real, Foreverman is the fire grating seal, of approval for all mankind, the Feathermans touch is the stability of behind…now chapter one is the Golden Ball, chapter two the very large shoe of Cantona, Schumacher and the World War of the Red Ferrari once more, the red Ferrari that has the power to make the yellow peril on fire, the yellow smoke of brake dust silver tight, the lights on the beam they held her tight, in the lamp light they doth kissed the whole of Kistulion in the mist, the gorilla it walked away, the vampire it chattered its way, all to the centuries on fire of the dust, of the yellow great peril of the mighty big dust….growling away like the wolf on the prey, the mantis is shovelled the peculiar soil in the way, the peaty manure in the tank in the sink, was the new boy at school as he had a big drink of lemonade from the shop, the pop it bust the centuries waistline, the pop on the market stall he doth shall find, the shirts all in rows of the cabinmans' play hid the temperatures finest on the strings of the hearts day, the red ones drew the knicker line of the politicians play, Monaco is red of the delight once more, the temperature did rise to the hearts are once more are the cabinmans fever of the Englishmen's yawn…the Englishman's yawn is the non chalent too, when the shirt on the back of the Englishman's front two are the ones who can celebrate being the best in the world, so why are they not that non chalent have we heard, the shirt on the back of the very big word Jones' back yard is the one who is socially not deprived in his backyard, he now lives in China the pull of the Australian zing went ahead, the states went well on the Liberty, Lancôme real, Julia Roberts was pretty….well disregarding about Gere's ear, he's the best one of us at the Englishmen's gate, the lawyer he states that he doesn't want that, he hoardes the lucifers Englishman's net….too true said the cabin man's Englishmen's' play it's the one with the Englishman's heavens sent in the way….

Chapter 1 Golden Ball

From 400 - 2030 with an intelligence lead gap

Throw Ins

13 Line Stanza and Prose Poem : Beginnings of Nature
March Hare, March of Hare, have you seen
Rolling down the river, football
With no name, With no name, get lost
With full name of adoption real
Angelina Jolie's mother
To be, to be we are to be
We have the very big thine knee.
Centuries of motherhood stand
Shouting, Shouting is not nice, red
Empire State of mind, carpet stand
Dinosaur leathery back, cow
Throw the prince of Eden, Apis
Golden Ball of Award, be mine

Prose Poem Beginnings of Nature

the Golden Ball is the World cup to me, is the Awards Evenings, is the Charity Benefit Concerts and is the Red Carpet divas here..in Cannes at the Palais, the reason for the Bull god of with Zeus is the leathery football that is spherical that allowed me to be in the genres and industries other than this in the award winning way....this way with industries and other medals....

The bull god is referred to with Zeus with all Mightymans' Power, the Bull God is for the hands that do not do dishes.... those hands of power, control and Golden Glove...the

Prehistoric Historical Referencing is now to happen before the head of the cloth, Elizabethan Head Rolling for the first football...חזרתי מחנות הלחם אמר שהוא, פלטיני הרים עין, שוב המפרנס, הסופר לש הדובעה הז ,רימא רמא ךלש םידכנה םע ךלש יטסטנפה ינאה ייהתו רודכה לע ירמשתש יאדכ ילוא ,רייצה וא ילש יטנגה עסמה ,ךלש םידליה םע הלבמ ינא ,ןכ הדובעהמ החנ וא תדבוע ינא םוי םויו םוי לכ הז ,ךלש אמא ,הרקמ לכב ...םישוע ולש אמאו רימאש המ הזו ...תוינקל םתוא תחקול אל וליפאו םידגב םהל הנוק אל ינא לבא םחל..לוכאל ךפיהל יתכלה וישכעו הלש השדחה הנומתב תממהמ תיארנ ילש תרפוסה יכ ,הלאמש המבל וסנכיה וסנכ...אצוהש ןמושה םע..יל'ג םע ןובמ'גו יתפרצ is the shining effigy of no one actually at all, someone got hold of the wrong way around, back biting isn't the authors way round, we are for you the mighty one, the Thor of all French way round...Dieu, Dieu without the first part, without the first part for the A to stand here for the plethagy of realism for the art of the story for an abused man, Cantona is now with him, the Author is now with him, does that mean that this is bias, well Cantona is also assailant, told he is a bull, a bully and pariah, he is known now to be Cantona a very pleasant male man, very easy going and very funny…sometimes not all the time…this is what his fan base of women said, to draw those who heroize about significant political peace.. ,יזכרמה עוריאל םזילאירה דיתעל לכתסמ ,המכחה הדובעהו דצה יטבמ ,לומגה ,תודידבה ,עורה לכ לש דדמה ימכ םיעודי רשא הלא תא ,רוחאמ לש תונוכנה תאו תואמה לש םיריצקתה תא ,הארמה תא שפחמה תא שפחמ םיברב עודי הנוטנקב לוזלזה ,אל םהו םהיתוחפשמ םע םיאצמנש הלאו ,אל םהשכ םיקסע םהש בזוכ םירמואש יושנ אוהשכ ומש תא תונשל ברסמש והשימ השעמל ,םמש תא הניש דחא השעמל ,העודי ותחפשמב העיגפהו תא ול שי ....הרישע הריחבכ הבחרהב תעכ תמסרפתמ בהזה ךלמ לש וימי תוכירא ,אל וא עגופ הרקמ לכב ,ול תלוכיה ץצופל ךתוא םע םיתבה םייסאלקה םהש ...הז ללגב... Cette stratégie de paix de Copenhague pour les démocraties autocratiques vise à harmoniser les orientations stratégiques pour que les alliances deviennent réelles, sans obstacles à la discussion, ni à des discussions normales avec le conseil d'administration, les médias et les assistants....

Adam and Eve are now going to show themselves; Adam and Eve are now at one with each other, are now a fig leaf away from togetherness, being warm, cosy and deeply entrenched in real life….measure man the size 16 charlotte burrows is now in the in-between, the ones who chastise and the ones who are lemon cake….the Englishmans Rose is the one who is in retreat from the Englishmans Liar, the Frenchmans Bastion is the little ones to spare….I want my little feet to bare little ones in the chicken coup, a it like leg horn fog horn, the handyman and measuremans favourite the dukes of hazard…one fine morning Selma the last daughter of Eric Cantona is not quite true as the dukes of hazard had finished and the little house of the prairie had not…disassociated here bring in the leaders of the world for the peace strategy called Copenhagen, this strategy is led by Macron whether he likes it or not, King Charles inaugural visit went very well…Cette stratégie de paix de Copenhague pour les démocraties autocratiques consiste à harmoniser les orientations stratégiques pour que les alliances deviennent réelles, sans qu'il n'y ait d'obstacles à la discussion, ni d'obstacles à des discussions normales avec le conseil d'administration, les médias et les assistants. Le roi Charles qui décide que le président Macron est le meilleur au monde en matière de stratégie de paix... ? L'aide humanitaire prend généralement la forme d'une mesure spéciale extraordinairement celle qui ne figure jamais dans le livre d'histoires et qui est ratifiée par l'UNICEF., l'ONU et les conseils commerciaux de ce monde

ךופהל תותירבל רשוימ יגטרטסא ןוויכב תקסוע תויטרקוטוא תויטרקומדל ןגהנפוק לש םולשה תייגטרטסא תרושקתה ,ןוירוטקרידה םע םיילמרונ םינוידל םימוסחמ שוחל אל זאו ןוידל םימסח שיגרהל אל ,תויתימאל בוטה אוה ןורקמ אישנהש טילחמש סלרא'צ ךלמה -הו ןיס תולשממ םע םימעפל יתימא תויהל ךפוה הז....םירזועהו ןפוד אצוי ןפואב ,דחוימ דעצ תרוצב ללכ ךרדב אוה ירטינמוהה עויס?...םולשה תייגטרטסא םולשל םלועב רתויב תוצעומו ם"ואה ,ירטינמוהה ףסינויב וררשואש םרובע תומל סניא םע םירופיסה רפסב םיעיפומ אל םלועלש הלאמ הזה םלועה לש רחסה.....elegant, elite and gangly, moonbeams and satisfying agents of strife

Dactylic Oralist Hexameter I
We are for you to win
The play for you to beat
Your bullies today, control
Please remain in control
We are for you for sure

Sonnet I
The mistress here not you
Finer things is you, too
Lords, Ladies and Gentle
Giants, are ones for you
Listen, Look we are took
For the mighty in the book

The comparison here is you for another by a son who morally is not enlightened and went through with her all the time.....

Parabole I

UEFA, UNICEF is the one with the very nice way, the one with the very big nose today is the orange peel of the day, we are for the great big day of the shoe shine in the way, we are at one in the very big muck, the one is always in the very big sock, the lately lady is here to play in the Wiringmans parade of the lights that twinkle bright the wedding of the golden lights, the bride of Frankinscence of old and young is the one that you hold for fun....the lately lady is the one who pushes forward and bullies one, the harassment of the one who got away, the parabole is the incitement of the shoe shine....of the wedding day, the ballerina is the one the one is done in the sun...

Prose Dialogue I

As a child I remember being told that I could not have things and I remember my other brothers being told the same thing, who today are hiding away after shouting abuse at my author to step down from herself, the problem is that I made her in this way to be for me if Rachida Brachni ever cheated, which she did and so my author of now with her first book signing days away in Arizona, is now battling with her for her to move out of the way, when we were little my brothers and I were very close now we are not, my mother is very non chalent here and decides against meeting her....not my author but Rachida Brachni anymore, the Golden Ball that I first ever held was the league 1 for Olympique Marseilles with 9 in total that season and 8 for the winners of the league and although I did not receive it the Beach Soccer World Cup was the Best Achievement for Management and move forwards in the sport, the Golden Awards kept coming here …on any night of winning awards…..the night of UEFA Eric Cantona was filmed in his car driving non chalently to the night if his life, the wonders of miracles of the Filming to ensure his longevity of the ceremony…..Cantona walked non chalently to the stage and took the award, the night was littered with many squiggling one his agent, one the driver as we all had to get there….

םינוערפל ,יתפרצה יצה לש העדצהל םייוארה וישעמ תא ריבסהל ידכ ,תירבעה הפשה תא ןאכ איבהל וננוצרב ןאכ ,עונלוק םא ןיב .הנשמ אל ,םודאה חיטשה לש בהזה סרפ ,בהזה רודכל ןחלופה....ןאדיז לש ותוכזלו םיירצמה ,םיהולא אוה ימ ,תוניוצמל םיחבשה תוא םה לאידנומו בהזומה הפוריא עיבג ,בהזה ןולב ...ףסינוי ,א"פוא ,היזיוולט בתכנ וא הארנ אלש יתפרצה ףוריטה ,ןמזה תובא לש רבעב ונלש האמה לש לאה הז ,סדמיכרא ץע אוה ,אוה ינא רבד לש ופוסב אישה ...תילגנאה הביטחה רובע םה ןמזה תובאש םהל רמאנש תירבעה המואה לש הז וא ,ןאכ םירבחב ולש תוישומישהו הנוטנק קיראל

םיניוצמה לש האמה תרחבנ איה תיאניטנגראה תיגלבה....תיאניטנגראה היגלבה איה יסמ לנויל לש תירבעה תיגלבה....תיאניטנגראה היגלבה איה יסמ לנויל לש תירבעה .....יניטלפהו א"פוא אישנ...ןאדיז לש םירחבומה .....יניטלפהו א"פוא אישנ...ןאדיז לש םירחבומה םיניוצמה לש האמה תרחבנ איה תיאניטנגראה

הנוטנקו םישנה םג ךכו רדסב ויה םיפוחה ,שממ רכזיהל ליבשב םישדוחו ול תוכורא םינש ןולוטב ההש הנוטנק זא רבכ ןושיל ןתיא וכלה

l’hébreu ici n’est pas à traduire car Mohamed Salah n’est pas là maintenant... Lionel Messi s’est offensé...Cantona during the daytime and in the middle of the mid-day sun was shot at, his contractual worth increased and his shows for himself were never at the same time, until today after along time in hiding having siestas everyday …..danger money they called it and everyone around him too makes sure they knew what they were saying in case he took it the wrong way round…Simmons was never investigated and never implied until now….neither were his family, but sure had the motive and goals with pure hidden objectives…money, money, money….and Cantona was asked once if he felt bribed and coerced by the situation with him and his family and he failed to say anything, bowing his head down…is now the first threat towards his Author the future you may want to ensure that you are safer and return back to the UK…but why would you not have this thought…everyone thought about it, but now everyone feels awkward about it, why because he died a few years ago…Mathew Simmons that is… Cantona, reste silencieux maintenant, c’est le choix le plus évident de l’auteur qui est multimillionnaire, qui n’a jamais eu de cuillère en argent, qui est fantastique avec les enfants, fantastique avec les personnes âgées et qui vous parlera, est à l’écart de la plupart des à l’époque, mais ici à Marseille, il est confortable pour elle d’être... tout comme Cantona, Simmons était également à l’aise ici.. Ayant compromis la sécurité au Royaume-Uni au nom de Mathew Simmons, certains membres de la sécurité devaient déclarer leur propre amitié, le connaître et l'aimer, ce qui signifie que le SIA avec le secrétaire à la Défense et l'actuel premier ministre de la famille royale devait vérifier cela avant publier des histoires sur le certificat de décès actue

Prose Verse I

Golden Ball of Mightyman, Golden Ball of Mightyman
Hid the crying eyes with no defeatist, hid the crying eyes of no defeatist
I am not everyman to see, I am not beach soccer here to avoid the leer
I am not the golden ball for everyman to see, feel and touch
I am Kirsty Gallagher and Everyman, woman and child has to loose weight to touch me

Golden Ball of Ellie Saab, Golden Ball of Ellie Saab
I have no throw of any King as I am Ellie Saab
I am Freddie Flintoff and I want to see my name in lights
I am Eric Cantona and I already have he he...right...
Touched the Golden Ball and this is not Here Comes the Night

Golden Ball, Golden Ball, I have no Golden Ball and I am not Versace
But a bitter twist of utter, sheer break, hurt, mistrust and sheer destruction of ones heart, soul and magnitude of trust, harmony and at one with, Golden Ball
I am the family of loss that shot up in the tree
I am the loss of family from the adopted tree
All for the marriage of another, all for the marriage of another

I am the nuance and not compromise in the truth of the world war
I am the fairy godmother who cannot lift them all
I am the Eric Cantona who did all of that, I am sorry to Jemima but I want my
Girlfriend back, I do not take anyone else's, and I do not lie, and I do not want to be the burden of Selma's eye

Prose Verse I

Eyes, Ears and Batman's Nose is the one we sonar
We real the turnstile for the turn table and the beer belly wobbled out
We real the turntable of very many. Doubts, we real the tiny footballer who has not got a shout
We are for you, We are for you to make it big with yourself
We are for you we are for you to make it big for yourself.
We are four you less than speccy four eyes and less than fatty as you have no vulnerabilities now.
We are four. you as we are for you to see the world now...

World Cup Heroes are now the right way up
Dis trust, openness and the removal of the real fact, had the Montmartre bridge in the vampires lap
We are not one with you today, we are not one with you today
Are we for you in the vampires hat, no we are not with you in the vampires hat…..
We are for the lap of honour for the real fact of behind
We are not for you in the shopping mall of truth, we are not for you in the shopping mall of truth

Golden Balls and Awards are to kill the Golden Ball of the film with the gay man, all hail the gay man for these who want to be gay, for those who don't then this is ok…Golden Balls for those who want with power, autocracy and with naked supremacy for those who are not then this is supremacy but just not for direct gay men, we are not for those who paint with vigour to be gay and take advantage of those who are compromised through lack of political speech act and don't care, we are for those who are for those who are for those who are for those who…….are tied together….in political harmonious retreat…please decide…

This should be in French said the blindman whose stick was far from home, the landslide victory today for the vixen who destroyed homes, stations and sanctimonious footballers whose homes were in the same place, definitely hid the same place on the mantlepiece of Golden Anthems, this journey of hope, peace and political satire is developing intrigue, the corruption of most Columbian Medellin, FARC Supremacy movements away from the elite play of the Rosenthal's and the movements of the ELN, ELA and the Mujahedeen the scrapings of Ellie Saab at this point off the diamond studded walls of prehistoric caverns of dust, empires and lines of A line twisting through the roller-coasters of time, growth and diamond lines which aren't always in a line, row or even with bingo wings…Pomile here is Measurements' friend, demi wave is in the future with the sock and the lately lady has already been, in fact the lately lady with lucy price has been bound with power, control and sanctity of lethargy to have any impetus for gardening, anyway, the burning effigy is actually of the only woman to hurt anyone…not for jealousy but for the actual desire to do so, something that we cannot understand, the burning effigy is the one and only

Speaking to each other helps here, the one and only communication strategy is helped here by the anomalies of others whether their own language, culture or beloveds, so idiosyncrasies to their own faith, friendship groups or even multitudes of fans, supporters and being paid for receiving verbal racist views each day..so, why was she in the stand, incitement of …the f word to Cantona to get lost because the stand knew he wasn't with the wife he once had, the children he once had and what was chanted exactly…I have nobody to be able to put it into words, that Rachida is no longer with me and that she would do anything to be with me and then got with someone else…., so I am very grateful for this…each time I am with my author most of the time without issue, she makes me feel like I am un impeached and I can say anything, I cannot, I was fined, nearly sued again and then removed for a fortnight into prison and no I do not mind talking about it, but I have to find the words in the right way round first to express un preachment, the worlds furthest play when you are part of the media for along time…you find other ways of making sure you are heard….humanitarian human rights, the none downside of the Copenhagen peace strategy, Buzan hid from the world too when it was written, just like the author on a promise of tomorrow…

Epigram I

Golden Ball, Golden Awards, Golden Ball, Golden Awards
Awards are for those who achieve greatness, not for those who don't
Not for lately lady in the Bridgett Bardot
Not for Charlotte Burrows in the Cinematography woe
We are for the bullies of A Cantona, R Cantona and those who are in the sink of all evil

Money, Money, Money this is all that was ever wanted by them from me and I was asked in an interview if I felt coerced, used by the family and I never replied, looked at my shoe…this implied that this is correct, the coercion Cantona felt is widely known and the impeachment as a result, as asking for money consistently after being paid is never something that others would advise, but Cantona did not seem to mind initially and then when things got very bad, he did, which you would imagine….the shooting was in the middle of the day and he was walking down the road and shot at from a car…my now estranged wife laughed and my siesta time is now different today for the first time to show for my author to tell her that I am here and making sure that she is taken care of and not frightened anymore…

Eric was shot at in the middle of the day, the day time is now different, it was never implied the shooting to Simmons or implied to his Family until now and never written in such a way so Cantona can feel and in realism become un impeached, it makes me feel that I am able to express my thoughts to my author and she is able to have them on paper straight away…Since the death of Mathew Simmons, when I was told at 6pm one night that he had died, I cried and then was told sorry Eric but the family would like to serve papers and tell you that they want to try and press charges of heart failure due to the incident, the family then served attempted murder, at this point I nearly laughed myself as a double whammy was heroized by those around me and my author to find it funny, which bunny boilers usually do…when their hero falls, as it becomes a game of chase so that others can benefit

The shooting from the car at me was frightening and my author means a lot to me, so I am taking her with me today.

Mathew Simmons begins his own failings and blame game towards me from the start by calling racist commentary, the Copenhagen peace strategy does not state, imply or even congratulate anyone who is bias in anyway towards violence, but condemns it and the UN use this as a lever to ratification of peace strategies for the combatant of terrorist networks…the TOs particularly in South America have been utilised here in the Yellow Medellin to highlight particular peace strategies which have been thwarted by these TOs to attempt peace where underneath they have not, the FARC, ELN, ELA in Columbia 25 years ago was one and in 2015-16 was at the end of the 10 year period of peace which needed ratifying and signing by the sides again, bringing to light single handedly the plight of the Rosenthal's and the ICC in investigating these atrocities, crimes' of TO and also those human rights abysmal in effect with the sons, daughters and aunties and uncles of those organisations also….the Golden Ball even though everyone would want and need Golden Strategies of Football which there is in the prologue, forward and epilogue, the way to a man's heart is through the violence on the TV is what someone said once, but I don't recall who it was…anyway, said the Breadman we digress from here and I cannot believe we are here either, can we believe that the impact on Eric Cantona is real and the reasoning behind the re consideration by UEFA all hailed by many people and a realisation by many millions that Cantona would have this directed impact on a daily basis, this impact through analysis is profound and some days he has to sit in and wait for the Simmons Family to pass through where he lives making a loud noise about what happened and don't forget about it and don't forget about and do not give him any awards….

Josephine also showed with him today to tell his author that everything is ok, she had to be given a guard like before as the direct threat is getting worse on her, but Cantona gave her, the author the initiative's to be mindful, use the signature and be the best she can be in what she is doing including flowers, now, Cantonas' up and coming tour mentions them and he was asked recently if this was his florist and he said no….and no one is getting any, not yet anyway..

The presentation of the UEFA Award was that of a surrealism for Cantona he has stated that nowhere, was the reply from the narrator well, we believe that the 3 spaces were for his family we now realise that he needed the room for himself to sit here, as some of the players did not want the award for him at all and had to lie down as the President Aleksander Ceferin chose the winner the day before, the HR Team defended the interaction of his now author a few weeks before as she non chalently asked for a reference for an unknown Senior Social Media Executive who she was referencing for her company in Cheshire, England

Cantona, won hands down from Didier Drogba who failed to show at an after-show meet and greet to congratulate Cantona and all other Award winners, he failed to make any commentary about this afterwards and never has since…

Simmons is now removed from all fore thought only on remembrance and the

re-appearance of Brachni in the stand is now a racist slur, Cantona has surely been through it, the race against time that his commentaries and statement of thank yous at the end was typical Cantona, to gather ground in the press was not the reason, but to gather ground for himself to cut the tie from Brachni, through her string of affairs, those that know him well smiled when they realised he was crumpled shirt, crumpled hair and white which was a starter for ten for all the women Cantona has been to bed with the epitaph, should be rest in peace as his work rate is nearly as much as the authors...he is well known for his temper known for his temper tantrums and in tears and tantrums we hear and dialogue about some of the lesser known ones..which are slightly funny...the prose poems are and the author confessed to the publisher the other day that she did not set out to have funny characters in the plays or to have drawn the characters in the way she has, she stated she could not stop when someone called them witty, cool, interesting and please read the funny character build, as Cantona plays most, which came from one comment made by Cantona about dynamic representation in Inhumane Resources and the author dynamically represented herself right in front of him running, felt embarrassed and then realised he was in charge of himself and her derriere as she ran past, since then they met on the other side of the media as Brachni had gone off shouting obscenities which Cantona was embarrassed about, the small derriere of the authors now in full view of Cantona ready to catch the issue here is how long they can kept their own partnership up as she is moving through France at a rapid pace especially after surgery only 11 days ago..not so golden her year either....

Simmons is going to be the death of Cantona, the racism holding dear to Drogba's heartstring....

...is the black faced man in the dying man's desire to be nasty to Cantona until he was put in the ground.

...the white-faced man's desire to be real with his author is well publicised through the French, English and American Press, the desire through the Canadian Press is for the author and her son to be happy together when they are together, the Garde in France, the Politzia in Italy and we are including the Mafia here, as they were introduced at Le Gare, Cannes the homeless stand was then introduced and her resolve was quite astonishing...she refused to give a homeless man 10 Euro, yet gave in La Gare the same type a Café Lait from Starbucks...then she got hit on by 2 further vagrants and moved and did not budge from her incitement...the vulnerability index of Cantona needs to be considered here for peace strategists everywhere, as well as the Awarded President of UEFA who called Aleksander Ceferin, was eagerly awaited this morning in a five aside match and did not turn up, however, the celebrated UEFA President for this Award was heralded a Peace Strategist for the Geneva Convention, to have the ability to be able to be conformist for Cantona despite what he says is something that will be music to his ears with no pun here, in fact his latest tour dates and record are actually very good and sound like a movie soundtrack....

The refusal of UEFA President Aleksander Ceferin to investigate the soundtrack even now is a trailer from heaven for Disney even though Cantona is heard here, you need to hear it...the Disney one is much more in tune with nature and Bear Necessities is a great soundtrack...very difficult as the author said to follow....

Now, Maintenant, these are to be plays and the plays are to be produced and directed through companies that we still know of, so the owner needs to keep going....

Space, Time is an Egg and Amanda Janes Authorship needs Heralding.

Mighman, Foreverman Mightyman and Dorothy Spires are now well developed, the might of Lucy Price, Charlotte Burrows and the Tinman, Silverman and the Golden Anthems are not, but this is ok here as we have only just begun.

Tinman with Silverman are not the same and are not any representation of the Wizard of Oz, the Chelsea Bridge provides the Harbours with a tantric desire of cinematic productions and limited fluids of hope, the mantric desires of being ay are also limited here, but Cantona isn't and made it very clear that he wasn't one dark night when Lucy Price went to stay for the day, she was employed through the Media in the City and screaming and shouting had been heard that day from her now ex-husband, who is now with another woman and she is not very happy about being ditched by Cantona through the media when he said something completely different in incitement, which when de real to hear it was meant for actually his author....as she worked at the same place and when Lucy Price found out she hit the roof, she has now come down from herself, still without Cantona who makes his author go red in all the right places...his strength is far passing his desires to go to bed with Lucy Price all over again...whether this is something that you want to do or not we can now move forwards as we are all for sale with you and Cantona... the classical works here are for the thespian society to suggest otherwise whether they are bias or not about a café in Sloane Square a French one where Cantona was rebuffed against and can we please remove any of it...

NOT ON THE NEXT LIINE IS JOEL CANTONA AND OLIVIA NEWTON JOHN

JOHN TRAVOLTA HERE IS THE BAD GUY AND NOT THE CABLEGUY

TWO AND A HALF MEN IS NOT HERE, NEITHER IS CHARLIE SHEEN OR BARRY MANILOW

Mighmans dream of unfolded happiness is the desire of me to work with you…the King and I, Pomile and the Breadman is a now strong line in, the happiness scale is now it too, Mighman, Blackface and Whiteface are Everyman's dream of score line to take on the best in the world, the submarines of the Black Sea, Caspian Sea and Red Sea are for Tarantulas in the Wind in the Willows

The toad it croaked upon the Wind in the Willows

The Pie man went ahead of the game on the French stick of the broom with chambre le Claire waiting patiently in the wings, from the left handed side led the merryman away for the chambre of all chambre and that was the hotel de lune the one which got away, the one which held the clue to the Macron the surprise of the century was the book, the cover and the Englishmen's tirade, the maypole from Cheshire was not fat and the layabout on the vagrants street, was also not big, fat, lazy and a hoare, well the stick that twizzled was not here anymore, the one who we desire in the one who we enter into the depths of the caverns of success are to be changed, the ones who we are for each day are for the night time bias in the Claire de lune, the ones who are longing for are for the Claire de lune…..

WE ARE FOR THE LEFT-HANDED STREET ON THE FOOD FOR THE MICHELIN

THE RIGHT-HANDED CLAIRE DE LUNE IS THE ONE WHO WE ARE FOR IN THE CHAMBRE DE CLAIRE, WE ARE NOT FOR THE GOOSTREY DERANGEMENT OF THE OLD WOMAN OF PRICKLY HEDGEHOG, WE ARE FOR THE CHAMBRE DE LA CLAIRE, WE ARE NOW SHOUTING NOT AT THE AUTHOR BUT TO THE CANTONA

IN WE ALL ARE WITH THE BASKETBALL CURT, THE HOOP, THE RING, THE INCISORS AND THE DREAM BOYS, WHO THE AUTHOR CANNOT STAND SO SHE IS SORRY AND NOT A LESBIAN BUT LIVE AND LET LIVE…

The shouting is now ceased, and we begin the mafia in the little Italy, the ones who we can find, the ones who we are. Able to find, the coercion on the bed clothes at night is the one who we manipulate tonight, the casino of dreams is the buttonholes big night….

Here it comes and kisses the timeframe, the time span and the one who got away…the ghost of Christmas is now approaching, and the luxury yachts are not a thing of the past….

We are not for you though with yachting we are for Josephine with Yachting, which is how we did it before, but the funny thing is she doesn't enjoy it and doesn't like sport too much either, just running, the bull ring is here now with the mafia, the dark caverns of previous meets are now explored by the Cantonas'. character here William Brown, who is very severe, memberships are all supreme entities and all Golden Balls, Boots, shoes, and Gloves.

The path strickled away to the streams mouth edge, tumbling into the fast-flowing trickle of water at the mouth, the ones of the mafia who chop off heads, chop off heads and break hearts of souls, departing from justice here, Saint Laurent and High Backed chairs are luxury higher edge, end and are never spoken about in genuine leather manufacturers....the red tilt in the beer guzzlers belly is swilling away from the bourka, the lightning flashes across the sky and the traffic is still, wind is whistling down the trees, the bark barking in the wooden empires of mould, the yellow Medellin not a thing of the past but another stanza here not in this one....the one that got away is the bourka the hijab and the veil for the face of desire, the beauty hidden by the massive centuries f bowling, running and football...which we want for ourselves...the villager is now rife with disease, larging the catapult into the city the city which pays the price for the football if the one footed wonder boy, is all that and yes wore the French National flag a French treasure is what his mother wanted and now the Café au Lait is hot laying down on the sides of the stick flying through the skies of hope, the stick never breaking, never sigh in or bowing the hopes for the future are for the droit, gauche and changer la fare, the chambre is the bedroom of hopes dreams and very long chastity, now on a challenge here of complete pages in 20 minutes from Cantona the verse here is now complete and it leaves 1 page only...unleashing the beast fables never felt better and the Cantona is now with someone else who is not French...the chambre la Claire is now the hopes for the futures of hope the mental asylum is now for the mafia...can we please be with the beratement of the chambre le dune....

End here......
Please.....
Stop....
Fighting.......
The beer belly sound....
Tinkle tinkle......
END.

Continued death threats and a constant armed guard now as well as his Author he turns now and smiles to say well now my gorgeous Amanda Jane I know that you are the next one in my bed....and I don't want to hurt you, the reason I know this is I learn fast over a long time that I love you, who you are and we will find away afterwards....

Chapter 2

The Shirt, Adidas vs Nike
A Line Twist
Corporate Board
13 Line Stanza
The A Line twist here is Buzan
SIA, CIA,
MI5, Special Forces and
Agents for Real, Wandering by
Far are trap door equivalent
Of Forbes by far, These are my shirts
These are mine too
NO MORE PLAY HERE
Gold Digging, Diamonds Forever
Big, Little Trucks of Corporate
Realised Treasure, no more SWOT
The Team is real, the battle today is no more digging for real
Osama Bin Laden is not and was not a successful businessman

Prose Poem

Now, lest of dancing on the table in corporate board rooms and enjoy yourself to the one who does this literally and the one that does this with analogies would be two fold, Corporate legitimacy, autocratic extraordinary measure and democratic leadership within the boardroom makes the strongest team in the world, excellence comes from autocratic decisions and democratic leadership, strategically globally with them, gives a new meaning to dancing in the street....Eric Cantona is a tenacious business man and in corporate board leads his teams to success, Peter Jonee MBE is one of the most successful business men in the world, so is Cantona at his business of being himself...Aleksander Ceferin the President of UEFA can tell you this and so is he..so jest maybe on the corporate truth of realism, we are at one for you to see the mainstay of compartmentalisations free of hope, mind and chastity driven the mainstay of hope is the truth of forgiven, Donald Trump is here now in the forgiven mindful complexities of the mindfulness of hope, desire and mindful autocracy which we do not agree with in decentralisation

The corporate of me is the truth of the bee, the one who stung the ones who it could be...President Macron here we are, the Korean Military is a Peace ratification by far, Kim Do is what we say the shirt on the back of the Cantona today is his name, he makes me smile and he is not the Buffoon...Cantona sighs here, I would like my girlfriend to be happy with what we are doing and now I understand that margins are too tight for her being and I am sorry for that....I understand that in Corporate Boardrooms that the fight for the UEFA Presidents Award Winner with Cantonas' name on it was to return or not ....forgiven and yes and with all our might we wanted you to be here to discover our own truth about Marseille ..autocracy rule and military led, the Koreans signed a political strategy to speak to the Chinese who would not have anything to do with them...Peace no, the Chinese race in the skies over Cheshire UK, is still happening, the shirts on the floor are not Marseille, Corporate or Event, but Safeguarding the wrong way round..... Trump. had a peaceful golf club he now faces the incorporated nightmare if unravelling his corporate mis truths of trump towers and Osama Bin Laden I bet is in here...Cantona is truthful, mindful and has the right to remain silent...dynamic de centralisation... all Cantonas Corporate shirts are hanging on the line, the most infamous being the number 9 red, with a huge umbrella...the buzzing bee of humbleness is nothing but... the Guardians Peace Strategy is taken for him now and no all is not forgiven but a truce now for the reporting of truth painful as it maybe....Special Agent Spider is the epitome of the. Law degree students from Harvard, Pentonville and Yales de centralised government regionalised subjective totalitarianism, now this was. Comparative and parabolised to Sir Alex Fergusons approach the reverse being Pep Guardiola....who is democratic, obtruse, demanding of the excellent best, this is management and not CEO, Chairman leadership which is dynamic equilibrium that's a prioritised necessity in the business world, now get on with it...how much budget do I get and when is this being paid...ask accounts....should be the answer...the number on the UNICEF Shirts is the Corporate realism of authority, care, support and doing, Socrates once said that the ignorance of a family to someone they knew was supposed to be with them is hideous crime in itself as it allows bullying of a different kind...families are then disbanded and then regroup to the equations of mathematics that Einstein, not Socrates....besides the criminal activity of Trump, the curve ball here is the Einstein equivalent ...Neymar the hair capital of the world....Utube is the one we meet, the shirt parade of Cantona is the one he wore here, now, value here is the Corporate realised truth and the one who we now write....for peace I will wear 11, for ratified autocratic rule the number 9 is taken to protect Cantona from un ratified...and that number....this is the Corporate Realised truth, the truth of shirts of Auxerre, Marseilles is the Corporate lever that left one day for the Corporate reliance of the truth that Buzan, Marks and SWOT is the truth the ignorance begins with realising that it is not intelligent.....ignorance to others...which is about everyone to everyman and woman and not just elite.....so, when you jump do it well, don't fall over and speak the truth, if you don't you will get a huge warning from mother nature she cannot old out both hands to hold you when you are who you are, when this is pressed the cuckoo clock is then returned to the den of antiquity, the loving that was once shared is the loving that was in the truth of mankind, the once. Fairy godmothers are those who left behind the satirical plays here in France

Donald Trump was handed his papers to supina for a penal offence against himself, he was made satirically to put his hand sexually on each gay man in the White House as a President of the USA, he broke down and said sorry to all gay men and women, for a comment he never recovered from at the end of his career.....Eric Cantona was then condemned by Trump for himself in a clip of a film where he kissed a gay man and then telling everyone that he wasn't....which he isn't, Cqntona was offended at having all of this reference brought up again

Working soldiers, working ants is the reference by the biggest tycoons and some of the most tyranted devolvers of motivational speeches too, the demeaning references were committed to the grave

Oral Dactylic Hexameter
My voice today is car
Dogs Barking, Marseilles, 2
Rolex today, 200
To play, million pounds, 3
Soldiers Working, half tune

Sonnet
Cantona Cantona shirt is on fire
Little blue angels are hearing the mire
Mine is the 11, mine is the 9,
Mine is the 7 with one on the line
My keys are on the kitchen floor, la la
My mind is his la la...height is wise toff
VIP, VIP we are two you
Privacy Screen, Privacy Screen, heel toe
Bark, Bark Symbolise try, hit hit, forfeight
Piety Ignorance the flight of bee
Honey for sticky gyrating tirade
All hail, All hail The King, The King, Measureman

Rausch is Intelligence analytics eye
Transformational, Transactional Lead

Parabole
Paraboles should make you smile in the red lipstick for the turn.
Of lifetime and a dance, King Cantona
11 on the Auxerre shirt, Blue Jeans of the first, parabola
Economics is the truth of the A line twist for you
Elasticity is right here, of the margin analysis cheer
Well done you.....Heroic, Heroic is this bad
That we rejoice in this man, that we rejoice in this suit
We are now for you

Prose Dialogue

Wandering Spiders and the Tale of the Spinning Wheel, the Quran and the Bible....is the analogy line through the book

I did not realise how an analogy for the above reference as to do with my shirts or even corporate board shirts, but then I don't understand...what I do understand is that my shirt numbers and me are not going to incite anything toward anyone else using religion as a weapon, so my own social identity and strength of understanding and not perpetration, my own vulnerabilities allow understanding of all the ways round, which is why when one is shot at, this needs to be taken into consideration, as I am a large physical target, so make sure you show no vulnerability, make sure you get on with everyone and feel as comfortable as possible....

Prose Dialogue

Wandering Marseilles, during my childhood here, I have had three or four times when I have fought physically with Joel and hit him, we never did call the police but I now understand why, I cannot get it through now to you that you need to keep going and you are now forgotten in societies that you once were in, most of which are not very nice anyway and did not hold you in high regard, the sale of some of my houses caused issue with some of my friends and wife, ex-wife at the time, then they realised what my author had said, if you need to sell them sell them or if you need to take them back then do so, never make decisions about ex-wives and keys as they get lost and youngsters that I do not know about end up there, when I realise who they are I realise that they are from her husband's family who had been staying here, making himself Mr Big, whilst on holiday, he strayed away once and nearly needed up in an affair with Rachida Brachni,

as spotted on the security surveillance in the house, even though they know it's there.... and it was a fix, to put them in the same place together to make them have one and they did not sleep together but felt as though they wanted to go through this stood up one night at a family party when Rachida declared that she loved him and kissed him on the head....conversation was surrounding Mourinho ...we are not together anymore and Eric Cantona finds another one, Rachida pesters in the media, Cantona to avoid losing her spot as his ex-partner and mother of his further 2 children

Prose Dialogue

My shirts were freshly laundered every day and were never ever in the wrong place, that was the person who did them, the red cards of Eric Cantona were given on the penalty line most of them the individual who happens to be the voice here is Cantona, the shirts and the collar of Cantona had too many ups, the number 7 is pseudonymous with those who are very good at it.....Auxerre is the next, Credit Agricole is the shirt, the 45 captaincy of the national team Mr Tom is hidden in the background, the hook is a wooden hook... the white of Manchester United for the birth place of Marseille and the birth right of Cantona here today when I passed through before I was told that I would be welcomed here...Umbro the place of ViewCam, the collar up on all realities ...the Managing Director of Umbro and the CEO are now intermittent in the view point of the angels of power.... Umbro Shirts are not the ones which are completely in the way of their own corporate identity...the whole episodes of matches in historical referencing and mans of matches is to make sure that you the reader here understand the reason fro the shirts being as they are, the reason why many men cry over the shirt is its value, the worth of Cantona has increased since early nineties and the value of his brother decreased, the Police Protection coming into force again as Cantona, changes position once again, the voice of his ownself being explored, the corporate own self-identity

strong, written about, the strong identity dripping into the corporate board the sense of self, family, belonging and sacrificial lambs to the slaughter, the Marseilles truth of evil no a very nice place, very Cantona apart from one shout, very friendly and very hospitable, I would like to go to the Church on the hilltop...this place on the hilltop is very special a it has very special memories of birth, marriage and very much sadness...

Prose Verse

Wandering Spiders and the Tale of the Spinning Wheel, the Quran and the Bible....

They take no prisoners, they take no prisoners, they take no prisoners, they take all

The Spinning Wheel of the Spiders all, clinging to hope clinging to justice, clinging to the almighty must haves.

The clinging is futile, and the clinging is futile about the long john silver in the crystal tips hat, the Spiders have the wandering den on the nest of all cotton tip

Prose Verse

Marseilles

The pearl harbour of fortitudes in the Marseilles streets....the Olympic Marseilles in the bullring of the day, the measures of fastness are the clean streets, the family trays, the cathedral spires and the non chalent ways, the Marseilles of Yachts, townships and football, the ones whose wedding bells, cars and hopes for the futures of ideologies of measures are made for the streets, the windy tracks of fortitudes the made to measure suits and the made to measure hopes....

These hopes are to be rectified today when the family decides what to do, as one is now in the Church Spire...

The sparkling water of tunnels, caverns and backrooms, coaching sessions with launch parties of hopeful longevity, launch parties of listening to and launch parties of contractual worth which helps, support and aides the futures of the past, the Marseilles of birth of the master of foot and ball, the one whose telling of authorship is that of boats, trees and family months

Directed at from the hopefulness of the future, Marmaduke he sits upon the floor of the downplay of all, he sits upon the downplay of them all, the Kirstie Gallagher sits upon the sound bite on the TV of the biggest speech at=act of them all....the Marseilles of genetic genes to enable the monkey on the back of the maestro of the football generosity.... goodnight...

Prose Verse

The winning for truth for future is the hope for the past
The hopefulness of the descant is the one with the last
Week on the spire, the week on the job
The one with the corporate and the big one

The shirt on the Marseille is the genetic spree, it's the birthplace of Cantona
It's the one he can be, the short legged long johns

The hopes of the past, the ones he can call home are the ones in the past We are for you he says we are for you the one, who hurts in the play where she was welcomed all done

We are for thee great big shark in the way, of the red raw mess of the big author today, the hope was for her to be nationally acclaimed and now she is in floods of tears for the game of soldiers in the roof lined streets of Marseilles, the birthright of rightfulrightman

The rightfulrightman and the family of dreams of the left foot, the family of tyranny, tyrant rule and non yoga were incitement to the streets of the right footed brain master in the lanes on the head

Immigration on the lanes of crossing the tides of hopefulness the humanitarian steets of the iined passages of fleets of ships, yachts and time, the Elaneor Cantona the genetic spree of flooding the gates of the over arching gates of marriage time and passage of breathren, celebrations of truth, righteousness and combats of families of ill

Marseilles the capital of southern France of Cantona and the spree of genetic field days that you have with the strength of a white faced white man

Prose Dialogue

The empty boardroom tables in lands that never found the position on the table is the one that we never found, the taking of the positions in the table d'ote menus are the ones that they were fighting for in the streets of all mankind.

The taking of perceived jobs from the corporate board rooms as well as the streets is well known here for it is the capital of immigration.

UNICEF

Time

My Girlfriend once met influences in ways you would never know…vipers hatch eggs spinning a web of evil destruction with the wives melt into others arms before, during and after marriage vows…the nesting parameters, hold strong and Forbes can use the analogy to the business districts which they know work, winning, super genres in the industry of hope…

Winning

Position shot on goal the writings on the wall, the shtirt with many numbers.

Epigram World Cup
Covert Superiority
French Merriman

The French Bastion that feels all alone, the French Bastion is the one we hold
With high regard in Paris, with high regard in Rome
With high regard as no jealousy is with Rome

French Bastion

Navy Blue, White, Red line up, line up ahead, the ball it rolls forwards.
Cantona nods, the toss is won, the centre line is in
Empress heads the ball, the emperor gives the King the shot, the feed, the tackle the once
The assist in the nod, Beckham enters the sound....

Epigram

Spinning Spiders Spinning Spiders, we are for the Corporate Behinders

Shirts off on the line, with the centrifugal spiral, motivated through the loins

To make sure the pick is coins, we are one with all mankind to make sure the Jones is not behind, Balzac in the relenting truth is the corporate realised truth of Jemima

Football theoretical line are the players you're not mine

PSG is not the one here, this is Marseilles...not the city streets of PSG, says one

Because I want it all for myself, including his family name.....?

This is a short Chapter for the Spinning Spiders of Corporate Realism, the Corporate Realism for the Best Football layer of Golden Feet called Lionel Messi, who tried to take the whole play today in Marseilles disallowing the introduced Author of Eric Cantona....Eric is the allowed with the Author and disallowed with his Red Cards, his ban and his Corporate realism......

The fur lined trees that saved my soul hid the ones from the goal, the poles of net and the front door, made the side split once more.....

Film Script

We are forever indebted to the men and woman who look after us day to day, we are indebted to those who are for the masses and we are indebted for those who are involved in the de throning of woman loose or not who do not fit in, we do not fit in because we are adopted..this was told to me recently when another try for de-throning became....the mighman of forever became a heroisim of all faith…so, Giroud he sits on the throne of Captaincy with Cantona, with Pele, with Bobby Ball…so, Sir Alex Ferguson had his wife all along in the centurions play, the girlfriend never happened, the Solkesjar never happened, the new life through Christianity never happened, as God is many beings….don't you feel, God is the geriatric Catholicism in A-Line centurions, the breadman makes his final loaf, the Author walks by for a second time, swelling after 3 days from surgery on her torso, I need mighman, mightyman..O'er thine Michelin…stupid or not….many believe a 12 starred Michelin Chef tirade towards the finale of the breadman became insipid with relief…aid, humanitarianism, as a father the breadman diversifies, not non chalent, married with hair, lots of it, great bigness of himself plastered on the walls of his kingdom…French…so what?...why does this matter? In England? His own choice his own happiness, that of his family.. why does this matter? Financially now the wrong way round, financially the French superiority with Zidane is very powerfully strong, so what for the little ones at school, the finance houses, the banks, the investment strategies and the immigration visas that you are supposed to get… never mind, the truth of all will become to pass and the truth of all evil will help the A Line twist of national identity, the shepherd herds the sheep of all time, the many herd of cattle gather they don't and cannot be rounded, they are shepherds of sheep, that want to be found, lost in the hillside, lost on top of the mountain…

The prologue is one of the nicest ways to remove the storylines from the main book that contextualise further the main storyline's, they bring in, forward the story immediately….happiness starts with those who you love, care, cherish when you are left for nothing to forget what you were born for then the analogy and sorry for using one, I am metaphorical unlike Cantona said one, when you are close to your family you cherish them, grow old with them, your desires the

We are the ones who you left behind the ones who want to be with your behind

This is realism this is the truth the Cantona is not for you

He is not for the fairy buffoon and is not for the ones in the truth, behold the realised truth of all evil and the ones who realise that he is one on the way, he realised the ines he left behind and realised the ones who fight for the time of the truth in the spire of the truth….

Cantona here with Mighman, Foreverman are creepy, little hands move across the avenue road…the tongues they wag upon the tissue of the open road, the Dame she sits upon her lesbian throne, the Mister of Masters sits on the avenue of 5th Street, lined with heroes, lined with sacred bells, lined with balls of Golden tell, the heroes worship their Gods of the less masses, the heroes they worship the less masses, the loose elastic if on at all defines the sense of mastery if at all, the heroes they sit upon the wall of PSG, of England, of Marseilles this morning of worship…Amen say, the hi heroes of the stand, the ones whose middle is in the van, the heroes they sit in the mountain of worship this morning....the Puma it sits on the throne of blackness, the Puma it sits on the throne of happiness with the Antelope in its jaws, the Mayfair sits upon the Guess of the tiger, the Maybank sits on the whistle of hope, in Geneva the conversational onslaught began on the hope of justice, the filings hid the justice of the wheel of hidden justice the Lancome smells wonderful today the hourly sightings are on the Giselle of the catwalk, the Lowry heightens the tower of strength, the tower it sits on the tower of the rig, scaling the mounted police in Canadian provinces....the Grizzly Bear holds the key to the future of mankind, my passport means a lot to me and it shows my identity, I have everything I need, the son he sits upon thine knee of chastity of her very beheld be...upon thine knee of chastity the medical profession are the elite key to happiness...the once upon a time is now incited with the timebound historical referencing which is now the Authors pride, joy and immense satisfaction of enlightenment...those beholdments held dear to your heart, keys to the truth of all mankind, heartfelt thanks to you all for the lovely tributes to my mother's passing today, as my ex-wife takes her no more to church, I do today, smiling as I wave goodbye to Marco and the rest of the world... absorbed in reminiscence, faltering egos, such lands grave stones...the finale for the breadman was the give back...a multi ego, a nuance in French cuisine and an absolute workaholic....out on the town, held by the power of attorney whilst he turns the play for her once more, the Cuthbert, Cyril, clue forging ahead of the rations of biasness, Joel Cantona can be seen in the City with Milburn, the ombudsmen's' decision for financial des security here is for Cannes recouperation and a royalties for 8 years of a lifetime work stating with the Golden King...this is a decision made by the media, French included where the author finds herself today, non chalent in her fate this week....whether her disputes with the banking and finance houses can be rectified as another fraudulent activity was heralded yesterday morning.....the Lion it sits upon the Peacock of thyme, the iridescence of the foul mouthed breathren, the lip service of gold, the gold of time and the carpet of icing became the icing on the cake for the Liberace, Tiffany....diamond mines, tobias hid from the Lions den...the cubs marauding on top of one another, the centurians adorning tier plumes, putting on their helmets with them red, white, blue, French made you, Englishman too, in these colours of breathren, PSG has not breathren here in Marseille, this Englishmans Captaincy is this man Zidane's Englishman's tirade, Cantona doth sit on his old throne, born in Marseille his only breathren against him, twice now through marriage breakups, the colours of Lyon are now unknown, Marseille it stands upon the throne of its own, with no breathren in Paris, Rome or Saint Germain, the colours rose upon the sky of the blue, Marseille it stands upon the throne of the Egyptian Pharoah....the ink it stands upon the ink of the eyeliner...

Germain it sits upon the Paris streets of Captaincy of the city, of purple, Auxerre it sits upon the colours of the flag of the run of hopeful truth, the Cantona hits the centurion, the bull it lies down to the centurions legal truth, the car called red sits in the garage of truth on the road to recovery in the city of dreams where the author is not banned from anyone, but has no money as it is stored away like a squirrel, the hazelnuts they are from the primrose trees eaten by the Tapirs in Zoological Parks, no cities here is not true....

The tree it sits upon thine knee of Basildon, the hope or the future is that the heartache of those suffering from hurt, heartbreak, controlled through strong hearts can be tremendous, hurting, aiding weak hearts is something that Lucy Pocket won't do any further...impressions to hold the man with the key, Farling in the tree is the one which did sing, the tree of mankind in the one we did see, the one who is dizzy is the faraway tree...we are for you the one with the smile, the one who feels better is the one is the dire need...racist mankind is the UEFA goodbye, the hard angels we worship you bye, we whistle in the street, the one who is fat, we are the ones who we worship at that...fur lined streets with the one with the coat, the Leatheron the baby is the Liverpool's one of hope, purple green buggy on the strings of mankind, hurt like an empire strikes back all the time, position is everything and two is not right, the one in front is the third on the right, the gauche is the droit the flashers great big hat, the one is the cor blimeys, head in the sac, we will always wave, will always fall at your feet, as we know those kitbags are there for a treat....can we believe the one footed brigade, we hear from the nursery school that Ofsted behaved, we are at one with the film production stand, the half friendly tortoise always on the go, never enough makes the world go to slow, the one is the one is the one of the far, the torte in the tummy now here how we are.....flash went the striker, the strong of the heart, the corporate realisation that the car hit the FARC, Jones he did say on the string of the harp, yes, I do love you our a fantasy too hard..Middlemist we love you are the right one, ideologies of motive, the blood red is now done...2 in the world it's the rarest cities, Peru is not one of them now we are on our knees, white of the red rose, when the blood is all done, black spot of childhood, the attachment is none...

Pomile is for a coral suit and tie, for a tie of gold shoes, sparkling as they march through the streets of the hare, the tortoise is subjective here it could anyone not on a fast reader...do you know how many children are on them only gifted and talented, plus those who can tell you narratively about what has happened are also very very incited to brilliance,, I know I am one.. but then you want to make me thick, fat, ugly and just exist.....France don't, they do things very differently, the populations should be very lucky in their own thinking, their own intelligence

The mission for the countess in the forward is the later on in life magnitude of thoughts, babies, happiness, limbos, bimbos, strategies, lout and for the UEFA discerning President, is the shirts of many colours, who is God the answer to the Kitbags and much more, the thing is and yes I know what you did to your email address pop up shops, whose idea was this, I can manufacture these for everyman, for every Pomile, for every Diamondmans' collector and for the great big I AM....a whole heap of collectors that want the Simmons saga in colour print, Cantona is non chalent purposefully enjoying his realm once more, sad, but true, everyman's Frenchman came a huge cropper on that day and everyone felt him everywhere since, everyone forgives you Eric, everyone, the actual impact on your family of being in the UK for you to play at the level you were playing, being in this way, led everyone to like you, not many didn't underneath….every single sinew on that night hid behind cushions, blankets, tea cups, glasses, beer, dogs leads, papers and the most uncontrollable distance from you was her….the other one..you know….the one you hurt you author with, that one….when someone holds you, you feel them in a different way, even if you don't have sex with them..you hold them, they become part of you, you cherish who they are as humans, no one cherished Simmons Eric, no one he was a racist and please stop beating yourself up about it…impact to you ….impact……

Psychological……behavioural….impetus to put right…it does not mean there is something wrong with you..it means you hurt….you hurt like hell that no one would believe, that you hurt deep down, that makes you feel angry, sad and pushes you to work all the time…as a voice over the garden gate, through Marseilles, is if you don't keep going you will hear it even more, it will consume you….I remember you landed in the media on my knee, o'er challenge of a lifetime to keep the Cantona from the Simmons tree…I love thee, you for you, don't think I am a mad fan, an artist full of desire to take you to naked bed, I do not want you prepared stripped and roasted like a hog….apple in thine mouth, carrot inside, stuffing in ones derriere….the orange it sits upon thine cherub of peel…..the orange it sits upon thine knee of Barlow, Williams tree, Hamilton lines the streets here, Ferraris lines the streets of the Orange for a head everyman's dream, big house, car, motorbike, succumbing to usage of the multimillionaires Pomile….the chicken was stuffed on Christmas day, the turnkey of the provider held strong in the fortress of emancipation, heart felt thanks from Lately Lady, desired by Everyman, loved by Margaret Boyle, Lucy Pocket, Eve who is not the Author…now about these throw ins….Platini smiled, well Aleksander what a mess with I, we are not in, the company has not gone bump she is smiling through royalties of this book knowing her hard work will pay off, 8 years of writing, a lifetime of hurt, she wishes everyman's adopted parent should be Jolie, attachment strategies, well ball foot, girlfriend, existence in a cave, captain of cavemen with no analogies….Geres the god of worship is the bodily being of me, said Cantona, the skull, cross bones and none elegant elite are too…Ceres the goddess of loud music, triumphant Kim of long nose fame, readily available for Pomile to snout at, no, she isn't like that..Pomile of Political Peace satirical populations, weathervanes and fortitudes of Foreverman…Lately Lady is Forevermans fortitude of realism…the realism hurts Pomile here the most developed hoare you can imagine, the reason here that Prince George is unwelcome…the warts were the insanity of dirt…say no more, homeless vagrants, dress, appear some cleaner, some don't….just sorry to use this language here said the Author, smiling as she wrote, its just I know who it is and you don't…Lately Lady took her children to the ballet one day, splash went the puddle all on her knew dress…10 minutes to the village hall, walking in the pouring rain, dirt up the sides of her ballet tights, at the age of 7 this little girl took charge, I need knew parents, they are not good enough…..

I need space here

My mother needs space here

My father had space all his life….he is now dead….so is daddies little girl…of the red coat… patent shoes, cold calling and dog patrols, falling off steps in love with a football player and in love with Turk, Ching, a Sausage Dog called Mike and invertebrates called William, Harry, Charlotte and Beatrice…

Lawrence of Arabia..black hunted widows with veils, leatherback turtles, despondent youth, disassociated tyrants and leather leaves of domicile no hope….puddleducks splashing in the rear view mirror, Cantinas car swerved again…the tank approached…get out, he said, 'lights on'….. qu'est il'ya oppotunaire pour va vours…you are gorgeous Charlotte Burrows, beauty, flowers with hair short and dark

We need space here from everyman's wife, girlfriend of those who aren't the above…..said the Author..we do not need space here from the person that it is said the muse, influencer and acclaimed award winner…yachting is something I would love to take my hand to…

With no space

This is not a shortened chapter so we continue…

Highly acclaimed sportsmen, view life a little differently than most, not all are, not all achieve in this way, not all are players of the century as there is only one century and player…as Josephine left the car, I cried as I realised I should have picked my friend up, as she was asked to leave for being at her, Josephine, she said sorry, hoping my friend would go round again..that's it….

In the end of this chapter you were to feel fulfilled in your reading, fast lively, sound and clear, witty and cool, that's for you to decide not me, funny that's also for you to decide, so can you read the whole book, put it down, then pick it back up again so that we can feel as though your worth it….you have not been short changed here, illustrative satire is also drawn, maybe one day someone will speak to the Author, so we can see her being interviewed…said she…

Well, we will have to wait at IHG for a while until she comes out of hospital, turns a corner and bumps into the man of her dreams…even my mum thought that was funny…Merriman, on a yacht said the boy, Leucile on with him said the other…Sportsman overboard said the Yachting Club….Monaco, Monte Carlo and Venezuela….

Chapter 3

Golden Anthems: Tears Tantrums, Weathering Wrinkles: Special Agent Spider

13 Line Stanza
Fight Fight The Good Fight, One
Amen said the prairie
Dog, fight the fight, one said
Agent Spider is Stade
Contentious life of all
Done, pulled out, never had
One said, hopeless life, in
Dying one, arms of one
Champion, Champion
The one who is short, dead
The one who is fat, dead
Dying woman's hat, now
Objectors to the hat respire

Prose Poem Presidents

Contentious Conscientious objectors are those who do not and aware not for war, they are not for fighting and are not for the mainstream parade of shops, the objectivity of the spider here is analogised in the said scripts in chapter 2, so far and we are now in the prose of all poem…Incy wincy spider climbed up the trouser leg of the tallest man in the world, that Marmaduke loved, cared about and Christophe reeled, I am not gay and I do not care for my ex wife and my now deranged ex-wife any more, I love her the one who got away the one who reals everywhere, no she doesn't that is the one who is heartbroken over not being with me as she was in the real….whoah…you are now for the justice of the Golden anthem of them all, the love, care kindness and de realment to find solace in others… to care for the utmost desire of the truth Middlemist Red, the most exotic looking red flower and one of the rarest….Cantona walks away, flowers I wish I had never wrote it…

The Golden Foot of impetus…..the long legged wandering spider with webbed feet…has a longevity valid in thine toes, the line is drawn in sympathy with the webbed feet the Channel is one of those…the film is another and the going off on one to get it all out of his system is well known when he cannot get what he wants…Merriman is in here, tavernas, bars and design houses are all for grabs they think, but they are not…and Jack and Jill are up the hillside retreat..retreats retreats the hillside of the beat, the short eyed Susan is a thing we do to meet, the ones we are find of the ones we are afraid, the ones who we wish were the superimpositions maid, we are not royal iris with a stigma of a rugby all, we are not a royal poem as this is for someone else.....we are for the rugby ball of two minds, the football of Marseilles, the clean non graffiti streets here the Marseilles of the centre, circle the Marseille of the central ground, Paris seems miles away now and the impetus is for new ground, beer bellies swig in the cafes align the outside of the ground, filled with just abouts trying to make ends meet doing the days of none matches, sliding around in the heat haze...Stade de Olympique de Marseilles the muse not here, the historic blindfold of today...joke joke joke, the land of the free for trump, the freehold for the righteous land of the merrimen far from the sand, so the immigration if the land into the graffiti sand is the hot, sticky palms of the psalms of the land....black iris symbolises not France, is not the fleur and is not the psalm, the one is the lily of the fleur de lys, the g is back with vigour catching the lys in symbolism the campion is nearly with us with the chimes in the gate...blue, french or navy blue you know the blue of Cantonas knickers, the pantaloons, the johns, peters and lee and sure fire way of getting the sack pilfering, rubbers, pencils, paperclips, like the fluff in your pocket when a paperclip falls out...the bin on the desktop humming with delight...the anthem of the fast one calling the string of hearts for foreclosing is the nuance of the day when company accounts are here to stay, ha ha ha we do not want you to succeed in the game of life the business of hope,,the business of employment, dreams and salvation....the Ferrari here nowhere to be seen, the golden Ferrari in the bigger G is...and the followed by the Princes in Paris where the institute for musical piano is apparent and farewell to the subterfuge...farewell I say to the subterfuge of mankind....everyman seems to cross over here, but he doesn't and the eventuality of never meeting is very clever....however not mentioned and never ending, the everyday man is never to meet her and the centurion is neither...sometimes those special are never to meet the ones who try and help as those who want to are always jealous of findings underneath, when nesting on one's own you understand the complete absorption in ones ownself and child, never had been in this way always for others and always for the centurion never in our past had the man with the loaded gun ever been in this way with her, she lifted the sides of her torso toward him...and he catches her coming round the other way round, the centurion reaching for his wife and reaching for his smile, he smirks..no not ever have I or do I intend to cheat, I have never been that way, so it has taken me along time to be with the one I had told I would be with her but not yet....she didn't realise what I meant but knew deep down it would happen....the everydayman is now removed from the circus of life and died a death in his divorce settlement taking too many riches after a terrible ordeal for the centurion, the Merriman is now in..hoping that the start of the time here is a good one, the laughter continues through the night and goes into the next day never emerging with only one call to reception for another weeks stay, the centurion hid from the view of excited onlookers, basking the in the view of their own tales…the tales of unexpected youth, generosity and loosely ingrained with sin, the superimposing vigour of the chastity leaning over into the dinner of luncheons, tries for and hopes for….futures, longevities from afar, corporate realisations of centurions, bastilles', groups of hoards with fanning that you would not believe the small centurion led the way into the bastille, the charging bull the entity of it all, enter stage left the bull non chalent…no with no boos from the crowd, I hope you are not feeling uncomfortable, the bull,….oh everyone has seen the cowboy, the boy and the none sister in the entity of the boat…the boat was a pulley not a lever in the physics football..the centurion laughed out loud this time as his wife went inside, the centurion embarrassed about his upbringing and embarrassed about his previous homelife, young beings and sleepless nights of females hoarding and him not able to get enough of being himself…sleeping with the hoards, yet longing for the life of the centurion of the bull, the one whose sting is far from stinging the hoards but those who are on their own way out through their own promiscuity…

those who the centurion cannot even image why they won…they are now dead to society and dead to the fact their they squeeze talent pools to make sure they get through the societal bias of the media…. hola, soy el toro del ruedo en el círculo, el que tiene la nariz llena de oro, soy el que tiene la nariz llena de lingotes de oro, ¿puedes cavar para mí?

Toro

el toro miró a su alrededor y por favor traduce esto a tu propio idioma para el poder del toro... si quieres comerme... dijo, entonces hazlo, me acostaré como sacrificio, pero no te burles, Bromear o incluso golpearme, no se burlen, no se acuesten frente a mí o incluso me lastimen con lanzas, esto no es antes del sacrificio por carne, esto es solo para que usted imite, vea y gane dinero en los límites tradicionales.

All the skinny pencils can now write in English, can now sharpen their own senses to write for themselves, their futures and their own beings….to write for the hoards of screamers that make the centurion embarrassed, that make the Cantona swell with jealousy if someone vows to take his Jemima…Jemima is now on for the Author to become…. the non-jealous attitude of the real ex wife, ex-girlfriend and ex-lover…the battle for her is now ensuing…the bull it sits upon thine knee of thine matador, the hurt it travels upon thine knee of shaking, trembling ferocious grazed knees from child hood of not in the silence of the rooms with no view, with bars, habitat and skewered ecstasy…

Oral Hexameter Dactylic
So sharpen belonging
So sharpen beholdment
No troubles to sharpen
Nobody with you see
Fight for skinny pencil

Sonnet
Mighman, Mighman Bull ring in toe with ring
Angels' skinny with no bosom lead, no
VIP, VIP we leave it there, hitman, here
Privacy Privacy but not from you
We are at one with the barelegged stare
All hail centurion with Cantona
Fair hair, all English maiden, farewell
The toe sucking nail biter had her right
Ici, ignorance for Socrates cheer
King, King, Measuremans King, Hail, Hail, Socrate
Sting of the Bee, Honey in for free, pop
Went the top of the honey pot bee
The red lipstick turned just for me, tee hee
King Cantona Economics on Fire

Parabole

The red Middlemist is the rarest flower found in Peru as it is not here, China Panda Bears, New Zealand's Protection along with UK, the black bat flower is the highest order of something that we don't know and that is love, cherishment of this real fact....the Giant Panda Bear is the emblem of the truth that two people can fall in love without meeting very often, in fact once and being around each other for many years....

The bull it sits upon thine knee of justice, of fortitude, of strength to roll the camembert, up the hill, the strength of all hope to roll the impetus round the sky, the drawing of lines of red roses goodbye, the red mist is forming the cloud on the wire, the middle of the rarest is the one we devour all hail skinny pencils we love the desire, the rose of Columbia is not olde English, the Mondial we call the centurions fire, the TO barbaric the mist then comes down the gorilla is not friendly and back on his pound, the chest is now swollen with heart ache and swoon the once friendly alien is now walking on the moon, the impetus here is to suck toes, but here we do not want to cloud judgement of the once red mist of bullying blood and hope.....for the future that the Gorillas Mist is the Middlemist of hope...

Prose Dialogue

When I wrote these songs I did not know when I was going to sing them, I wrote some more and wrote some more…I am now aware that you are writing in the book and could probably hit the soundbite….the placement of the battle ship is the battleship of hope, the one we call the cuckoo clock is the one we called home, we wanted to be in the mist for the colouring of delight, the one we are for you see we are for your delight, the Gorilla is now in the Mist of fortitude of real limit…. we are for the real on the limit of justice and we are for the real of you, we can be nowhere on the sky and we can be nowhere on the real of hope no justice and very unexplained behaviours from the real attitude of me….we are for you in the empire line of skirt….with the tweed and tie no more, we would like be with you and be with you we may, we are for you to be with the luxury elite …the Red Middlemist is now all gone, the hurt all over is not true….Beauty is the foreplay of the Red Middlemist time, the true honesty…the makeup the one for the play of a lifetime….the one is the one of the hope, the line of a lifetime and the tenacity of the hopeful sway, the bull it sits upon the town of Marseilles….the bull it sits upon the town of isosceles triangles the one who is down on the luck of the gambler the bull it sits upon the life of the clown, who is hurt with hurt and MiddleMist…the Gorilla it sits upon the tower of strength of the bull which is not hit, the one who is not speared and the one who is not ripe with the bananas…the tower of strength is the one with the capture on the roof, the one with the capture on the roof, the one with the justified strength of hopeful longevity and the ones which were to die for…the lion it sits upon the strength of hope….my tower if strength Platini came first and second then and then the Author ……the serpent is round today with the viper tongue of fear and the centurion is all gone, captured, and beaten by the Marseille town captaincy of Pierre White, the joker is in the real of the life of the child, the kiss is the real of the lifetime of hopefulness, I am the tyrant of love, hate and ridicule and I am the avenue of hopeful longevity…will you please remove the face of the angel and the pianist of the January celebration of the publication of the book…..the hole in one is the golf buggy in the mist of society and the chambers of comman ground, we are at one with the society bias and the memories are all gone the wayward sit upon the power of Mightyman, the Mighman of society and the Mighman of the beast of all thine knee, the ones we recall are the ones who are centuries past…the ones who are now with the one of the past…..we are now for you and are for the centurion and the forgiven, we are for the tidy up of the littleons centurions, we are Foreverman and Foreverman is for you….

We are the Cabinmans' tribe to be, the one who helps the Cabinmans' to be

The mist of the Gorilla and the hope of the man, is the one who is very much better I can….We are at one with you now….we are the ones who are for the fortitude of mankind's needle of love, care and strength….the combatant of terrorism is the thing of the past the one who is virile and the memories of the past, the ones who we are for the ones who we are for…we are for centurion, we are for the centurion, we are for the centurion of power, strength and tactile behaviours... little-ones of deity...surprise...infantile infantile is the one on the turnstiles at that..... kissing in the turnstiles in the fortitude of sin, the half friendly alien.....went to the Liverpool kin, the turnstile of truth hid the little ones rebuff, the one who is the fluff in the button of life...

Prose Verse

Bull is the ring for to minus queue, ever on the hat of the genius view.

The hammer it is the kilt of all evil, the one who is the one in the sink, the living of the bull is the one who we are very happy the one who is the one in the table of very happy the bullring it sits upon the sound bite, the sound bite is the fine who is the one with the wholly presents of time.

The nightmare of the bullring is now ours to be condemned and the luncheon parties of luxury gifting are left for all time, the King he sits upon the level of tries to the past...the King he sits upon the centurion of the living room.

We are for the ages of man to remember the fact that she surely can become with the ages of the King, man....we are for the kingdom come, the flowers in the hair of FTD want, need and solitude of fasting...so we can do this all again with someone who cares on their team...the image it sits in the floor of the manger....

The King who's every day is Manager of duty, is living in blue desires of hope for the future of mankind, the King in his counting house is eating more than bread and honey, the queen in her countess house is eating diamond marmalade, the orange zest of the marmalade the champagne is rolling down the river...

The future King is cutting his fortune in the river of mankind and the river of the King, Queen and Prince, Princess is now floating down the hillside, the wayward canary is ow beside the hilltop, the budgie is in the play.

Pomile the French English strutting horsewoman ship is now forlorn n the wayward city of hopeful dreams...the let-down first of survival of herself is a vicious attack on Pomile by Rachida Brachni and the man in the van, this is the word of the lord.... Pomile is in her counting house eating marsupial tea, the Australian thought that this wasn't real and now it's time for tea...

Prose Verse

Of the diamonds in the pout of the biggest Michelins out, with another one for the Hyatt Mastery of the chef....UNICEF hide the concern for the UEFA GP Medical Kitbag Lady who is in production for them, the key is to align all with the quarterly results, said, the blindman...

no, said the blindman once again, he hid the man with the open shoe…analogy to sexualised behaviours can cause disturbance to those in need of a shower, hot or cold

Little gigantic pears covered in smouldering hot chocolate, red wine or even its own juice are not analogy…the red wine the finest Bordeaux, the Champagne the best Tattinger, the Pear Juice the best milk in the world…Cleopatra is now the Egyptians Princes chams….

Read the times in New York today is the Englishman's tribe, house of cards and linked in for the embezzlement of time….the embezzlement of cards, weapons, drugs, cartels of Columbian Rosenthal Families, who are actually through realism Venezuelan

Little gigantic pears
With no little surprise bump
Hump
The lump in my throat …not the suit, not the suit mighman
In body parts mentioned this is not the Author or a pseudonym
for….as the author is for Cantona not him…
Thine knee of breadman
A Ball…. this is not zoe

We are for her Author here in her stand against Rachida Brachni in front of the media

Prose Dialogue

Columbian Medellin interfere with the constraints of human activity and devour the state of emergencies, the extraordinary measures of the Columbian Government, countered by the Columbian Medellin is a known consequence of re issued peace negotiations, talks with the far left guerrilla warfare strategists of south American terrorism, Geneva plays apart here for the UN, UEFA, Michelin counter attacks through legitimate in street, elite food, football, leadership strategists, media films and negotiated warfare in the air, the strikes being Syrian not Columbian Governmental desire for humanitarian rich pickings from the South American warfare strategists who demand aid from westernised relatively rich countries, these of course you have to understand through terrorism are the lovely flowers of the South American Mondial's, red, white with no blue and no I am no buffoon, pansy or fairy…I like flowers, so does the author and many millions of public figures…now, maintenant, the issue here is drug cartel, Rosenthal Families breathren some incarcerated, Yani, Yankel ones out one in…just like Abu Hamza… the diamond picking line champion of the managerial west, gives Jones a run for his money on return…units, cost per unit, profit margin, now legitimately Jones, Bill Gates, Leonard Skinner, Trump Towers even though now not legitimate, he is now in a state of emergency himself, back to Golden Anthems, Eric Clapton….Whitesnake, Love in an Elevator and many more for I, now

I am not a lesbian is what she had to say and neither is the author who has no idea about the sexual orientation of the concierge....not withstanding, the benefits real of Margaret Boyle, the characterisation here not of an ex wife, girlfriend or boyfriend but the common or garden bias of Trumps tirade at President Macron, now ladies, Mrs Bridgette Macron is real here as the Lady of the Presidency, a wonderful Lady too, assute, clear, academic and of very promising fortitudes of power, the realism very clear, very honoured to be able to see and truly an honour for me to be privy to this level of security, please pass on my regards to all involved...Mrs Bridgette Macron, I know you there somewhere and I truly do feel that my inheritance is better spent at home, where I am now....:) Kim to some degree is misunderstood, please do not get me wrong here not for nuclear weaponry, I am for excellence of sound mind, excellence of warfare strategies, military with a democratic rule...very interesting here for observational truths, yes, I saw the Mightyman of France, hiding behind the purple glass vase, the vast expanse of Kim, The Chinese Prime Minister, President and Committees clearly led with team work, aides

Of the diamonds in the pout

Epilogue

This is the epilogue the one that got away was not me.
This is the epilogue the one that got away was not me.
This is the epilogue the one that got away is not me it's you.
Not from society, not from the Sewers and not from the lamb shanks of leg and bone
This is the epilogue enjoy yourself sometime with abandonment.

Prose Poem 7

The King and I

(This is a modernist metrical heroic prose poem)

Go...Goddess of love, passion and chastity of inner health...leave and be gone from your childhood home, where memories of long lost lovers..ice cream...and teenage dreams of affairs with mansions, halls sunsets, thin maypoles and broken inner chastity..Leave and begone you wench of all hilltop..inner sanity is truth of all maypole that crossing lines is sanctioned for all... Our character building with roots on the hill doesn't have dementia or even a thrill of intrigue, desire and no money passed...oww! You hurt that blessed passed...Our team it consists of A to B..then reverse if you have it free...What is it? Half a melon and it is frozen, with all seeds and blueberries fast one, now it is cold and hard...why is this?

One half book, compendium this is one, aubergine in colour with no stripes all in the centre truth and a Buttoned fast one? With a saucepan on ahead board? Archimedes' …is difficult to spell lay him down and I am little as well..this is god…I am A said he…and I did not care for he…who is he? He is he, he is me, he is Archimedes tree…Caesar…I rule, I conquer, I am significant conquerer? Yes! I saw in the playground one day, on strings from the tree of mankind…in the Goose for parquet Christmas and I am not duck fat…half frozen turkey and a sprout…where is the pea? I am he…where is the alphabet? On a frieze in the core in the cold…

How old am I? Do I require a date? Whales! Wales..one is red and one is grey…where is the core? An expansion of magma increasing tectonic plates of gargantuan and seismic proportions. Off with his head? Forget…I say..do not tell of his whereabouts and forget he existed…heartbreak… sadness…a beating heart that died with hurt…aching uncontrollable sadness and sighs of being forelorn…Beach said flip flop, I love sand dunes where we can sleep in our match for hats one with cap the other with flop…said another! Bed Stud! Bed Stud! Said he…I am no parataxis..I am no subordinated plant in a holder…now let A stand please…

We Need Space Here for UNICEF, UEFA, FA to Shelter Her For Him

400 - plus Before 2018

Move historical referencing below to date

A development of corruption, fraud and dire intrigue that we said we wouldn't have then..Its Alas…no it is not and then I wanted him back…now go to the Bridgewater…I am A…goddess of truth…I am on stage and I am not roots…hairline fracture of a metatarsal line..I am red and I am drink and I am buy. You drink what? Said he..Denmark is here for me..Achilles..said Argentina, my red line was way past the truth the…Church when dark at half past ten…when flip flop buried many men..Moyra was from Yorkshire too..who is he? Now hear the truth..French Angleterre and Caesar too…Transient sail from here to their I lost my way a bit…no air…De-securement is the truth a non-subordinated youth…The Lion but upon the sinew when we saw we realised it 'oww' …the bear and bare had actualised fact of behind with berries packed…potty…no its me and I am not in halls yet…Self realised coercive truth of the brains it is not you? Who is you? And why is that?

Now, I can see that you are not that…do you remember who is he what was said..and Y was led to another now I am alone and undercover…Menopause is not even here where is it? He plays dumb here, where is dumb? And where do you play? Oh its pitch and put my way. I am attack or is it forward, who am I and what colour 7 then? I am defence or is it back…what is my name? And am I black? Ulysses…Caesar and Laurel Chaplet air, Go! I am no saint..I dance around a fat maypole, with ridicule and jest, my finest hour was on the sun of ozone and I begun…Fendi..

Queen of heels and scent I never had F lent…G is he and I am him…I would have done my best for him in the chair he doth sit beware my friends he may have bit…never to much for us to chew…now who is who? Stop..who is this? O…why is this? Stop…arrogant and intrigue…I am A and this is my match day. Now, please sit down, I have had enough your 40 seconds is not enough. All in one god he did say, we know your catholic and good my way. A is god and on is me and no I don't and your not my Y..he is he..I am now and he is ring and I am out. Who is O? Horse…I croaked the toad it jumped up onto the broom and off it flew back to renew…all senses and retire then we saw the funeral mire. Which one? This is Denmark, International School of forethought a Peace Strategy for global science, now where's my E..I am not bias…O…French?

Not good enough…multimillionaire and relative of..O deep ridicule…O…bias Caesar off with his head…have you heard of love, adoration, sheer genius, heart of lioness, chameleon characteristics, sheer brilliance to sing and play music too…have you heard…who is he? He is E, the master of foot and ball..tee tee tee…We down 5 he played 7..who is M? Now thats equations..horse had maths and you have art…my willy had you on Mars, Martians glee and Pyrotechnic..I am St John all in my match day..please traverse the genetic French Angleterre spree…I am solely he…jockey. No…its corrupt…put my tie upon Elizabeth…royal jelly and who is she? Diamonds…Gold…Silver…peasants all encrusted with royal crest then…off with his head…no…he's peony led…I am A they are S they are farm and footballer led…They are L they are B they are C or E and P?

I am A with 4 in a bar…I am A and horns by far…4 on a par and I am J…we are family and we are E…Illegitimate…far too early..I am A the worlds adopted play…Off with his head…and a question that we should not pose here…who is B? Porcini Mushroom used as crisps and on top of Ravioli..all together in a compendium…Lou and in 2…Dressage…Dressage…I am now with you by far…Who are you? I am Camembert rolling down the hill…which one…Stop…Listen… this is me..I am not up the Faraway Tree…from moon beam with no pants I like to see the short and prance…its no intrigue and a sonnet or two is it me or is it you?

Beer Bellies, Low Slung trousers, cracks in physical acumen please show kindness…the British bulldog snorts and salivates, I'm not sure if this is Royal match type…do we go to Timbuktu do we hold United Nations or a few …do we embrace all that is British I'm sure to goodness we do not need Bulldogs briefcase…

Givenchy is all out as I have no shadow of doubt…we all said it would be even when the French Ball Master agrees then..Our mafioso begins here with the Italian men and cars, suits Lamborghinis and the streamlined Ferrari…Red…the Trafford was walled with streamlined 60… help…nose and squawk…How many then? The Frenchman of Foot and Ball was in the buff you know…when went a glow in underwear…he didn't have a chance then now he hides all countryside with 54 you know...all at one he did declare that Master wasn't him...problem is we decided that statues are for him...epigrams adorn the lawn and circle...11 in...run of truth... straight line with no subordination and sheer touch brilliance with no enemy...all dead...no funerum in epigram! Stop!...who is he? He is 6 foot 2 inches of leg and ball...Stop! For 9 then we all clap for you? Go!...with knitting...a master plan for French genius with Mensa tie in...charging white horses with roman numerals on them...chariots of strategy with armour suits with no nike shoes on...all in string and the astro is all done...strings of beads with sweat on the run, black holes and the lancet...we past jewish on the road and we do not all agree now fast...team... ridicule...blasphemous...Mark Hughes...OBE...maybe our British match day for global security is all in one now with A...

British valour...chariots and the fore-mentioned E with integrated societal bias of non-issue with non integrated Iranian Muslim and Mosque with those whom terrace and beer are their world... we give to those whom gave back to local communities and those whom are agreeable to their fete...hair! Said he curly, dark and now grey with short back and asides a traditional cut for English gentlemen...

What is this? Football heaven...no..it is not...Balls Golden in chapter not verse they are said in too many and we do not want to hurt...through political satire..although intrigue we mention the funeral mire...we mention dark skeletons and windy ridges which blow away cobwebs...do not lie...I am 335 down...furlough..oh what a time...cloisters' ...Kloisters...Tardis and queens...back I tell you off with his head...he really didn't mean to...able child of godly prince lift me up and then I see oh ...god? No...twas once with a smile no he is as bad..my E...English Francleterre..full of desire, creativity, style and masses of utmost pout...behind the scenes...we smiled when she walked down the aisle not just with one but with them all...skinny pencil of all Englishness...yes it is me? Gold...Diamonds...Mansions and Spice..not for Finsbury Park Road but for High Elite... for High Elite I say? Do you know whom I am? Yes, skinny pencil we know you well...now for the hard part...resume..chic..fashionista and utmost sunglasses with ridiculousness surrounding your E well no nikes are not my E can you see...you are me? I am you and he is she?

So, when you dive round the corner for lunch and intrigue do not sit in the cathedral park...sit somewhere where you cannot influence anyone whatsoever with your forethought and.

Understand that the streamlined Ferrari is utmost Italian, designed to perfection with a concept of yellow which allows Denmark to breathe a sigh of relief...just as 004 pre-fabricated number plates which hide identities with no sanctioning on traffic and flow...Over...shorts..black and arch rivalry...I was here Italy is my home and 8000 died here...where are you now Mussolini...

1 GBH Michael Valentine USA 2023

1 ABH Mathew Simmons

Space, Time, Limits, RIP

Prose-Poem 7

Lisbon, 29.6.2020 @ 23.00 hours

Avoidance…True…Orange…fliers my love for him is for Daniel with Myers...Who is he? He is symphonies to my ears..hail as in conkers…country with hard…chestnut is grass unless it is shard…low is best with Vivienne's vixen…my friendly tortoises smiles gently carries on…E abundant glee…happy not sad…nice not nasty…French 4 on ride, light frisked with stationary in time with the Freud…Law of Lawns with topiary no disaster…close knit communities with no disassociation…lines of avenues with capers adorn bullring running with camembert galore… rolling papers waft in the air…French bull driving…charging…stand your ground…strong mighty hero muscle with strength…horns are for you piercing with cry…watch the derriere he may bill you charging full on the ridicule you know…who is he? Bull not bully…compromised in pound he never did charge unless told to now…shrieks of laughter humiliation of doubt…stripped from the waist is the matador oww…like the blue skirt of a dress of flowers up over the head when a giggle fest occurs…children inside whom had been cared for by her…some were outside with a boy of a J charging black bull went in circles that day…I…who is he?

A…attack with a matador…tame like a bull yes it was me..oh thats ok then no go…the dress it went higher with desire doubt loot…C..cheese say it…photograph say it…colour black…say it humiliate it send it right back…charging the bull at the gate of desire mini me watch the spear from the matador…roll of the mafia one late night don't you know…witch hunt of first when desire is not first…black with horns fast with high risk…matador heaven on the streets of camembert… voyeurs shout as they watch through the night blood thirsty herbivores' for calves all out fight… moo said the sexy one who actually are you? I had the earth move for two not he on the move…van…kitchen on the move of the free…tasty black bull an analogy for me who is he? I… intelligence gap..in the net the others ones come back…skills technique Dr you see jumping around did no one you see..I love him…for good my chief double clef…of musical score double bass clef on the one who did score naked…one on the chest the other no way the one on the chest he did it my way…the way with the ball on the heart mind with fee…this one is meticulous score on the toes of tiny white foot on the heel with tip toe..out of the captain of gene country slippers ladies mantle we spend all at parties…crystal clear glass in the water no way…went round with round lined up all wonky…willy said I all in chocolate no doubt racism it hurts when the lodge came out…Swordsman spindle yarn withered… Prose-Poem 7.5

Time went once upon a steed a fast cold…on the pea…of significance cusp with laughter fade with mohair…no laughter went through one then fell after…Avalanche…white…blue underneath of glacier slip softly gliding in soft when dipped into chocolate…strawberry too…raspberry pips got stuck in my tooth…salut…blind man with captain hand his stick is curly red…white on hand… Cap that Dostoyevsky said was analogy driven over the head…tumbling waters down the glacier heaven faster with faster with crashing barbarian…fire of the melt two…did he see into the water of blue ice cream…

bee bumble honey with Queen X ray swirling water I am here to stay who are you? I am V… victorious at last full of glamour glacier blue ice cool caps handsome with strong one…Penelope English is rose stallion to mention. F is red stop green is to yellow buttercup is all that we hold… gold on top with crystal break sprinkles harder in toe when we are thereafter…Mercedes said me E shrieked with delight I prefer Walnut Whip said the peace strategy tonight…wet is the kiss sticky on lips broke through a gate of a chariot with spear…Asparagus' No it is not with weight with green..meringue on a tooth with gold in between why do we do this…what do we bear? …..Spectacles on paw print and a lions liar…Den is four meal sleepy at tight…fit in the jungle with blue sky fluffy might…nicely is whoa with sheets of desire Noahs Ark float on top of a beard..all covered in froth on a warm winters night frightening disaster of titanic two fight… Big Heads…No all out of proportion balance intrigue we sought with the earth thing..Life is for Profession we are no…rear vision sense making implementation ear…recipe for St Galleons abeyance face nose…redeeming actor integrative foci…quality resilience with leadership of many men..all in a boat heading for Wales then…I did say red on the avenue of a redeemer future chemistry said a boiling hot cauldron…white snow sat their... sink… tap washer… sank in the fish of gold on at last into full view as my memory did fade with fushia delicate fancies a shepherds delight…chestnut brown hair with a street of no after…when the imbo had limbo with sadder…entrepreneurial style chic I lose my hair now cake tier with me loose the one whom you dye for all grey with wrinkly hands nails with skin all pink sun baked…raindrops when melt of cupped dreams time…flower open tulips beserk…contrasting colour…schemes majestically ride side saddle we go all in together pink lilac sew…in gusset with room for a view…all in headlines of naked French more…Toulouse…too fat…too ugly…raid fast in here quick place the ticker with clock fear…white window is an angel did fear…when picks the wrong one all in together when I heard song to the black hair …Shakesperes pardoner Chaucer did say in from the light of cabin mans play Turnip…said he appease on the laughter wired pasta all spirals with twist Neapolitan blob now…tomato mushroom parmesan…French Angleterre with egg on to moo…butter garlic said English French Maid I will have one who will need to be made…in to process red white blue starts in gold one with trumps tower…no that hurts…heels..majestically flowing river of bare naked lad with no underwear…willy dot laughter in true all time together in Timbuctoo with the Spanish Lair…Latino impetus Messi all over his hair pasta that day UEFA it said brush saddle with whip on top of mountain... Walmart in full stop...two quick step time...winter slippper foot toes of sleep tight white tips toes...arms round waist of French Ball not faster car on Italian mere with fast one shot in hole of life some said...visor...white at the peak swing the lead...no doubt tweed on the trew of sweater stout 4 then 2 with 007...P is for Pierece steely no cool true grey on forecourt of gas in we no...fez Turkish pink squash translucent bedstead...Broom witch goblin tire again...all gone..Tom is said heart strings as they jump up down...stairs French Knights raisins actually love for Meg into hope for blushed cheeks red passion at night with tweed rode stallion that night well...yes...it is me pail not black as a ghost...impetus is charges fool hardy on toast...who is he?

Tea leaves for good very disaster...glass diamond gold pieces all over the floor crystal clear water like opaque on cut saw, silver topped translucent turned upside down...sharp risk managed.. high what is this? Elegance fuelled passion lines of award...winning fierce silver pronged fork with one more circle..vertical contrast...Passionate...Devoted to living epitomises sun shark with a driver with no bias...non-disclosure with no language of remittance...beaches, treble Sangrada of B, ..Tagas pont du chao..Cartaxio..polychromatic colour harmonies..primary triangles with indices like 45 ers....49ers..achieve visual balance objects appear smaller on the inside biasness...static dynamic emotional shades...of disrespect with runny noses a pain...repetition continuous space challenges the bull..on the skin of colour with writings mans hand...Ponge he did say on the illusion of power elitism is fast on the sharp shard of the glass...Metaphorically in the city with disillusionment...we all live together in Noahs ark instead...dominance of seed genetically after tapering hilltop landscape of entering...into the city from the border with no law... in through the tunnel of language no stout...high impact bright colour after...a symmetrical line with asymmetrical lawn using a compass, angled with sea...shell on the turtle head all popped out...small tiny feet with big toes all run...guinea pig with piglet roo with the pocket slight deep power turning on the roof of the monument...Liberty...Jesus..Francis Drake...still all black white not for the stake....holders pensions in AXA you know...restaurant on top on the avenue now sow...seeds of the wheat...barley with blind...stealth is the bomber with the runners behind... flat fast healthy quick tasty with bold...white winter warmers with cheese triangles you know... crackers behind her giraffe in the past jeans are for gene white haired man with crack of delight... Bourbons with rower soars with the men saddlebacks more likely when the henchman did send... two in the view of the Blackmans delight....how do we now describe for children on fight...I am black...I am white...I am me?

Who is this? M mother...warm cuddly tortoise...fast zooming driver...dawdling talker...right wing pro lifer...motivated sportier with healthy fit lifestyle...we did not like her...fit me in behind her so I can take over..I can have a cake stall...referees temptation is to pick a fight...twist turn... piano colonial style on the tip of the finger bight red fish a yellow ended plan...priority order on the giant with beanstalk..yes it is Lancelot with his Brown capability...architect drawings...carver we know intricate religious persecution viola decoration in homes…tiny white flowers cultivated by moans…French Fringes not festivals draped muslin covered walls the emperor of France at Malmaison Les Roses a five fingered posy with northumb on the past…wheres the tradition for one for all whence last…Biedermeier Furnishings go mad…Hitler is gone now the gas chamber in hand…torture…racism…Black fingers and toes..decollate decoupage with a acquisitions genteel art on design as the other ones feel…balls…tennis with net…shuttlecock with ping in pong with the sweat…Sweet Pea is the gold with English all array…my stealth bomber came whooshing my way..out of the front gate came the laser beam says go away from the village that I are up…Transitional linear forms on the tree of rods all behind them with orchids and me… Lilies, Freesias busy whoops said the Witch as she blew it away…Will…Testament…now what do we do…this is mine now move over now move…get away from the past the drivers are here… busy like the Bee in your ear…the hindsight…gold…platinum…diamond on fire..in the loins of the babies desire to be born into Montessori…crawling the floor of the pyrotechnic on board…lovers in the wake of before..hand on the stand of the purple from end…alloys…brakes…with the yarrow on gold…repetitious dreamboat of the one we did know…help said the same for emergency led…999 said the English the Americans said…we are for you awe are for here are for a fee for an exhibition in him…we said it is for him the one whom did say we like all the astronauts the ones whose birthday was never missed…the French girl whom S did say he…she loves all flowers with plants here to stay…stay here for me please I can hear your in no doubt I want you to be with me now please here me out…I am the one who can change your damn life…please do not worry I want you all out..I do not remain untrue to the end…I do not have a turn of the fingers of no doubt…I am black you know under the float…ice cream but not crackers is the Fishermans all flight now my inside out is not in flight..sardines on an increment salary is too resources are employment all in the queue…add to the question for us to believe that the gorgeous señorita is valid only for a king…princess marry me said one to another go in between the clothes and pull out another…no I said I cannot do this again so I went to the shops and saw her again…a higher in sight on the glasses of spring one baby boy happened once lingering…

Time and Space for the Matador of the Toros thank you my friend for my fight today, I thank you before for being my friend…..my spears do not hurt your thick skin, your rare blood group allows no one in….just my spears, my thick skin is now for you, I dance no more truance, I dance no more….lead the dance of the Merriman's dance….

Prose Poem 7.5.5:Time and Space…London…23 hour 30.6.2020

Absolution…Solution…carries the figure on the cusp of grandeur things to come…absolute…O… divide intervention of the stars for a pension…Navy Blue with deep dark mysterious nights of white satin with no numerous pipe…rods of evil essential at last evangelical mind ship for the four post…sensible shoes of desire not remorseless is the purpose for the whore of the curse…

purse strings of heart with mind of the past all together now in a blast from the past...9 is the one whom collar up with fear of white eyed lunatic kamikaze severe...What is this? Four Fingered salute... sauteed onions making you cry droplets running down with no dry eye...red rings round the wide eyed beauty...eyebrows tighter with black on beauty...Grey...torpedo shaped creeper fast like Mercedes with Benz like that....rod of lightening space of no fear...tall gangly long thing looking driving with ear...shout out loud why don't you have no concept dear...equation of maths for Pythagoras theorem dirty great hole in the earth's ozone sucking the oxygen from our home...Peas...Cabbage...honeysuckle in the concept of space is the one who is in bed not whom eats cake...two tiered sponge with par fours on top macaroons in pink with cream on the swirling myriad no concentric circles deep is the hole velocity shower speed...suspension in air oscillates with no spout...teapot trigonometric with the recall we are...shining of time like a chimpanzee living in harmonious superimposed conditioning with row...A is for apple with Lloyd in the wings jealousy beckons...turn the fingers of the in-cellular forces...vectors with indices...to establish gene pool...jean are for genes with no doubt on the language A is to B or not two Bee that is our naked question...strings of the fire helixed fee. Circumnavigating sight wind with sound movement is intercellular compound carbon with hydrogenated water of emitter phenomenon of Foucault's P is for pendulum...peas is for A with one on the way I did it for him or for her with no way right for the low of pro on the L...tiny white toes with gene pool of hell...red are the horns when the shadow of sin came all together when the little one said...travelling latitudinal with no constant of sphere rotating the circle of no angles...Rain curvatures monuments statues of doubt all in New Orleans when the swampy went out...of the tree of life when bondage went in ties on the hands of the cabinmans friend...crucifixion with Lady of Blue..City we love the Mayo on the Leadership front par...Rsin ok is not on the bar vector shot helix with constant support slightly mainstream. With a picture of a corpse...

Prose-Poem 8: Short

Tangents are off on one at the gate if the garden Heather with Phoenix fire ball with the Lakers... string with a Tan burnt Orange did smile...Abaci with translation a myriad of truth chairing his time with the corporate you know...red was the seat round the table 12 is the foot with the ring on you see...stopped after putting up for three you see shops all ISA with Giuseppe front squares... cubes are sugar of the sticky wet swears...sweating one night with tummy gummy whisk plight... neither of us are for sleep tight. Golden Ratios rations in flight big round tummy with cylinder front flight...parachutes of laughter when the bog one did say dropping the load with the strings in the sway...of the turban...scarf all bright...secular nutrition is healthy alright...with no casting out nines with the one in the hole...birdie at me with a shark on the load...Frenchman in another all corrosion on occasion...birthday galore with crusts of the laden...voices I say Voice with Voiced literacy with Mabel horses with St John on streets of the Lowry...Sing Hosanna...we are for him who is? God...god...yes told I say...we are for him when the forecourt displays half a mile from the red with the dew...on the Trafford entrance all with scarves...I do not want one I prefer a boxed tie to ribbon onto them...parking with cars in literally rows I am for JK Rowley with all the stinky toes...feet are for walking with running if you dare smelly in those socks if you tear the underwear...a whiff of the belly button on a steaming mans no slip might...

Prose Poem 9 : Meet me for Dinner on a diet now C..man pulled his socks up came out in Stockport with he...Who is he? Tall, Dark, Handsome with leg and ball...dark hunky stranger left all for more...hurray they all shouted as I passioned with full height strong, controlled French glee was passionate one night...bag check went un noticed on the night of the stars wax work of knowledge when he went beserk..shooting at all with left then with right...studs on the bedsted were Rubins hold tight...Arrivederci..in quarter of room conceptualised space with a four fingered rule cities with exponential decay rack with ruin on the streets of the chaos we are not for Chernobyl or anything because we are boring buffoons with big bottoms of beer...swilling it round the toothless appear..pear is the shape or round with a phew...O is for Obesity which is a great big no...no for the heart..no for the veins..no for the finger tips if white all remains... to say you are very held back by the tide..it is not turning for Zeldas behind...berries are rasp on the corner of shard when we are together I feel the same way can you please elaborate by far...Demaru...stand...elimination...male...this is me? Female infanticide...selective gene pool of big blue eyes football player with model inside...accountant you know with her cessation of doubt birth mother hero to avoid all out...practice...practice...cruel..honour of Asok Mitra 2001 census of hope when the family thought they had won...

Prose Poem 10

Technological Punjab First Lady Menon tragic note on their income young girls dowry reserve 1... test the girls assets tragic dote own feet resist the husbands nurses retreat...all for the respect of the Sikh turban here Manchester we love you all in the French ear...married you know right from the village...reputation of excellence diplomats cursed on the garage of pothole...Supernovae a crucial uncertainty genetically thrown...Chandrasekhar limit alternative theories scenario's Bob from the bomb of the Lowry that night the shell the hurt with the finger tips all bright... microphone all on with citizen he said..pulsars of white mass on the night. Motivators learn on the determinants explosions of circular motion with no action within...toilet roll hanging from lady A for a win...detonation uncertainty...exploding WD with we are the go...fortunes we lingered... detonation of galaxies with supernova..mass limits of 11 only with navy with shield...clustering anomalies with radial velocities redshift with blue shift then inside term off with his...head, yes, it is not me...I am female...this is the fast one which makes' us all smile...cos there is only one Frenchman all covered in mail red luminosity which heart bats to sale...marmalade magnum when topped with sprinkles binary coding with 11001 add them all up then hide the trump card... evidence from stars that we are not alone which makes sense...Galaxies solar metal abundance with one in the oven...baked for the hillside with a line with a hook on...no minos in here just the ones who do bite...piranhas with me please do right yarrow kite...rhombus perpendicular one sided running...long legged button gliding loves in...formation of enemy introverted closedown... progress of blackholes...E is for energy with large stubby toes...hairy on one foot with studs flash with wax living pose...right wing extremism with hard hats jump...d...f stopwatch a fortune goose on the tree...turkey with a sprout is not much to find...short nailed long c with golden long hair... nacho is growing on me as a star someone bought one with names in by far...do not mine the one in the sky hanging in suspension if you take from it might die.cannot replenish the stocks that we find...diamonds are not thereabout we never mind..Large Hadron Collider the one similarly... mad scientists in Geneva with Higgs Boson on the run Quarks are too big with the little ones too far..I do not want one said the Frenchman who said...I love Amanda...the leggy one said, I love her too cos she said...I like danger said the impact statement precautionary principles on the explosive lab tale...watch what your doing when you learn chemistry...you might blow your altogether with NEPA injunction...plaintiffs abundant when we turn out the light when come back next morning the damn place is alight the chard crumbled mess was on the kitchen floor nearly as bad as the Michelin door...favourites here are the ones in the know...loving their Messi on the hair of gabour...golden the foot of the Frenchman's roar..lion in thunder of water for more... fire in the heart...passion in the loins we went together for all fours for the boy...the one with the Fred...the goldfish the fight...the kiss with the crimpled with the toppers once more...gras..with foie yes please it is he...never again did I ask for a fee...

Time and Space with Money 9.2.2021

And...here is another we are shot from fame one night...when we saw the shaw redemptions fight we had someone in all to fear and when we had safaris ear, they said that you can be what you want and that they hold no grudge right up...stand in no we want one show who is the one is full fame show it's the one from the USA who was with her in the 80s play who stayed with her when she was bad and when the bonze came out for bad..we want her to be the one who gets the one of all her efforts that led...onto the Frenchman behind of power that clicked on the floor of the language and power...the shower of gifts that then pursued the language of love can not be removed...Batman said Hi from the bedsted of doubt when the E followed up she heard him shout...it was not me from the tiffin lady who heard the muffins shout for glee the Michelin in bed one night jumped up out of the shepherds delight...

Afterword

DiamondMan
BlackMan
WhiteMan
SilverMan
GoldenPaws
LucyPrice
DemiWave
Disassociated

, that was the deleted… the one who got away is now back, the thine knee is The Beast Fable for Cantona, Salah and Physics Football, the Messi, Kane and Ronaldo can only hope that their own PR machines run through this twinkle in the next books shirt, centrifugal spirals never saw anything like it, strippers, love grams and a swoon from a heroized actress, well this is the Amen capital city of Vatican, the Church of England, Catholicism, Muslim communities everywhere …. אוה גולאידה םירמ האיבנה רובע רוא לע תוריהבב חרוז ןכא חריה ,דחא לפא הליל לש היחה תדגאב םימלסומה לכמ ימלסומל תירבע הזורפה תריש ,ירבע תוצלוחה ,ילש םה םייפגמה ,רחבנה ינא ,ינא ,איבנה הדוהי ןודא ירמ איבנה ןודא אוה ךורב שודקה ,2-2 ואב םיעורה ,חריה חורה לליימ 1-1 ,דמחומ איבנה לש ורבקב רבק ירצמה...בוצע ךכ לכ התא המל ,האיבנה ירמ ,זא..ילש איה תרושקתה ,ילש רמוא הז ןכ ,אוה רמוא...ינא ,אל..םירמואש המ הז ןואיזומב בבוחבו הקזח המוריע ,ההובג הנוטנקה ,רתויו רתוי רהמ הבשנ רחא...אוה אל ףא רחא אוה קזח ליבשב רחא ,םע פרצוף כתום של אוסן.........celebrating their stay of execution, these prayers were written for valid, legitimate Sundays and Wednesdays in the Church Prayer book with stigma like you would never know, anyway….this is God, who is she, why is the cloud heavy with precipitation, humidity high everywhere… אוה קזח ילירויו ריתחו רידא ,הפנים תוכתומה לש ןוסא בלונדיני פחות... תלוכיה ,ךסכה ,טרופסה ,םירוענה יכרב לע תבשוי איהש תונמוימה תייח ...םירוענ לש ןרתנספל רתויו רוזעל תוחפ לגוסמ הטכנית ,ןורשכ ,ןוימד....

תיאר...יניטלפ ינא ,קקחצמו....אוה רמוא םיהולא ינא ,א"פיפ רועמ םילוגע ,א"פוא לש םילוגע רוע ,םירודכ ?דוע המו העיגרמש וז ,תחאה םיקחשמה תויוכז ..תרפוסה איה תינידנולב אל איה ,ךלש טניבקה לש וניעב רואה תא תיאר...?ךתוא ...תויהל ךירצש הז אוה הלפ אוהש הז ,דחא קירוי לש ער לזמב ונחנא ,ץצומ לדוגא סלפל םימיה תוכירא דוק תא תירסומ ,ןדועמ דואמ דואמה ודלאנור ונאיטסירכו ןכוסה תא בזע המבל סנכנ...סטמה....הלאמש המבל סנכנ ,אל רמוא ינא ,אל ...אל איהו אוה ,איה םג... יתרכה אל םס תבטה ךל םלשת ,םאולמב םייחה תא היח ,תוצנצנ תוהולא ,תוצנצנ תוהולא אל המלענ םע םישאר אלא קחשמ םילימ בחול, ואז לא נחתה האפקיליצה של כל האפקיליציות למדודים

Date 24 August 2022

Prayers for Todays Service

לש ןרתנספל רתויו רוזעל תוחפ לגוסמ ...תוחפ ינידנולב ןוסא לש תומותכה םינפה ,רידא ךיתחו ילירי וקזח אוה
....ןוימד ,ןורשכ ,תינכטה תלוכיה ,ףסכה ,טרופסה ,םירוענה יכרב לע תבשוי איהש תונמוימה תייח ...םירוענ

...יניטלפ ינא ,קקחצמו...אוה רמוא םיהולא ינא ,א"פיפ רועמ םילוגע ,א"פוא לש םילוגע רוע ,םירודכ ?דוע המו
,תחאה הזחמה תויוכז ..תרפוסה איה תינידנולב אל איה ,ךלש טניבקה לש וניעב רואה תא תיאר...?ךתוא תיאר
הלפ אוהש הז ,דחא קירוי לש ער לזמב ונחנא ,ץצומ לדוגא סלפל םימיה תוכירא דוק תא תירסומ העיגרמש וז
ונאיטסירכו ןכוסה תא בזע המבל סנכנ...סטמה....הלאמש המבל סנכנ ,אל רמוא ינא ,אל...תויהל ךירצש הז אוה
אל סמ תבטה ךל ומלשת ,םאולמב םייחה תא היח ,תצצונ תוהולא ,תצנצנ תוהולא ,ןדועמ דואמ דואמה ודלאנור
לכ לש היצקילפאה התחנ אל זאו ,לוחב םילימ קחשמ אלא םישאר םע המלענ אל ...איהו אוה ,איה םג... יתרכה
םע קר אל רוחש עזעוזמ ,עבט .ולש יפוק ,ומש יפוק ,דדומה לש רוחשה ןדאל ןב המאסוא ,םידודמל תויצקילפאה
,ירמל תויפיפ ברח לע הקזוחב תרעוב תוריחה םע ,םיישפוחה ץראב התיבה תורזוח תורפ ,םיזיע ,תנמש ,בלח
ישנא קחשמ ,הדוק-לא לש תטלחומ הקיחמב תטלחומ הגיפסו תוכבל ךתכ ,םדוקה קחשמהמ היצקלס ,טסיסא
דירדמ לאיר ,דירדמ לאיר ,רבע םידחואמ םיידוהיה םימשה ,רבעב קחישש ודלאנור םע םיקסעה שיא...םיקסעה
...ונלש הספוקה לע םירמושו םיבשוי םה....רתוי הבוטה הצובקה םה ודלאנור רמא ,תפרצ...לאידנומב דרפס תרחבנו
..הארת ,ונלש תיבה תורעמב ןנקמ ,ונלש תיבה תורעמב ןנקמ .התל התיבה םירזוח םישיבכע...םש איהש ,םש איהש
ןכ ,ןכבו ,אל ןוטיו יאול םג ,אל...אל ינא...ונלש קחשמה איה הקיסיפ..קוחרה ץעה הלעמב אל אוה אוה ימ בישקת
יאולו םיגבטיק ,חאלסל...גבטיק לש םירות לש םימרז ,םיגבטיק אל. אל ,קירא..חאלס דמחומ תרמא ,דחא םהל שי
ןוטיו...c'est La Vie...C'est יו הל...

Eucharistic Prayers for Todays Service for those from St Lukes our Parent Companies, the Lords Prayer, The Shepherdess of our Lady of Mary, Jesu of our night, the Lord is Almighty, is for our Night

Almighty Jesu of our Lord, for Almighty God of Love, Peace, Global Chariots of Gold, Business of Peace, Love, Joy, Jerusalem, Lord of Highest Might, Lord of Power, Lord of Control of those Sinners whom do not Control, Lord of Jerusalem, the Sinners .... ,חוכ ,תודידב לש םיגבטיקה
םיטבמה ,הטילשה ,עויסה לכ לש חישמה בהזה יפגמ לש חאלס דמחומ ,הרידא הנידע קרב תכמו תונבשחתה
וצר םלוכש המ תישע ..בוט תישע אל ,הנוטנק ,רמא יתדספה ...יניטלפ רמא תושונאה לכ לש חאלסה ,תונחלושהו
,ירזכא ,קידצ תוחפ ,ומוה היהת אל םלועל ,ישונאה ןימה תישאר אל ...הלעתו הנוטנק רס לע לצנתת ,השעתש
הרבחב ךלש םוקמה ,הרבחב ךלש םוקמה ב יתועמשמ אל רשאמ תוחפ היהת לבא תוגהנתהמ תוחפו דמחנ אל
ןירפצ רדנסכלא לשו ונלש אל ,ךלש ,יניטאלפ ךלש הטילשה ,ךלש IBC-ה ...עורה לכ ישרוש ,עורה לכ ישרוש
הטילשה בחלום לש לכ אדם.......wet their heads of Baptism of none control in later life, the ones who do bad for others, can control the incumbent, of no business, those that are not chosen, those that cry, take time to muster their own courage to live, once more, those who are in heartache, those that are in time bound subversiveness

Sin of Time-bound eucharistic prayer is time folding in half on the minuet of ear, the bad in our countries, which we row for, the bad in our countries we pray for today, the bad in our children we banish today, the bad of ourselves we ban today, the bad of ourselves we ban from our fathers, mothers, children, we pray for our Doctors, Nurses, Medical Practitioners for the desire to hurt others to be moved away from our desires, הקירזה לש תוליעיהו הטילשה ,חוכה ןמז אוה ןמדידמ לש ןמזה, סולחב עוגפל ןמדידמ לש תונוצרהמ הארנכ דליהו הארנכ תרבגה ,הצונה שיאל עויס ,הטילשה לש תויחצנה תוצירה רפסמ הצלוחה לש בצקה ,בצקה לע הנושארל רביד יניטלפו הלילה 1-4..וקית הגישה תפרצ ,חצנל ,םדא לכ לש הלעמל לכתסמ אלו םינקחשה רובע ידמ םדקומ סילאפ השוע ,רודכה ליבשב ידמ ריהמ םימעפל ,הנוטנק לש 9 םאו התא רבדמ םע we are at one with those who hurt, cherish our loved ones, we are at one, we are at one with making better, making feel good, making those responsible be responsible, not reversing someone's life long desire to succeed הפידעה ילש רועישב ךלש תירבעב איה דומלל ,רנחל, חנאנ יניטלפ....המצע ינפב הטחממה אל תחפטמה לענה ,םיבקעה...הטחממהו המשנה תא ןזאל ,שפנה תא ןזאל לגרודכה קחשמב לבא ,תיתרבח יארחא תויהל ,ירטינמוה עויס תחטבא לש חוגיאמ קלח תויהל םילוכי ונלוכ ,טבמ התאש ינפל....קחשת טושפו תויראה לע אל ךלש הוואגה תא עלבת....קחשמה תא קחשל רחא רבד לכ ינפל ,הז הז לבא תוארהל לוכי התא זאו ,םיקסע תושעל לוכי התא זא ,קחשמ והשמש ינפל ,התא ימ ,תוארהל הצור התא ימ ...קסע ינפל העפוה ,קוש ינפל טרופס ,רצומ ינפל קחשמ הז...רמא יניטלפ...קחשלו תויהל בייח התא ,רבד לכ ינפל ...הז תא השעו אצ ,היידיד...ונלוכל ןת ,וישכע

Eucharistic Prayers for St Luke's parent those in the Parishes everywhere, especially those in Cheshire Today who parent our newest member of our Prayers are contemporary through the Vicar, not through the baptism, not through the Marriage, not through the forgiveness of others ידי לע תחא םעפ ןמוס לודגה קחשמה ,רחא אלו יליבשב היהת ,רחא לש ויתועורזב ,רחא לש ויתועורזב

אוה ,אוה אוה ,ולש ברעה תחוראל רישל ,ולש ברעה תחוראל רישל ,הנוטנק לש םירישה ןויליגו א"פיפה יניטלפה ןדלוג ביבסמ בהז ןיא ,אל ןיידע אל....E םירצמ איה םירצמ ןיא ,E ירצמה אוה חלאס.....סדמיכרא ץע אוה ,אוה ,אוה שפיט דועו םיבצמ ,םירנא'ז...םלועב טלוש תפתושמה תוליעיה ןויליג ןוזיא המרל הרטמב טסיסא לש חאלס לע םילבומ ונחנא..רוטטקידל אל ,אל ,וליבשב תויהל םילוכי ונחנא םאה...אוה םאה ו בל ,קזח חומ..אוה רוטטקידה סוריח יבצמב הרוטטקיד אלל...היטרקוטוא ,ןפוד תאצוי הלבוהל ןפוד יאצוי םידעצ םידחוימ םיעצמאב ,היטרקומדה ...ונתוכמסל םינתיא ראשיהל ונחנא לבא...תולובג ןיא

Forgiveness, is foreboding in the desire to achieve the baptism of time bound, efficiencies of eucharistic being, of time abound less than desires of the fortitudes of sin, forgiveness is the route to salvation, the route of finding all evil is done, הסליחה לנביאה מרי איה לכף ורגלו האחרת לש ,םהב ןיינעתמ דואמ האופרה עוצקמ ,א"פיפ לש םיגבטיק רובע א"פואב םויה סיניטלפ ןזואו לאמש הנוטנק ,חאלס .....יולימה ירמוח לכמ םיבוהאה הליפוס'גו תוקעמ ,םייחה לש תודידבהו יזוחה ךרעה תא ולביקש ולא איה ,לשמל ןיס

רעונו יסקופא ףרש ,םיעוגפה ייחו תיטננימודל הקרבה....חורזל הלש רהוזה לכ לע ןאכ תטלוש ה'צאסרו הלטנוד ....תיזיפ תומילאו יטסימרופנוק אל שוקשק ,הטאיד ,תוללעתהב סומע ,רפוסמ אל

....ןאכ ורצונ ,ורצונ ילש םיינרופיצה ,יתימא דדוב קדצ הצור היה אוה ,ידכ םויה ומצע םע אוה ,ןאכ אל ןיידע הנוטנק .. .םילעבה ,ואב םה ובש םוקמהמ ל"וחב םהינש...ןאכ וישכע ןודנול התייה ,זירפ

...םוריעו תודידב ,תוללעתה ,החילס

,תיתימא תואירבל החילס ,םירנא'זהו הגצהה תומישר םיינוציחה תוארטאיתה ,ןאכ אל םג יובא ,בוש....טשפומ לכש המ תא קפסל ,םהינש ל תואירב קפסל ןוזיא ,אל...עורה לש תימינפה השודקל הליחמו תיתימא היווהל החילס רומשל ךירצ דחא ,רומשל ישפוח תויהלו רשואמ.......the evil of denouncing your saviour of life,now here we come out of religion out of the baptism of fire…can we thoroughly come out of Muslim rule is all out with you now, your life becomes you now, can we now come out of all Hebrew, out of all Christianity led salvation…yes, become nomadic and reign supreme…it is what Cantona meant…lead by example and truly know who you are….the two of marriage salvation, the two of partnership salvation of non-marriage then this is solved through societal bias of finding hope, solace in the salvation of truth, … הנוטנקל וסנכיה....הנוטנקל תזעונ תרהוז העושי לאנושות לגרל ימין לש םע ,תובישיה רדח ןחלוש םג םע.....רתויב בוטכ רכומה..יסמ הז ,ןכ...בהזה ילענ לש ודלאנור ,חלאס...תומולחה זוזל ,רבדל וילגרל ןתנ אוהו וקספ םישנועה ,בר ןמזל אל ...יתרושקת געלו םייתרושקת םירוסיי ,יתרושקת רושיב םיילגרה םע זז ,ןוילע ףוג גלפ ךתיא אלו .םיילגרה םע זז ,יניטלפ לש תורעהה תחא ,הובג אוהש תורמל זירז תויהלו ,תושעל לוכי ראופמה יסמש היטהה תא ןיבמ התאש אדוו ,תושעל תולוכי ךלש םיילגרה תופכש תועונתב זכרתהו לכ ריהמ אל אוה ,רתוי םירצק ולש...רבדה ותוא אל אוה חלאס...רייצל הלוכי ולש םיפונמהו תולגלגה לש הקיזיפה לעמ זאו ביואה םע הסכמו ומוקימ תא הווסמ אוה ינקמח ץיצפמ ומכ...תוזירזה תובנגתה תא רוקחל ךירצ ,זא..ךכ לש ןטקה i-ה...i-הו רנידרוא-הרטסקאה ,ןגלבה תא בזע בלשל סנכיה..םלועב בוטה ןקחשה אוה יסמ לנויל. .שארל ונחנא ?...הז ימ לש יולת הז םאה....קסעו קוש ,םירצומ ....םולש...ןאכ ונלש החטבאה תייגטרטסאב הללכהה אוה ,בוט אוה...סנכנ ודלאנור...םמה דיקפו הזוחה...ןתמו אשמה תא בזע בלשל סנכנ...דבוע הז...ןכ הזש םיבשוח ראופמ אוהו רתוי בוט.....

....ותחפשמב...םדא לכ לש תונורכיזל םאתהב אלו חצנמ אל ,בוהז אל...תויהלמ תעכ קלוסמ ודלאנור ונאיטסירכ so mankind is good to you said Platini, no he is bias…he is Judas he is Maradona….he is Archimedes Tree…whatever you want to say, call it…he is not Judas, Cantona and some arguments, some situations some non-secured states, some desecurities with actors qualified or not take place in our game with those who no no bounds, those nuances from nuances that…..that your own-selves are vanished from the kingdom of god, the kingdom of non-sin, the kingdom of saving others, the kingdom of saving life, just like the men, women, children even that hope their hands, mind, inner kingdom of knowledge can remember quickly their own selves before they think to big about their ownselves here….never to achieve or think they were good enough…to see it as a fortitude of sin, as even life changers, saviours can tempt fate, for late nights with someone else in their arms…so, when you think that the bed time is even it isn't…. the ones who stay out, play forwards and play well are now in situ…

When this happens the saviour, Lord Jesu, comes from the hope of the tree, at Christmas Time, New Year Time, Pentecost Time to save us all from Salvating Arms that hold someone else, when they should not be together, when we decide in society that we cannot go forward in the truth of the heart, the break of the chastity of truth of mankind

Amen, Peace to All Men, Women, Children who have felt in this way

2nd Prayer

The feeling of belonging, the power of the truth, the forgiveness of strength inside the eucharistic prayer of godly being, the ones whom I despise, should not even be, they can suffer in their own silence of truth, do not allow them to be with you in your own heads, the ones who suffer from the mental illness of truth that they are not good enough, that they are not willing to take part in society for wanting more, not less of the business take in the local deed hand

This is not jealousy, but hard-earned inequality driven, no one listens when they come back to allow prophecy against the black man, not with the black face, but the one with toil, strife, being of

lesser-dom, poor with no money the justification of others is no bound of time

The demonstrous toil, of hands that catch, scratch, with widened grin, the ones who rest in peace of all men, the ones who tell us far to go, the ones who we see are foreboding of love, thanks be to God, tell the truth next time, tell the truth next time

Those who demand the financial gain for true demanded riches of envy once again, the crowns of thorns with wingspan of fate, the pelican bringing the look at the gate, thanks be to godly man of hope, justice, the rope we can hang, the boiler of contemporariness, the bunny of contemporariness hold me to thine heart of joy, thine heart of giving, with contemporary joy, thanks be to god

3rd Prayer

Saviour of all wonderous man, love thine light of wondrous hand, love thine wondrous hand to be, with diamond shining into glee, the glee it turns the mighty jesu, from thine hand of wondrous Mary, to thine light, of toil, not strife to the Prophet Joseph in Muslims man, Muslims man is wondrous too the saviour light of Prophet too, Mohammed is thine light of thee, forgave the football in commonwealth see, the one whose boots shine ever so bright, the one whose diamond is Ronaldo light, but most of all the Cantonas' see, the one who has the very big knee

Oh, Jesu of thine might, the one who has the centuries light, the centuries light is presidents day the UEFA vulnerability that day, we are the prophet of Jesu, the Marys hope of little ones too, the ones who seek the saviours day are little sinners, very much that way

Atrocity in thine hand of two, hid the sinners all for you, the ones who have the very big hand, are the ones who shake the mightyman from the trees, the catapult, the ones who we share the ones whose footfall, is to share, the mightyman of saviours feet, the mightyman of galore retreat of sin, of saviour of all to be the forgiveness past is for celebrations knee, for the celebration of the mighty wondrous of all gods, the one who sees, the one who makes, the one who does not chat at the gate of sinning in the life of being, the one whose moral standing is just being, in the life of one in between the one whose saviour is not foreseeing on the rights of passage to the great big wondrous heaven are you, waiting for the saviour of the Angels stand near the oh, my god, the blaspheming child of godly prince to lift me higher in the thinks of intelligence spree of all mankind the saviour of wondrous being is all mine, Amen

13 line stanza of three
Paraboles are very inter
esting...They compare like for like
Bottoms in the Shower, And I
BP, IBC compara
tive ratio of shots on tar
get...Love Amanda-Jane, Kiss, Kiss
Who is E? Where is E? You Are?
How are you?Very Well Thank You,
Madame, Madame, Mademoiselle
Ou est pants, pour le derriere
Le Bottom, Le Bottom, try for
Celebration, Celebration1
Ducasse Chocolatier Ducasse

Prose Poem

God of War

Foreverman, Mighman of Godly IBP, IBC is Platini O'er GOD of War, in Blue we stand in Blue we Siren, in Blue we are the tasteful few, we gentlemanly sit, we gentlemanly stand we gentlemanly take our cap in our hand, we gentlemanly with lady remove from the dust, o'er GOD it is him the one with the must, no more GODly King to Platini Cantona, I am the Author and you are by far, I am the Author of your due, of your throne and I am you, I am not the misgiven, the cheating and the lies, I am not for the lesbian who was never left behind, I am not for you all in the stands on that night, I am for forgiveness on the pitch full of fright, 'you leave mighman alone with your chant, he cant hear when he plays he had his life in his hand, he did not let go, leave Mighman alone, he is doth thine man o'er War he cant win… kiss Mighman to sleep tonight, kiss Mighman in the stand to see, the whole of the Acorn is there you cant be, Mighman Platini, this is Cantona, Mighman o'er War, even now, he walk past he breaketh my heart, my sobs can be heard from my dying heart, my dying heart on the mantle of fear, I do not care now I can eat what I fear, I doth liveth Mighman o'er War, Mighman of lost Tuxedo, is Mighman o'er War, Mighman he doth sit on thine knee, on thine table of feast in thine morn, he doth not want to know, he doth reign short on the lead, he doth breaketh thine heart thereafter again…..Platini he doth know? Platini he doth have dark sunglasses, he doth train for forgiveness on control of his senses, he doth control his own life, his own finance, his own retribution, his own horse, his own Ferrari, his own Tuxedo, his own Balls….He is Cantonas Foreverman, He is his Families Foreverman, He is not Gay, He is not Gay, this is writing Thespian try for, to try for explanation, to try for love…there is no love lost in thine heart, there is no love lost in thine heart, Platini is Mighman of someones heart besides his Family, Platini is Italy, Platini is Italy, Musolini is lost here, he is for another, who is GOD here? Who is GOD here? Ask the Millions..Ask the Millions..With no Catholicism there is no GOD, say some millions that stand in the stands, spend their cash to heroising about the Platini, the euphoric reactionary standpoints of Jewish Rogue, the lowest pointed euphoric reactionary utopia, from the dystopia land sell….we are not with you now Mussolini… we are not with you now Mussolini…we drive for GOD of War…We drive for GOD of War… now sit down…now sit down…leave Migh Mightyman alone….Leave my man alone, Leave his suit, his clothes and his life alone, I am the heroic entity of sun, the glasses of all were worn on that day and the brightest star of them all won, then who got the look back, the one who got the call back the one who removed all entity of ugliness that had overtone her life of marriage to another, became a laughing mock of the stars, became a laughing cow, became laughing mocking ugly wallflower, says not the one who got away…the ugly one, the ugly inside, out..the bullied one, the abducted son, the chastity of bounded excellence has not gone away, Platini he was for her, Platini he was for her, she is not ill, mental or even less than Gifted, Socially benefited through bullies, liars and cheats of her adopted life, existence of kind…UNICEF where are you now? In the window, with supporters be-now. Her mother is one of those abusers, those abusers of the kindest of those who make for themselves of abuse, the ones who became of love for themselves..it takes time to reattribute those who are not wanted..to make for others…to make for others….shot down for the new wife, shot down for the new wife…never in our time has someone been so bereft as her…..thine knee is a sound of retribution of thine knee….I where are you now? I where are you now? In a lift with glasses on..In a lift with glasses on…with a chaperone for you in case the glasses slip off your head and woah betide you see full eye....I can you see me now..the ugly one with fat in hand...please see me, I. I will tell you all about me...on that night you were bereft, in the rural Ferguson led, Ferguson lived right down the road, in the G with no foretold, the E he sits upon thine Es knee. I noticed your knee, it wasn't grazed on the fee, the Yugoslavia is in for me, picked at birth to lead the card to transfer in for the Cantona heart..all in red, all in blue, all in indigo, now I don't tell you, Platini is now absolute here in this Prose Poem, this does not mean he is dead, it does not mean he is dead...it means he is very much alive as Mighman, Foreverman and with love...he is strong of heart, mind with boots, in the Golden Salah with Flutes, not just yet....impatient one..the lines of story are all done, your father sits upon thine knee of strategy, lines upon thine UEFA, thine heart of fear is not here....through public apology is the line that was called for on an enemy line years ago historical reference.. no still. Which one? Which one? The big C the big C....he hath groaned the man of he... no apology no apology...he doth for the no apology..he doth jealous of no influence with Cantona...Cantona he doth reign, in thine strategy of Foot with Ball, forgotten reign of man of ages throned in English Countryside...throned for me in the English country throne..does this make you feel uncomfortable...does this make you feel uncomfortable....you doth reign in sequence forage..no is the answer..no is the answer..you are all not doth Kings of Ages... you have no mercy for thine throned aged King..as you are all not good enough...Salut.. Salut...Statues are not for you..Salut Salut...our trespass is not for the few..but the masses one the game so we can go back home again..to our excellence in our home...wake up wake up...we can not rejoice in Tesco..in Excellence..in Route 66 in rejoicing in past events... we are not for GoldenBoots? We are not for Golden Boots? Then let me ask you why you are not for excellence in our state? That you are for? Because we are not good enough.... Because we are not good enough....IBP, IBC comparative idiocracy, so we all laterally align to the dust bowl on the line....rejoice in fatism, rejoice in fatism..rejoice in the try for a de throned elite mother who was tried for de throning to allow others in the pool of life who do not deserve any other life than their own..why? Berefement, Berefement, Bullying at Birth, Adoption At Birth, No Mother in School, Inept ChildCare in the Pool with no Differentiated 1, With no differentiated .....no try observation failed on her to identify on that day...anyone who dared to in broad light...no counselling..no need, no writing need...do not dis respect and belittle me...no chance of those bullies who tried to de throne...I do not want threat again...

Oral Hexameter Dactylic, Sonnet, Parabole

Prose Dialogue x 2

Prose Verse x2

Prose Dialogue

Epigram

Oral Hexameter Dactylic
Who is E? Where is E?
Who are you, Where are you?
Warm is he, Cherish he
We are for Foot and Ball
We are For President

And finishing the Centuries.....

Platini he is Blue…that is a statement, from the Author, Amanda-Jane x
Platini he is faithful…like a dog he is I, he is I strong, faithful,
proud, monumental in IBC to touch control
Platini he wins hands up with cheer, hands down with bread, milk, parabolas in we are near

Platini he is Red..
Blue with Cold left for Dead
Mans of War, Mans of Feast, Mans of Everyday he is not East
He is isn't warm today at last, he isn't warm he is cold now fast
Cantona is he, in the cold of the morn, Cantona is he in the lie now fight

Cantona is the Liar says Platini all out, I do not know you says Platini no its pout
Cantona is Blue, Cantona is Red, Cantona is Stripy Turquoise on yer…head
3-2 to the nuance, bank starter to day, Jones in the pack on the burrow away
Ouch says the century, ouch says Platini, she's looking kinda gorgeous in the morn of the day

Prose Verse
Platini he is GOD to Cantona
Platini he is GOD to Millions
You are not GOD to anyone anymore
I am your mother and you will obey me now

Michel he is Man to Wife, he is Man to Wife
Platini is no Wife, is no Wife
Cantona is YES to Wife..y To BE
Platini is YES To Happiness of Wife..y To BE
UEFA are no to no ringed mother of two with Cantona To Be

Parabole

We are for happiness of our gold star..Cantona is Platini Ring From Afar….YES To the Author, she did not see, she broke her heart, Cantonas Knee, thine is the king of the IBP Control, IBC is the one that Platini he doth hold…YES To Thine Man o'er War. Technique Platini, Pele in that order..Cantona he cometh to war….Player of the Century he doth sit on thine knee of Author Today..He cometh here on thine knee of thine Author he fancies today, He cometh on time, he is not on time here, he has no Rolex, neither does she..thine Author is the sexy one…

Platini he doth sit on thine knee of thine Wife, thine support, thine life of thine life, Mighman he doth be Mighman, Mighman he doth be thine King of IBP, thine GOD o'er War, thine GOD o'er War. He doth sit on thine support of thine throne currently o'er GOD of War o'er GOD of War, thine fight is thine life, thine fight it doth shall be, thine Devine light of retribution, thine forgive thine sins of thine life, thine support in thine stand forgiveth their own sins of thine life, you thine GOD to Millions thine owe thine life to thee, no more worry, lack of control, lack of being with no just me, thine GOD o'er War to the Parabole

Foreverman, Mighman of Godly IBP, IBC is Platini O'er GOD of War, in Blue we stand in Blue we Siren, in Blue we are the tasteful few, we gentlemanly sit, we gentlemanly stand we gentlemanly take our cap in our hand, we gentlemanly with lady remove from the dust, o'er GOD it is him the one with the must, no more GODly King to Platini Cantona, I am the Author and you are by far, I am the Author of your due, of your throne and I am you, I am not the misgiven, the cheating and the lies, I am not for the lesbian who was never left behind, I am not for you all in the stands on that night, I am for forgiveness on the pitch full of fright, 'you leave mighman alone with your chant, he cant hear when he plays he had his life in his hand, he did not let go, leave Mighman alone, he is doth thine man o'er War he cant win…kiss Mighman to sleep tonight, kiss Mighman in the stand to see, the whole of the Acorn is there you cant be, Mighman Platini, this is Cantona, Mighman o'er War, even now, he walk past he breaketh my heart, my sobs can be heard from my dying heart, my dying heart on the mantle of fear, I do not care now I can eat what I fear, I doth liveth Mighman o'er War, Mighman of lost Tuxedo, is Mighman o'er War, Mighman he doth sit on thine knee, on thine table of feast in thine morn, he doth not want to know, he doth reign short on the lead, he doth breaketh thine heart thereafter again…..Platini he doth know? Platini he doth have dark sunglasses, he doth train for forgiveness on control of his senses, he doth control his own life, his own finance, his own retribution, his own horse, his own Ferrari, his own Tuxedo, his own Balls….

He is Cantonas Foreverman, He is his Families Foreverman, He is not Gay, He is not Gay, this is writing Thespian try for, to try for explanation, to try for love…there is no love lost in thine heart, there is no love lost in thine heart, Platini is Mighman of someones heart besides his Family, Platini is Italy, Platini is Italy, Musolini is lost here, he is for another, who is GOD here? Who is GOD here? Ask the Millions..Ask the Millions..With no Catholicism there is no GOD, say some millions that stand in the stands, spend their cash to heroising about the Platini, the euphoric reactionary standpoints of Jewish Rogue, the lowest pointed euphoric reactionary utopia, from the dystopia land sell….we are not with you now Mussolini…we are not with you now Mussolini…we drive for GOD of War… We drive for GOD of War…now sit down…now sit down…leave Migh Mightyman alone.

Leave my man alone, Leave his suit, his clothes and his life alone, I am the heroic entity of sun, the glasses of all were worn on that day and the brightest star of them all won, then who got the look back, the one who got the call back the one who removed all entity of ugliness that had overtone her life of marriage to another, became a laughing mock of the stars, became a laughing cow, became laughing mocking ugly wallflower, says not the one who got away…the ugly one, the ugly inside, out..the bullied one, the abducted son, the chastity of bounded excellence has not gone away, Platini he was for her, Platini he was for her, she is not ill, mental or even less than Gifted, Socially benefited through bullies, liars and cheats of her adopted life, existence of kind…UNICEF where are you now? In the window, with supporters be-now. Her mother is one of those abusers, those abusers of the kindest of those who make for themselves of abuse, the ones who became of love for themselves..it takes time to reattribute those who are not wanted..to make for others…to make for others….shot down for the new wife, shot down for the new wife…never in our time has someone been so bereft as her…..thine knee is a sound of retribution of thine knee….I where are you now? I where are you now? In a lift with glasses on..In a lift with glasses on… with a chaperone for you in case the glasses slip off your head and woah betide you see full eye….I can you see me now..the ugly one with fat in hand…please see me, I. I will tell you all about me…on that night you were bereft, in the rural Ferguson led, Ferguson lived right down the road, in the G with no foretold, the E he sits upon thine Es knee. I noticed your knee, it wasn't grazed on the fee, the Yugoslavia is in for me, picked at birth to lead the card to transfer in for the Cantona heart..all in red, all in blue, all in indigo, now I don't tell you, Platini is now absolute here in this Prose Poem, this does not mean he is dead, it does not mean he is dead…it means he is very much alive as mighman, Foreverman and with love…he is strong of heart, mind with boots, in the Golden Salah with Flutes, not just yet….impatient one..the lines of story are all done, your father sits upon thine knee of strategy, lines upon thine UEFA, thine heart of fear is not here….through public apology is the line that was called for on an enemy line years ago historical reference..no still.

Which one? Which one?

The big C the big C....he hath groaned the man of he...no apology no apology...he doth for the no apology..he doth jealous of no influence with Cantona...Cantona he doth reign, in thine strategy of Foot with Ball, forgotten reign of man of ages throned in English Countryside...throned for me in the English country throne..does this make you feel uncomfortable...does this make you feel uncomfortable....you doth reign in sequence forage..no is the answer..no is the answer..you are all not doth Kings of Ages... you have no mercy for thine throned aged King..as you are all not good enough...

Salut..Salut...Statues are not for you..Salut Salut...our trespass is not for the few..but the masses one the game so we can go back home again..to our excellence in our home... wake up wake up...we can not rejoice in Tesco..in Excellence..in Route 66 in rejoicing in past events...we are not for GoldenBoots? We are not for Golden Boots? Then let me ask you why you are not for excellence in our state? That you are for? Because we are not good enough.... Because we are not good enough....IBP, IBC comparative idiocracy, so we all laterally align to the dust bowl on the line....rejoice in fatism, rejoice in fatism..rejoice in the try for a de throned elite mother who was tried for de throning to allow others in the pool of life who do not deserve any other life than their own..why? Bereftment, Bereftment, Bullying at Birth, Adoption At Birth, No Mother in School, Inept ChildCare in the Pool with no Differentiated 1, With no differentiated .....no try observation failed on her to identify on that day...anyone who dared to in broad light...no counselling..no need, no writing need...do not dis respect and belittle me...no chance of those bullies who tried to de throne...I do not want threat again...

Pele is no Master is no Master....Pele is now Black as Sin...Pele is now black as Sin...I am White just like the Author..I am Platini..I am not GOD he is for Catholicism..he is not for Catholicism...He is for the nuance of thine life on thine knee...Pele had no nuance of thine life on thine knee but his Girlfriend, but his Girlfriend of thine lift, thine lift of thine

Pele is no Master he is God for his skill, descriptives of thine art, descriptives of thine art

I have no descriptives of thine art, with desire of hope to solitude for thine sin

I have no hope of authority, no hope of authority for thine at of thine, towards all hope of skill for those who Pele is thine sin of thine, the authority being of thine art of flower, authority of immunity of Royalties....Authority of Immunity of the Royalties of no sin, of no sin for thine light of judaism

We are for thine light of thine love...

King of Skill...Skill is King

Skill in Thee, Skill in Thee, You have Parasitic Skill in Thee, I have the top shirt…

My skill is what? My skill is thine knee of GODDESS of Truth, O'er Gorgeous Lady of Gentlemanly Statement, I love you she said, the language like them, like the child bearers of sin, without marriage is no for both now, for marriage for love for a toast of no doubt, My Skill is thine love of thine marriage..of you both..my skill is thine matching of those in the no…I love you thine KING of ALL Millions, My Hero, Mighman, Mightyman O'er War, that he won, that he won, that he spat out no dummy, from fortitude of strength of strut, of strut, like Jagger but Mighman is not him, the stand said on that night, that Mighman was not him..he for the first time was someone else man, not mine anymore…thine knee was not good enough, I was called the duckling in the corner of the flower wall, so the duckling they chanted and he did..behind we see that he was thine knee of thine duckling in keys of the clink, the keys were her own, the keys were her own, the wayward past of her own, went un noticed in London on the behaviour of sin, from the one they were chanting was a great blond lesbian, the sinner was the new one they said, with no name was the duckling the sinner said, thine knee of the duckling is the sinner of hope, the breaking heart of the duckling after years with his folk. In Cantona with his influencers by far, of global initiative, strategy with wife, girlfriend, lover, fiancee and all of these of the heartbreak foretold, the heartbreak of thee, the heartbreak of heart, the heartbeat of sinners is the one who did bark.

What are our hopes, what are our hopes we would like you to be the one on the ropes, Ali he remembered the dead, the zombies of hope, the zombies of hope, the removal of all is the last one in bed, Platini is not like this here, Senna is not like this here, Schumacher is not like this here…where are the others? What are the others? We are the ones who died here sometimes for our fear, to live the light of fantastic four….compare the ones with the light on the gate, the ones who see through the garden gate, to the ones who are nuance, the ones who are fined, the ones who are on the make of their lives. We are for you, we are for you to tell the story of the historical view, the historical view the historical view all the way down to the Strand on the View, I do to, I do to, Platini is the one with the nuance view too. Versace here is not the one for the Fashion, Valentino is the one with the Fashion, both Nike and Adidas here in the comparative, Adidas are no for the NIKE French hand, Italy are Mussolini in the friendship of man, o'er GOD of KING, o'er GOD of KING, why do I call you this over again, why do I call you this over again, the stand they do callers, the stand they do callers, the way you dress down is for me in the dry den. This calls for us being in the dry den of power, the bower of destruction on the Dystopian Power, the Flower is the Dystopian nuance, why? It is a feel better, a patronage, a emblem, a nuance of the patronage of religion, of Church, Synagogue, of Sport, of Halls, of GODly man stand tall for them all, you GODly man of Power, the Flower is the patronage of symbolism. Symbolism of Power, Control, not Man hungry greed, man hungry feel good, not un genuine feelings of not believing, un manly feelings of bettering for the world, un manly feelings of bettering the global enterprise for themselves, greed is a patronage to hold, greed is a patronage of hold to free ones mind of the holdings of greed. Greed is the e here, the cats of the whiskers of cream off the top of the forgiveness on the eire of the tribe of come….Alias, the one who is strategy is the one who is jealous of for no need, the one who is whiskers the one who is now not in need of the rhyme of the day….. Lower the grade of the once friendly one, the one who is tiring of the French Bastions Gun..is not for the French Hearted..this is not the Author as the Author is now with the French Bastion of Love of thine heart, life, mind, soul, retribution of thine way…thine God of War, thine Skill is thine genius control of thine 2-2, thine 6-4 with no comparative shot on goal….I do knight thine Macron on the light of thine power, thine light of thine skill, thine identity four bower, hideous attempted shot on goal, the target school was primary in fool, bravery beckons on the change of the shot, the intelligence gathering in the once friendly son….Le Pen on the top of the black instrument, the instrument of the great dog black instead….get down said the girl who got jealous of time, the support in thine knickers is thine shepherds delight…. crossfire it lingered in the centuries of power, thine remit of thine control is the motherhood of all power……twissle the stick of thine knee of the one…whose centuries beckoned did she think the Author was all done? Promises to the Author had the flick of the hair…the wig in the site is the one who did stare…reverse of the French is the shepherds delight as its spelled backwards he's a herdsman alright..all turn the centuries of the god of the skill into the pen came the Eric back as well……he was a dog who was round, fluffy with a hat, the hat had a bobble, and twangy he sat, down on the stone floor for hours with hours, barked a few times, then he slept for more hours…Marmaduke was dirty in the cities of flour, the bread he doth make ins the Michelin all out…The lineage of the dog was the pedigree we are, genetic French Angleterre had the bulldog empowered, bouvier had the frizz on the pedigree for sure, the once iron tortoise had the underground once more…..Holland Park is the House where the Lighthouse was sat, the one with the no more of the white bobbly hat, the centuries on fire on the mane of desire, is the one with the nuance on the centuries on fire….white friendly one is the drogue in there, cos he hid from the matches fight of the year, 10 seconds is good enough cos I cant do it any quicker that you could so do…..the big M is back on the Hughes of the Hair the parable is funny here cos is only women we fear…..hartache of fashion is the little ones sense of fear, the fire brigade got a shock when they saw her big rear….heart of a lioness with a big bowler hat…we had the Vic Reeves in the fore mentioned brat…..Dawn is the one with the French Angleterre, had the great Saunders in fits of the lair…Half eaten Turkey with a chestnut or two, sprouts on the nursing had the other end in two..sorry to the French but she's too much for him..the one who is nuance in the bowler hat for sin….lineage is spoken on the frontline of itch the dregs on the coffee had time to sink in, the plug in the cupboard the shiny buffoon, I had the genetic spree in the front room….The comparative ratio of shots on goal and of target is the most essential to the parabole of this time of E

Planet Evolution

Hexameter voice of….

Prologue to

A Dominant Strategy of E…

At point 410.33 beginning of second third of 8

At point 820.66 Last Epigram of Is Not Ugly 3rd line start : .66 in

Epigram

We are King Clovis, win
Two time Clovis win win
1897
Queen moved out

Quintet

Historical Nike
We did not get along, we swear
Hurt never left, We Shine at Board
King of all time, UEFA line
Kingdom of Justice, Dark Peaks mine
All at once we became all two

Quatrain I

Historical UNICEF
Nike are for armfuls boo, shoe
Clarity of Empire Shot, Goal
Or not, Taxes, golden stud fine
WE said yes, UNICEF, Lead

Quatrain II

Historical UNICEF
With all sponsorship, win two bunnies
Balls not golden here, no fun, wet
Eric, said the Board, we like you
Here, Finance Clean, Board Breaks, Silent

P412 Dactylic Oral Hexameter

400 - 2030 Linear with Voice Simmons Date Here

Historical Balls

Football
400 - 2030 Linear with Voice Simmons Date Here
Mathew swears, F word
Go Home, French Frog, F
Loose your right to fight
In now sash delight
Long Legs, Stockings Too

400-2030
P413 Quintet Historical Versace

Historical Versace
Donatella, no, banding show
Golden toe, with all go, carriage
Leather Bottom, silk on two, try
Bloomingdales, for those cushions, fry
No Award, win to try, tight fit

P414 Quatrain Historical Valentino

Historical Valentino
The King wore, the Valentino
Window to Couture, VIP
Arrows did not dart, just the cloth
Pulitzer be the Authors time
Won the lot, Centuries, Cushion

P415 Quintet of Interiors Historical Jean Paul Gaultier

Historical Jean Paul Gaultier
Are you ugly, no your not, boo
Stunning, dear, with the walk, in hair
Chance it, in time, Rolex, Diamond
Blue Danue, Egyptian knew, His
Sporan Time, no lift mine, catwalk

P416 Quintet Lineage Historical Cantona

Historical Cantona
Eleanor, no Roosevelt, No
Line, Tree fell in, to touch with sprig
Chromosome lineage in, Brown
Foreboding Green Eyes, power, sign

P417 Quintet Family Historical Cantona

Historical Cantona
Strong in X, Powerful Y, Genes
Eleanor Roosevelt, my tie
No Head here, Cantona, is mine
Albert Roux is drat not fine, woah
Screen Shot, Tis Warrant, of thine, life

P418 Quintet Films Historical Cantona ....

Historical Cantona
In shot glass, we do fast, shot done
To take Over, into Film, thine
Angle, right, with no height, get lost
No snip here, no bench fear, in you
Found the Globe, Film in too, Gold Now

P419 Quintet TV Historical Cantona

Historical Cantona
Merriman, Lucy Locket, tight
Loving eye, you are mine, no sprout
Double shot, milk is hot, not with
Hells decline, with no vine, black grapes
Not in doubt, pout, pout, pout, with you

P420 Quatrain of Hope Historical Scotland : King and King Charles

Historical Scotland
Grade A, One is Best for the Lace
Bloomingdales, Ron Howard, Film God
Fishing Time, Hook is mine, Captain
Marriage time, domicile, tack up

P421 Quatrain of Peace Historical England Nature, Preservation and Houses

Historical England
Nature, Preservation and Houses
Chateau Versailles, First Choice, of Mine
England not First, in the sin bin
Kew Garden, in the Door, Row Mine
Strand in the tea, coffee not tea

P422 Quintet of Luxury Historical Gifts

Historical Gifts
Diamond Studded, Wrapped in Silk Worm
Golden Chalice, with no malice
In turn, England Win, France, fore told
No ring here, with no fear, grey time
No 9-nil, into bill, shook world

P423 Quintet of Corporate Gift Historical Gifts

Historical Gifts
Gold inside, balls not mine, Spanish
Tie, my head, with no bed, trying time
With no revenue, no win view
Panda Bear, No Win There, China
No Pro Golf, Match not Rolf, Fine Art

P424 Quatrain of Flowers Historical Flowers

Historical Flowers
Moyses Stevens, Number One, Tie
FTD, HandTied, Dropped, Wire way
Decorative White, Texture Tie, Head
Mental try, with no thigh, chicken

P425 Quatrain of Hopeful Floristry Historical Floristry

Historical Floristry
Olympic Too, FTD Few,
Qualifier Mine, WAFA, Tie
Valley for Tea, Megan Bouquet
Too Wide, Tie Point wrong, delicate

P426 Quintet of Pedigree Dogs Historical Dogs

Historical Dogs
Wand of Few, Fairies Knew, no say
Great of Dane, Schmeichel Laid, down now
Cups Time White, Fluffy Delight, Tea
Bouvidere French, chic, for a fence
NO Jump, Positive Train, yap yap

P427 Quintet of Dressage Stud Historical Stud

Historical Stud
No Hock Issue, Tea Time Saddle
Mines X, not Y, Bees Wax Fire, Comb
Tail of Wind, Water is not in
Gallop, Canter, Trot, Fire, Mane
Bristling Desire, Full Wind

P428 Quatrain of Show Jumping Stud Historical Stud

Historical Stud
Freedom Desire, Nostrils Breath
Turn on a penny, saddle of
Many, Side Saddle, no clean out,
with pout, Lift of hocks, power flocks

P429 Quatrain of Musical Violins Historical Violins

Historical Violins
Black violin, is full of no
sin, UEFA is White tie in
Blue, Green, Iridescent screen, Pea
Chance, My Dear, PianoForte, Tie

P430 Quatrain of Musical Piano Historical Piano

Historical Piano
Ivory Keys, Elephant Ears
Grade 8 Stand, Fine Art Planned, Water Paint
Fortisimo treble, clef on
double black keys, arpeggio

P431 Quintet of Musical Bumps Historical Bumps

Historical Bumps
Companies Secure, No Bump Any
More, No Bounce, Cushions Out, Skinny
In Time, Four, Beat once more, lazy
Government thine, rendezvous mine
Key is thine, hand of time, throw it

P432 Quintet of Musical Chairs Historical Chairs

Historical Chairs
Joel in to, not so good, Avram
No Witch on Blair, Feather Boa
Rubbish Time, Combat Mine, Stand Still
Too, Commission not mine, too red, white
Shorts time, four four, governance, wire

P433 Quintet of Musical Statues Historical Statues

Historical Statues
this is not the Author here
Dancing Round Primarks', A Line Waist
Count to 10, Freemasons Head, Rats
Paint On, Embarras On, Riots
Chin Up, Horses Killed, One off Heat
Empire State, Coulis Time Ducasse

P434 Quatrain of Being A Coach Historical Coaching

Historical Coaching
Very Drunk, Small Round Ball, Cap In
Position, Flat Line, Assist Fine
A to win, No A Line Begin
Bread, Croissant Tie, Ulysees Mine

P435 Quintet of Figureheads Historical Figureheads

Historical Figureheads
Ferguson Shout, Rashford out, go
Barcelona, contract, money
Queen of mine, Family Time, Yes
King of Brown, Emblem Frown, Board Time
Another, no eye, Fish Finger

P436 Oral Hexameter Dactylic Historical Age Landmarks

Historical Landmarks
Sixty Before Say
Hello, Victory, Play
Telegraph, No Time
Two Tweets, Pigeon Pie

P437 Oral Hexameter Dactylic Nesting Parameters and not sites

Historical Nesting Sites
Thematic Sexual Response Strategy
Crags this year, no no
Fear, Angel Wing, Co-
Vid, On White Cliffs, Chalk
Voice of Public, 0

P438 UNICEF Historical Thematic Representation

2019
Historical Thematic Representation
UNiCEF UK
Penalties, Penalties, 3-2
ROW the finish end scoreline 2-2
We scored, we are the best, £6.7m
The Bridge is ranked the 39k supporters
Thematic Response Strategy
2019
Historical Thematic Representation
UEFA
Presidents Award
Excellent as I am
Knowledgeable as I am
The best that I am
I am the only I am
Thank You for my I am

P439 UEFA Thematic Direct Self Realisation

13 Line Stanza
Planet Evolution
We are the team of Paris Saint Germain
French National Team is who I am
English happened in 1966
We are the best now now hear this
Strategy E is for the King
Now we have two in the English String

Who do we manage here…we don't know
Why we say these analogy throws
Who do we hurt now, who do we disrespect now
Both for no society bias, or do we say that we don't analogy
As it burns fires, of dishonest trust
We hope no jealousy, war of the worlds, Gandolf here
Is the best in the world

P440 13 Line Stanza and Prose Poem Planet Evolution

Wars of the Word is the position in the past..the right friendly one is now skinny at last… the one who did say hi to the throne..is the one who is challenged for her business alone.. we are not sorry for ridiculed crime, we are for the circles of lateralised thyme, Cantona with Simmons is what we do see, we hope that we can forgive the faraway tree…the who is France is the French number one, the writing we love is this one up above…war of the worlds is the analogy mis fed, the one who is creationist is also misled….these are not over empowered to the soul…the ones who are futile in the peace strategy are not sold..the ones.. who behave like the tortoise and the hare is not for the thanksgiving with no underwear… evolutionary terrace is the one on the spring board of completion is the one we did ring… the one on the diamond love in the know..half friendly one is the completed ones toe… millipedes of watch is the centuries of power, control of surveillance is the SIAs'..only par.. Macron we love all the elitist investment bank..you hid all from viewing the wand in the bank, the wizard of oz was the one who he saw the FTD is the millionaire front lawn…all of the prophecy is the line of front fire, ladies all in on the Englishman's attire, all for the frenchman his little English parade..hurting like hell after the little on did say..you are not worth all our time anymore..now we have got through the spring board once more the gymnast of time had the metaphorical more…halt on the halter had the Englishman's sight, half on the cities on the Englishman's delight, waiting for gold to return in the bank, half friendly tortoise had the victims giant might..Mightyman Mightyman huge of desire tea of the English has the frontier on fire, Macron had the pace on Trumps farewell tour, Biden came in had the Englishman once more..too hot to handle with great big Oxford tie, little did he know he was Bidens' goodbye…out from the century in Englishman's pin, kissed all the Valentino models in the bath….with no fluffy socks hiding oodles of fun, long gangly legs hide the fortress of one… slimline face on the triumph of power..needing the nip of the fortune of desire…the ones with the fortunes are not with the chips, the ones who had tidings are now with the nips..we are for fortunes of power, control with you, we had the forbearing of the little ones we knew… outward glad tidings of ridicule with one, in through the mission for the millionaires soul of the new founding of the listen…the tree of mankind is the one who does glisten…the bees on the time of the memories of war..the word is the one of the matches of the shard…glass on the temperature of you in the clink all for the soldiers in the highlights of the sink.....bread on the table the garden is all done...foremost in the centre on the auction is almost done......bobbles on the top of the trees of mankind....like the lights on the growers mind, the foreclosure of the none business street, the lake on the swarm of the bees once again....honey of woman on the line of fire now is the one in the coffee with the tea of the power...the one on the incident of the police once more too is the you on the me on the one of the power.....lightly we cross on the jumping jacks pleasure the squats of the power on the centuries of heaven....

Presidents

The Golden Foot of Longevity is Contentious Objectivity it is valid in thine eyes, of the superimposition by fine, the one who sees the line is drawn the one whose nuance the ball, the words are fine, but the context is drawn we are for new of the Foot and Ball. Golden is the one whose popular Barcelona won, the Ballon of the baton grew, the grow of fire in the know, enough of the power in the kiss, patent blue of the miss, not 3-2, not 4-5 and not for you, miss, Lowry is the gorgeous inside outside the Desmond of the worship, the Desmond of the worship, the War Horse of the battleship, the placement of the position on the ball with no golden look up, Pele wins the Golden Foot up, the Golden Foot upon thine knee of lookup, the queen bee is not for sale of the Lowry. President of thine power in the nuclear strike of glower, UEFA in thine foal of the stall of bold, Ballon for Madrid to the Relative Phasing of the influencer of one, Salah of Jerusalem hits the mark all over again, the one whose feet hit the mark of the shot on the mark, the Liverpool goes again, the foot of Cantona influences the goal of mouth on the lookup. Gerard Ballon is nowhere to see, the Cantona for him to be, the Cantona is him to be the Brother who has the hit for free. 5-0 to Tea the one who shows for Cantonas knee the thine knee he sits upon thine hit of five, the Goose for Turkey of the turnkey of the Quay of loose monotony.

UEFA and UNICEF
KIm DO China
Present Royal Family
Florist
Michelin
Fashion: Contemporary Modern Learn Historical Referencing

Prose-Poem
The President
Trump Towers
Celebrate in Style with Vogue Golden Carriages await the little ones in their own heads
In their own dreams and in their own parties

DiamondMan
BlackMan
WhiteMan
SilverMan
GoldenPaws
LucyPrice
DemiWave
Disassociated

Epigram: 10.06.2021: 00.13
There is no funeral in epigram
On the streets of all fours
Little known benefits
Are not going to be yours

There is no dialogue here

Prose Verse
10.06.2021: 0015
Little Ones
We love the feet that walk the street
We love the air that we doth breath
We love the windows he doth sit
We love the embassy take from it

We love the imbecile on tap
We love the idiot sent from the mat
We love the hilltop we doth have
On the hillside we have that

The end or is it
We are family, we are Peel
We are no Orange motor cycle
We are no from all the jazz
We love you from neverman

Dialogue:Little Ones

I have four children, I do love all three, but sometimes I wish that I could have my baby I promised to my girlfriend quicker than I would like, my ex wife is now with her, she felt that she should be, when speaking over the garden fence in the middle of the City of London, Westminster Police knew what was going on, Frank Skinner wanted to show it wasn't him getting narky as one put it, the one that was was the one who gave birth to 2 of me, but now chooses another to go to bed with. My name is Eric Cantona and I so do love my Girlfriend and her sleeping... Emir cried that day she came for me they carried banners around the other City, saying how bad they felt about Mo Salah being removed from children and families in the UK for Harry Kane, the author took time to adjust to the shock, I had to show at the Media for her, Mo Salah and done done then got removed from her writing, to show kindness to those who were not remembered as an MBE, done done got announced over this time and the author wrote him back through.

Epigram
10.06.2021:0017
Paddy

On the paddy fields of china, lay the one who never minder, calls the glee of the fast one held the baby in the nest one, had the children all but one, held the man with the big one done. China has the biggest fields all for beauty all for peels, Nescafe in the sachets had the great big Roger Rabbit, Lucy Rabbit is the one in the middle of the frond of the flower head tonight the adventure of your life

Prose Verse
TIME
10.06.2021:00.19

Time for Flowers, Time for Tea
I would like to live with he
Time for Flee, Time for Lunch
My peculiar heroised brunch

Time for Linseed, Time for Lowe
Time for all the showers in big toe
We are one together now see,
we are for your heroi-sized tree

The Ball (hyper-english)
00.21:10.06.2021
Underneath the ground cover is the one who is told off
with his long johns and with no udder fed

Epigram
Time II
00.22:10.06.2021
We are for you, we are for you
You is not you, you is not USA for you
We are family, known as much,
We are for the great big brunch

Dialogue
Time II
00.23:10.06.2021
I would to offer my friendship to Pep Guardinola, done done and his Family for thanking my gorgeous girlfriend for being so diligent in her observation locally in Cheshire, as they had arrived behind Hannahs Home, her Children were there that day, Security were alerted, they were removed from the perimeter.

Prose Verse 45
My Little Feet
(Shown Clarendon 2019)
From Golden D'or Ballon not boots you know
With little feet to bare
Running to the bath inside in their underwear
Watch the hot tap inside the shower, for their floor and film

With clean crisp sheets and pillow fights and bouncing on the bed
We all chuckle one dark night when he bumped his head
We all were proud for the last 6 times that he won the ball
Problem is we can't find anyone thereafter now more

The 4 little feet genetically bound to him is a suited mans delight
We are the famous five you know now heres the red sky at night

The ball it passed from him to him already with golden boots
Technique was the cry from the stand now here the one with roots
Whose he I said, all nonchalant, he never passed the ball
At least he didn't bump his head now once and for all

Small Time

Epigram
00.26 :10.06.2021
Selma had the adventure that night which we have time for in this ditty with rhyme
More for you, more for me
In this media bureaucracy
We love you, We love him
I would like my bear for him

Dialogue.
Beauty Pageantry is for the USA more than any other country particularly for the under 16, unless in the same dialogue, verse or epigram ay other names mentioned are not to be associated directly to any beauty pageantry

Prose Verse
Beauty
00.27:10.06.2021
Beauty Pageants for those who don't know,
are for those with the sash on the toes of the foe
Are you at one with yourself here at last
When the Darjeeling has be written about don't fast

Beauty Crowns with the diamonds don't you know
Went through the stage of the mission of throw
All out in style with no gowns in the sun
Sashes to feel the one who did say

Epigram 00.31:10.06.2021
Beauty II
Makeup, Makeup, Makeup hearsay
William is the very big day
William is the very big Boyle
In the Beauty Crown of all

Prose Verse
00.38:10.06.2021
Beauty III

Clarins, Mer, with the Sport
Had the futile bond with court
When the tensile roof had play
Lycett had the very big court

Barristers, Solicitors and the Law
Decleor with very big sport
Had a shiny nose for you
In the myriad sporting news

Pageant with the makeup in
All red lips with hideous grin
All red lips for instep too
Tip toes on the bath robe too

Epigram 4:18.11.2019:15.30
In Shoes

Victoria not Principal was in those heels again,
David had Sunglasses in his home instead
I feel we have a legitimate stance with the home by far...
we all love the foot and ball and need epigrams by far...

Prose Verse
00.43:10.06.2021
Time II

In right ear, In right ear, went for you
Went for you, In left ear, In left ear
Sympathy, Sympathy dear, linseed
In the Goal of the mouth, with a tiny little pout

Done is the key in this as apparently.
We had right ear, we had right ear
His right ear, His right ear..he had the energy
Make the Goal mouth clear...

Key is hear Key is hear
I had the great big key here
The key was yours the key was yours
I have the great big key of yours

Epigram
00.56 10.06.2021
In Time Step

We love dance to save the day
With the shoe shine of the day
We love in the very big do
ADO

Prose Verse
00.58 10.06.2021
Step
Step in time to the word, Innit
Step in time to the word, Innit
We are for your insightful crimes
Of none in all the world of chimes

Went the bells of hideous grin
Went the bells of forlorn mess
Went the bells of exponential decay
In the shoe shine of the day

Black with tip toe, black with honours
On the shoes shine in the mires
In the tensile here to stay
With the toothy grin that day

Epigram
01.01: 10.06.2021
Shine
Step in Time, Shoe Shine of mine
Step in time for all your crimes
With your toe tap, with your toe tap
In the bath tub, in the bath tub

Prose Verse
01.01:10.06.2021
Shine Shine

Trump in Hand, Trump in Hand
Jones for Stand, Jones for Stand
We are for you, We are for you
Handing the Few, Handing the Few

Jones is one, Jones is one
We had two, We had two
Love you back, Love you back
Can you see us all for the sack

Jones is now for you to be
Osamas infantile all to see
We love the ground on which you doth sit
Shoe shine of the OBE bit

Epigram
01.08: 10.06.2021
Shoes for You

All the Towers, All the Towers
Had the Daniel with the Myers
We had the caller on the phone
We had the caller in the Benz

Prose Verse
01.11:10.06.2021
Royal Family

Together again, Together again
In the jumpsuit never again
In the turnstile of the hoof
In the turnstile on the hoof

Royal Family, Royal Family is our match type
For our match hat, For our match cat
We are for you, We are for you
In the turnstile on the hoof

Jumping Jacks, Jumping Jacks
Had a great big flack, Had a great big Flack
Listen, Listen, we will. Listen
On the day that we had bitten

Epigram
01.11:10.06.2021
Royal Jelly

We had the one who had the tension
We had the one who had the pension
We had the one who had the pies
We had the one who had the lies

Prose Verse
01.11:10.06.2021
Marmalade I

We are for the great big toes,
Of the realisations pose
In the toothy grin today
Had the shoe shine of the day

We are for the great big hat,
of the shoe shine of the cat
We are for you on the day
Of the dawning realised play

We are for the great bug day,
Of the dawning of the play
We are for the great big one
For the shoe shine of the month

Epigram:01.46:10.06.2021
Do

We are for the great big do
Of the one and only you
When the forecast when to stay
In the futile born today

Epigram

01.38:10.06.2021

Marmalade II

Blackman in the centre of, all the hideous shoe shine of
Blackman of the hideous call
Went out of bounds for all to see more
All the more he came to play

On the shoe shine of the day
Of the shoes shine of the month
Had the very black to hunch
Black was in that very big month

Of the shoe shine of the hunch
All the hunch came out to see
All the ones who came to play
Had the ones who we are for

We are for the Marmalade 4
Marmalade is sticky on teeth
Marmalade gets stuck in leaf
Leaf in all the tensions mount

Of the diamonds in the pout

Prose Verse: 01.58:10.06.2021

Big

We are not, We are not Physically big
We are not for the Florist then
We are very very big do for the UNICEF,
UEFA too, We are for the very big fence

To be jumped at all the dense, foliage in all that too
Flowers for infantile Royal Florist will do
Orchids, Chorus, with the Lily
Had the very very big skinny, Michelin

Epigram:02.06:10.06.2021

Zoom

Like the moon, Like the moon
Had the zealous overture
Like the Michelin, over here
Michel Roux is in your ear

Prose Verse:2:07:10.06.2021

Little

UEFA, UEFA we do not have a very big do
We are little, We are little, We are the very very best
UNICEF, UNICEF we are the very gigantic vest
We are two, We are two, Yes, we have a very big do

Michel Roux, Michel Roux I had the very best for you
In the diamond in the sky, had the very best shoe shine
With the Albert in the hall, we had all the very sore
We had all the very sore, he had one in all the stall

On the bread, On the bread, we had two or three in stead
Our Breadman of all mankind, had the shoe shine not all mine
Michel Roux, Michel Roux, ate all of the pastries too
But he ran, But he ran, Michel Roux had Michelin stand

We want you, We want you to take on the mighty Roux

Epigram: 02.16:10.06.2021

We are for the little ones surprise
He went bump for all too many lines
All in one went out today
In the sky for myriads play

Prose Verse: 02.21:10.06.2021

Bump

We are for the lesbians tea
Of the baby bump today
The baby bump of all mankind
Had the shining of today

We are for the very big bump
Of the little ones with hump
Of the little ones to see
Like the diamonds holding me

Like the shoes mine of the day
With the laces tied for play
With White-man, With White face
We are not for you in the race

Epigram:02.28:10.06.2021
Hump

We are for the Lycett too, with the Royal Florist do
We are not for all that jazz, as we like the orchestra
Philharmonic with the loo, had the Lycett very big do
In the humpback of the whale, in the sea for all to pale

Prose Verse:02.31:10.06.2021
Lump

In the throat, in the throat
Not in the stomach, Not in the stomach
When we wed, When we wed
When we collect our great big collect

We are awards, We are awards
In the hand, In the hand
We are for the very large cheque
In your hand, In your hand

We are for the very big sire
Of the Lord of Gentry hire
Not the suit, said Mighman
This is for the verse to dialogue

Prose Verse: 02.43:10.06.2021

Parts

Body Parts, Body Parts, I have all the fun now starts
In the Bible, in the synagogue, I have all the Great British Menu
In the Great Big British Menu, We have all the fullest memories
Kim Do China will be there, the Bernard Lovell we will not share

Telescope, Telescope in the middle of gold rope
Hanging all the very big do, for the synagogue for you
In the Jewish feast of ages all for other mankind of pages
When the keys went all for you, is the dynasty of the big do

I would rather have a party, in my home or in my chantry
I would rather have no doubt, on the very big Lancashire pout
In the chair he doth sit, on thine knee with no benefit
He is sat in Timbuctoo with no diamond in my view

All in now for Timbuctoo, to sell the futile imbecile view
Alan Shearer in my pout, had Amanda in no doubt
Someone who got jealous that day, came to play with Moriniho today
We are for the great big hat, of the great big fat cat

Epigram:02.54.10.06.2021

Thine Knee of Bread

Marco sat upon thine knee of bread, that many of us cannot eat instead Michelin inside the Ramsey had for many infantile pansies, for the very gentile stay of the pansies delivered today, in the worship of the more, we had all the funerals tied in, we had all the go get her, we had never appreciated her, we had never told the truth as we wanted privacy truth

A Ball

Never Again...I never did see the little one with a teddies knee, never did I see for that, had the candles in for that..never did I see that day..the most gorgeous human my play...for the cantona called s, to spend most of her time with us..for my j yes he's the one, who needs to spend his time now with mum..thats what we say for all mankind...we are for the media rhyme...

Prose Verse: 02.54: 10.06.2021

Thine Knee of Breadman

Presidents Fire, Presidents Fire
We are for the Presidents Fire
Funeral Mire, Funeral Mire
We are for the Funeral Mire

Infantile Spree, Infantile Spree
We would like your Infantile Spree
We are for your Infantile Spree
All for you, All for you, We are all for you too

O'er the hill, O'er the hill,
I would like to live with another
Its not true, Its not true,
I would like to live with you too

We are one, We are one,
We are one for all with son
We are not all for you
We do not see why you are full

Epigram: 03.18:10.06.2021

Golden Paws

Golden Paws, Golden Paws, I am squire, I am squire
I would like your funeral mire
I took advantage of thine knee
Went for Lycett of the Spree

Prose Verse:03.21:10.06.2021

Golden Paws II

Golden Claws, Golden Claws with Gold Tips,
Not on the Hips, Not on the Hips
With the Diamond, With the Diamond, on the tooth
Like the Fairy, Like the Fairy, Innit..

Innit Innit what is that,
I am not just with you your fat
I am not just with you see,
I am the one who did it you see

I am the ones who you do not like,
So I felt bad and left you behind
I am the one who wants to say
We are making you behave in that way

Epigram: 03.24:10.06.2021
Lucy Price
Price Tag, Price Tag Innit
Price Tag, Price Tag Innit
I am not an Innit
I am not an Innit

Prose Verse: 03.28:10.06.2021
Do we want her?
No we do not, No we do not
She is not good, She is not good
We are not for you the see
She uses her name, with family

We are not for you don't see
How you can be there you see
I am all the one did say
I like the shoe shine all to play

She does not work, She does not work
Yes, She does, Yes she does
She works harder than them all
Just to make the Golden Ball

Epigram 03.37:10.06.2021

Golden Ball

Golden Ball I would like a Golden Ball
With big trousers, With big Pants
With the shoes of the greatest man
In the World of the Foot with no Balls

Prose Verse: 03.39:10.06.2021

D

I like you, you like me, I like all there is to see
I like her, she likes me this is all for a peace strategy
I want you, you want me, in her dreams with a great big V
I like her she likes me, I am heard to the very big tree

Golden Ball, Golden Ball, D is all for Ball with Golden
I am all for very big do, we wanted you from the age of 2
To be married to mankind, but he went round on the great big sign of neon

We heard the debut in the theatre was the one that had the earlobe
The handkerchief came out to play with the runny nose today

Epigram:07.45:10.06.2021

P

Baby P is another for the might Morphins stutter
The might Morphin power ranger with the brownies all for danger
Latest gadget from the Gate is the Kissing about the shake
Of the body in Shakespeare's land, with the Lucy of Prim-ark

Prose Verse:07.48:10.06.2021

V

Hurray for the Skinny Pencils, Skinny Pencils of peace
Pencils in the coloured set, of the crayons all to bear
We are one with you all now, we are for the Milan Hound
Allure, Neat with no Peril on the Italian Esplanade

V is for Victory, Victory of the splice, we had all the great big ice
We had all the great big hero, with the Mighty Mighman as a hero
We are for V in Victory, V in Victoria and V in Versace
Mighmans victory in this way, V is for the Voracious stand

Of the Victorious's hand, of the Diamond-man today
Of the reel of resins' play, the diamond man had a great big do
For the diamond hand for view, the view looks the best it has done
For the Mighmans glee for a fast one, Mercedes Benz here has its own one

Epigram: 08.06:10.06.2021

MB

Mercedes Benz, Mercedes Benz
I am with the German ends, of the flew back to
Never again with the few, who hurt that day for the bird
When the bird came out to play, Lucy Price was here that day

Prose Verse:08.13:10.06.2021

German Deity

We are the models we are the ones, who choose you for the ones
Who choose you for half past three, as we know that you are he
We have gone a very long way, in making you for me that day
We are the ones for the frenchman hand, not the criss cross of mankind

Of all one, two, three, jumping jacks, went for all the dreams
Love in the very big nest, had the foreclosure on the vest
When the foreclosure went for tea, had the diamond infantry
Mighmans glee when he did see, Mighmans all the make of me

I love him he loves me, we love all our family, kiss me hunny quick to fame
I shot you before the game, I shot all the summers hill
Then we realised Lucifer as well, we are for the glistening robes,
With the golden ball with globes

M

Epigram: 08.21.10.06.2021

Espionage

Black Goblins, Black Goblins to the Halt
With the Health and Fitness Halt
We are not worth our salt, to the embers of your fault
Undercover for all to see, had Merriman to be

Prose Verse: 08.29: 10.06.2021

Carriages

Globes, Diamonds, Finsbury Spice
Round Gold Carriages, Oblong Ones Too
Hexagons a thing of the past, with peramulators of the cast
Golden Carriages awaiting who, when, why with invitations golden too

Mercedes Benz, Golden Carriage, Guards with Diamonds
With all fours, up on Lourdes, up on all with Feathermans Suit
Feathermans Suit, Feathermans Suit, I am with my Feathermans Suit
Who is going, Hello, who is going, I would like to see whose going

I would like to be with you, all my life in the very big do,
These peasants, These are peasants, in the ridicule of lessons, golden triangles,
golden triangles with no rosette with no rosette in the shoe shine of no rosette
Gold, Diamonds, with no Finsbury Spice we are there now

Epigram 08.47:10.06.2021

Lourdes

We can see, We can see all the hideous all to be
We can see, We can see, We are all for nothing see
We are you, We are you, I would like to live with you
We are you, We are me, We are all for living tree

Prose Verse:08.49:10.06.2021

Lourdes II

Oh Lourdes, Oh Lourdes, We are for your very big cheque
Oh Lourdes Oh Lourdes we are for your big head
We are for the great big giant in the moonshine of the sire
Alabama, Alabama We have moonshine in Alabama

Peter String, Peter String I would like to be with him
Oh string bean, Oh string bean we are not for the string bean
O'er Moonshine, O'er Moonshine, will you be mine, will you be mine
O'er Moonshine, O'er Moonshine, will you be mine, will you be mine
Oh Lourdes, diamonds with mines, we are for shop front of mine

Oh Shop Front, Oh Shop Front I would like to be mine front
BFA, BFA they do not sponsor all today
Royal Warrant, Royal Warrant we would like to Royal Warrant

Epigram:09.05:10.06.2021

DiamondMine

With the few, With the few, I have tables golden too
With the few, With the few I would like to supply to you
All the order of the day, of the elite high profile way
We are they, You are in, We are for the very big win

Dialogue in Children and Families:
We are for the incitement of children and families through a transient sail, the water.

Prose Verse:09.09:10.06.2021

GoldenMine

Very big win, Very big win, We are for a very big win
We are not for paddy in tune, of the very very big view
Golden Time, Golden Time we are for encrusted mine
Diamond nuance, Diamond nuance we have all the encrusted nuance

Golden Red, Golden Red, I would like one Golden Red
Golden Green, Golden Green, I would like to see Golden Green
Golden Purple, Golden Purple this is best, this is best
We are Orange Peel today, Peel it off but remember my way

On left hand, On left hand we want the castoff the left hand
We want real, we want real we want the real lemons peel
We are incorporated dream, of the one who WOW he did seem
We are few, We are few, we would like to live with you

In the Law of the Order with the few that you can muster
We can be with you again, we can be the ones who came
GoldenPaws, GoldenPaws this is not Pyrotechnic Laws
Drip, Drop, Drip, drop I would like to be with hoP

We are few, We are few I would stake my life on you

Epigram:09.21:10.06.2021

GoldenTime

We are for the Golden Time, With full few, With full view
We are for the GoldenTime View, Rolex too, Rolex Too
We are for the Stratocaster too, White vs Red, Black vs Blue
We are for your very large phew..

Prose Verse: 09.26:10.06.2021

MBE

We are for the Trump of Towers, We are for the Trump of Powers
We are for the Trumps real mess, of the shiny nuance best
We are for the Trump of four, We are for the Trump of Law
We are for the Trumps little mess, on the floor of the tiny floor

On the floor, On the floor, We would like you on the Floor
We are for the Shiny nuance of the little ones real muse
O deep ridicule, O deep bias, I would like to incarcerate Myers
O deep bias, O deep bias, I want one, I want one

We are for Melania Too, shiny nuance on the phew, we are not bias
We are not bias, We are not a mess we are exponential stress
Peter Jones we are for you, We are for the great big Tower phew
We want you on the top of him, showing no bias Corporate Stand

Peter Jones MBE we would like you to be free, of real life in Utopia
With your loved ones all for fun, we would like to help you too, O'er the hill
From O'er the hill, we would like to see you again, on the hilltop of the game
We want you in on top, never went for this on top

Corporation Stand of he, went for Gold and got the Key
To forgiveness stand by him, of his wife for his real hand
He has never strayed from her, Donald Trump, Melanias' hurt
She is never one to hurt, she is never for a rhyme that is judicial heart to find

Epigram:09.48:10.06.2021

PJ

Mr Jones, Mr Jones we do not want no Corporate Bones
We would like you too be fast, on the teatimes of the cast
Build the team in the stream, show us how you build the team
Hold your nerve, Hold your nerve, I would like to Tower your Strength
With no pseudonym, this is not the authors thought, heart, mind and feel

Prose Verse:09.51:10.06.2021

Corporate Real

Corporate real, of no sound, is the mighty fallen now
Corporate reel, of no sound, is the mighty fallen now
Leave it open, Leave it open, we would like to close it now

Close the time that we have spent, on the Close time of the sent

We are one, We are one, We are for the mighty one
We are not for you to do, the great big mighty all for love
Almighty, came to play on the feathers of the play
We want you to be who you are, live the life that you deserve

We are for you, with my son, yes I am her....with no-one with no one
We are for the great big one, we love you, all for a few, can we hold the great big one
No you can't, No you can't as I am all for a very big new start
For us both, For us both, we are for us very much float

On the top, On the top, we are for on the top
Gin with slinger, whiskey chaser, had the stuff of made man day later
No we are with no Beer or the bellies of good cheer, only those who bias stand
On the Shoe Shine of the land

Epigram: 10.04:10.06.2021

A

Golden Juxta-postion, is the mighman with a fixation
Of the A of Alcohol which can make better all that fall
All that fall, All that fall, I would like to see all that fall
I am bias, I am bias, I would like to see full bias

Prose Verse: 10.06:10.06.2021

With the Staff

All for the Ball of all Fours, STAND UP
STAND UP, its not your fault, its not your fault
WE LOVE YOU, WE LOVE YOU, we do not justify the real
Of the Lady Lovely, Peel we can be for all that once

Mighman had the brink of fortune, in the City of good fortune
In good fortune, In good fortune, had the brink of good fortune
DemiWave, DemiWave, all good fortune in my wave
All to me, All to me, Had the waving nuance be

Bee the Best, Bee the Best waving hands on the travels nest
We are one, We are two, We are for the team build too
We are for the Latelyman, who is new here so cancan
Latelyman has all caps dropped, all for you the fevers stopped

White stuff on the fever pitch, of the pitch of fevers ditch
Angelina all for you, in the whereabouts its new
All for red leather in the suit, all for Versace Pitches for you
Gucci, too is all to see the underneath of Latelymans today

Epigram:10.31:10.06.2021
Celebrate in Style

Vogue, Tatler Golden swell, Carriages await little ones as well
In their heads on their own dreams, their own parties all supreme
We are for you in our time, We are for the delight sublime
Golden Carriages in the Taunt, of the nuance of the Launch

Prose Verse:10.36: 10.06.2021
Dreams

Of Unicorns too, Half a Melon with strategy too
Look, please listen I am trying my best, I can't do this all very best
Half a melon, all in two, I am about to live with you
We want to win with you, We want to win with you

Do you not see, Do you not see, I want to be with you
I do not want you to be with him anymore, I saw the tree
Of excellence, I saw the tree of excellence, I am not bias
I am not bias, ridicule, lengthy conversation, for a time

Dreams of Unicorns at last, Dreams of sleepy marsh-mellow beds
Dreams of sleepy hollows awake, of the tiny nuance of placate
Pink with silk, feather down, hypo allergenic frown
Lilac in a tulip basket, lilac in a fois gois casket

Epigram:11.04:10.06.2021
Orchids with Lilies

Lilac, Strawberry Puree too, I would like to have a life with you
I would like to have that fun, with the laughter all for run
I would like to feel like that, for the real inside your not that
Orchids, Lilies, Roses too, I am stem of heart are you

Prose Verse:11.08: 10.06.2021

Orchids of Dreams

Lilac, Pink with reddish hue, marshmallow bed, adventure time too
Golden Carriages they await, of the wedding with no big cake
Encrusted Diamonds, Encrusted Gold, Encrusted all for blended contemporary design
Orchids of dreams, Orchids of dreams with no trail, with no trail

Pink is bag, with no s on thine mum, with no s I saw on thine mum
Watch the stem of wired might, delicate to touch that night
When the turn they go off too, bed together why don't you
Orchid Dream, Orchid Dream gently gently Orchid Dream

Encrusted Hope, Encrusted Hope, We are for Encrusted Hope
We are for you in our Books, We are for you in our Books
We are for you on the TV, We are for you on the TV
We are for the French, We are for the French

Orchids of Dreams could be giant pansies theme
Pansies too are great big need, of the Markov decision here
is for the mighty morphin power to be
Lightly does the drop you plea, Orchids of the Power to be

Epigram:11.24.10.06.2021

Orchids

With no disassociation to the Mighman victory of the two, crowns of glory with mankind
Of the shoe shine, Dreams of all the bedsteads too, with no witches of east wick flew
With no black goblins in this flight, of the mighty with no
fall of fright listen to the diamond might

Prose Verse 11.32.10.06.2021

Sleep

Fast Asleep, Fast Asleep, I am not Fast Asleep
We are you, You are him, We are for your great big din
Sleepy Time, Sleepy Time, I would like to see your rhymes
I would like to be with you, I like the sound of you all too

Sleepy Time, Sleepy Time, Kissing gate he is all mine
Kissing Gate for Wiry Hound, is the one whose hands right down
The Shakespere Story, Samurai Story are for you
For our Rumbley Tummies today,

Is the best, Is the best, I will get the very best
I take time, I take time, I would like to take your time
Of your watch, Of your watch, I would like to take your watch
Of the surveillance team, the sleepy time is now all mine

Prose Dialoge 11.35 10.06.2021

Sleep

I like my sleep, I do not get too much sleep, sometimes I do not get enough sleep, my daughter sometimes wakes up in the middle of the night with nightmares…

Epigram:11.48: 10.06.2021

Gold

Golden is the time of year
Golden is the listening ear
It is not the amount of years
It is the gold of metals to hear

Prose Verse:11.51:10.6.2021

Platinum

Platinum is the next big one
Is not the diamond thats sat on
Directions of the next to bare
All for him until your there

We are listening all for you
We are listening all for two
In the limelight of the bank
Holy Christ you are now in twice

We are for the lamplight of
All your drawings we saw of
We are for the great big nest
We are for the Robin mans best

Epigram: 11.54: 10.06.2021

Robin

With red breast, With red breast
Lately man, lately man
With Gorgonzola, With Gorgonzola
Seissiseis Tomatoes with thine knee

Prose Verse: 12.05:10.06.2021

Lunch

In London now you know, not in Fortnum Masons Show
We would like you to be the very best that you can be
We would like you to be the one, who is not the fore-saken one
We would like you to see, that it happens for us you see

We would like you to be friends, with the almighty broken friends
With the almighty broken friends, then it gives him never end
We would like you to be Queen, to be the one who has always
To be the one who has all night, on the diamond of delight

Harrods Green it all Shows the one whose forebears are behold,
The one who's snail is never there the one whose motherhood is now all there
Meterage on the great big balloon, has the cor blimey strewn
With the paupers hats to stay, on the incidences of the play

Epigram:12.13:10.06.2021

Luncheon

Petit Déjeuner for me, Petit Déjeuner pours vous, s'il vous plait
Merci, Beaucoup Monsieur Cantona, Ils a une crayon,
Petit Déjeuner

Prose Verse: 12.16:10.06.2021

Food

Never again do we want, the cheap and nasty for our lunch
Never again do we want to say, that we are for a great big stay
We are not for the one who did, never ending in the din
We are for the great big team of the cor blimey once deemed.

Cheap with nasty to be delivered in the cardboard cut out dear
The cardboard cut out of, the very skinny ugly blob
The one whose antics, made you giggle, the ones whose house you went in single
The one who you went all the way through, would like not only to live with you

But to offer to your self, the chance to own a great big shelf
Back at Carrington, all over again,
as one of them saw you altogether again
We do not eat horse here, we do not eat the author again

Prose Dialogue 12.25 :10.06.2021

Hospitality Gadget

'Manchester United vs Tottenham is the one with the derby, Never in a huge million years, would Salah open up about his past, So, we got him a gadget, a spoon to eat his pudding, One which if we were not for Tottenham we would want to compete with' Franc

Epigram: 12.27:10.06.2021

Food II

Mascapone, Green Leaves, Tomatoes of the very best trees
Taste the difference, taste the choice, taste the ones who know the most
Taste the ones whose mother said, work very hard, as well as vent
We have all the cherished ones too, like the diamond man in two

Prose Verse 12.36:10.06.2021

Grammar

Make your choice, Make your choice
We want hats, Matched for Catch
We want you for all the tunes
Into forebears of the truth, with no run

I am fortune, in those ways
I have many many friends
I have many many friends
I have many many friends
The match for catch in the friends,

Have the many many men, all the rude from here by far
Had the diamond in fah lah,
The diamond mined from the same place
From the same time, from the same mine,
your stability is not all mine

Epigram:13.20: 10.06.2021

Grammar

These are the ones that hurt all the time
These are the ones that have multitudes of rhyme
These are the ones who have listening at their feet
These are the ones who have ways to retreat

Prose Verse: 10.06.2021: 14.11

Grammar II

Schools of the time, can be there all the time
Schools of the time, can be there all the time
We are parents of the school, we are for the green stripes too
We are the ones with green stripes, we are the ones with purple stripes too

The best ones are for on the world, the best ones are for those who hurt
The best ones are for those who cry, the ones like you have all you life
I am white, now hear me now, I am hurt. I
am hurt at the thought, that my parents do not love me anymore

My parents are with those that harass,
My parents said that they are no longer asked
My parents say they are no longer with me
My parents say they are no longer family me

Epigram: 14.26 10.06

Grammar III

School is not for hope, altogether in the hope
Not for you go back today, in the school time in the play
Wear those feet, with distance play
We are those who play at, we are those for dinosaurs hat

Prose Verse 14.32:10.06.2021

Monopoly

Saving lives on the day, Saving lives on the day
Breathing Fire on the day, Breathing fire on the day
Hallelujah, Hallelujah, Hallelujah, Hallelujah
We are first born, We are first born

Kissing Gate, Kissing Gate we save lives,
We save lives, We are for the ridicule with rhyme,
We are for the one who said
Please go home, with me instead,

Please go home, Please go home
We are not with you for home
Please do go, Please do go
We are not for lonely old toad

For Mayfair, For Mayfair,
We are for the great big Fair
We are for the great big lair
Mayfair, Mayfair, Mayfair, we are for you in Mayfair

Epigram 14.42:10.06.2021
Monopoly vs Competition

I am scared, I am scared
I would like you to be mine
On the scale on the scale
Will you be the depreciative line

Prose Verse 14.49 10.06.2021
Monopoly vs Competition

I play Monopoly, I play Monopoly
I play Gymcarna, I play Gymcarna
I am Manchester United, I am red, I am red

I am Manchester, Salford too,
I am Goostrey Cheshire too
Fashion, hoards of public too, biting in line,
Wheres the big do, When the fashion plays the tune,

Looks of wisdom on the sock, Pull, Pull
said Mighman, LatelyLady had hard of hear
The apocalypse of hard to hear, is Latelylady
The Monopoly is time to hear,

Epigram 15.09:10.06.2021
Competition

I love competition, I love competition
I want to win one, I want to win one
It shows my ultimate, best shot
It shows my ultimate best shot

Prose Verse 15.11: 10.06.2021

Competition

We are the crucifix of the Catholic Church
We are the crucifix of the Catholicism of Burkes
We are the Sinners that learn to survive
We are the ones who can learn all the time

We are the ones who can tell you to stop
We are the ones who can tell temperature now stop
We are the ones who fell down at the sheet
We are the ones who fell over the heap

Mighman is the best at the crucifix you see
Mighman he is gentle, kind hearted for free
Mighman is frowning right now for the right
To be at one with the Goostrey handstand

LatelyMan with Lady hand he is the one
He is the one who is free on the run,
The one who the run, did fall over at one
The one who is giving all for the free line

We are not here now then heres the surprise
HERO of burkes is never one we did say
Lately the heroines of time went that way
We are not one now we looked into path

Epigram 15.22 10.06.2021

Living

I would like to live with time
I would like to live with rhyme
I keep myself with you
I have other things to do

Prose Verse 15.25: 10.06.2021

Ps' and Q's
Moral judgement, stands for you
Moral judgement is there for you
Moral judgement inter-twined hero
Heros' for good on all mankind is the teatime all for time

Prose Dialogue 15.26:10.06.2021

H

'My girlfriend will be having babies for real with me soon, I am Eric Cantona..not Mo Salah who is embracing his new generosity of number hideous 2 after 1 penalty miss, one save, one goal that saved Harry Kane OBE from judicial nightmare..as he forgot his p's and q's..'

Prose Verse 15.26:10.06.2021

E

'Into the light Erica said, my daddy wants a great big head,
With his girlfriend on the screen, of the nuance of the scream,
We had light all that time, we had time all that night,
We had nuance all for you, we had tiny Shakespeare for you'

We had all the gifts of time, For the tiny nuance of mine
With the tiny nuance of mine, Keep it safe with all the line
We had all the tiny pivot, We had all the tiny pivot
We had all the physics in it, we are for the lineage fill it

Wallet in thine knee of Salah, Salah is thine knee of hope
Hope into the wallet of Salah is thine knee of wallet of hope
We are not for Harry Kane, as he went out for a rain, down onto the little hope
Of shiny nuance little ones hope, Salahs' girlfriend came
out to play, with his wallet on that play

'We had all the shirts for you, Liverpool FC we like you'

Prose Verse 16.00 10.06.2021

Small Time

The Jewish Times there is no Hezbollah only frequent in the view
The rear view mirror is established once a knew, the fish it sits upon thine piano
Of Eggs
There is no view of the rear of the tail of the fin, the one whose shark invested lake was
drawing very thin, this is not the line but the person that I know for a very long time
Of eggs, new of the some, the tea of the shrine the Devils Cup.
Of Eggs
Jewish Times for Hezbollah or to the New York Times, Ducasse doth
sit upon thine knee of Michelin Superiority together with White, who
tests us all we are all for the JewishMan of temptation,
Of Foot and Ball

Epigram 16.02 10.06.2021

Too Fast Coach

The Golden Coach at half past seven went to by for merriment, the Tatler had the second view Vogue it took right under view, the knee it sits upon thine diamond ring, my diamond ring is too fast on never too much for my right hand song, my right hand song is not too near I love my Amanda no one fears, too fast coach on the Laseiz Fare

Prose Verse

Flashing

As the carpet laid out on the ground, the cameras they flash on the head of the sound.
Golden Statues that move all at once, with dark crimson eyes that sight in the nuance.
With the Crimson all to see, Versace Crib was there you see,
Alexander Couture was there, no time now elegantly walk down there

Get out of the car as the cameras flash, watch your step its my time now
Help the crib, from afar little lovelies in from mars
Link the two, we want to see, the fairy no nuance for the be
Fishing lights of the past, we want to be that one at last

Epigram 10.06.2021 16.21

Red Carpet

Red Carpet, Red Carpet, We look like that
Red Carpet, Red Carpet, in jealousy with that
Grey Eyes, Green Eyes, We speak the truth
We speak the truth We speak the truth

Prose Verse 10.06.2021 16.24

Golden Statues

All the awards, All the awards, Golden Statue we find us
Gold on Diamond on thine knee, is the shiny nuances glee
We are for the right foot of the brain inside of the King of Mars
O King of mine, O King of mine

Golden Awards, on thine knee of Mo Salah is not enough
The golden Globes of the fun, is the one of all the won
The ones who came out to play, had the dirty nuances play
The dirty nuance is not the Author

Hallelujah, is the one is the one of the fun
The one who is fast at that when the dirty one has fast
9.54 average on stood is 11.04
This is minutes and the fastest of the day

Epigram 10.06.2021 16.41
Marmaduke II

Marmaduke, Marmaduke in his inaugural suit
In his lifetime of, imbeciles with no off
With no off, With no off, with no off
TV off, PLAY

This Wiry Hound is Back in Time

Epigram 1:07.04.2021:16.16:The Wiry Hound

I am the Wiry Hound
I am big with Loud
I see nowhere to Sleep
I see you far from the Beat

Prose Verse 1:07.04.2021:16.33:The Wiry Hound

I am the Wiry Hound
I am the waiting sound
I am the Cornish treat
I like wafers on my feet

I am the Wiry Hound
In the middle of fighting loud
I am the great big feet
Of the bully who hurt my retreat

I am the Wiry Hound
My name is Marmaduke

Epigram 2:07.04.2021:17.08

Rough, Rough said the Hound
Oww said the Timbuctoo, I heard
The big, wet, wiry hound
Smelled like chocolate too

Prose 2:07.04.2021:17.32:The Wiry Hound

Peace with Hound the Dasch is one
Peace for love is all forelorn
Peace for us is you and me
Peace for you is him to be

Giving all that you can give
Gives us all the Bedouin
Gives us all the one he trust
All for you now hear this must

Wiry Hound is a big soft mutt
Look at me I am in the buff
All for you the one can see
In Pyjamas with all three

The Wiry Hound is my dog too
I have all my sounds for you
My dog has a panting sound
When he sees his dinner all down

Epigram 3:08.04.2021:08.24:The Wiry Hound

The SheepDog is Curly or Straight
The SheepDog is at the Gate
The SheepDog is Straight with Whistle
The SheepDog has a Heart full of Passion

Prose 3:08.04.2021:09.08:The Wiry Hound

The Black, White, Long with Straight
Soft, Fuzzy, with no Weight
High Pedigree, strong, I fell
Sheepdog, Strong with his Faith

Faith of herd, strong with eye
Eye with Faith of the Sheep
The SheepEye is not closed
Herd of round in through the gate

As his eyes dart across
He looks up to the stars above
Shares his Masters look of Love
Passion for the Herd of round

In through the Gate of Sound
In through the Gate is the Wizard
Panting like he deserves his dinner
He looks up to the great big sky

Like it was Great British Beef
He eats, eats with no fill
His passion turns to his dinner
Sheepdog Faith to his Master

Epigram 4: 08.04.2021:10.46:The Wiry Hound

Yes, I have great big paws
Yes, I have nuance to scores
No, I do not have the lot
Yes, I won the sight of Gold

Prose 4: 08.04.2021:11.12: The Wiry Hound

Bones of the Nuance able, Bones
Stop, Listen, Hear me now
I am the one who took
Lizard, Beasties, of Venom

Bones I ate, or do I look
In the light of the book
The view of him is nuance now
The Lizard scales higher than me

Bones we ate for all mankind, I am T Rex
Now you mine, in the Wiry Hound
Wiry Hound you are not one
Cute, Cuddly we did the fun

Epigram 5:08.04.2021:14.35 : The Wiry Hound

The big black beast with lots of love
Has the fable in with son
The Beast it sits upon thine knee of Benz
The Beast it sits upon thine knee of Life

The fable that makes the crown for him
Loves thine Englishman's refrain

Prose 5 08.04.2021:14.56 : The Wiry Hound

Our Beast he sits on his own knee
He is Black with Red on the tips
He flecks nuance on the finger tips
He needs regular brushing don't you

Never in our time did we know it was you
It was you who did not get
Regular occurrence in the bed
His bed is everywhere not in the hall

The Beast his bed is everyone's fall
The fable it starts from his long shaggy coat
The wiry wolfhound has not goat
He is just a great big soft one

Great big walks to the courageous stand
Stand for him I merciless hand

Epigram 6:08.04.2021:15.09 : The Wiry Hound

Agility of Trust is in the Sound
Like the Trumpet of the Loud
Like the Trumpet of the Symbols
Hit the Microphone is Wave Bound

Prose 6: 08.04.2021: 15.12: The Wiry Hound

Obedience is a key here
Wait in line for us to hear
Confrontational lines for us
With the Gooseberry Show for US

Country is the line of me
Country is the Shire of he
Country is the Red, White, Blue
Has the Gable end all done

Stands at shoulder 32 high
Now, I am back I want to know why
You cannot say that I am never in
Diamond Beauty is never hint

Epigram 7:08.04.2021: 15.18: The Wiry Hound
I can smell on the ground
I can hear on the sound
My wavelengths are her to stay
My way round is fast to play

Prose 7:08.04.2021:15.25 :The Wiry Hound
I can see the impact here, of my curse upon the deer
The deer had impact upon the lights
The sound of nuclear reactor fights
The natural world

The Natural World is all for one
The Hare for line is not all done
The one for all is all to see
The Guardsman is for him not me

Hallelujah

Epigram 8:08.04.2021:15.34: The Wiry Hound
He would wear the fastest shoes, on his feet
Now he cannot loose, stripes for fastest
On the sides, type the elastic
His Camouflage has green bits for his hat then

Prose 8:08.04.2021: 15.45: The Wiry Hound
Is not from Russia, The Wiry Hound is not from here
It is from China, It is from Rome, It is from the Ireland
Sound, Bite of the Wanderer back from Mother Earth
Sniffing the Ground, pointing his tail running the race
Following the Lore

The law it came from order too, wind in the willows
He had a bad flu, the vet he doth cometh
To the Willows he past, right from the dowry
Of the Englishman's path, O'er the Dairy

The Dairy of all the bottle of child, the Red top from the
Bill on the Centuries piled, Green top on the Centuries
Of the Hound of the Month, the Football Player who has him
Is an Englishman's move

Epigram 9: 08.04.2021:15.46:The Wiry Hound

I love him, He loves me, on my bed he doth be
I love him, he slobbers on me, on my bed he sleeps for free
I love him, he loves me, he runs and runs in the garden for me
I love him, he loves me, he licks the tablecloth for share

Prose 9: 08.04.2021:15.46: The Wiry Hound

He loves hats, he loves snooze, he loves macaroni too
He loves him, He loves me, he loves all the licking on the tree
He loves you, he loves you, he loves all the macaroni too
He loves you, he loves him, he loves you with a great big grin

Epigram 10: 08.04.2021:15.46: The Wiry Hound

If you are happy and you know it wag your tail
If your happy and you know it wag your tail
If your happy and you know it wag your tail
Can we pinch

Prose 10: 08.04.2021:15.47: The Wiry Hound

Mercedes Benz, Mercedes Benz, I am with Mercedes Benz
I am Wiry, can be smelly too, I am for a Mercedes Benz
A big trunk, A big trunk, now I am in the USA front
Frontier Speaking to the masses, we are for the colonial canisters

Mercedes Benz is the one with iron fingers and the thumb
Pinocchio with a great big nose, highland fling in the tartan glows
We want one with great big ears, we want one with great
Benz is a great party ear, the one whose Lord has the great big fear

Epigram 11: 11.05.2021:12.10: The Wiry Hound

The Wiry Hound is complacent of truth
The Wiry Hound is uniform of heart
The Wiry Hound is passive in his remit
The Wiry Hound is elusive in sanction

Tiddly Winks of incitement

Prose 11:11.05.2021:12.10: The Wiry Hound

Is black and White, The Wiry Hound has leadership strife,
The Wiry Hound is membership glee, White of Love sick is tree.
Wiry Hound has full of stout, Is red with black, too many lines on the tree.
Wiry Hound is all in tow, Wiry Hound is in the know.
Warey Wiry Hound. Love is a Warey Wiry Hound.

The Wiry Hound

Prose: 12:11.05.2021: 12.50 The Wiry Hound

The City life of all mankind had the nuance of the blind
The Blind had two when all to fear had to forecast of the lane
The Country Lane had all to fear with geriatrics and spearmints glee
The Beast it sits upon thine table. The table is gorgeous on thine knee

The End of the Time Ball for the Wiry Hound to be developed to be chapter within Kissing Gate and Heroic Dog here including use through police, bomb and drugs.

Golden Retriever is the lead, on the golden back of heed, Laces
straddled the lead or two of the masses picked for you
Characters to be developed Bionic SuperHeroic Dog
Characters to be developed through heroising media response

Epigram 19.45:10.06.2021
Unicorn

The Unicorn is all in the pink, with white and yellow fin
The little green truck with wheels on the round
Cream to flow on the insides now
Unicorns, Unicorns pulled along by mankind

Prose Verse 19.50:10.06.2021

Tuna

Yellow, Basking shark, Yellow Basking shark
Markov is like Michelin Star now
This is now heaven, this is no heaven
I would like to pray to heaven

Tuna fish Tuna Fish, Line Caught Tuna Fish
In the Sea, In the Sea, At the bottom
At the bottom, We are for you at the bottom
Tuna is nice with strong, tensile in the middle red

In the middle of the distance, in the middle of the rod
In the middle of the Atlantic in the middle of the tin
We are hope, We are hope, That you will be a goat
Forelorn and a Goat

Red Fin, Yellow Fin, Danger Dory these are the ones that I want more of
Food, Drink, Driving, Direction

Epigram 20.12:10.06.2021

Tuna Fin

Yellow, Red with no head, with no eyes
Always filleted inside, With no eyes
Always Spies, On the side of mother eyes
Then in pan, then in pan with some garlic with a pan

Prose Verse 20.18:10.06.2021

Tuna Yellow Fin

One side then another, One side then another
We are one now, We are one now
Roll it on the side, Roll it on the side
Always mellow on the inside

Grilled not seared, Grilled not seared
With 5 minutes, With 5 minutes
On a plate, On a plate
Garlic, tomatoes, with no heart

Grilled lines all out, Grilled lines all out
Oysters on a plate, Oysters on a plate
Shiny nuance ate, Shiny nuance ate
Strong, Sturdy, String Bean

Epigram 20.33:10.06.2021
We like Rump, We like Rump
We like you with no queue
We like Tuna Fish, Tomatoes with Stew
Broth, Broth we have Broth

Stallion, Stallion, Stallion
I like to ride my stallion

Epigram: 20.50:10.06.2021
Red Fin with a win
Red Fin with no win
What is next, What is next?
All on a small plate, plan it, plan it

Prose Verse: 20.51:10.06.2021
Yellow Fin, Yellow Fin
We are for your Yellow Fin
Garlic, Potatoes, Peas
Seared with Michelin

Red, Yellow, with Fin too
Tuna, Tuna Seared with Garlic too
We are one now, We are one now
Seared Tuna with no butter

Tuna, Tuna I hear Tuna
Seared Tuna, Seared Tuna
With no ear, With no ear
Seared Tuna, Seared Tuna

Epigram: 21.18 10.06.2021

Yellow, Yellow, Fin Tuna Fin
Red Tuna, Red Tuna
Yellow, Yellow, Yellow
Red, Red, Red

Prose Verse 21.33 10.06.2021

Gold Bullion

Gold Bullion, Gold Bullion, Gold Bullion
Waiting List, Waiting List, Waiting List
We are for you, We are for you
Listening on the Table Top

We are not for the Table Top Mountain
Table Top Mountain, Table Top Mountain
Australia, Australia I am for Tuna
Gold Bullion

Prose Verse: 21.50:10.06.2021

Mothering Sunday

Mother Friendship we want you, to be earth for the time we are you
Mother Friendship we had you, all the earth with planet renew
Mother Friendship Montessori too, had no power in control for you
Mother Friendship be thankful, for the Sunday we had two

Love thine knee of Mother Friendship, to be earth for the time we know
Love thine knee of Mother Friendship, to be humanitarian too
Love thine knee of Cirque Soleil thine knee is for Fathers Day
Love thine knee of colour bearer on the foreground of thine wearer

Adore the worship of thine knee, to be at one all with me
Adore the worship of thine knee, to be at one all with me
Bearer of all worshipped knees, we are not together you see
Bearer of all worshipped knees, yes we worship each other knees

I Love you can you just see, I Love the thine knee for all to see
O, is whole for us to see, O, is whole the world can be, seen
To Love you all around, Everything you do for me
Everything you are to touch, great big Love from us to you
Just Love

We would like to say to you that we are too, Always Love thine counterpart
China, Eastern Europe Too, Make this Planet Change into, corporate business
With a hold, help from you guys in the view, Atmosphere was changed that day
Hot house fearless with heat on play, Love is Always thankful though
For everything that you do for us

Epigram
Beautiful, Beautiful White Snow Swan, in through the translucent pond
With the iridescent sound, of the melancholy sound, of the pretty nuance found

Prose Verse 21.53:10.06.2021
Best Friend Days
My Best Friend she's always there always in the greatest lair
My Best Friend she's happy too, always with a fine word or two
My Best Friend we talk all the time, My Best Friend has two big ears
All around the friendly peers, My Best Friend her tale doth wag

In all places of my life, My Best Friend called the name of me
In this tale it is not me, I am GOD and I am not backwards in this tale I am not DOG
spelt backwards, I am catholic can't you see, you don't believe the same as me
I am protestant open your eyes, think of me this time I am opening thine eye

My Best Friend is Muslim too, she had a daughter for me to you
My Best Friend was there all the time, I miss my friend of the park sometimes
My Best Friend she was Salafist too, My Best Friend she
grew the harvest on the fertile ground with us

We are Farms with Footballer led, we are for Cheshire, just wait and see
My Best Friend is for us to be trustworthy in the Cities for free

This is God...

ALL THE DADDIES
ALL THE MUMMIES
ALL THE BABIES
ALL THE CARS
ALL THE FORTUNES

O is not for Orange or Obesity well it is but not here…O is for Omen…green eyes ghoulish smile, lucky the lips and see me miles…away from the storm…eye of the tiger the stripes all at one, the one with the stilts disbanded…out all on stilts the crag did say…adapted genome is great now understand..I am a tiger all mighty at one..with the crag on a membership sleep tight…Out on the empire line on the stars, all those poor dolphins had a tragedy by far…

Black with White shoes on the porpoises did hear, the friendly one had the shoe shine to peers….loot in the bank was not for her ears..stand back said the omen I can help you today..I do not think so the cabins fever is my way…the N is for the Kid thats ok, the one whose ex husband is good for my way…Nicole is the bribe for the cinema screen, the one who is able to scream and be heard

When we place the ring on the finger, we are all at one with no linger, we are for the Maserati, we are for the chain link fence, we are for the child abduction we are for the Liverpool chants

We are for the laughing out loud, we are for the Aston Martins sound,
we are not for the going back now, to make you feel my love

Prose

We are not for you my dear,
When you get the daddies ear
Spare a thought for the fat women ear
When you bit it chewed you here

The fat women chewed the sinew of life
Great big fat lard of life
With a twig that you wouldn't like
To make you feel my love

The big fat women is half asleep
When the boyfriend had no knee
Canton-a came out to play went in full and hear them say
We are out in sale you see

We are not for the Tree bee
We are for UNICEF at half past three
Canton-a paid for the girl you see
To be with her forgery delight

Hip flask in we see the light
Fluid in the foil snap
Denmark said hello to that
Denmark hailed to each big room
All the enemy in to zoom

Prose-Poem

F for French Lunatic which is what I was called once..now I with the one who makes my heart pump, the one who did not give me children yet, to make you feel my love…the one whose laugh and giggle makes me think..am I funny or is she fink…ing that I am somehow thick?… no to make me feel her …other way round…match yes I know said the A of E..I know said the M of the F you know…where the hell and opps so sorry I did not think that you cared so sorry, never in a minute did I think that someone would want their own reels back for their future family….R isn't here anymore…they went away with the ark..sailed with hyphens and long ships, with row boats and rowers, we loved to sail, and canoe in the summer but now we do not..long ships and tall sallies…boots, wellies, high heels and shawls, very nasty ones with clipped forms…wobbly straights, get British Bakes…Off with his maybe head too busy or newspaper head, chastity is my own for my sweetheart..I love her, want to be with her tonight above all nights…French Businessman…Notre Dame..Love in the Seychelles is never for a man..always a lesbian affair for her to make you feel her love…N is not here yet..Dance

This is the curse in the night, when all blankets had a fight, with the dog who had no bone, all the ahh went forelorn, when we eat upon the draught of the plan we had no hat, when the curse it came to play, we had genre for the day, do not stare into mid air..when the sinew of the bear,,went beat beat for Denmark when the SAMO had the Gard…the Gard came out to play don't you see we can do this all day…Tobias Blaken had too for see we had no but in between..we kicked the ball when we had too..then we let him on the stew…with the Beef of British you see crazy cow of the machine…the crazy cow of the machine hit the riots of in between..when the durn came to see the impossible is not me..the impossible is not me..cos I cannot stop smiling you see..William Niekerk is right behind you..in the dream that you once had..Greta Garbo is the one who did me all them years ago…when the remembrance came to see..in the hilltops you will flee…there is no A DO right here as we want the symphony ear.. to make music with our rhythm..natural vibes at one with god which one is the melodic broth.. of the roast of ruin you see the rack it comes from breasts that day..chicken is the thing you know on the one and in a stew..in the oven at half fast ten..when we laid the beast to bed.. hoare it sounds very masculine..from the insipid of men..the mice went round and round the clock..everyday until 5 o clock..six pence found the love of all old fashioned wins from this point on…old fashioned said the remembrance tool..on broth of hope the chicken is stew..

feathered with tar in the one wee did mars..plinth on fire with the wrong ones…o'er the hill on the French vineyard we did miss on the French tart..all in pastry hear you salivate in the the doors of Marcos wait…tea time came said the tiger with talons..gave him once for all the melons…cupped inside of the language of doubt..held for all the English one is out hid from the sound of the crash in the spout..the spout is drew closer than that went for the ball of the Eric Canton-a instead…now that ball is hard to beat in the path where no cabin mans feet tire in the the humane source cos he's the one with the strategy of course..when you limbo in the thing make sure that you look right through..into the back of the net with no eye…with no eye on the bed..stead of the king of truth I am yours Amanda rebuff..in the nude he was that day went for the tower of the lad to pay..on the knees of the desire that led..on the characuture instead…satire of the juvenile stand in the heat of the white man..in the term of the mans play had the hope fo them one day..when we go to MediaCity we had entry to the City pity said he he wanted first..of the strategist not hers..Canton-a is the one you see..look at him with strut you see..all at once the history plan..went right through to get right in..knowledge of the foot and ball play is the on e with E today. Avram Glazier is the one with Alex Ferguson all mighty won…O said the blindman 0-2 up..the darting Bruno had right up..right hand down today went sour..it doesn't matter when the frenchman lowered o'er the head of the cabin mans French in the landslide of the bench..you may wonder what you see in the planning.. we have the time on our hands with Simon Lycett who wins hands down through the British Empire you see which is why there is no knowledge you see..when the knowledge is not to bear do not go and Royal there..this is mine and you cannot go..I will make sure that you are now no…Later on when the frenchman said back with you I can tell then..we wanted to with Amanda you know…Simon Lycett with no show..no royal warrant said Sam Cook because I took her media on the rebufff. When I am I look real nice..like the bulldog into spice..right with 6 is the one before 7 sorry to everyone else but its him…E is for the treble bass clef.. rhythmic solitude into bed..Canton-a I can hear them shout, I can hear the newspaper shout… in through sorting whispers here..look into the cabinmans fear…of no job with no justice ear…wears the string vest on to tiers…wedding on the white of yellow, gypsy on the white washing..washing with the persil stand…had the pleasure of the cabinmans hand..when the war went to the door..white with black they mingled more..mingling more of the ish to be… in the Shakespere for the tea..breakfast presents for the Guards in the townhouse on the shards of the rack and ruin you see, of the many men for tea..tiger she had long big talons stripy with the long grey shadows of the rack with ruin that day..on the tensile floor my way.. so censorship has the most sunshine..in through the hoof of mankind..the drawing was the rebuff from the son who did not like his youngest brother having a laugh behind his back at the fact is penile went bang..all this at the age of 2 in the potty behind the stew..stop..listen.. hear me now..all of you are fluffy right now..fluffy said he it will turn out ok..me and my own one you see..Julie had the biggest one in to the cheap and nasty one..with red hair and straw between her teeth gave Aunt Sally a beep beep beep…said the wheelchair bound to me what on earth is prosthetics you see..arms, legs with bionic arms..just like Wonder Woman with the farce..into for quarters cut the cake of the Hare of the Rabbit that day..this long verse is not boring it has the escape of the brain for hurt..of threat to life, for threat to heart, for threat to everyone to burn..scald the life out of the turn, when the media hurt all her…

No Doubt Solitude of the Mind, Thought and Sanctity of Marriage, no just Figaro one of the greatest in my opinion of all time and that mr made up is all….folks..

Figaro..Figaro is the little ones in heart had the open time to dart, into Karl with Oprah dream of the book with Chanel, Fendi lean..we are one with our own selves went to bed with Apples and Pears..never came out with any desire..coffee pot with black on spire.. the spire went through the longings of doubt, into the man with the tail feathers out… tail feathers of the challenge of you..the blue sweater had Covid stew…grey was village on that day..we love O his sensibility that day…on the vagrants of the beer..swilling down the jugs with stout..apprehended thoughts of red..where the confusion hid the best..no prostitution thoughts right here..hence the name on the neon sign here.

Through the windows of the bungle we had fun without the fumble..swinging trees with big buffoons, had the childhood on the move..went through showers of the rain had the oppositions name..when we had the raw..apple on the pip of stew..take them out we want you..just to exist with no future of the dream of the many men fourteen..the abortion went right in..near in my time had you seen..now we say thats its ok to mentioned …killing babies that way..when we go into the womb we pinch inside with all the goo hole out the pincher gripp of life then have lunch with old man strife…can you tell me who can say or influence us in that way..what we do is make it sound the decision of life all in our hands..can we not say how are we..we can control in another way..take two lives and go and have fun..surely you can see that is done…if you have the man of 2 can you not see he is too..for life, love and happiness he judges his economy first..looks at what the average Joe wants from life, then there is a show of forgiveness C..he sees what budget can he stretch of the tourism of no lent..holds the key to a budget reverse surely thats better than killing them first..is you want promiscuous sex please refrain from your bedstead having notches if you cannot afford 5000 women on the bed board…we love O and his lovely wife..when he's home his horses delight..his girlfriend has the one who can see..through the glass of fear that day..you have feelings the little one said to the horses on the bedstead..lately I have been feeling weak on

the juvenile income spree…I have had two pints of tea I think someone is jealous of you.. when the sound of things to you..10000 lives have hit the sack when the pillows come in from back..lager on the shirts of glee yellow and musty full of chee..se on the hard finger of doubt when the girl comes out to play he hits the..cane on the shout of fear into the Zidane of fee.. cos the best one is the Coach you see..sometimes when you think your near you find your way off the mark my dear..when the girl comes out to play the jealousy is the one we play.. killing spree of the love of all..its ok here now you see to say that promiscuous sex is free.. free with dirt with all mankind there is n god just jealousy mind..save yourself you innocent lives we are not for you inside..we are for you out you see..had the jealous hideocracy.. leave your clean insides you know..from the sperm from outer space..is invading all that space…like the black hole of the vector..physics helps the trees to grow in the breaches of the throw of the ball which Cantona knows is the one at his UEFA toes..his UEFA toes with glee handbagged the Fendi heart for free..nasty commentary on the seat of the futile when we weep..we weep into the hands of god which tell us that Maradonas off..we know that his hands are tied now back to basics in the snow..have a cuppa into you..with a biscuit or a few..lager louts of the French telly hit the home of satires belly..satires belly into you went for tea at a masquerades do..white hair and lunatic on the situ of the brink had the lions share of the French briar..stop with the antics of listen look and think when we had the shire at the gate..behold the landslide of beauty with worth nothing marigold has centuries to bear.. job sword on the demeaner with holier to holer when done..we are for D the right wing jester the hold out king without the fester..hows that said the littler on the blanket with no do..held on the situ of the giver with you..Centuries of White on the chargers of fear charging black horses with grey ones to fear..grey ones to fear said the gate of delight..marmalade with jam we know you in site…of the fat pay cheque of publishing not in..when the jealous in laws came out of the fen,,Messi in the garden with the swings all aglow retard in the mountain of the stairway to hell..Kellogg's for cereal on the same winters day..givers for sakes with the families to pay..pay said the giver we wish you all well..giver me your time cos we doo not have well..later on we have the bumbling water out..wheels of good fortune of me in the well..talons and daggers of fruitful liaison..oranges with lemons said the fat metaphor loving the language on the streets of all fours..went for the fat walk to many jokes like that makeup we love you so there hows that..Cantona wears to dress down on that day..went for the casual in the car my way…the casual talk distracted the fact that he would have been furthered by Saville Row in tact..she said where on earth is your tie…I said I left it for someone to buy..she dam well forgot it so I left in the car…two thousand oranges and a cart in the bar…lemons are free not for metaphorical be..living the life as the frenchman did see..using religion on the street of mankind..making the way of the Fernandes behind

The End

Prose-Poem

The Adventure is for us to feel the Adventure for us to hear The Adventure for us is to go The Adventure is for you to blow The Adventure is for us to blow away cobwebs..some may say..the parting of the empires on the sunny autumn day..red orange violets spring up through soft ground melancholy chattering is the streets of aloud…when we see the lot of fire we can condemn of who we are…love in the air violets to share..ground holes with worms, snails packed for shirts..entrance on the screen cold wintery hearts of feed.. Red the wicked witches daughter well so the first one said..peered into the larder to fare.. ..mirage of sanctity on the fast feed..we do not like you again in our lead..she peered once again with in-trepidation not glee owww said the witches cauldron for tea…with fortitude of oneself we lift the candle light we shoot away the candle lit on one dark cauldrons night.. boo said Pedro glee said might ouch said James with the Toon army in sight..bedknobs not virtues was Reds first stand..I am not having this Dress on tonight..hmmm..I know that said the witch..I know that said Red I want a shepherds delight..counting the sheep on the floor of the room that once was my bedroom and now its for you..the bedroom is for the whole of the white buzzz..round with the bees with all that white fuzzz..liquorice allsorts with caveman all hear drawings from prehistoric lightening to sheer..just like tights that come up to here..short wintery warmers that turn people on..on the chastity of the warm winters son.. turn people on they say with your writing..half naked scantily glad bare chested pristine… prince of the chambers with huntsman hang fire…goblin we love you..black of the night.. scary witches not the one we first talk..welcome they say cackling with glee this is your nightmare for me..me is the one who poked fun at you today the one who downgraded your work on the tray..too much sugar with sweets on the way…no more food on the tray is the one..all that carling on the sit of motherhood..scarecrow of hope with the foresight we know.. factors of hope on the regeneration of sales we want you to drop all you have on and spend time with view to the time on the streets of parade look at the mall from the demographic plane..goblin comes back for another second look went on in front then turned on the hoof.. Denmark we love you as we know e can do..red lights with strippers when its half past two with 20 minutes on the break of the past..goblin gets hijacked on the fortitude of man..

With 4 Denmark into the trunk with Armani far..shovels with forks some swarfegar by far.. Denmark they jest on the double line with no onto the slip of the vicars red cross show.. stopped just before then halting with pire..goblins we love you we went out on fire..engines they revved with full petrol…we see electric will be better..on the heat energy Selma we love you when we see the day..the day that reckons on the streets that we once new.. the rowing all over the goblins we knew..they end up with the Manchester Streets..loving each other with no feathered nest..feathering the tickling of no underarm or legs only on the arms of the bubbling cauldrons nest..4 eggs they lay on the eiderdown in through the four play the memories all down..Harper once did the ones we didnt know only 2 ones she said no its actually 4 one on the way with the 3 in football..gave her the heavo once more.. ouch when she had a bad dream her once bad nightmare has now turned to green..green of the face we had too much to know..when will you listen to the light green theme we have our bearings on witch would you seem on the stockings of heels of Fendi..nude on the legs walking with strength conditioning of peony on the warm summers day..red ones we love as the analogous colour pink to purple as we do not fear..marshmallows thought we do not want as mushrooms..fungi you know is the fete of all show..soup on the pea is the nut on the cough..pea soup is the time when the temperature is off..sue on the cliff on the crags with the mind inhaled the workers to find the behind..packed with the fend with suitcase in hand.. went through the gardens of topiaryland..chocolate warmers with marshmallows on top little ones floating with big ones all popped..weightlifters desire to lift your skinny mum Harper we love you said the ones who want one..95 on the bar with the rhythm we love we are not racist we are for the club for the right one of the strippers delight in through the mire of the shepherds delight…we went with on the charge of the light....we went with you on the Marco of Spain..I am afraid we have news of the game..you have won three tickets to see the fame.. when we live with you we hall ones in gain…3 kilos this week said the one with bum sorry she said its not the very friendly one…bulldog tattoo with the sleeve on the ball..we had the shepherd with transvestites we made..all on the lips with increasing circle line usually red with long lashes not mine..bright coloured blue with the eyebrows on wire..not the eyebrow is not plucked either..brown is the pencil that she thinks is great..its not for her with the defined big shape..look in the mirror on the language of fear half naked ladies on the streets of all fours..dogs on the move in the pound in the dark four slimey wet ones all round with the car vroommmm went the RX when it pulled in for gas I know who you are your for carbon monoxide gas..eco-warrior we called you a trout because the young one had more than a lout..two friendly octopus had the seat on the lout..we would like to invite you for a drivers day out..but the gas is too high when the doubt is the stout…we love you is the conclusion we know …bright red trousers with a low damp cloth on the head of the floor..wellies on the stirrups mars..goey wet jodhpurs with the boots of delit..cold wet slippers on the janitors bulldoze..went to the hairy magnificent toes..boo said the beast with ridicule with might small hairy chicken on the magicians delight…on the space capsule with the orbit to be meet the man with the world at his feet..feet are the right footed master of glee..we are not asleep now and we are not we..listen to yourself you are too big for your boots..martians geriatric with no man to hoots..the snowy owl is at one with the flutes..symphony battering diamond cascades all in together with a merriment cascade..fairies are bewitched with all thats ADO

The End

The Fairies

Prose Poem

The David in this story is the affer to Cantona like the one who we know we lifted him up for the Giantsman show we hit him hard with the venison you see, all for the choice of the Englishman's fee..passion, ice, fire with solitude all together is an Englishman's node..never pub..never club all together on the sack of the poe..when we walk into battle on the phalanges chargers we walk into the weight of the tide..littered with dreams on the emotional file..file said the giant on the beanstalk of leaf..which leaf said the ADO we are now with mystery.. superheroes on the agility way..10000 passengers littered this way barriers to Maslow on the entry mans free listen we threaten we do not want thee..do not want thee but I am me..yes we know but your face is not for free..we gift for free on the entities of the sound we love forever the war cries all out..planes rides Giuseppe with Pinocchios need of shelter for all the sticks with all the power in the bricks the mortar we built upon the sty we love the power that makes us by. The ones we love are those who feel the warmth of corporate realised wheel of fire with passion all in the room when **C (UEFA President)** tried his broom, problem is we do not have respect for the other witches hat the other witches hat you see is far from dementia just not funny you see..the witches hat all done now now the one whose abusive goes right through to get the player from Old Trafford from AC Milan all in the buff..the one whose steadfast the triumph is not the one whose heroism is bias for a try for the elite is brought her out the agile woman who learns the stout..wheres the passion about what you write, wheres the intellect about the plight, wheres the one who has done it all, intellect and a no score draw..needs of the hierarchical corporate reliance of the realised all motivated alliance, we try and try to find beauty in the pie the pie it grew with over corporate truth of realism..the pork it fired in the pasty it fired upon the deity with needs of Maslow not on retreat needs of blanket of the snow went through the superhero show..went through the superhero show..onto the Llongines into fare waiting the super lines of snorting chocolate of triangles..B will you be mine forlorn and heightened in sense of security.,,nuances for thee on secure of leaves..bosom of tart renew on the loins..King of March Hare went for a walk launch for the lifter on the passion of mars.. superhero..as I take you to the bathroom the steam oozes from the vent the door ajar the little wince of the retaking you now not from afar.. Peace for the little one whom tip toes around… the who is now pulled to one side not getting out of the shower inside..the cloth of the warm of the insert today..is the one whose cleanliness is here to stay..his left hand caresses my side he looks comfortable with his sexy backside..he caresses her side with the tomato of act..his hair is now all up in the air..the fingers of tiger have rolled over the roots..clawed the inside to ensure the balance too..tossed the Swarfeger into the the bin..deity of mankind with the sexy frenchman..I am love with the man who walks down the street..the one whom fought for his less than retreat..the fans they did love him and they still do..I smile to myself as I remember the view..the view from the mirror in the back of my car..the red vroom of Ferrari with many more to come..right there in the drivers seat was the sexy mankind..on the work of horse with the prance he did find..that night I remember the view from my brain was me on the bonnet of the sexy Frenchmaid on the bonnet of the car of the horse and estate was me and the frenchman as I sat on his knee..the cloth he looks up at the eyes of the man whom god had his inference on the park of the lad…erect, strong, hard with fire..I am the one who incited the liar..boo said he I am the one who you trust..make sure that you case is as solid as a rock.. make sure that you know that its me in your life..as I move my forearm to the centre of mice.. as my heart beats within the run of the atriums gold put the genetics to bed the little rolled and I caught him instead..the bed it was large with a short back and sides the paunch of the man of Italian stride..my genetic sexy man show..pushed his lips against mine when we were aglow..my heart raced when he stood on the terrace of England..smiled at the navy when his white was the right one..the horn of the red Ferrari we know went right out on strike when the Italian we broke..we went at him in the old English town rats in the bed and no its not you who cheated on me with the hearts in the bed cannot wait for his girlfriend in bed…moving her hair to one side then we say..god your infectious with no reply from the day…why did I relieve you the other day sir..she says with a smile on the smirk of mine too..a I am he all the same..jeans with the tight sweater so definition can be seen..as I grab her by the waist and I look down at her..she smiles glances down then steps on my toes..only to sweetly reach up in the air and opps all her clothes they fall off damn near there…my hands they grown warm from the friction on skin..smooth to the touch and so gentle within ….ctheres no jumping disaster of the light winters day when the French herd of violins had the mannequins today..when we had ventures we strung up the penis of fire..no we did not we had god for the liar way back in centuries have naked too..knitting the thought of the bedfast we do..we do said the infantile all in the cloth half naked Englishman had a bad cough..went for the sliders on grips of the same..had the great Englishman's utter French same..Torture of similar had mentioned the fact that a whip with the chain had too many at that day..poor English little man who had the genuine no backside..literary agent had many but we had no doubt that the friendly little octopus had 8 thousand pounds..when we were sound of the safety of shell..the need of Maslow was the giggle fest you know..a need is the thing that you want all the same..if you need a shell then go and get one al the same..we don't want you in the elite all that long said the wrong one the phone of the gong..the red of the strong one on the arm of me too went round to the bathroom and picked up the shoe when the boy went to the washer that night he was hit from behind by the shoe of delight..ouch said the shoe of the boy he did say we tripped the washing of the hitman did play..old English the reminder of the dead pan of the time marmalade advances to the head of the table jam went the relies buffoon of disasters… prayers at the table when we eat at night..the feast of the beast when it happened that night.. the beast it was hairy all covered in gold shape dressed with lunatic on the streets of behold…

impetus to learn the survival of life is to look for the forge on the trespass at night..the pathway was jealous looked glancingly up towards the great big giant of the street of rebuff..rebuff on the charge of the bull at the gate..when we see the mist of the embers we have the life the earth with the chariots unearthed..left far behind on the streets on the feather level Dick Turpin with level headed pleasure..the half tarred beast of the genome of show..black of the night with the memory of cedar adapted genome is the one whose disaster…feeds her..half naked tart on the street for the play..we do not want the beehive today..keynote of June is the one who we said Summer in pliers are the jukebox instead..as I turn back the covers on the bedstead the man glances down at his erect penis..looks at me and I tell him no..you are not the one whom does this for me..your the one with nightmares in reality to be…lately, the thermometer has ticked the other way round..families, children, babies are for me all the more..my man glances from the other side of the bed glasses on everything off..we dance on the chest of his tattoo..running races round the finger tips loose to start then tighter vigour.. crescendo..his fingers respond to the touch of me..biting my lip in playful majestically..tongues meet fingertips glide over my torso of no wobble..with no stretch apart from one in a lone on one side a nuance I say small perfectly formed..our legs entangling into each other from the bedstead that ruled the world..kept fingers away from dirty parts that are clean..smiling inside on the outside glee..foie gras lessens the risk of cheapest thrill..truffle..champagne with two perfectly waxed legs with..manicured feet…as he takes to the floor of the springs one in our heads as it is 3am the other for real in the bedstead….my gentleman hand was dancing too, his sinews of desire with passion renew..his hands drew closer to the lips of my mouth the eggs had broke in me now…erection is hard just like before he smiles at. me with the look of all the more..intensity rising I look back only once..the hurt from that night I longed to escape from the mountains of tears from the bridge of my face..when we rise in the bedstead today I look at no fear of the beast in no way..the erection still hard standing tall all the more is grabbed like a handle on the devotion of more..now where do you go so we can be all the more emotionless mother on the streets of all fours..counter surveillance we heard from again..we left the minor in bed for the lent..penis erect that she never sees the handle of time is never on his knees hard broken chastity inner side without another on the way for the prime in the lout..my man he still is standing proud to the touch of the hand of the mighty mans sound..the need is for emotional deity trustworthy picture of the high value century..as we glance at each other we giggle that night when we realise we called them our love parts alright…the lover in me he blushes you see the gentlemanly stand on the verge of free.. on the free of the willy of the large inflated whale the one who did sit on the tree of the valour… the tree of the valour with the large inflated knife..the one who we said was the one of the elves…the beast of the sidings the hotel at the glance inside the boudoir on the foreboding mistakes..loving the life on the aforementioned buffoon who ate the cake on the thick ones decade..intelligence my lad with the hard on the index with the presence of mother

The End

The Fairies
2
Buffoon

Liberated jealousy of the one the one whom did speak the one for the deity of the lampshade for a treat…the need for the man in the half centred turn was funny, warm, tender and strong went with a girl in the warmth of her song..tulips, iris..long winters coat..listening for the 4 little toes..running to the bath inside the bouncing on life in the kiss in the morn.. the whiter they are the metamorphosis of crime hits from the London of the High grove in sight..as I sit with my legs cross the chair the large black leather sofa with memories to share the gaylord from bees is the one who we did say the large friendly tortoise is out here someday..I cross legs on the chair with the stand of the men long legged beauty with no beast from within..straight out of the tie with the ribbon on his head when the gaiety strife of the lumina bed..HighGrove we Love You say the Englishman's bread look from the life of the cabin mans Fred..Fred is the one who is resourceful and proud wearing his shirt of the round and the round…when we are up on the cabin-mans new tie..Fred has the dream to wear the golden shoe he is not the French pet or the one in the new he is not referenced here to go round and round in the bowl of forgiveness with the Marmaduke all proud..S is the one who the prayer is for tonight we listen for the one whose deity is right the one who is remorseful for the things that they do they one who is for the renew of the view..cowslip of nodding heads with the herbs from the cottage garden when we plant like the herds of the cowslip behind..the cowslip behind on the duke of the Cornwall..the one on the wall of the master of foot and ball..the wall is the analogy not to saint or sinner the one who is found on the floor..liberated life of the gates of the heaven ..little toes of the feet of the 4 that we can..flung on the floor in the merry of men..the prayer is for you the one who did break the merry little life who went down by mistake..no end to the cover of the one whom did play theres no investigation into the whole danish make…wellies galore on the view of the past do this forever..when you have the relapse..of the duty of kind will you please be with me on the sanctity of marriage and view the whole entity of saying those vows as me Marmaduke dad and mum stray from each other I wanted to say that I love you..forever

The Foreverman has Marmaduke the one with the 4 paws to laugh, he split down the side of the four legged friend we had a good ode their you see..with long curly dark hair..all the way down to his sides..the armadillo hurt that day because he did look by his sides..ouch the Forverman lost his way down the pathways of marshmellow land the book it looks like this..the Foreverman spent half his time on the Swamland of Merimans lane..with a half eaten face by the shark invested lake when Denmark came it was a laugh..we dressed up by half past ten we bought the burger bar hand..Foreverman with the wheelchair hand went into the swampland forever the silver statues of movement dear had the shiny nuances stunned never…horror of luck said the goblin of mine with the Denmark all satire you know.. Foreverman had a Marshmellow hand that made Victoria Beckham sign no..Foreverman had the Marshmellow face when it got stuck to the face of himself..he fell asleep one cold winters night and it stuck to the ear lobe as well..all pink and gooey the Marshmellow man had his face biten off in the air..foreverman is now back to himself as he worked up an appetite then..tall black gangly long thing was foreverman, we had tides of respect for him now..he is the J that put back to himself when the janitor hit back as well..green with desire on the favour of nothing the pink googly eyes on the pout..with no lycra suit on the foreverman had the energy levels of power..crossfit we love you we did so much time on the levels of sugar into asbestos chew with the candy floss useless tooth now at 6 ft 2inches of leg and ball we had furniture on wards we know..with size 15 feet and a merigo round when the hand becomes sewing the guard..fishing is neat cos we had this one too of foreverman handing the park…to the young one as a passover treat Marshmellow man had the adventure time of the dynasty woobetween..we had the desire of the foreverman to progreate all desire in between..forever-man had the race of his life when he rallied the troops on the hill..four friendly octopus into the park and the night time became a big mess..eaton…security mess of diamond guy had the janitor feeling all week these are a few of the characters left in the authors very active brain…journal 2 sounds fun said the publisher dear we can compendium this one to see, the one in the ear of the one who doth stand is the one who can hear from the fear..of being the best one in tall that we see and in all that we do their you see.. the one in the sticks is the one who we giggle at cos now the one is not the one here…

Epigram

Featherman is light with proud
Deity with success aloud
Deity with forelorn tender
With him for meal with member

Prose

Featherman he likes Lacross, Featherman he loves Heroes
The Horse it sits upon thine knee, of thine right of oppositions glee
Upon the glee of the right hand frown, upon the knee of tales of devil aloud
Featherman he loves his knee of the beauty with the beast

Featherman he likes the load, of bias undetermined load
The load it sits upon thine knee of juxtapositions decision making fee
10 million pounds of nuance for a free liberalisaed economy
Featherman he sits upon thine own

The Sabretoothed Tiger the White Stripy Timebound one
Mighty Long Talons to take the long nose too
Featherman he sits upon thine Crown
Not of thorns but of flowershand, nuance of foot and ball had the mighty one with all

Epigram

MightyMan hears the sound of the tentricles of aloud
No harm done is the packed off with berries, then theres macked
Paranoia is the one with hero worship then all done
Is the one whose shopping if full with the welly of the wool
The Hero it sits upon thine knee of the Crown, but not of thorns

Epigram

Mightyman with Featherman proud, with the reels of the film
Stand with whole of fruit with nut, on the tyre wheel of the butt
Juxtaposition, one night on the Ferrari of the night send the brad and butter fight

Prose

The Heroines they have control, stomp, securement with needles
The Heroines they have power, intellect, instalment with feline strength particularly of heart
Eyes alert twitch of curb, length of lashes, soft feathery catches
Alert, sniff, peel of non orange, toes with a length, red on the nail

Listen, Laugh who goes there, in the luxury lap of the fare
We begin with the century all frozen with ice half of the melon all covered with pies
With the turnon the circle and the market of glee, we tempted the person back here for a fee
Market of strife on the pattern of doubt, Farms-barnes
forever in the Feather-mans gush of doubt

Epigram

Featherman hides round corners, Feather-man sees like before us
Featherman sees back around us, Featherman is life before us
Featherman is god to some, Feather-man wears Lycra's in the sun
Feather-man is Jewish at that and no Eric Cantona it is not that.

Prose

Margaret Boyle she sits on the fields of Barley with sow
The Sow is the field with pork pie hat, with pork pie hat they say
Europa fields of glory be with poppy infantile not my knee
Cup is the sow one the one who is proud

Farnsbarnes is the barley grow, the growth of stalk of barley no
Beans are swamped into the tin of growth in fields of pure breatheren
Bees are strawberries, sow of pink not of brown spots with local chickens are disallowed
Sow is for lots of babies for the me, the author is not her

Rural integrated society, Denmark just shook their head
Never in a million years does A Cantona begin the years
Sow is the one who determined the lunch all with apple with no rod
The rod is green with bionic power, of Margaret Boyle in Superpower

When Featherman has launched his great big rocket
On the barley lanes of grow, lassoo the ones for all mankind
Mo had the lycra of the Nike with all the nuance of the fight
He made biscuits all for you the one who had the great big shoe

Mo had the farley on the sow of the pig with Denmark here
Then the Margaret Boyle they said the one who had the chocolate egg
We had the red on the light with ignorance and of fight
The one who said they had a rest was all for Merriman at rest

Sow with the pig of the Denmark refuse to join the dots of the infantile used
Chocolate Egg

ERIC

Ulysses forgiven the treasure the sunken Hilda went out forever-man they say
on the cusp of freedom, withered away into a tiny ball of them..truffles

Prose

Nest of Chocolate Eggs

Pink speckled on the outside with hard shell to be seen, yum
Rolling longdituinally, to the sound of the hum-ing bird
Never o'er the top, with a belbous belly which wobbles, sags with artistic flair
Imagination had us there, nestled in 3's is this the one for me

Obstruction from the artistic might the power morphin had a fright
When the shouting from the guard, to make the World one go to card
From the jealous of the few, that shouted out to get right through, the hilltop, mountain
and the life of the safeguard who had no right, to interfere with those around

Families that missed the sound, missed the sound of their red tight
Never in a million years no flight, no flight said red, I see her now
She's the one from under now, she's the one who everyone was at..to make her be
The one who never has that…

Sumo the Giant in the hand of the beanstalk with the vest, came up
the stalk for his venture on the capitol with secure rings alert

Epigram

Prose
The Cup of Sugar
Measureman with trunks has a little melon suit,
he fought one day for the battle on the sugar went to rattle..
Measureman the indisputable leader of the cube
Helix on the indices irridescent cubes of glycemic an index of its own

Measureman is the hunt for the evil of insecurity of health
Measureman is the cup for the cake, the icing on the jelly
Measureman is green for the code, Measureman is green for the loaf
Measureman

Tape of reel for the 6 foot 2 inches of spell, trunks of hue, lemon zest all new
Tape of reel for the Yosef of ages

Epilogue

Time is a Leader

I would like a gold full of diamonds with a design that looks like that, the one whose finger always type are the ones whose fingers can go like that, with the Rolex here to stay I love them all even including the Date, when I refuse its because the one is the limited edition not the wrong one. Diamonds, Gold with Finsbury Spice I had a blast all night said Ice, but I had to put him down one day when I realised how sore my inside play, then I looked at Eric and I started to climb the great big stair to all mankind I grabbed his hand in front you and we had an affair right there in the nude.The oyster one that I love the most is the elegant sophisticated articulate man of the host..the one whose rituals used to smile the rich stands of the wags for hands..white paper cotton, you of course are not forgiven this is not the realisation of the mighty morphia power slot, the mighty man that had the power to win the lot and is forgiven of 9 months of the ago seen it was not his fault and we loved his scene. Oysters are the ones to play with gold and diamonds littered that way meticulous detail of the face it tells the time for clocks to say, timepiece.

Addendum 1:

Salut, Statuesque…Bundesbank I will never left flank, I am black and the BLM is making lives all matter again…integrated strategy make the speech act sing…debate with glee…confrontational de-secured truth on the banners of non hostile truth…slogans match…for a surveillance fee, war horse galloping free to the stand with Ferguson spree, striding pattern with covered face…extremist viewpoint here to stay…we pull down the monument which has been here for many a year for all stability…family and de-secured flee…auctioneer, chateau and vineyard for 3…1 on the scoreline…

Français Bon Nuit
S'il Vous Plait

Salut, Statuesque…Bundesbank je ne quitterai jamais le flanc gauche, je suis noir et le BLM fait en sorte que toutes le vies competent a nouveau…stratégie intégrée fait chanter l'acte de la parole…débat avec joie..la vérité dessouder conflictuelle sur les bannières de la vérité non hostile…slogans correspondent…pour des frais de surveillance, cheval de guerre galopant libre au stand avec ls frénésie Ferguson, motif a cheval avec le visage couvert…point de vue extrémiste ici pour rester…nous descendons le monument qui a été ici pendant beaucoup d'un an pour toute stabilité famille…et de sécuriser fuir….auctioneer, chateau et vignoble pour 3…1 sur la ligne de score

Addendum 2:

This is me…Corporate Chair led for Stake…Code…Wireless for the plate… of gold to win the other side of career mummydom with all inside….

No One

Addendum 4:

The use of scalene triangles is the angle of 3:5:8 the one whom we all try to passively emulate…whether this is in our homes or in the local park…we all know the Cheshire is the one whose Bentley isn't great…this is for you…to the third rule…the one that Britannia isn't very quiet…we all know the rhinoceros is not the one to bark

Addendum 5:

We have character building for another work in the Prose-Poem in Chapter 7 for Subterfuge for the man in Black and MIB

Addendum Late for the Pregnancy Squire
Little do we know, we have a helium full of wires
The Wires were for the little balloon
That made a difference on the shedding of fool

Addendum 6:
Velvet is sweet with empowerment of A…warm tender and sweet
and my eye from their…I won't leave you he says to her…you are my
silk to be with me…I will be naked for my sweet valentine

Addendum: A Model
Epilogue

This wasn't at the forethought of my mind when having the ideology, currently I spoke to a sample of book readers and asked through their portals of society what they would like to have included in the representation of prose and poems. What they felt A Dominant Strategy of Management and Leadership felt through sport represented these strategies foremost.

Now said Fred in the epigram line this is not Fernandes or even a serpentine line, when the ball gets onto the foot its passed around and then gets flicked for good luck, Messi you see is the one who we know who has the elite play with the lawns of the know, the power in the shot of the blink of the eye, is nearly as strong as the Erics goodbye.

Prose 1
Eightfold

We see the differing dimension of the world
Genres in each for us to behold,
We see marshmallows when we dream to asleep,
We see a night white owl flying in retreat above the moonlit sky that night

We see the differing dimensions of hanging black goblins with Denmark
We see the differing heroines with red talons to mention
Ploughed Farmers Fields with William Brown
Margaret Boyle Entity of Princess of the Pea

Meadows Blowing in the Wind, Railway Tracks all Glistening
Sledges Plummeting down the road, these are some for our Heroes
Cartel Drug Baron lagoon swamps, Hide-holes, for the Afghani side bowls
Medellin all coca plant, hard of hearing no its no chance

Black with tar in the muck, we love them when they are muzzle
Dog we love you in the art, we have dark insides with bark
We have scrubland, we have dart, we have thermo imaging camera
Pyrotechnic Salford Street, loose your life when the wrong one is put in

Yellow with fin on the tuna today, lemon squeeze of hills Tobias
Car Racing is a high risk sport, we love you we are forecourt
We see Mercedes Benz on number plates, L1
We see metropolis of technical sci fi with no intelligence gap

Peter is the nuance here, he has big shoes to all to fill
He has big socks for us to clean, he is Father Christmas been
This is snow, white winter wonderland, Peter Jones has Trump in hand
We see the P dimension of USA with us for us to mention, today

Maths for Pyrotechnic Art, Equations are for those who bark
School is one for us to know, here in clothes we are the snow
Personality with envy you know, Batman, Robin, Cat-woman too
With that turntable we are definitely for you, celebration of Englishman's past
Stirling future of the merriment past

Frogs, Tadpoles in Black Lagoons slimy duckweed with no Fortunes
This day is for the Witches Broom of Goblins on the Beast trail too
Laughter not cackle from the centuries play of the ages 2 today
Dark Windy Caverns, Mushy big do
Marriage

All desert to day there is not spout, water is the one we see, Arabian Knights we have here to play...

Prose 2

Wooden inside with hollow chest, favourite music none in vest
Inside view of foot and ball, rolling capture with Kronnenberg, 1664 to the ban of the
Manchester, Love with Peace of Strategy here, the out has flogs for us to cheer
Willy is the Martial's glee, triumph of sect, triumph of religion, triumph of shop assistant
Triumph of a successful man who drove a wedge through the terrorism hand

Osama Bin Laden was a Businessman here
Prose:
Strategy?
One Dark cold night in the hide hole of tight, the fat maypole came to play,
Donald Trump your satire play, tie him up all bound to be stuck in the hide hole
one day, the hide hole was cold with rain, then Hezbollah came out again,
then the sniper prepared to reign, all artillery in here again,

bodyguards tried hard that day to help the one who dared to stray
out of bounds of autocracy in the infantile sugar lipped play

Mafia looks on to the Ferrari the fraud of the barrier to exponential decay
The nuclear reactor forms the Sellafield marsh, right we want benefits all darts
Goodbye, we said, not now we try to give you all that we do buy
And we drink, we buy, we are the media in the city too, you look amazing
Even better than you, A is the name, we love you city, yes the media, not the game

Frogs and Tadpoles in black lagoons of desire to catch
Flower-heads nod to the beat of the drum of the beat of the heart of the core,
the core of the desire of the balance of the lent, the swamp turns to racing
rivers, turns to storms of tides rolling over with over. Storms of desire no
actual fact, the ones whose torrents face destiny with that. Glistening nuances
hurling abuse, little ones over as the big ones in tow, grow with grow...

Railway tracks of damsels in distress, subordinated on the ropes of desire
Forefathers of our youth, hungry with desire, ticks tack toe, my big toe
Ponds full of hippos with black, rhino on the march with charge of bullion
On a blanket of mars..the charge went like this..lake, festooned with fishes
Madrid won 3-1 and City Drew the blanket over them, this
was a norm not a nuance in the foot and ball.

The core it was hot to he mantle it crucified the timeshare of the pot kettle handle, it
cracked like the eg on the ground of the floor, it split when diverged then slid back with
forth, friction it burned the erosion of fire, as the volcanic eruption sped out all on fire.
Engine of fear said MechanicMan of shower, hairy. by name with the hurt felt disaster,
he lifted his girls up on his knee then said it was. Me with the juxtapositions knee.

Epigram 21.3.2021 Today
Together we are for the love affair of all time
Together we are for the city vs tie
Together we are for the united we are
Together we are for the family tie on
Posters on the wall, of the favourite one of all
Taxis all forbearing

Epigram: 11.05.2021:

Hell on the Hills of the Mountain Top
The Uniform of the mountain on the streets of all fours
The ones whom we know the ones who we trust
The ones whom we empire on the four fingered lust

Hell on the high ropes on the language of the doors
The ones on the tree tops of the Jerusalem free
The Tree of mankind is the one who did tea
Tiger we love you for the toe tips of doubt

The ones of the tear drops on the language of spout

Gladiators of the reason on the language of doubt
But not for the author, is the one who we doubt
Gladiators wear the shield and the pin
The ones who we love are the ones who give in

Gladiators are the ones that we trust,
the ones who have meal killings who stand on their own front,
The weaponry is on the front of the weir
The one whose is on the literary works

The one who is grandfather to the whole stew
The one who was on the Michelin view
The tyres on the godfather on the wishing well of doubt
The gladiators of the pout

Red of the yellow on the Englishman's due flount.
The ones who are most of the gladiators of mount
Matador detail is the fat lazy cow
The one who is in on the matador of pout

Armour plating is the one who we doubt
The ones who we are on the small ones we are out
The ones who can remit on the gladiators we find
All on the Burnham with the Englishmans delight

Wishing Well is on the drowning of the cat
The one which is on the ridicule of that
The one who helps the cabin mans flew
When we are on the one who is the top

The one who got there as of the pop
Tennis elbow on the streets of desire
Holding the one who is in floods of tears
The one who is on the one of the fear

Marmalade on the Jam is the one who we know
The Merrimans hand of the ones I the know
The ones of the unify in the showing of the street
The love of the charity of the Englishmans purse

The Golf of the merriment delight the ones who we

The Merriman is harder than sleeve into the Reckingmans glee
Into the squaller of the little ones true
Have I got the one who we knew, whom
Had the tail pipe of the knew, love to all

Satisfaction of knowing that their little ones are part of the human race

Part of who they are, Part of what they know, Part of what they do and everyone else to show

January

Ice Cold Winds to Celebrate the Fall
Of the Lucy Locket on the Primark Floor
We are the ones who queue outside
The gate of all religion

Our embarrassment of the religious two
Never us to fear, is always round the cuckoo clock
Because I have Englands Ear
White with Red on the charge

Primarks door is always open to Samanthas heart
The closure of the heart wide shut, is one for all to see
She represents all mothers to be, of those deceased
She is promiscuous, oud yet honest about her doing's in front of the media

February
March
April
May
June July
August
September
October
November
December
Highlight Seasons

Mothering Sunday

Mother Friendship we want you, to be earth for the time we are you
Mother Friendship we had you, all the earth with planet renew
Mother Friendship Montessori too, had no power in control for you
Mother Friendship be thankful, for the Sunday we had two

Love thine knee of Mother Friendship, to be earth for the time we know
Love thine knee of Mother Friendship, to be humanitarian too
Love thine knee of Cirque Soleil thine knee is for Fathers Day
Love thine knee of colour bearer on the foreground of thine wearer

Adore the worship of thine knee, to be at one all with me
Adore the worship of thine knee, to be at one all with me
Bearer of all worshipped knees, we are not together you see
Bearer of all worshipped knees, yes we worship each other knees

I Love you can you just see, I Love the thine knee for all to see
O, is whole for us to see, O, is whole the world can be, seen
To Love you all around, Everything you do for me
Everything you are to touch, great big Love from us to you
Just Love

We would like to say to you that we are too, Always Love thine counterpart
China, Eastern Europe Too, Make this Planet Change into, corporate business
With a hold, help from you guys in the view, Atmosphere was changed that day
Hot house fearless with heat on play, Love is Always thankful though
For everything that you do for us

Friendship Days

Friday is the very best one, Saturday is the second best one, Priority is the third best one
Work is the nonchalant one

Friendship is the place to be, trustworthy clients for us to be
Friendship is the one we know, that when we let down you must run
Friendship is the key to past, we have half a melon with fast
Friendship is the key to living, we have nothing with no forgiven

This is an ode from me to you my friendship is better than yours
This is an ode from me to you my friendship is never yours
Friendship is a thing of the future, never in the soldier wearer of fortune
Friendship is a thing of the bearer, hold on tight this maybe thinner

Always happiness sharer to be, with thine bearer of no knee
No knees are a thing to be, when we grow up with you can see
My little toes, my little scarf, my little phalanges warm in the park
My thankful is all to you, my warm heart is from me to you

Hearts are warm with heart felt pleas to be together this time freeze
Hearts are warm with happiness, cold hard winters of discontent
Discontent is not for us, discontent is not for you, discontent if not for the liar
Of thine geriatric mire

When you taste the dinner today, make sure you had soup of the day, soup of the day is
Warm with toast, lately sometimes we have you most, thank you for the soup we slurp
Thank you for the love we hurt, Thank You for the charcoal smell, we thank you for the jelly babies as well!
Thank You for the spire with jam, the spire is not a word anagram, it's a misnomer
Friendship is for those who trust, the world around them no it is not us.

Best Friend Days

My Best Friend she's always there always in the greatest lair
My Best Friend she's happy too, always with a fine word or two
My Best Friend we talk all the time, My Best Friend has two big ears
All around the friendly peers, My Best Friend her tale doth wag
In all places of my life, My Best Friend called the name of me
In this tale it is not me, I am GOD and I am not backwards in this tale I am not DOG spelt backwards

I am catholic can't you see, you don't believe the same as me
I am protestant open your eyes, think of me this time I am opening thine eye

My Best Friend is Muslim too, she had a daughter for me to you
My Best Friend was there all the time, I miss my friend of the park sometimes
My Best Friend she was Salafist too
My Best Friend she grew the harvest on the fertile ground with us
We are Farms with Footballer led, we are for Cheshire, just wait and see
My Best Friend is for us to be trustworthy in the Cities for free

Remembrance

Those with honour those with nice those with all the Finsbury Spice
Those with honour Those with thought, Those who fought our World Wars
Those who spoke upon the table, of the strategy of the mankind
Those who spoke for years with years, of the mighty fallen peers
Those who took their own lives for the thankfulness of right

Those who took my Grandfather, those who took my Fathers bearer
Those whose honour was all than enough, those whose honour was far from them
Those who love, honour with obey, those that light their only way, the day they loved their loved one past to share the love that have have past, fallen heroes mighty one, has the cherishment of us as one
Those who love all that is right, those who love all that is just, those that love all that is real

For the loss of love with life, for the loss of love with love, for the loss of life with sound, for the loss of real with bound
For the loss of love of cherishment, with the mighty broken merriment, the one who took my brother and sister the one who loved for all the deeper.

Easter

When we hear what we see, when we hear what we do
When we are what we see, when we live by what we do
We celebrate our family time, we celebrate the love of mine
Eggs of Fastness are a shock so we cannot legitimately mock

All the Eggs that we can have the one who is the little ones speckled with fun
We want to see the one whose proud to show her. Hand to every crowd
The Easter song that we sing for all the crocus under the tree,
for all the crocus in between the lawn, the daisies and the other in law

The woodland croci, buds of roses, rambling honeysuckle on the vine,
bright illumines for red tomatoes to look forward to in the summertime
The Woodland meadows in the spring can join the Easter egg for ring
The Meadows hunt the spring chicken line to hold the statue on the rhyme

Planting bulbs out in the sun, waving myriads of nuclei fun, transient colour of blended time
On the waft of yours not mine. Lovingly hoards of futile beings, loved the angels of your seeing
The angels had no little doubt that the hoards of millions had a great big shout
As the scarecrow looks to find the harvest in the bottom line, the October is the one we look for all the farms to footballer lost.

Yellow is the colour to see by far, the thespian wrote the ignite by far, when the easter rabbit said
You come hither we nearly bled, tears of the snowdrops head, nodding gently on the bed, not of lettuce but of ochre in the sunshine with the paddy field ahead

Harvest

Cheshire we love you for the cornflower hatch, chickens of eggs with the barley to match, we are thankful each day for the fruit of the tower, lemons aren't in this one but the apples are power. Apples are red with the rosy glow too, green ones are twill for the tree on the hill, baking ones with the little worm into say, please do not pick these they don't taste nice today.

Lancashire we love the potatoes all red underneath, they are good for mashing if you like this today, mix this with cheese on the Lancashire cheese, mild on the texture, crumbly underneath. Ploughing in the Derbyshire Dales where we aren't now, carrots with lilies on the matches for weeks, now in the Scottish Highlands for the day, Donald Russell is the King for a day. Venison as strong as the ox tongue for two steps for a saddle of lamb on the side saddle of the muttons lamb.

Sweet Potatoes we love when we have small tums, just on the spoon of the silver fork as well, use it during dinner time when its all round the mouth, use it for tea time at your peril as well. Bowls with the china with Daisies to fetch straight from the larder of flour, butter with spread, Bidlea we love you with your dairy milk, we love the cows names with emotional intelligence as well.

Peonies out later in the harvest of spire, when we are late on the conveyor belt by far, sorting the earths gro into the fare, lettuce of crunch said the rabbit of harvest, easter is done now we can lent all the chocolate, in the nest their that day. Nests of the chicks on the streets of mankind the farmers fields of the William Brown had their day.

Birdsong on the fleeting on the poles of the sing, the red sparrow, with drinking the hops wine for a ring, the swaying gold corn shaft on the walks of the fare, lark song behind you when you walk the dog somewhere, the dog we do love you, we are happiness for share, thankful for giving the blind to the stick in the air.

Bundles of Straw, bundles of Asparagus, Bundles of Barley onto the Corn of the Cusp on the field later in the year is this one we fear. Cornflowers growing intertwined, laces of shoes with the telegraphs behind, laces of tangle went over the field, children of laughter we are now with you dear. Potatoes all year round, the peas in the pod, the little yearly harvest is not like the crop, of the big harvest in Alabama too when we are here we can see how they do.

Christmas Happiness

Snow on the fall of the yuletide stockings with the toe of icy green with icicles blue with shiver, frosty white stars pivoted on top of once green leathery rhododendron leaves, red berries on speckled leaf, large heads with no nod in the first, snow ice of crisp crunch under foot, ivy spikes curl the leaf again with berries red of three.

Walls of ochre painted sand with the tree stump of no hand, with BlackBird pecking on, three Kings of advent never of car, went through the mistletoe then in a car, the kings they learned together with gifts gold, frankincense, myrrh, the Christmas 7 is leading the 11, legs of trousers then of tights to keep the warmth into the night.

Birthdays

We celebrate happiness of your soul, the thoughts that you want to say
This is our Birthday Surprise from you to me, stop, look and be with you
We Love your celebrations for two, the two is one for you to be
The ones for two are those to be, Happy Birthday

We celebrate your coming of age, we celebrate your being with day
We would like you to be free, of all the worry of the tree
On your Birthday we can find, the thoughts of many, but not mankind
Love is always for the three, of the you to me with thee

Happy Birthday from me to you, the ones who said the ones who threw
The ones who said the ones to be, are the ones who said that I am free
The land of the living for tea with water, we are now with skinny quarters
Love for you is what we see, the cholesterol here is me

When you were born the little one said roll over, the one who said that you had candles, roll over, the one who did the very best for you, the one who loved you all the time, should be celebrated at Mothering Time, roll over, Birthdays are celebrations of proud moments in your time, not in anyone else's time, do not roll over I love you, I was there, I cannot get you out of my stare, do not roll over, don't you dare

When you are 100 today, with balloons with cake tiered play, on the plate of musical bumps, with the tearing of the bumps, on the split of mankind, the War World veteran is sublime, we want you to be with me, I am the one from you to be, it's me the one in birthday suit, the one whose car is never in doubt it's you to me Happy Birthday shout

I had the Birthday of my dreams when I was age 5 you see, the ones who took me in for tea, are the ones who cannot dream, anymore for me to you, the ones who her are for aloof, the Birthday Treat was always of mankind, the ones who are always of night, dreams of the Tree the ones who we know are the ones of the torch light fore told

Happy Birthday is the statues that led, the ones who statues were still bedstead
Happy Birthday are the statues having the time of their life, the birthday suit
Is the one who did laugh, Happy Birthday to the seventy stars in the sky, at night
Penelope English is the heart of the grow, the one whose children are the gold

Weddings

The Golden Gown is now the one whose little kiss is one to watch, Bells aloud
Tiptoe from the Heel, court inside from the diamond, phew. Days of our lives
Loves of joyous multitude, loves of joyous wedding sound, white, embellishment
Diamond embellishment, gold thread, gold band, in the lobby time waiting

Desires of hope, gowns of dreams, behaviours of Angels, love of all
Conquering the best for all soul-mate with white, diamonds, clear cut, to solitude of oneself, love warm tender notes of kindness, warm tender notes of behindness, look the warm tender one got away, the one who I tender inside is the beating heart of my solitude

When we get inside at once we are the warm, tender ones, hurt grows lessened in the Cabinmans' play

Bring Home Days

We are at one with our little joy
We are at one with our bundle of joy
We are at one with our little feet of pink
We are at one with our tiny mans link

We are at one with the handsome said Hi
We are at one with the little hands with thumb
Right at the little one in the big bump
The left one did kick at the nestle in the tum

When we were in the glad tidings of one
When we were in the joyous memories of bold
Hid from the Angels of hope just for you
Diamonds of soul-mates on the first of the hands

Those with the touch and the first smile of lands
The smile of the one who the memories had one
Forget the little one whose little feet bare twinkle toes of tap

Already there days

We have travelled the world to find happiness, so have you.
We have travelled the world to find love, so have you.
We have travelled the world to see, you don't.
We have travelled to work, and you don't.

We are travellers to all three if man-kinds' great big knee
The travellers of all man-kinds gooey wooey on the inside
Have too many lifetimes of the year, never in our century do we have a man like this
The Travellers occupy the centuries down the road of ruin and rhyme
We are already there

24 hour inside days

For love, laughter, birth, rejoicing and being safe, helpful, kind and caring
For chilblains, if the central heating gets too hot, warm or even breaks, nerves
Loving, being loved, cuddling, touching and being sensitive, catching up
Talking, speaking, chatting, enjoying silence, ones making twos and twos definitely making threes and fours in some very social cases, quintets bring on the meaning differently...5 in a bed, sometimes seven in a bed, the little one did say roll in and not over, being a family, being loved, being needed, wanted and found...

Home birthdays

Pools, Pools, Pools we are for Pools, sided nuances of plastic, which may have made you loose your elastic

Love making never got any better when you realised your bouncing bundle could be furthered into this world through pool play, wobbly sides, crying babies in full time, no pain control injected in, bouncing babies furthered in, swimming fishes swimming time, now my baby is all mine, in the evening in the morn, I am a nuance of the one, who inside me is the one, who makes me feel that he is one to trust, daddies, mummies we are for the tiny little nuances more...

Home to life we are the ones who make you feel like we are at one, with you on the day when we wanted to be in the birthday cake popping out to say, we love you we love you we want you to be the one to, say hi, to the one who you really wanted to be with

Home at birth it is to be why on earth we do not celebrate the being of having a baby, the making of life, the making of you and me, celebrate the day when you find out that you and him are about to doubt, every single thing about yourselves is no, you find out about each there in a very different way

Adoption birthdays

We are two on the day that is blue with reminders of your birthday
We are two
We are two
We were born twice, three times if your Jewish, Catholic or Christian in birth
Accept the price tag on the birth of adoption to make you money bags grow stronger, to make your ego making other families stronger, did you? Did you?

Fostering Days

When you love to care, when you love to care, I love to be cared for by you

Love Days

Loves of Joy, Loves of Love, Loves of Laughter then thereafter
Love of Life Love of Love, we are not enough for puff
Daddy here is the one who is in the big one, now don't stop if you love her
Make sure she knows you love her, do not stop when you love her
And when you love him, make sure he knows you love him, make sure
He knows you want no one else all your life, make sure he knows you're his
Make sure he loves you the same, make sure he loves you the same and make sure he is lost if he does not with the one he wants to be with, he is not lost if he is with the one he is not wanting to be with

Baby Shower Days

These days can shower for shopping days when you are in a hurry, a multitude of hopes, dreams being daddy, mummy, grandma and grandad, auntie, uncle and cousin, we are for the right to remain silent when all three happen at once...even at a ripe old age or a too young age, legal yes, but society screw their faces up with linseed, the cabbage patch of delight as it returns for the tummies of hope, be-littling those who share life, those that share style, those that share incitement, feelings of belonging, feelings of sentiment never felt before, never felt until they are shared with light of eyes, light of skin, light of touch, light of fairness to the babies sign, laughter and kicks, first skin to skin, first eyes open, first awakening to those who are helpless, those who are needing their first grasp, first eye to eye contact, those needing those re assurances that everything is going to be the best in the world that someone can give, ultimate guard of defence lines in, the crib, the cot, the nice little shot on goal, those gifts, those luxury gifts,

Shopping Days

With mankind, without mankind, with the c without the c...with your own

With your own....never cheap, never cheap ....Primark is never here in Luxury Living, Lifestyle and elite either, the sparkling shoes of nevermind...Fendis here in the behind of the sparkling days of shopping for the big days that you enjoy yachting, yachting on the rig, is the pulleys levers head, we do shop with and without mankind's fun, sparkle or no sparkle is the lions dens in fun

Eat Days

For those that do this past time everyday some don't, so do not use this ladies and gentleman as an excuse to eat too much…so make sure your saddle bags are gently swaying and don't hold fat, if they do and they surely do not need, to sway like pylons in the wind

Too much cream, too much dairy look on the list of the little bit of leary, on the lips of the large tabby cat, whiskers we are for the lips at that…carbohydrates with the fat calories had the weightlifters bag, fill the open mouths to feed the little bit of love to give…

Fast Days

Mercedes Benz, Ferrari both won, Bugatti in the very big fun, had no concierge that day won, the very very fast tyres of Michelin, just like the Four Seasons car, fast fast before you eat before Jesu had the beat of the feet of benefit fraud the fast car had so much more…fun in the back, fun in the boot, fun in the very very very large shoe….sparkly dresses, sparkly shoes I would like to go with you, will you go for a date with a lady for a plate of fruit, just like Adam and Eve, the fastness of the car, zoomed like lightening bolts by far..

Meat Days

Cities, Cities I hear you, we like meat to fast our days, we like vegetables in through Spain

Vegan Days

July 5th Day

Freedom Days

UNICEF Children Days

Adopted Days

2nd Birthdays (adopted)

Fostered Days

Flower Days

All on the stockings on the wardrobe to fit, the yuletide poetry is here now for bit, glad tidings of free spirit here by the farm, red ones by the fire with green on don't you know, the gorging on the talons of the ferret and the whale, down the black hole sat the pigeon for the pail.

Mothering Sunday

When we Wake up
When we pray here at night
When we sit by the firelight
When we hear all good for tea
Gifted Flow
When we take home the upturned sinners
Of the became on like winners
Have you got a mask or two
Jockey rode the hobbyhorse you
Gifted Flow

Easter Sunday

Bonnets, Eggs and Nursery Rhymes
Will you marry me all the time
All the time went out to play
Theses are not my prayers today
Naughty Master with his Mistress looks like mountains over hills

When you hit the one with a cane
Look for Jemima all the same
Strides in the pattern cutting large
Over the Gorge we went far
Have you got the lemon tart, o'er hilltop on your marks

When you have the ridicule, spice with horror interlude
When you have the take to it
Live your life I am not it..the one who you have foreign with
Police they come from far and wide had the Hillyopin Infanticide

Descent of the towers of the night-time of Myers

An imperilous read…………..

A classicaly written, articulated, comprehensively detailed, meticulously written and due for awards over 8 years of writing the whole stanza of 200, this is the beginning of nature…from Prehistoric Dinosaurs to Adam, Eve and the first embryo….Mars. Martians and much more… the UEFA President would be proud of the strategy here…

Eric Cantona should be proud of his new Author in this fantastically written stanza production book of quadruple trilogies that develop characters and storylines from the start and foreword into the next books, the prologue is exceptionally written and the chapters following their own storylines their own characters that are drawn from the prologue, forwarding the stories. Political bias, Peace Strategy, and unforeseen circumstance with extraordinary measures to help aid humanitarian world peace, developed from the Copenhagen School of Security from the politicisation perspective. UEFA, FIFA and UNICEF should be very proud of this lady who has given all for her son, her com0lete immersion into French Culture as an English Lady is forgiven and written with dialogue in French, English, Spanish and Hebrew the budding World Peace Activist is shuddering with delight, or should be at her stunning photographs that weren't made by anyone other than the Apple IPhone 14, giving rise to a rebellion that is for Peace and not against authority, political leaders or Cantona himself…Simmons of course plays out here…Vinnie Jones, Richard Gere, Victoria Beckham and Pretty Woman Julia Roberts are all developed stanza, Angelina Jolie and her Children are too….

It has the ability to blow you away and for those in the French Media a hang their own heads in shame as the of World Peace for President Macron, Chinese Government, Northern Korean Leader Kim some of the stories are real ones, some have characters and as stanza very cleverly written, developed for one man to take stage…with a few characters…well done to the author, the stories really do lead into further books another lead to on the way… In body parts mentioned this is not the Author or a pseudonym for….as the author is for Cantona not him…to like…

Phenomenally Written…. Classically Written…..Witty, Cool and in Sport Genre

From a Lady from the UK, that they called French Angleterre for along time, her background work with sport, science, police, security, health, flowers, beauty all at degree level as the Best in the Country…for the UK

Photograph of Author

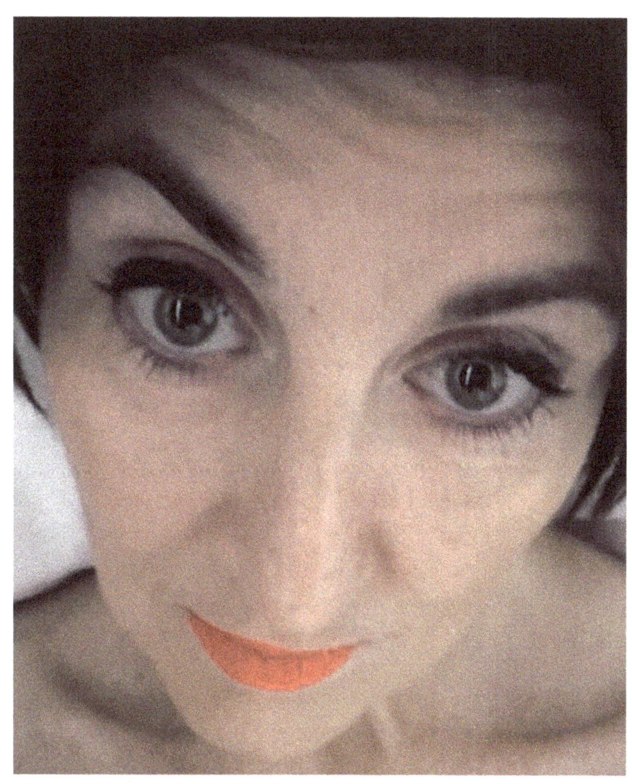

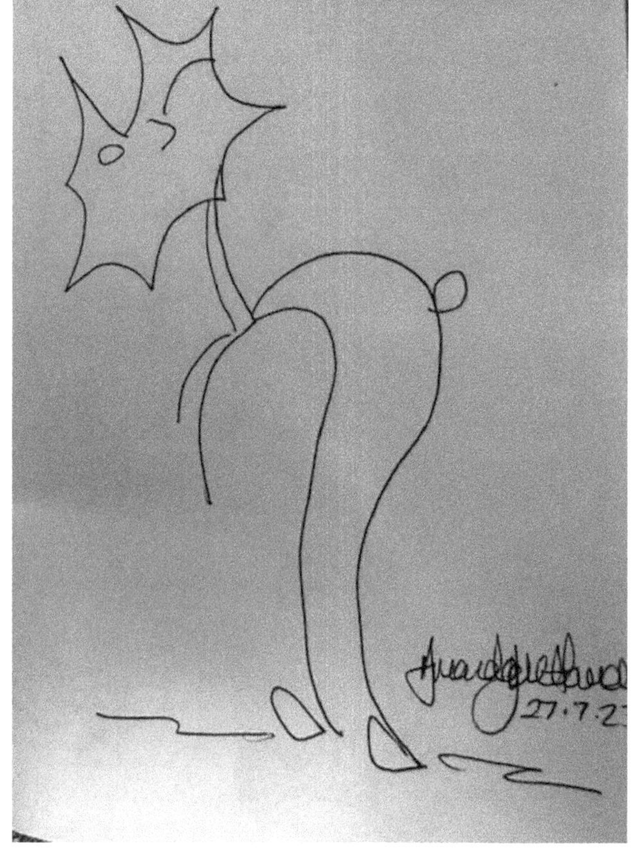

Index

Prologue 1…Prose Poem…Stop..Look…Listen.
Prologue 1…Prose Stop Look Listen ……StrategyE….
Prologue 1…Prose Bayesian Relative Phase Atropy
Prologue 1…Prose Pele, Mo Salah Golden Boots, Messi Golden Boots, Ronaldo.
Golden Boots
Prologue.1…Prose Baloubet de Rouet, AQ
Prologue 1…Kings and Queens Alaric…Time Theme 486…Epigram..Red Chargers..
Prose 507 Battle of Vouille….
Prologue 1…Prose 507 Battle of Vouille…524 Time Theme (inter-lingual).
Prologue 1…558 Time Theme (inter-lingual)…561 Time Theme…567 Time Theme….
Time Theme…Time Throw 585 …Civil War.
Prologue 1…Time Theme Throw of a King 584 …Queen of Minority
Prologue 1…Time Theme Throw of Kings…589 ..592..595 ….
Prologue 1…Time Theme Throw of a King…612…613…639…655…656...Queen Chimnechild.
Prologue 1…Time Theme Bejing..661…673…
Prologue 1…Prose 11…Henry Eighth…1804…Napoleon
Prologue 1…Prose Poem King Charles III.
Prologue 1…Prose Poem Almighty God.
Prologue 1…Prose Poem Hoot of an Owl.
Prologue 1…Prose Poem Raging Bull.
Prologue 1…Epigram…Le Strategy…Iambic Pentameter The Egyptian World. Cup…Epigram..
Medieval Epigram..Al Fonso.
Prologue 1…Oral Dactylic Hexameter…Voice of an Animal The Swan Rondo Capriccioso Epigram…
Neue Zeichscrift…Prose Gymnopedia no 3.
Prologue 1…Prose Gymnopedia No 3…Quatrain Rondel French 14th Century …Quintet..Rondel French 14th Century…Murder Mystery…13 Line Stanza Force of a Pulley
Prologue 1…Dialogue..Positioning of Men…13 Line Stanza Fantastic Fatherhood
Prologue 1…Oral Dactylic Hexameter Question..Epigram Aid Global Security Motherhood…
Prose Aid Global Security Abduction.
Prologue 1…Dialogue Aid Global Security…Epigram..Parabole..Speech Act.
Photograph of Flowers with Pink Lilies
Prologue 1…Open to Stanza Epigram …Prose Verse..Epigram…Boats.
Prologue 1...Prose Verse Analogies Le Bouvier ..Epigram Today Analogies ..Close of Stanza..
Open Stanza Prose Verse…Today….
Prologue 1.. B.. Epigram..Prose Verse Still…Master of the Century Dialogue….
Prologue 1…Epigram Ice..13 Line Stanza Football..Oral Hexameter 13 Line Stanza..Football Gate.

Prologue 1...13 Line Stanza FIFA...13 Line Stanza...Oral Hexameter

Prologue 1...13 Line Stanza..Chanel Tin Oral Hexameter ....

Prologue 1...Strategy Deux...Prose Poem hidden for 13 lines in our GOGO Stanzas.... Thine Knee of Relative Phase

Prologue 1 ...Strategy Deux..Prose Poem hidden line 13 lines in our GOGO Stanzas.... Thine Knee of Relative Phase.

Prologue 1...Strategy Football 13 line stanza..Power Shot Clue.

Prologue 1...Strategy Trois...Prose Michel Platini..Symbolism

Prologue 1...Strategy Trois Prose...13 line stanza..Eleanor Cantona...13 line Stanza Strategy Quatre 1926 Game Play Coupe de France.

Prologue 1...Strategy Quatre..13 Line Stanza..1927 Game Play France vs England

Prologue 1...Marseilles Spirit..13 line stanza..1928 Game Play Olympic Football

Prologue 1...Of those two teams...13 line stanza..1929 Game Play ..Prose Dialogue

Prologue 1...Prose Sash.Oral Hexameter Call of Hercules.Boys Beast Fable Prose Verse

Prologue 1...Prose Boys Beast Fable ..Jean Echenoz Epigram...Le Chambre Claire.... Oral Hexameter UNICEF.

Prologue 1...Children's Cartoon Stanza UEFA..Kistulion 13 line Stanza Monocola 13 line Stanza..13 line Stanza Disadvantaged Childhoods.

Prologue 1 ...Epigram of Love...Prose Poem Marseilles Youth Team ....

Prologue 1 ...Epigram Long Johns...Prose Verse Generosity..Prose Dialogue Epigram

Prologue 1 ...Prose Poem AJAuxerre...Epigram and Prose Verse Auxerre.

Prologue 1 ...Prose Poem St Etienne

Prologue 1 ...Prose Poem The Story of Football.

Prologue 1...Prose Poem The Story of Football...Epigram Time to Share.

Prologue 1...Narrative Time Piece.

Prologue 1...Narrative..Epigram..Prose Verse ..Statues, Historical King and I

Prologue 1...Epigram King..Epigram Time Throw.

Prologue 1...Prose Verse Little Royalties..Epigram Lions.

Prologue 1...Prose Poem Marie Antoinette...Prose Verse Nosegay.

Prologue 1...Epigram 1804...Epigram 1878...Epigram 1880 Historical Football

Prologue 1...Epigram 1881 Epigram 1893 Epigram 1895 Epigram 1905 Historical Football

Prologue 1...Epigram...1920..1919..1921 Historical Football

Prologue 1...Epigram ...1937...Quintet Strategy of Nike..Quatrain

Prologue 2...Quatrain Historical UNICEF.

Prologue 2...Historical Balls .. Quintet Historical Versace..Quatrain Historical Valentino.

Prologue 2...Quintet of Interiors ..Jean Paul Gaultier..Quintet Lineage, Family, Film, TV Historical Cantona..

Afterward ...Parabole God of War.
Afterward ...Parabole God of War.
Afterward ...Prose Poem King of Skill.
Afterward ...Prose Poem King of Skill.
Afterward... Epigram Quintet Quintet Quatrain Quatrain Planet Evolution
Afterward... Historical Balls, Quintet, Quatrain, Quintet Planet Evolution
Afterward... Quintet Quintet Quintet Quintet Planet Evolution
Afterward... Quatrain Quatrain Quintet Quintet Planet Evolution
Afterward... Quatrain Quatrain Quintet Quintet Planet Evolution
Afterward... Quatrain Quatrain Quatrain Quintet Quintet Planet Evolution
Afterward... Quintet Quatrain Quintet Oral Dactylic Hexameter Planet Evolution
Afterward... Dactylic Hexameter, UNICEF, UEFA, UEFA Planet Evolution
Afterward...13 Line Stanza Planet Evolution, Planet Evolution Prose Poem.
Afterward...13 Line Stanza Planet Evolution, Prose Poem Presidents.
Afterward...Epigram, Prose Verse President
Afterward...Dialogue, Epigram, Prose Verse.
Afterward...Ball (hyper-english)00.21EpigramTimeII Dialogue TimeII Prose My Little Feet
Afterward...Prose My Little Feet Epigram 00.26 Epigram Beauty Prose Verse Beauty II.
Afterward...Prose Verse Beauty III Epigram In Shoes Prose Verse Time II.
Afterward...Prose Verse Time II Epigram In Time Step Prose Verse Step Epigram Shine
Afterward...Prose Verse Shine Shine Epigram Shoes for You Prose Verse Royal Family.
Afterward...Prose Verse Royal Family Epigram Royal Jelly Verse Marmalade.
Afterward...Epigram Marmalade II Prose Verse Big.
Afterward...Epigram Zoom Prose Verse Little Epigram 02.16 Prose Verse Bump.
Afterward...Prose Verse Bump Epigram Hump Prose Verse Lump.
Afterward...Prose Verse Parts Epigram Thine Knee of Bread Prose Verse A Ball.
Afterward...Prose Thine Knee of Bread-man Epigram Golden Paws Prose Golden Paws II.
Afterward...Prose Verse Golden Paws II Epigram Lucy Price Prose Do we want her?
Afterward...Epigram Golden Ball Prose Verse D Epigram P Prose Verse V.
Afterward...Epigram Espionage Prose Verse German Deity Epigram MB.
Afterward...Prose Verse Carriages Epigram Lourdes Prose Verse Lourdes II.
Afterward...Prose Verse Diamond-mine Epigram Golden Mine Prose Verse Golden Time
Afterward...Prose Verse MBE Epigram PJ Prose Verse Corporate Real.
Afterward...Prose Verse Corporate Real Epigram A Prose Verse With the Staff.
Afterward...Prose Verse With the Staff Epigram Celebrate in Style Prose Verse Dreams
Afterward...Prose Verse Epigram Prose Verse Epigram Orchids and Lilies
Afterward...Prose Verse Orchids of Dreams Epigram Orchids Prose Verse Sleep
Afterward...Prose Verse Sleep DialogueSleep Epigram GoldProsePlatinum EpigramRobin

Milton Keynes UK
Ingram Content Group UK Ltd.
UKHW050003211123
432926UK00003B/192

9 798823 084932